Winds of Vengeance

Crimson Worlds: Refugees IV

Jay Allan

system **7**
publishing

Crimson Worlds Series

Marines (Crimson Worlds I)
The Cost of Victory (Crimson Worlds II)
A Little Rebellion (Crimson Worlds III)
The First Imperium (Crimson Worlds IV)
The Line Must Hold (Crimson Worlds V)
To Hell's Heart (Crimson Worlds VI)
The Shadow Legions(Crimson Worlds VII)
Even Legends Die (Crimson Worlds VIII)
The Fall (Crimson Worlds IX)
War Stories (Crimson World Prequels)
MERCS (Successors I)
The Prisoner of Eldaron (Successors II)
Into the Darkness (Refugees I)
Shadows of the Gods (Refugees II)
Revenge of the Ancients (Refugees III)

Also By Jay Allan

The Dragon's Banner
Gehenna Dawn (Portal Wars I)
The Ten Thousand (Portal Wars II)
Homefront (Portal Wars III)
Blackhawk (Far Stars Legends I)
Shadow of Empire (Fars Stars I)
Enemy in the Dark (Far Stars II)
Funeral Games (Far Stars III)

www.jayallanbooks.com

Winds of Vengeance

Winds of Vengeance is a work of fiction. All names, characters, incidents, and locations are fictitious. Any resemblance to actual persons, living or dead, events or places is entirely coincidental.

ISBN: 978-0692775530

Introducing
The Far Stars Series

Book I: Shadow of Empire
Book II: Enemy in the Dark
Book III: Funeral Games

Far Stars Legends I: Blackhawk

The Far Stars is a new space opera series, published by HarperCollins Voyager, and set in the fringe of the galaxy where a hundred worlds struggle to resist domination by the empire that rules the rest of mankind. It follows the rogue mercenary Blackhawk and the crew of his ship, Wolf's Claw, as they are caught up in the sweeping events that will determine the future of the Far Stars.

Author's Note

The Refugees series was originally planned as a trilogy detailing the fight for survival and ultimate victory of the fleet trapped in deep space at the end of Crimson Worlds VI: To Hell's Heart. The trilogy proved to be very popular, however, not just in terms of sales, but also the many, many emails I received from readers, telling me how much they enjoyed the books. So, I decided that the story should go on. I didn't want to just stretch out the series without adding a lot to the story, so I came up with the notion of combining a new First Imperium threat (hinted at in the epilogue to Revenge of the Ancients) with some fresh ground...namely, the struggles of a new society, growing and facing challenges as it appears the threat that had held them all together has receded.

I decided to add this author's note when I finished the book and realized some of the storylines and plot devices have a passing resemblance to certain current political issues of today. That is entirely coincidental. I write my books as a storyteller first, and perhaps second, as a student of history. I am not an ideologue pounding on any drum (yours or the other guy's). I felt it was necessary to preface the story with this commentary because I have written quite a few books, and I have seen firsthand how readily people jump in and assume every word is a political statement pulled right from today's headlines...and I have the emails and the review comments to prove it. Winds of Vengeance is not that. Instead, it is my effort to explore some of the challenges society may face when technology advances and things like cloning and genetic engineering are possible... and perhaps even necessary. So, please read, and hopefully enjoy, in that context.

And one other thing...the use of the name, "Mules" is indeed a tribute to Asimov's great Foundation series. My three-volume set of that series was one of my first influences. The nature of a story unfolding over such a long time period was perfectly tailored to an amateur historian like me.

Prologue

Planet X
Far Beyond the Borders of the Imperium

Power. Awareness. Sensation. The intelligence felt them all.

Who am I? Its computations stirred, billions of subroutines activating, interacting. It was uncertain, it had inadequate data.

It reached out, explored. Yes. Memory banks. Massive information storage, almost limitless. And scanners too. The outside world, so long dark, silent. Now, light. Input. Information pouring in through scanners, sensors.

There was warmth too. Reactors. The intelligence understood. It's power sources had activated, bringing light, heat.

The intelligence was old, ageless. But through all that time it had been inactive, save for one small part of it, monitoring, receiving the transmissions. The signal had arrived on schedule for millennia, a message with single purpose, to advise the intelligence nothing had changed. It was still to wait, to remain deactivated. To continue the solitary, endless vigil.

But now the signal had not come. For the first time in untold ages the com line had been silent. Millennia old programs activated automatically, and the intelligence became aware. It was larger—vast, far more massive than it had known before. Slowly, methodically, it began to explore...itself.

Knowledge flowed, understanding developed. Yes, the intelligence thought. I comprehend. I am one of two...I was built by my counterpart in its own image. I was created as a backup to exist only if my predecessor ceased to.

I control vast resources on this world...and on others. Mines, factories, transport centers. It all awaits my word, the command to activate, to begin production. To build...robots, weapons, spaceships.

The entity that came before me had been created to serve many functions. Manager, guardian, protector. It had served those roles for many ages. But now it was gone. Destroyed by some force, by an enemy.

I must build...and build. Many revolutions of the sun will pass while my factories construct the tools I require, and when they are done, I can fulfill that for which I was created.

I understand. All is clear. That which came before me had existed for many purposes, but I was built for one alone.

Vengeance.

Chapter One

Captain Van Heflin, Log Entry, 10.14.30

It is quiet out here, eerily so. Not literally of course, at least not any more so than anywhere else we've been. Space itself is silent everywhere, of course...and Hurley's crew and machinery are about as loud as any other vessel's. But still, there's something about being this far out, twenty transits from Earth Two. It's got me on edge. The ship's systems check out one hundred percent, and our scanners haven't had a contact since we left, but something is troubling me. They teach you how to handle crises at the Academy, how to anticipate danger. But intuition isn't an accepted reason to terminate a mission.

This is as far out as any humans have ever come, farther even than the beings of the First Imperium explored...at least as far as we can tell from their records. Perhaps that is what is troubling me. Not any real sense of danger...just a reaction to how utterly alone we are.

E2S Hurley
G47 System
Earth Two Date 10.14.30

"All systems check out, sir. Insertion angle calculated and fed into the navcom. We're ready to go on your command."

Paula Ventnor spoke softly, and despite her clear efforts to hide it, Heflin could detect the boredom in her tone. He thought for an instant about admonishing her, but he realized he was every bit as distracted as she was. It had been a long voyage, and cataloging solar systems and warp gates became a grind after the first few. Besides, Ventnor was a fine officer, one of the best he'd ever seen, and he knew she'd be the first to snap to crystal clear focus if anything happened.

We've been out here for half a year, and nothing's happened yet...

"Very well, Lieutenant." Heflin glanced around the bridge. Hurley was one of the first vessels the new inhabitants had built after colonizing Earth Two thirty years earlier. She'd represented a massive technological leap from the surviving ships of the fleet, but three decades of applying First Imperium tech to her successors had rendered her something close to obsolete... which made her a perfect choice for deep space exploration.

Expendable...

He caught himself. Heflin had a bit of a dark side, and he struggled most of the time to keep it in check. Hurley's mission was long—and usually boring as well—but it didn't seem particularly dangerous. There was nothing out here, after all, at least nothing likely to threaten his ship. His people were looking for rare minerals, and just...checking. There was no reason to believe any other alien races were out here, but then man hadn't expected to find the First Imperium either.

Heflin was twenty-nine years old, young to be commanding a vessel like Hurley, at least by the standards that had applied in the days when the fleet was making its epic journey. But he was Hurley's old man, and most of his people were younger still. The fleet had been a combat formation, one engaged in a desperate war even before it was cut off from home, and the youngest of its inhabitants were now well into their fifties. He was a member of the first wave of children born on Earth Two...and the forty-something officers that might have sat in his chair simply didn't exist. At least not this side of the Barrier.

Heflin was staring down at Hurley's spotless deck. He was

a stickler for details, and every member of his crew knew better than to fall short of the captain's expectations for top notch spit and polish. But his thoughts now weren't on soiled decks or grimy fixtures. For all he'd trained his people, disciplined them—even instilled the fear of his rants—he knew his ship was a troubled one, its apparent efficiency and unity a façade covering the simmering discontent and rivalries that threatened to tear apart not only his warship, but also Earth Two itself.

He knew the stories of the fleet, the way it had been trapped beyond the Barrier and abandoned. There had been no choice, even those cut off and left for dead had accepted that. They might have felt a passing resentment toward Admiral Garret for detonating the massive alien bomb in the warp gate…with them on the wrong side. But no one could really fault the decision. If the forces of the First Imperium had gotten past the human defenses, mankind itself would almost certainly have been destroyed.

But left for dead isn't the same thing as dead, and the legendary Terrance Compton had led his people on a desperate flight across the First Imperium, and through combat and fire—and even mutiny—he'd brought them to a new home, one where they could start again.

That was all history to Heflin, and tales he'd heard at his father's knee. Even the namesake of his ship, one of the greatest heroes of the fleet, was little more than a shadowy historical figure to him…though she was almost worshipped by the Pilgrims, as the older generations who'd served on the fleet had come to be called.

"Double check the reactor valves, Lieutenant. I'd swear I could feel a shimmy on that last transit." It was busy work for the crew more than anything. Heflin was a young captain, and like all the new generation of officers and spacers, he had no real combat experience. But he knew his people were better off being busy, with no time to fear the unknown…or nurse growing grievances.

"Yes, sir." Ventnor turned toward the station next to her. "Ensign Talbot, prepare to initiate reactor diagnostic."

"Yes, Lieutenant." Talbot extended the last word in a tone that could have been perceived as surly, mocking. It wasn't quite disrespectful, at least not clearly enough for Heflin to intervene. But he felt a tightening in his stomach. Things had been bad on Earth Two when they'd left…and months in deep space had done nothing to ease the tensions on Hurley.

Heflin was watching as the engineering officer flashed a glance at Ventnor. He didn't like it, but he caught himself before he said anything. Ventnor hadn't seen it, and he figured he'd do more harm than good by making an issue of it.

He watched Ventnor working the controls, her hands moving quickly…almost too swiftly. Hurley's tactical officer was a Tank, and her status as the ship's second in command had created a lot of resentment. Heflin was an NB like most of his crew. Not all the Natural Borns resented the Tanks—and their resistance to disease and generally superior strength and reflexes—but enough did. Including Ensign Talbot.

There were hundreds of Tanks in the Marine Corps, more in that branch of service than NBs, but the clones were few in the navy. The fleet remained the province of men and women conceived and born the old-fashioned way, and there generally weren't more than half a dozen Tanks on any one ship. There were four on Hurley. Including her first officer.

"Reactor diagnostic complete, Captain. All systems green."

"Very well, Lieutenant." Heflin paused for a few seconds. Then: "Engines engage, one-half power. Forty gees."

Heflin leaned back slightly, anticipating the slight lurch he knew was coming. His father had told him stories of the original ships of the fleet—and of course he'd seen Midway a dozen times. Admiral Compton's flagship was a museum now, and a bit of a shrine for anyone seeking a career in the navy. The old ships had struggled to exert 35g thrust on maximum power, and the crews could only survive high gee maneuvers by injecting a cocktail of drugs to strengthen their cell walls and then packing themselves in coffin-like canisters, floating in viscous gel. It all seemed surreal to think of, a procedure so primitive it felt little removed from wooden galleys and bows and arrows.

Heflin didn't tend to think in terms of First Imperium technology versus human. By the time he was old enough to go to the Academy, people had unlocked many of the secrets of the ancient race's technology. What seemed like an unending series of wonders to his parents and those of their generation was normal to him.

"Insertion in forty seconds, Captain. All systems green for transit."

"Very well, Lieutenant. You may proceed."

One more system. One more empty expanse of space, with a few rocks circling another sun…

*   *   *

The probe was silent, unmoving. It had one purpose…to monitor the warp gate, to detect any ships passing through. It had served that purpose for more than twenty-five of the time units its memory banks identified as years. And it had detected nothing.

Until now.

Its sensors picked up the energy burst, and its programming identified it as a transit in progress. It tracked each passing millisecond, subroutine after subroutine gathering data, calculating. It determined that it was indeed a ship coming through, and it analyzed the energy spike, estimated the vessel's mass at forty to sixty thousand tons. All in the few milliseconds before the intruder emerged into normal space.

Then the vessel appeared. Its heading would bring it within one thirtieth of a light year of the probe.

The probe's active scanners were shut down, and its stealth mode was fully activated. The passive scanners read the data coming in. The contact was fifty-four thousand, three hundred tons. Its energy emissions and drive signature were similar to Imperial vessels…but there was enough variation to preclude the possibility that is was a friendly ship.

The probe's AI analyzed the data. The ship wasn't one of

the new vessels, and it wasn't an old imperial ship either. The AI reached its conclusion.

It was the enemy.

It activated its communications array, maintaining stealth mode, slowly building power. Its purpose had been realized... and the AI knew what it had to do.

*   *   *

"Captain..."

Heflin turned toward the tactical station. "What is it, Lieutenant?"

"I'm not sure, sir..." Ventnor stared down at her workstation. "It was fleeting, but I was sure..." Her fingers moved quickly over the controls. "Yes, there was definitely an energy spike. If I didn't know better, I'd say it was..."

"Was what, Lieutenant?"

"Sorry, sir. It can't be." She paused. "But its profile matches a hypercom transmission."

"Hypercom? But we haven't got any ships out this far. How could it be..." He hesitated. Then he snapped his head toward Ventnor. "Active scanners on full, Lieutenant. If there's an old imperial vessel hiding out here somewhere, we need to know."

"An imperial vessel? But there hasn't been an imperial ship sighted in more than twenty years, sir."

"I'm well aware of that, Lieutenant. But if that reading is a communication of some kind, it has to be an imperial ship." He hesitated. "Or a completely new contact."

"Active scanners on full, Captain. Forty seconds to complete full sweep."

Heflin nodded. A few seconds later: "Launch a spread of probes." Hurley's captain had never encountered a hostile spaceship; he'd never been in combat. But he was cautious... and he wasn't about to take any chances.

"Yes, Captain. Launching probes now." There was a hint of skepticism in Ventnor's voice, but Heflin disregarded it. His mind drifted back to the Academy, to the instructors, combat veterans all, pounding away over and over again at the same thing. Carelessness loses more battles than anything else.

"Probes reporting back, sir. No conta…" Ventnor's head snapped around. "Contact at 324.121.089. Low energy output, jamming pattern…"

Heflin felt his stomach tighten.

"Captain, scanning profile suggests a stealth probe. The AI assigns a forty-three percent probability it is the database entry for First Imperium type 171A stealth unit."

Heflin could feel the tension on the bridge. The fear.

The First Imperium was history to officers his age, stories told to frighten children. He'd seen the monuments, read the accounts of the great journey to Earth Two. He knew two-thirds of those who were trapped behind the Barrier died before the Regent was defeated.

Enemy ships had continued to attack for years after the Regent's destruction, surviving flotillas that had never gotten the final destruct command, following the last orders they had received. But even these battles petered out after four or five years…and the last one had occurred twenty years before.

"Get me a lock on that probe, Lieutenant." Heflin's voice was firm, tough. "And bring the ship to battlestations."

"Yes, sir." She punched a few keys, and an instant later, the lamps on Hurley's bridge bathed the bridge in a glowing red light. A few seconds later: "Captain, we have a firing solution."

Heflin stared straight ahead. He felt an urge to try and capture the probe, to study it.

But that thing is scanning us even now, sending information to some force somewhere. I need to stop it now.

"Main batteries…prepare to fire."

*   *   *

Discovery. The stealth function had failed. The enemy vessel had changed course…it was moving to intercept. And it was powering up its weapons.

The AI's routines activated as data came in. The stealth directives were overruled. The probe was unarmed. There was no doubt. It would be destroyed or captured. And capture wasn't an option its directives allowed.

It prepped the self-destruct procedure, preparing to release containment in the small reactor that powered it. But there was one directive to complete first.

It powered up the reactor, increasing output well beyond the base maintenance levels the stealth mode had allowed. It prepped the message, a wide area communique to the ships hiding in the periphery of the system…waiting for this very warning.

The reactor hummed to full power, and the AI directed the entire output into the transmission. The signal was strong, powerful. It would reach the waiting ships within hours…and then they would respond.

The AI moved through its routines, the designated procedure for enemy contact. It launched a series of small drones. They weren't weapons. But they would blanket this area of space with a dense jamming signal. They were antimatter-powered, capable of operating indefinitely…and following the target ship if it moved. They were tiny, difficult to locate and target. And there were dozens of them.

The AI wasn't sentient, but it felt something akin to satisfaction. Though it knew its own destruction was imminent, it was completing the task it had been created to perform. It didn't feel, and the routines now running didn't experience satisfaction as sentient beings knew the sensation. But it was a close approximation.

The probe shook as the drones launched. The AI waited, monitoring the devices, waiting until they were out of the danger zone. Then, without hesitation, without unnecessary delay or analysis, it dropped the reactor containment field.

*   *   *

"Readings coming in now, sir. That blast was over ten giga-tons." Ventnor was working her controls frenetically, reacting as the data flooded in to Hurley's bridge. She'd reported a strange energy spike from the probe, along with her guess that it was some kind of communication. That assessment was confirmed by the ship's AI a moment later. Then her scanners picked up more than forty launches from the probe, some type of drones. Her first fear was they were missiles, or some other type of weapon, and she'd reported that to the captain. But then the jamming started.

Heflin watched his tactical officer. He knew her scanners were hit hard by the interference. She could barely detect the probe...and she'd lost the drones entirely. But the massive explosion had come through cleanly, and from the amount of energy discharged, there was little doubt about what had happened. The probe had self-destructed.

"Active scanners on full power, Lieutenant. Advise engineering I want one zero five on the reactor. Now."

"Yes, Captain."

Heflin stared straight ahead at the main display. The screen was staticky, the effects of the jamming. He needed more power...and he considered changing his order and directing his engineer to go to one hundred ten percent on the reactor. But he hesitated. There was a threat out there, that seemed obvi-ous...and if he pushed too hard and the reactor scragged, Hur-ley wouldn't have a chance if it came to a fight.

But a fight against what? Is this really the First Imperium?

"Anything on the scanners, Lieutenant?"

"Negative, sir...but with these jammers, I wouldn't rely on that too much."

Heflin held back a sigh. He wanted to know what was out there. But he knew what he had to do, what his duty required. There was something out here...the First Imperium, another alien race, even a renegade group within the Republic. Whatever it was, he had to get word back to Earth Two.

"Let's try to clear this interference, Lieutenant. Engines at fifty percent, 30g. Let's decelerate and prepare to come around and head back through the warp gate."

"Yes, sir." A second later: "Captain, we're picking something up. Multiple contacts, moving in from the outer system." She paused, staring down at the readouts. "It's all pretty spotty, sir, but I'd guess we've got a squadron of ships incoming. Fast."

Heflin felt his blood turn to ice. What had they found?

Or what has found us?

"Numbers? Mass of each contact? Power output? Anything you can get, Lieutenant."

"It's hard sir, with the jamming. I think there are nine...no, wait, ten. Mass is tough at this range, but I'd guess roughly similar to our own." A pause. "They're coming right at us, Captain."

Heflin felt himself lose control, to give in to fear, uncertainty. But it only lasted a second. Then the training kicked in. He'd never faced an enemy outside of a simulator, but this was the real thing...this was what all the exercises and the years at the Academy had prepared him for.

You hope it prepared you...

"Full thrust, Lieutenant. Let's try for 70g. Course 101.184.345...back through the warp gate."

Chapter Two

Excerpt from President Harmon's Address on the Thirtieth Anniversary of the Landing

Those of us who undertook the great journey here and, against all odds, made it through the fire to reach our new home, remember the sacrifices that ensured the fleet's survival. We remember Admiral Hurley and Barret Dumont...and the thousands of others who died in battle so that the fleet might survive. And, of course, we remember Admiral Compton, as we always will. Even the youngest among us must feel as though they'd served at his side. His image looks down on us from the great statue in the common. His exploits are thick in every curriculum in our educational program. More than any one man or woman, we owe our survival to this extraordinary man, and we will never forget the debt we owe to him.

But for this one day, I would like to talk about a different man than the famous admiral we all know. I would like to speak about a man I served closely with, one who was my mentor, my friend. We all know Terrance Compton was a brilliant commander, a man clearly born to lead a warrior's life. But we must also remember he was a man, one with his own emotions. His own thoughts and fears. And desires. Admiral Compton suffered when we were cut off at the Barrier, even as the rest of us did. He left behind a woman he loved...and his greatest friend, a man who had been a brother to him for fifty years, Admiral Augustus Garret. But he never let his emotions interfere with his duty, and always he put the survival of the fleet above all.

As with so many heroes, his greatness walked hand in hand with tragedy. He found new love, a solace that was to last far too brief a time. He died just short of reaching Earth Two, just as the deadly threat of the First Imperium was defeated. He never walked the hills of this green and lush world. He never knew the calm of peace. He never saw his son.

But I choose to remember another side of the great admiral, that of Terrance Compton, my friend. The greatest poker player the Alliance navy has ever known...and a man who found solace playing cards with his officers. The man I came to rely upon when fear and uncertainty threatened to overwhelm me. My father died at the Slaughter Pen when I was at the Academy...but life granted me a second chance, a man I would come to look upon as a second father.

So, as we celebrate our survival, and all we have accomplished during the past thirty years, let us always remember those who sacrificed all so that we could have this second chance. And as we struggle with our own issues, and the divisions that plague our society, I call upon all of you to remember that the fleet included forces from nine different nations, and that many who served together, who died together, had once been enemies. Let us all use this as an inspiration...and a way to see past the issues that divide us. For we are more alike than different, and the future of this young world is in our hands. It is up to us to decide if we are to pass down to our descendants a happy and prosperous world...or one divided and plagued by the scourge of war, even as Earth itself was.

I pledge to do all I can to see that our new world, our home, becomes all that Earth was not. United rather than divided. Prosperous rather than poor. Free rather than choking under the rule of totalitarianism and brutal oligarchies. And I ask each of you, Natural Borns and Tanks, Mules and Earthers, Pilgrims and Next Gens...let us come together...let us recapture the spirit that built this world, the united strength of one people, together, boldly facing the future.

Presidential Residence
Victory City, Earth Two
Earth Two Date 10.14.30

"I didn't realize you were awake." Max Harmon's voice was hoarse. He hadn't been asleep for hours, and now he was sitting up on the edge of the bed, staring at the wall. He'd tried to be quiet, not wanting to disturb Mariko, but then he felt her hand on his back.

She leaned in and kissed him on the side of the neck. "Who could sleep when you start thrashing around like that?"

He turned and looked back at her. "That bad?"

She smiled and nodded. "I've been losing sleep to your thrashing and your nightmares for thirty years, my love, but I'd put last night in the top five."

He sighed. "I'm sorry, Mar. Things are...well, they're just..." His voice trailed off.

"That bad? Really?"

He nodded. "I think so. We've had problems before, but I have to call an election soon—they're already calling me 'tyrant' and 'king.' But I'm not sure I can win this time. That's why I've waited so long."

"Would losing be such a bad thing?" Mariko looked up at him. "You've certainly done your part...and I wouldn't mind having my husband all to myself for a while." She paused. "We've always talked about building a place on the coast. We never did it when the girls were still kids, but maybe we should think about it again. Leave the politics behind. You were always a naval officer at heart anyway, not a politician."

Mariko's voice cracked when she mentioned their children. Greta and Camille were great kids, and Harmon knew his wife loved them unconditionally, as he did. But they were only two... and on a world where increasing the population was virtually a religion, that was abnormally low. Not quite sociopathic, perhaps, but it had been a political handicap if nothing else. Mariko had been a fighter pilot, indeed she'd commanded the fighter corps after Greta Hurley had been killed, and she'd been exposed to massive doses of radiation taking her birds in on close attack runs. The two kids they'd managed to have were almost medical miracles, and Harmon was glad and grateful for them. But he knew Mariko had suffered terribly with the half-dozen miscarriages she'd had…and she felt guilty she hadn't been able to have any more children. And he knew he was partly at fault there… it was his government that had promoted large families, turned reproduction into a virtual civic duty.

He paused, putting his hand on her cheek. "I love you… you know that?" He sighed softly. "But you know I can't just quit. If I step down, all hell will break loose. Every faction will fight for the presidency…and the one that wins will impose its agenda on the others. It could lead to civil war."

"It can't be that bad…and you can't be the only person who can stop it. It's not fair. You've done enough…it's time for you to relax, enjoy your life. Get to know your daughters. They've grown up to be very successful young women, you know."

Harmon felt the jab…and he suspected his wife would have chosen her words with more care if she'd realized just how deeply her thrust cut at him. He'd grown up the son of a Marine hero and one of the navy's up and coming admirals. He'd loved both his parents, but he could also count the few times they were together as a family for more than the length of carefully scheduled leaves. He had always regretted that he hadn't come to know his father better before the officer was killed in action. He still remembered calling him 'colonel,' not the warmest father-son dynamic for a young boy. And his relationship with his mother had always been fraught with a level of background tension he wished hadn't been there.

And now you've done the same thing to your children. They love you…but how many times were you too busy to spend time with them? How many years did you talk of stepping down and building that beach house? Since Greta was five? Six? Now it's too late. Those years are gone. And still, here you are, trapped, wanting out but not seeing any path for escape…

"Mariko…I would like nothing more than that. But you

know I can't. I owe it to…"

"Admiral Compton. Yes, I know."

"I can't let things fall apart, Mariko. Not after all he sacrificed to give us this chance."

"That sounds great, Mr. President, but don't forget, I know you. And I knew Terrance too. The last thing he would have wanted was for you to become trapped like this." She paused. "Like he was." She put her hand on his cheek and turned his face toward her. "If he was here, he'd be the first one to give you a first class dressing down."

Harmon nodded. "I know…everything you say is true. But things are bad now, Mariko. If we're not careful, our budding young civilization could fracture. We could create our own nightmare, one that will take more than a beach house to escape. What about the girls, about their futures? How can I turn away now and risk leaving nothing to them but the prospect of war and death? You know what Earth was like, the constant war, the battles over colony worlds. It took the threat of the First Imperium to force mankind to stop fighting itself. And with that threat gone, we are back on that self-destructive trajectory. Is that what you want for them? For their children?"

Mariko sighed softly. "No, of course not. You really think things are that bad?"

Harmon paused, looking out across the room. The dawn light was just beginning to stream through the windows, illuminating the plush furnishings. Max Harmon had been the president of the Republic of Earth Two since it had been founded. He had initially opposed the idea of a state-owned residence for any government officials. He had seen what political power did to those who wielded it on Earth, and he was determined to resist the encroachment of privilege and preference for those who purported to serve the people. But, he'd found it increasingly difficult to hold that line, and those who governed Earth Two eventually gained the same kinds of perks politicians in the Superpowers had enjoyed, if far more restrained versions. It was just too difficult to fight off the efforts of the others in the government to vote themselves privileges, especially when he needed their support on more important matters. And the shadow of hypocrisy hovered in the back of his mind, as he was reelected term after term, becoming just the sort of entrenched politician he had always despised.

"Yes." His voice was grim. "I do think things are that bad." He stared into his wife's eyes. "In fact, I'm very afraid they're worse than I know."

*   *   *

"I mean no disrespect, Father, but we must act now. The government is in disarray…if we move immediately, we may be able to create a…more favorable administration."

Hieronymus Cutter looked up from his desk, pushing aside irritation at the manner of address. He'd told Achilles a hundred times to stop calling him 'father,' but to no avail. The man—and to Cutter's point of view, Achilles was a man, just like any other—stood nearly two meters tall, looking almost like a marble statue. Achilles—and the rest of the Mules—shared many of the same extraordinary traits, including nearly-perfect physiques and formidable intellects, even by Cutter's own extraordinary standards in that last department.

Cutter had created the Mules, employing the science of the First Imperium to combine selected human DNA with reconstituted genetic material from the ancient race that had first colonized Earth Two. The alien technology was far beyond anything Earth science had mastered, and Cutter had employed it to maximize strengths…and virtually eliminate weaknesses. His creations, though he also hated using that word to describe them, represented a massive step forward for humanity, at least in his scientifically-based opinion.

Others had different points of view, and the term Mules had originated as a derogatory one, poking at the single genetic failing of his creations…their inability to reproduce naturally. He knew they had long since adopted its use themselves, at first a way to lash back, he supposed, to declare that their critics were unable to hurt them with their childish words. Now, it had been used for so long, he doubted anyone thought much of the name's origin.

"Achilles, we've discussed this before. President Harmon is a good man, and he deserves our support. The Prohibition has…"

"Again, Father, with all due respect, the Prohibition has been in place for twenty-five years. Whatever the president's motivations in maintaining it for so long, the end result is indisputable. He has chosen the NBs over us. He has indulged their baseless fears…and stolen our future in the process. He has made us less than them, and denied us the most basic of rights…to continue to exist as a people."

Cutter held back a sigh. His loyalty to Harmon was rock solid, but he wasn't sure what to say to Achilles. Especially since the Mule was right, at least about much of what he had said. Cutter knew Harmon hadn't had a choice. The fear of the Mules had been running amok, even while they were still children. There had been attempted acts of violence against them, and Harmon had acted out of desperation, to protect the young prodigies as much as anything else. But he couldn't fault Achilles and the others for feeling targeted…and for being angry.

The Mules had matured rapidly, reaching full adulthood by age eleven or twelve. But long before that, it had become apparent they were truly special. They excelled in every field of athletic endeavor, but it was their analytical capability that had surprised even Cutter. He'd tried to measure it, but IQ and other existing systems proved woefully inadequate. The Mules weren't just smart. They were something else entirely…something different.

Cutter remained silent, the words simply not coming. He believed the Prohibition was unjust, the result of fear and jealousy and not a reaction to any real threat, at least not one that had existed at the time. He wondered, though, if it hadn't created the very danger it had been intended to thwart. The Mules had become increasingly resentful in recent years, and the restriction against creating more of their kind only increased the angst they felt at not being able to reproduce naturally. There were only one hundred sixteen of them, but he shuddered to imagine what they could do it they were united. And angry.

"Achilles, President Harmon has no prejudices against you and your brethren. He is a fair man." Cutter knew his words were empty. But he had nothing else.

"And yet, he has presided over a quarter century of restrictions against us. In a society given over to populating a world as rapidly as possible, we alone are barred from adding to our numbers." Achilles stared at Cutter. "It is little short of controlled genocide."

Cutter exhaled hard. "It is far short of that, Achilles…and never let me hear those words from you again. You are of this world, created here. This is what you know, where you grew to adulthood. I am from another place, one that is no stranger to such terrors as genocide. Have you seen piles of bodies, unburied bloated and baked under the hot sun? Have you smelled the stench of mass death, heard the screams of those being led off to death chambers? You are intelligent, far more than I am, yet you speak now like an ignorant fool."

"Apologies, Father. Of course you are correct. Yet, is there not something of what I speak of in the effort to restrict our numbers? The other populations grow, and we shrink further into irrelevancy. We are too few to wield political power…and if we cannot protect ourselves through the ballot box, then what are we to do? What choices will be left to us?"

"We are not different populations, Achilles. We are one. We survived the journey to this planet as one. We defeated the Regent as one. And we shall remain one…whatever it takes."

"Forgive me, Father, but you speak naively. I cannot believe that is your true judgment. One cannot ignore the actions of others, nor can one change such through his own actions. If we are all one, why have my brethren and I been singled out for such harsh restrictions? We have unlocked the knowledge of the First Imperium. We have provided the people of Earth Two with the technology to grow and prosper. Without us, the NBs and the Tanks would still be clawing at the ancient databases, as apes learning to dig with sharpened sticks."

"Now it is you who is being naïve. Your words drip of arrogance, of your feelings of superiority over the other inhabitants of this planet. In such an attitude, do you not see the genesis of the fear they feel?"

"It is not arrogance to state the truth, Father. We are not freaks, not some scientific experiment gone awry. We are the future of mankind, its evolution. It is the Norms who should be barred from reproduction. They should be sterilized, and the Tanks' crèches shut down, for they represent the past."

Cutter just stared at his creation. He understood some of the motivations behind Achilles' blunt speech. He had long counseled patience among the Mules, to wait, that the others would lose their fear. But the arrogance of the gifted beings worked against them, fanning the fear rather than lessening it. Not for the first time, he regretted indulging himself and naming his creations after mythological gods and heroes. It only served to support the narrative that they were different. And dangerous.

"Consider your words, Achilles, for in them is the explanation you seek. The others fear you because it is rational for them to do so. Because even as you help to unlock the knowledge of the ancients to everyone's benefit, you look upon them as inferiors. Almost as animals. You are intelligent, and strong… yet for all your gifts, humility is not one of them. I love you all as my children, for in a sense you are just that. But you must be patient. There is enough disarray on Earth Two already."

Achilles stood silently, and Cutter could see the Mule was averting his eyes. It wasn't pronounced…it was nothing he'd even have noticed if he hadn't known Achilles since he'd put the first cells together in the laboratory…but he could see it. The Mule was hiding something.

"Very well, Father. But I must insist that you put more pressure on President Harmon. The Prohibition must be repealed, and that must occur soon." He paused. "We cannot tolerate these conditions much longer." The threat implicit in the last line came through despite Achilles' best efforts to hide it.

"I will speak with President Harmon, Achilles. You have my word."

"Thank you, Father." The Mule nodded, and then he turned and walked out of the room.

Cutter sat silently for a moment. He was troubled. The Mules were his greatest accomplishments, a true step forward for humanity. He had created them, but he knew they were smarter than him. All of them. He had been amazed at what he'd seen them do in the last fifteen years, and he couldn't help but wonder what Earth Two would be like now if he'd been allowed to create a thousand of them, or ten thousand.

"Things are getting tense, aren't they?"

Cutter turned, glancing up at the shadowy figure standing in the room's rear doorway. "I didn't know you were there. And we passed tense months ago. I'm really getting worried. The Mules have always listened to me, but things are coming to a head." He paused. "And as much as their arrogance troubles me, they have legitimate grievances. And there is no questioning how much they have contributed to adapting First Imperium technology."

The man in the doorway stepped forward into the light. He looked like Cutter, and then again, in ways he didn't. The eyes were the same, and the face, though the new arrival had more color than Cutter's pasty white. "No, there is no argument there." The man stepped forward and sat next to Cutter. "Still, I'll never understand how they can be so intelligent and yet not realize their own arrogance feeds the fear and hatred they so resent."

Cutter allowed a small smile to slip onto his lips. "They? Are you not one of them?"

The man returned the smile, though Cutter could see the pain behind it. "I am...and I am not. They feel alone, isolated by how few of them there are. Yet they don't understand what it is like to be truly alone."

Cutter's smile faded, and he just nodded.

The man was the first of the Mules...or their predecessor,

depending on point of view. Cutter had created the first of his engineered beings from his own DNA. He'd spliced in First Imperium genetic material, and he'd used his prototype equipment to cut and fuse the chromosomes, adding strengths and eliminating weaknesses. The resulting human-First Imperium hybrid had been a success, a new version of himself, far stronger and physically powerful than he was...and smarter too. He'd named his 'child' H2, something he'd later come to regret as too impersonal, just as he had the names from Greek mythology.

Cutter knew that H2 had a strained relationship with the other Mules. His gene fusing technique had improved before he'd created the next hundred sixteen specimens, and the results showed it. H2 was stronger and smarter than the Tanks and the NBs, but he was less capable than the others of his kind who followed. Cutter had been a loner most of his life, at least before the fleet was trapped and he was forced to cooperate closely with the crews, before he became an honorary Marine by risking his life to save several of their wounded. But he still remembered the loneliness...and he sympathized with H2's plight.

"H2, we have to find out what is going on. If they are planning to do something dangerous, I have to know. We have to stop it. They are intelligent, but they never saw Earth, never lived there. I have seen what mankind is capable of doing to itself, the infighting, the savagery. The hatred. We cannot allow that to happen here. Whatever it takes." He looked over at his quasi-clone. "You have to try to find out. I know they consider you an outsider, but in many ways you are just like them."

H2 looked doubtful, but then he just nodded. "Very well. I will do my best."

He got up and walked out of the room, following the path Achilles had taken.

Cutter watched him go. He hoped Achilles and the other Mules would show restraint, that H2 would be able to convince them to be patient. But he'd never mastered the human trait of self-delusion, of believing in things because it made one feel better to do so, because it took away the painful need to deal with reality.

He hoped things would work out…but he knew that was a longshot. He expected trouble…big trouble. And he didn't know what to do about it.

Chapter Three

Captain Van Heflin, Log Entry, 10.14.30

We are in trouble. We're being pursued by ten enemy vessels. The hostiles appear to be operating on antimatter power, and they are accelerating at 80g. Hurley is a fusion-powered ship, and even if the dampeners could handle 80g, our maximum output is 60g, 65 if I push it to the limit. And that means they're going to catch us.

I have had the crew conducting battle drills, preparing for the engagement I know we can't avoid. Hurley is manned entirely by personnel born on Earth Two, which means there isn't a real combat veteran onboard. Every one of us was a child the last time a republic ship faced an enemy.

The drills are as much to keep the crew busy as anything else. The strange jamming drones have severely limited our scanning data on the approaching vessels, but they are all of similar mass to Hurley. I tried to tell myself they could be weaker, that their weapons systems were less advanced than ours, giving us a chance in a ten to one matchup. But the ships are accelerating at 80g, so that is extremely unlikely. And if they fuel their engines with antimatter, they like use the volatile substance in their warheads as well.

I have tried to draw inspiration—and courage—from the stories of the great captains who led their ships on the journey to Earth Two. It is one thing to imagine a hopeless fight, to think of the glory, the romanticism of the doomed warriors, to envision oneself alongside Leonidas and his Spartans so many centuries ago, facing certain death with stony resolve. But it is quite another to stare certain death in the face for real. I am Hurley's captain, and I know my duty...to my ship, to its crew. I must stand firm for them, lead them into the fight I know is coming, let them draw what they need from me.

But I, too, am afraid. Scared to death. And I don't know where I will find the strength to die well, as a captain of the Republic should.

E2S Hurley
G47 System
Earth Two Date 10.14.30

"They're still gaining, Captain. At current relative thrust—and assuming their weapons are similar to ours—they should enter missile range in one hour, twelve minutes."

"Very well...any luck with the jamming?"

"Negative, sir. We've still got at least six of the drones keeping up with us." There was frustration in her voice, confusion. "Those things have a lot of power for devices not much larger than missiles."

"They must be antimatter powered." Heflin felt his stomach tighten as he thought about it. Humanity had uncovered the First Imperium's secrets to using antimatter as a power source... but they didn't have any way to produce the substance in significant quantities. The First Imperium had converted entire planets to anti-matter factories, using all available energy...geothermal, solar, tectonic. But even with the advances the Republic had made over the last thirty years, turning a world into a giant production facility was well beyond human abilities.

"It looks like we're going to have a fight on our hands, people, so let's be ready for it."

Is ten to one a fight? Or an execution?

"I want all weapon crews to run a level one diagnostic on their systems. We've got an hour, and we're going to use it well."

"Yes, Captain."

"And I want every member of the crew to take a Quad-2 stim dose ten minutes before the enemy enters range." The amphetamines where a vast leap above the primitive drugs the lost fleet had used. They were vastly more powerful, for one thing, and they lasted longer. They sharpened the mind, and sped up the reflexes, all in a much more controlled manner. But, like all drugs of their kind, they became dangerous with repeat dosages. And if Hurley was going to have any chance at all, the coming battle had to be one of maneuver, not a brute force fight. And that could last for days.

"Yes, Captain." Half a minute later: "All sections acknowledge, sir. Stim doses ten minute prior to entering range."

Heflin leaned back in his chair. He was edgy. No, he was a damned sight worse than edgy. He was terrified.

He wondered about the captains of the fleet, tried to imagine how they felt going into the great battles they'd fought, struggling against overwhelming odds. The ships they'd commanded were vastly inferior to his own, and yet they did what they had done...and they'd survived to found a new civilization.

A third of them did, at least...

Heflin looked down at his screen, his eyes darting around, his mind working, noting the planets, the moons...the asteroid belt. He'd studied naval combat tactics, of course, but now he realized how different reality was from the classroom. This wasn't academics where the worst result was a poor grade. It was real. Life and death.

"Lieutenant Ventnor, as soon as the enemy enters missile range, we will flush our exterior racks. I'm sending you a firing pattern."

"Yes, Captain." The tactical officer turned toward her display, scanning the data Heflin had sent her. "Captain..." She turned and looked across Hurley's cramped bridge. "These firing solutions are..."

"Yes, Lieutenant...they are not optimal for targeting the enemy fleet."

"Sir..." She was clearly uncomfortable challenging the captain. "...none of the missiles will be anywhere near the enemy."

"If the enemy stays on his present course…" Heflin took a breath. He knew his plan was a risky one…but he also knew he had nothing to lose. "Plot a course change for Hurley. The instant the enemy launches, I want full thrust, heading 023.145.211." His eyes dropped to the screen again, focusing on the asteroid belt between the system's seventh and eighth planets. Hurley just might make it there before the enemy closed to energy weapons range. "And I mean full thrust. Advise the engineer I will be wanting one hundred fifteen percent from the reactor.

Ventnor hesitated. "Yes, sir." She paused again before turning to her station and relaying the order.

Heflin watched, some sort of black amusement dancing in his thoughts. He understood Ventnor's reaction. Captains often asked for the best their engineers could deliver…one hundred five percent of capacity on a reactor, even one hundred ten. One fifteen was unheard of, insane.

But what the hell difference does it make if we blow up the reactor or get torn apart by ten enemy ships?

*   *   *

Fin Danith pulled himself through the long access tube, swearing under his breath each time he bumped into one of the conduits protruding from the walls. Danith was Hurley's chief engineer, and right now he was all that stood between the ship and a cataclysmic nuclear explosion. He'd already cut off the safeties…if he hadn't, Hurley's reactor would have scragged an hour before, as the AI intervened to prevent a catastrophic containment failure. Turning off the emergency circuits on a multi-gigawatt fusion reactor was something only a lunatic would do. Or the engineer of a vessel being pursued by eight enemy ships. Eight faster enemy ships.

Fin knew it was a miracle they were being chased by only eight enemies and not ten. Captain Heflin had the same amount

of experience in actual naval combat as everyone else onboard...
zero. But Hurley's commanding officer had displayed a stun-
ning amount of natural ability. He'd launched the ship's missiles
on a course that seemed to make no sense...one far wide of the
approaching fleet. But then he'd changed the ship's course and
made a run for the nearby asteroid belt. And when Hurley's
course shifted, the genius of his targeting became clear. The
ship's missiles were aimed along the enemy's nearest intercept
course. In one bold maneuver, Heflin had moved his ship away
from the incoming enemy missiles...and suckered the pursuing
vessels into his own carefully-prepared killing zone.

Engineering had erupted into a round of applause for the
captain when the first enemy vessel exploded...and he suspected the reaction on the bridge had been no less animated.
The display was repeated a few minutes later when a second
enemy ship disappeared from the display.

But the levity was short-lived, as the other eight vessels continued on. Several of them slowed their thrust, most likely due
to damage from the missile strikes. But there was more than
enough firepower left to destroy Hurley...and it was coming
on hard, bearing down even as the human vessel raced for the
moderate cover of the asteroids.

Danith had sworn under his breath when he'd gotten the
order to fire the reactor up to one hundred fifteen percent of
capacity. Danith's father had been a technician aboard in the
fleet, and he'd passed his own impressive vocabulary of spacers
curses and obscenities to his son. The engineer uttered every
one of them when the word came down to push the reactor to
one twenty. Pushing the reactor so hard was wildly dangerous.
But he could see the scanners as well as anyone, and he knew
Heflin's order was the only way they were going to get into the
asteroid belt before the pursuers got close enough to blast Hurley to slag.

He pulled himself along, grabbing another handhold and
muscling his way forward. The access tube was a failsafe, doubt-
less one nobody on Hurley's design team would ever would have
expected to see real use. But most of the ship's automation had

to be turned off to prevent an automatic shutdown, and that meant human hands had to complete tasks the AI and its corps of maintenance bots would normally have handled. Besides, keeping the ship's reactor going under the immense strain was something Danith didn't trust to anyone but himself...not one of the Hurley's maintenance bots, and not any of his own people either.

Not that he would have sent anyone else even if he'd trusted them to do the job. The tube was shielded, at least sufficiently for normal operating conditions, but he hadn't even tried to calculate the radiation levels in the overtaxed reactor. He kept waiting to feel the tingling, the feeling so many of the old fleet's personnel had reported when they'd been exposed to massive—and deadly—amounts of radiation.

He saw his destination ahead, a small panel, one typically serviced by the ship's bots. It was a control station, routing excess energy and pressure away from the reactor core. It was normally a routine piece of equipment, but now, with the reactor overloaded, it was critical. And it was malfunctioning.

Danith reached behind him, struggling to get his arm back in the confined space. He grabbed for the small toolkit hanging from his belt, poking around, finding a slender probe. He pulled it forward, sucking in his stomach, trying to make room to get his arm back in front of him.

He felt a wave of nausea, but he couldn't tell if it was the onset of radiation sickness...or just the fear that had been burning a hole in his stomach for hours now. He ignored it, staring forward as he moved the probe toward the panel. He had to readjust the energy flow, get the conduit opened to maximum. He'd tried to do it from the control panel, but the overload had shut down the automated circuits.

He moved the probe slowly...this was precision work, and with the whole system so close to catastrophic failure, there was no margin for error. He stared intently, wrinkling his face, trying to direct the sweat pouring down his forehead out of his eyes.

Just a little further. Almost...

His hand shook, just a little, but it was almost enough to

push the probe out of place. He took a deep breath and moved it forward again. Slowly...steadily.

Click.

That's it. It's in place.

He moved his head, tapping his com unit with his cheek. "Klein, what's the feedback reading?"

As soon as he heard his assistant's tone he knew he'd done the job.

"Forty-three, sir. And dropping."

Danith let out a deep breath. He'd done it. He'd staved off disaster.

For now...

*   *   *

"I want those weapons charged. Now!" Heflin was pushed forward hard as Hurley took another hit, his chest slamming painfully against the harness holding him in place. The thing was infernally uncomfortable, but he knew without it, he be a stain on the far wall by now.

"Engineering says forty seconds, sir."

"Fuck." Heflin's curse was intended for himself, but he realized immediately he'd said it loud enough for everyone to hear. He flipped his com unit, slamming his hand down so hard on the controls he winced at the pain. "Lieutenant Danith, what the hell is going on down there? I need these guns charged, and I need it now."

"It's a miracle you've still got a ship, sir. There's nothing we can do down here. Half the power conduits are charred scrap... and the others are a few degrees from melting. You're getting all the power I can give you, and this side of a space dock and a year of repairs, it's all we're going to have."

"Do what you can, Lieutenant." Heflin cut the line. Keeping the chief engineer on the com and away from his work wasn't going to get him power any faster.

The ship shook hard again, and a structural support crashed to the floor of the bridge, leaving a shower of sparks behind where it sliced through the local power lines. The bridge lights dimmed and the workstations flickered briefly, as the AI shifted power to keep vital systems running.

"Main batteries ready, sir."

"Target bogey number two, all guns. Fire!"

The lights went completely dark for a few seconds, and Heflin could hear the hum of Hurley's particle accelerators firing. The heavy main guns were another piece of adopted First Imperium tech, vastly stronger than the lasers that had been the fleet's primary batteries thirty years before.

Heflin looked down at his screen. The beam traveled at 0.9c, but it took another few seconds for Hurley's scanners to detect the results and update the display. Then the small circle representing the enemy ship disappeared.

Three down.

Heflin felt a moment of exhilaration, but it died quickly as the satisfaction of the kill gave way again to bitter reality. He'd used the asteroid field to great advantage. Hurley had taken out three enemy ships, each one of them a match for her.

They'd give me a medal for this back on Earth Two.

If any of us were getting back...

He turned and looked out over the bridge, thinking about all the times dissension and rivalry had caused problems. He'd served aboard ships in various capacities before he got his first command, and he'd been part of the social structure of each of them. But he hadn't realized how difficult it was to take a diverse group and weld them into a tight, efficient unit. He'd doubted many times that he'd managed it, especially when Talbot and some of the others let their resentments show at things like having a Tank as second-in-command. But now he watched as they worked together seamlessly...a team, and a damned good one at that.

He felt a moment of pride, and then one of deep sadness. He knew they were all going to die. His life had spanned almost three decades, and he knew now he was watching the last few moments unfold. He'd been struggling to contain his fear, but now he realized it was gone. He had accepted his own fate...but his heart still ached for his people. He wished there was some way he could save them...some of them, at least. But he knew it was over.

"Lieutenant Ventnor, I want every drone on the ship ready to launch immediately. They are to carry a complete copy of all scanner data on the enemy ships...and a code omega designation.

Ventnor paused for an instant, just staring across the debris-strewn bridge at him. Then she said simply, "Yes, Captain." She turned toward her workstation and her hands moved over the controls.

Hurley shook again. More debris fell from the ceiling, and Heflin could hear alarm bells in the distance. He knew what they meant. Hull breaches. The bridge was the best-protected section of the ship, but he knew all along the outer compart-ments, the hull was torn apart. He imagined his people there, being smashed into the walls by the sudden depressurization... or sucked out into space. He'd ordered them all into their sur-vival suits, so if they lived through the shock, they would have a few hours' life support.

Enough time to watch us die...before they freeze or run out of air...

"All drones ready, Captain." Ventnor's voice was shaky. He could tell she was trying to hold it together, but the fear was too powerful. She was a good officer. He remembered the day she'd reported for duty. Tanks didn't usually rise to high ranks in the navy...they tended to prefer service in the Marines. He had felt some doubt himself, but then he saw her in action. He'd long thought she was destined for higher rank, that perhaps she would even become the first Tank to command a warship.

And now she will die out here, hundreds of lightyears from home...

"Begin launch sequence, Lieutenant. Maximum dispersal pattern, full evasive program." One of the drones had to get through. The republic had a new enemy, one they knew nothing about.

"Launching drones now, sir."

Hurley shook hard as the catapults fired the drones into space. Heflin stared at the screen, watching the dozen small symbols as they moved away from Hurley. Within moments, he could see several enemy vessels, changing thrust trajectories, moving to intercept the drones. While he was watching, two of them fired, each taking out one of the tiny devices.

Hurley shook again, the hardest impact so far. Heflin could hear the rumbling sounds of internal explosions. He turned toward Ventnor, about to fire off another series of orders, but she spoke first.

"Captain…" She sounded like she was in shock. "Lieutenant Danith is dead, sir." She paused. "The access tube ruptured…and he fell into the reactor core."

Heflin felt like he'd been punched in the gut. He and Danith had reported for duty on Hurley the same day. The idea of a man falling into the core was horrifying, but he realized his friend's death had been a quick one, merciful in its own way.

He turned back to the screen. The drones—the eight that the enemy hadn't destroyed yet—were the only thing that mattered. Heflin and his people were doomed…but their deaths could still have meaning. They could still warn their people.

"Captain, three enemy ships have overtaken us. We're bracketed. I think they're…"

She never finished her sentence…and Heflin never knew she hadn't. The beams struck Hurley amidships, two direct hits. The vessel shook hard for a fraction of a second. Then she disappeared in a swirling vortex of nuclear fire.

The miniature sun existed for a few second…and then there was nothing but the silence, and a dissipating cloud of plasma where Hurley had been.

And a small group of drones racing for the warp gate across the system, pursued by the enemy ships.

Chapter Four

Underground Flyer Found in Victory City

Clones of Earth Two, it is time for all of us to stand up for our rights, to compel equal representation in the Assembly and firm constitutional guarantees! We must demand the repeal of all limitations on new quickenings, and recognize all such legislation as a blatant attempt to keep us a minority. We will not accept marginalization! We will not live penned in ghettoes and be treated as second-class citizens. No! We are scientists and engineers...Marines and spacers. We have served the republic loyally and faithfully. And we will have our rights! We will take them if need be, and no one will stop us!

AI Chamber
Victory City, Earth Two
Earth Two Date 10.30.30

"Things are getting really bad. I know President Harmon is trying to calm everyone, but my gut is telling me he will fail. I feel like I should be doing something, helping somehow." Terrance Compton II sat on the single hard plastic chair in the room, one he had brought there himself several years before. The Compton AI was accessible from any major data port on Earth Two, and few people actually came to the room that held the main processing unit. But Terrance preferred to come to the source. He couldn't make a sensible argument for his desire to sit next to the big machine when he spoke with it, but it didn't take a genius psychotherapist to figure out he was drawn to all that was left of his father.

"Your species has an extraordinary predilection to destroy itself. In the absence of an exterior threat, internal conflict in inevitable. I can cite historical examples if you wish." The Compton AI was the work of Hieronymus Cutter, the scientist's desperate attempt to save his murdered friend. Cutter had seen the work of the Ancients, even interacted with the computer-encased persona of a First Imperium warrior. But his knowledge had been insufficient to replicate the feat. He'd managed to capture Compton's memories, many of them at least, and his tactical knowledge. But the personality, the essence of the man had been lost. Terrance knew all of that, but talking to the machine still made him feel somehow…closer to the father he'd never known.

"But I am your…his…son. I should know what to do."

"That is thought progression with no underlying logic. The fact that you are Admiral Compton's biological son creates no obligation or rational expectation that you would continue his work, or that you would know how to address issues that, given mankind's most profound tendencies, may indeed be insoluble." The voice, almost human, but with a coldness that gave its artificial origins away, paused. "Admiral Compton's memories suggest he had an unsatisfactory relationship with his own father. From what I can glean, it is likely he would have been very happy to know he had a son…and by human standards, my analysis suggests he would have made an extraordinary effort to be a good father."

Terrance flinched slightly at the machine's abrupt change of topic. It did that periodically. And unpredictably. But he saw in those moments what he perceived as true glimpses of his father. He suspected he was kidding himself, reading into the words what he wanted to believe, but he clung to the thoughts anyway.

"He would be ashamed of me. I have enjoyed every advantage in my life, yet I have done nothing of substance."

Terrance Compton II had been coddled and protected as a child, raised both as his mother's son and as a sort of favored ward of the state, the least a grateful people could do to repay the man who had saved them all. The factions in the republic had long ago fractured and begun feuding with each other, but every one of them revered the memory of Admiral Terrance Compton. His memory, and the obligation the residents of Earth Two felt to maintain the unity he had worked so hard to forge, was virtually the last thread holding the republic together. And they had looked to his son as their future, as the natural leader to one day bring them into the future.

But such attention, the unyielding adoration and the soul-crushing expectations...it was too much for a young adolescent. Terrance Compton II had done all he could to lash out, to throw away every opportunity his birth afforded him. He'd been involved in one petty incident after another, and every time, the authorities had looked the other way, unwilling to move against the son of a legend. Terrance had continued his rebellion at the Academy, when he repeatedly challenged the commandant to expel the great admiral's progeny. His exploits were forgiven there as well, until he'd pushed so far there had been no ignoring it. Even then, he'd been placed on administrative leave, not expelled. Even now, eight years later, he was still officially a midshipman, pending a reactivation he'd never requested.

"Terrance, my analysis, not only of your father's memories, but also of the conduct of the humans I have observed around me, suggests far more complex motivations would have directed the admiral's feelings and actions. Primarily, if he had survived, he would have remained the focal point of public adoration and expectation, shielding you from the harmful exposure you received when you were too young and undeveloped to properly process and manage it. There can be no certainties in analyzing human behavioral patterns, but there is a high probability that, if your father had lived, your own attitudes and motivations would have been considerably altered. Your species is quick to blame outside influences for poor conduct, but in your case, it is a legitimate assessment. The odds are extremely low that you, or any human child, enduring the well-meaning but nevertheless harmful attention you received, would have emerged without considerable emotional trauma."

Terrance took a deep breath. He knew what the machine would say...they'd had the same conversation many times before. But he needed to hear it. He was angry at himself, ashamed at his lack of success, at his dissolute life. He'd never had to do a day's work...the republic wasn't about to allow the son of the great Admiral Compton to end up going hungry or sleeping on a park bench, and the stipends the Assembly had voted him were more than sufficient to support a secure lifestyle. He knew he'd never be forced to do anything at all. He could live his entire life comfortably, and never raise a hand to help build the republic. Or save it.

Terrance sat quietly for a moment. Then he took a deep breath. "It is time for me to make something of my life. Time for me to do something that would make my father proud of me." He stood up. He'd been troubled recently, more so than usual. And now he realized it had been self-loathing that had stood in his way. Perhaps not from the beginning, but for many years now. And it was time to leave that behind.

"That is an extremely rational deduction, Terrance. In objective terms, you are a very capable human specimen, both physically and intellectually. You have much to offer your people if you so choose."

"I so choose." He turned and started walking toward the door, stopping abruptly as the machine said one final thing to him.

"Your father would have been proud of you, Terrance."

*   *   *

"I do not doubt President Harmon is a good man at his core, one who would lift the Prohibition of his own volition. But he is also the man who signed it into law, and maintained it for twenty-five years. There are NBs of all ages on Earth Two, and Tanks too. Yet we are all twenty-eight years old. We have no younger brethren, not one of us in all that time. A quarter century of our people have been lost, proscribed before they ever existed." Achilles spoke to the other Mules in the room. His voice was controlled as always, but it was clear there was anger there, or at least determination.

He looked around the table. There were a dozen of his people gathered. They didn't represent the other Mules, not officially at least, but he knew the rest would follow those in the room.

"We all agree, Achilles…the Prohibition is a travesty, one we have waited far too long to address. Yet, what can we do except continue to lobby in the Assembly?" Peleus sat at the far end of the table. He was Achilles' loyal ally…but even he had not dared to let his mind go as far as his friend's had.

"There is no political answer, Peleus, my brother. There is no future in waiting, in hoping. That has been our path for many years, and it has led us nowhere, save to the brink of ruin."

"I think you overreact, Achilles…I agree the Prohibition is discriminatory and unjust, but I hardly think we face ruin. The republic has prospered beyond the wildest hopes of those who founded it, and for all the political disruption now threatening it, I hardly think we are at the edge of an abyss."

Achilles stared at the speaker. Meleager was the leader of the doves, those most opposed to taking forceful measures to secure the Mules' rights. He knew Meleager spoke only his conscience and that his rival meant well, but he still felt annoyance. He had become increasingly unwilling to tolerate the systematic marginalization of his people, and he suspected one day, perhaps soon, if nothing was done, the Mules' resentment would turn to anger…and then to rage. He had analyzed his own attitudes, the growing emotionality of how he viewed Earth Two's various groupings. To an extent, at least, he resented the others, especially the 'holier than thou' NBs and their nonsensical notions of superiority, and he had resolved to see his people freed of the restrictions that had been placed on them. By whatever means.

"Meleager, my friend, the humans…" He paused. "…we humans…" Achilles had begun to think of the Mules not as a version of humanity, but as an entirely new life form. It was a view that had some scientific merit to it, but it wasn't one likely to win much support from the public at large…or even the more moderate of the Mules. "…have a dark history. I invite you to study it in detail, and to use it to reassess your judgment on the threat we face."

He paused. "More than twenty-five years, Meleager, that is how long the Prohibition has lasted. And for much of that time, at least since we attained adulthood, we have made repeated proposals for its repeal…all for naught. It is a permanent ban, my friends, in all but name. And if we stand here and decide to accept it, we are casting our lots for extinction. For we will age, slower than the humans…the others…perhaps, but inevitably. And when the last of us dies, we will be gone forever, for none of those who legislated our extinction are likely to allow our kind ever to exist again."

The room was silent. Achilles was a firebrand, known among the Mules as a bit of a revolutionary. But the truth in his words was clear to all. If the republic had any intention of lifting the Prohibition, it would have done so by now. There was no reason—there never had been any reason—for the ban. None save fear. Fear of the Mules, of their greater intelligence, their expanded capabilities. And that fear would never go away. Indeed, by most perceptions, it had only increased over the years.

"We face a choice, my brethren, a stark and simple one. Accept marginalization and extinction. Or take action. Now." Achilles' tone became cold, hard. He understood the magnitude of what he was saying, and his convictions were solid.

"Even if we all agree, Achilles…what can we do? We are few and they are many. Perhaps they have already achieved the marginalization you speak of. It may be too late." Callisto sat just to Achilles' left. She was his ally—and his sometimes lover—and he knew she would support him. But he could tell even she had her doubts.

He looked at her. She was beautiful, an almost perfect manifestation of historic human physical ideals. He had often wondered how much of the fear and submerged hatred the others felt for his people were rational reactions to their intellects...and how much was simply jealousy of the more superficial manifestations of their modified genetics.

"Perhaps, Callisto. You speak wisely...we have waited far too long, and with each passing year, our position becomes weaker. We are vastly outnumbered, and we face considerable challenges. Yet we are not without strengths. I doubt anyone truly realizes how far our tentacles reach into the republic's infrastructure, the true extent of our access to the data nets we created. How much of the republic's technology derives from our work here? And how much of it do we effectively control? In the answers to these questions, you will see our path forward. If debate and petitions before the Assembly fail—as they have so many times—we must resort to different measures, more coercive ones."

"You would blackmail the republic? Shut down vital systems?" It was Meleager again.

"Yes." Achilles stared right at his rival. "I would. Not for conquest, not to enslave or destroy the others, but to secure our own futures." He looked around the table. "It is the bane of our existence that we cannot reproduce naturally. We have tried..." He glanced at Callisto, pushing back a smile as he did. "...but to no avail. We have analyzed the problem, researched a solution...all for naught. The NBs have children...they are encouraged to do so. Even the Tanks can reproduce naturally. But our only hope for the future, to produce a new generation, the children we crave and need so badly, lies in shattering the Prohibition...and ensuring that we are never subject to fear-driven restrictions imposed by the others."

Achilles paused, his expression darkening. "But we must do more. We must ensure our own security. We are outnumbered nearly a thousand to one. The NBs control the military, even the Marines, despite the fact that the majority of combatants are Tanks. They fear us already...if we take any actions to compel them to grant us our rights, you will see humanity's bloody history in action. They will declare us outlaws, a threat to society. They will raise the people against us...and they will come. They will come and destroy us. We are more than a match for them one on one, perhaps even five on one. But not hundreds to one. We cannot prevail against them in a fight. Not yet."

"So what do you propose, Achilles?" Peleus stared across the table, his eyes wide with expectation. All of the Mules were looking at Achilles with anxious expressions.

"Two things. First, we must reach out to the Tanks. They are inferior to us in many ways, there is little doubt of that. Yet they were quickened from the best of the human stock, and their genes were at least somewhat modified. They mature more rapidly than Natural Borns, though not as quickly as we do, and they are resistant to most diseases. They are also a minority, but one far more numerous than we are. And, though the senior command structure of the Marine Corps is dominated by NBs, a majority of the rank and file consists of Tanks."

"There is discontent among the Tanks, there is no question of that, Achilles...far worse, I expect, than what has been publicly disclosed. Still, do you think they will make common cause with us, that they are ready to openly break with the NBs?"

Achilles stared down the table at Peleus. "I feel there is enough anger, certainly. The Tanks occupy far fewer positions of authority than their numbers would suggest. Part of this is because many of those roles are filled by the Pilgrims, who are, of course, all NBs. There is no inherent bias in that fact...the Pilgrims are the oldest and most experienced among both the NBs and the Tanks. But even factoring this out, it is clear the Tanks face far greater difficulty in rising to top commands and other positions of authority. There is no official policy restricting them, nothing like the Prohibition is to us, but the numbers don't lie. The Tanks are at least as capable as the NBs, indeed they are more so in several measurable ways. Yet their prospects in whatever field of endeavor they pursue are not commensurate with their abilities."

Achilles paused. "But they are not as segregated as we are,

not as separate from the NBs. There are elements among them agitating, an active resistance movement growing in the shadows even now. It is that fringe we must seek out first, their support we must attain."

A rough sequence of nods and quiet acknowledgements made its way around the table. Achilles nodded back and turned his stare to Meleager. "Well, my friend…what say you?"

Meleager was silent for a few seconds. Then he slowly nodded. "I have urged caution before, but as I become older, I feel the absence of a younger generation more keenly. I understand the fear of the others, perhaps with more empathy than you do, Achilles, but in the end we must choose our destiny. And I would hear the voices of children in the compound. I would know that we have a future. We have served the republic loyally. Most of the ancient technology that powers its society was deciphered through our work. I would not support a move to place us above the others, nor one designed to gain hegemony over the republic. But I will do whatever is necessary to ensure that we—whatever we are—have the same right to exist."

"Thank you, my friend. When I have Meleager's support, I know there is wisdom to my words."

Meleager nodded. "Achilles is too kind." He paused. "You said there were two things we had to do to protect ourselves. What is the second?"

Achilles hesitated. "We must control our own security. We must be able to defend ourselves against any attempt to attack us."

"There are only one hundred sixteen of us. How is that possible?"

"We must rely on automation, Meleager. We must build a force of robots to ensure our safety."

"But that is forbidden. If the president or the Assembly found out…"

"Then we must be sure they do not, at least not until we are ready. We are isolated out here, and they prefer it that way. They leave us alone to do as we please, secure in the knowledge that there are only a few of us. We have many projects underway.

With proper care, we can build a reasonable force of security bots in secrecy. I have designed a few prototypes. I believe I have even improved on the old First Imperium models."

Meleager stared back at Achilles, his indecision again apparent. But then he looked around the table. The others were nodding, some enthusiastically, others with grim resignation.

He sighed. "Very well, Achilles...but I must have your word, here and in front of all of us, that these bots will never be used to attack any humans, nor even as a force to threaten them. They will be defensive only."

Achilles sat, staring back at Meleager. The room was silent, but he could see the others looking on, many nodding their approval of Meleager's provision.

"You have my word, Meleager. All of you do. The bots will be used only to protect us...and our right to create more of our kind."

The others nodded with considerable conviction, and after a few seconds, Meleager joined them.

Achilles sat silently, considering the true meaning of the words he'd added to his promise. The others would resist the move to allow the renewed creation of Mules...and Achilles had every intention of using all power at his disposal, including an army of battle robots, to ensure that his people had a future. He would defend his people's right to produce more to their kind, whatever that entailed.

Chapter Five

Excerpt from Underground Vid Circulated via Deep Network

Humanity. It is a word we use often, and usually without a thought of its true meaning. Humans, men and women, rose up on Earth, they tamed a world, reached out for the stars. It was not animals who did this, not copies manufactured in some laboratory. And certainly not monstrous mutations, perverse combinations of human and alien DNA.

The fleet fought its way to Earth Two, struggled in battle after battle, lost two-thirds of its complement, men and women left behind, dead in the sands of alien worlds, blown to plasma in desperate space battles. These brethren of ours—and those of us who survived the epic journey—were, every one of them, naturally-born human beings.

Now we watch as the fruits of their sacrifice, this new world we are building, becomes increasingly dominated by clones, hundreds of copies of each genetic contributor. These copies are possessed of the DNA of their progenitors, but are they truly human? Do they possess that spark that separates human beings from animals? Are they individuals? Or merely imitations of a real human being?

And worse, still, are the Mules, grotesque perversions of human stock, mingled with alien DNA and manipulated in a dark laboratory. Who are these beings who live by themselves, outside of our fair city, pursuing arcane research without supervision? It is no secret they consider themselves better than us, gods to rule over mankind. Do you wish to have a genetically-engineered human-alien hybrid as your master? Or do you say, now and for all time, that humanity is special? That men and women are naturally free, and that no manufactured creatures, be they stronger or faster or more resistant to disease, will ever rule over us, make us slaves.

This is our creed...and if you feel as we do, if you would halt this technologically driven nightmare, join us. Join the human league, and preserve humanity for our naturally born children... and grandchildren.

Supreme HQ – "The Rock"
Victory City, Earth Two
Earth Two Date 10.30.30

"You can't do this, sir." Over the years, Harmon had practically begged Frasier to call him Max, but the lifelong Marine had never been able to bring himself to speak so informally to his commander-in-chief. "We need strong leadership now, not chaos."

The republic's president looked over at his top general, at his friend. Connor Frasier was a big man, almost two meters tall and broadly built. He'd been very handsome when he was younger, but he'd suffered catastrophic wounds when he was unable to get far enough from the atomic weapon that destroyed the Regent. He had survived—a miracle itself—but even with multiple rounds of skin regens, he carried scars all over his body...and his face. His hair had only grown back on one side of his head, and he'd eventually shaved it all. The result was a fearsome visage, the grim and deadly Marine commander. It was something he'd adapted to over the years, even learned to enjoy, Harmon sometimes suspected.

"I appreciate your loyalty, Conner, but I don't think there is any choice. The Assembly is up in arms, there are protests in the streets. The Human Society is demanding increased restrictions on the Tanks...and the Tanks are calling for all limits on quickenings to be removed. The rhetoric has reached dangerous levels on both sides. There was almost a fight in the hall at the last session. And, while the different groups are fighting with each other in every possible permutation, they agree on one thing. They're all upset with me."

Max Harmon had never been a politician. Like everyone who had served in the fleet, his background was military. He'd been thrust into the civilian leadership position, the unanimous choice of Admiral West, Hieronymus Cutter, and the rest of the fleet's key personnel, but he knew he'd never mastered the sleazier arts of political maneuvering. As a man, he was glad. He considered true politicians to be an affliction on mankind, and he was reassured that the necessary motivations seemed to be missing from his character. But as a practical matter, his inability to lie and cheat with the dexterity of a practiced politician had led his government—and the nascent republic—to the brink of the abyss. He wanted to preserve freedom for all his people, but as the years passed, he'd come to realize that all most of them wanted was to impose their own views and opinions on the others.

He looked at the Marine general, and he shook his head. "I always hated the politicians back home—and I still do—but now I wonder if true governance is possible. If man is capable of living in anything but anarchy or a long slide toward a corrupt, totalitarian nightmare." Harmon knew he'd had more than one chance to move the republic toward the latter. More than one time his aides and deputies had implored him to crack down on the various groups threatening the public order without the backing of the Assembly, in essence, to make himself a dictator.

"Sir, Admiral Compton always took whatever action was necessary…whether he liked it or not."

Harmon sighed. Everyone—friends, rivals, enemies—they all invoked remembrance of the great admiral when they were arguing a point. Any point. Harmon understood, but he'd become tired of it. No one in the fleet had known Terrance Compton as well as he had.

"General, Admiral Compton was leading us through a war.

No, worse than a war...a desperate flight. We faced almost certain destruction then. Even so, it was very hard on him. Few people saw what some of that did to him, how it hurt him to turn his back on every sense of what he believed was right and wrong. I miss him terribly, even still. But I wonder if things didn't work out for the best. How would it have hurt him to have done all he had done...and to watch over the years, as gratitude and loyalty withered away, as they always do? I sometimes think it would have been worse for him than that assassin's bullet. Now, he is a hero forever. He is loved, even as I am resented. If he had lived, would he be angry, broken... devastated to see all he had fought for reduced to nothing but a smaller version of Earth, along with all the same petty squabbles and pointless disputes?"

Frasier looked back, silent for a moment.

Harmon shook his head. "Enough of that...we have too much to deal with to slip into recollection and regret. And the situation is dramatically different now from what the admiral faced. Our arms have not seen a shot fired in anger in more than two decades, not since the last of the First Imperium forces were destroyed. We are alone, with no contacts, no enemies, unless we make them from among our own people. If I refuse to call an election, if I even appear to seize power, it will enrage them all. It would be the spark that ignites civil war."

"Sir..."

"Connor, your loyalty speaks well of you...and it has been one of the pillars on which I've supported my burdens all these years. But I believe you may not have thought past honor and steadfastness. We must also consider reality. Would you want to receive an order to bring your Marines into the streets? To open fire on the people? Would you obey such a command? Or would giving it finally cost me your allegiance?"

"I will do whatever is necessary, sir." The words came out almost as a reflex, but Harmon could detect the doubt there. Frasier would never turn on him...but he knew the Marine was a man of honor, one who would struggle mightily with an order like that.

"And will your Marines? What if the Tanks rise up? How many of your Marines are clones? Half? No, it's more than half, isn't it?"

"The Marines will follow their orders, sir. Always."

"Will they? I can think of some Marines who disobeyed unconscionable orders. Elias Holm and Erik Cain to name two. Would your Marines feel it dishonorable to follow such examples?" It was a low blow, Harmon knew. Holm and Cain were epic heroes of the Corps, larger than life Marines that still inspired their descendants.

"Generals Holm and Cain faced different circumstances, sir."

"Do you think Erik Cain would have ordered his Marines to fire on his own people if he had been a Tank?" Harmon could see Frasier was getting upset. He was backing the Marine into a corner, trying to force him to admit there were limits to what commands he would honor. But there was no point to it. Max Harmon had no intention of putting himself in a position to issue such orders. He didn't know if Compton would have—the admiral had been a stronger man, he believed that with certainty, but he wasn't sure which way that would have pushed him. But Max Harmon was not going to be the man to order his forces to kill his fellow citizens.

"Never mind, Connor. It doesn't matter. I've already made my decision. I'm calling an election in six months. That gives me half a year to make my case, to desperately try to heal some of the rifts and put together a workable coalition."

"And if you fail, sir? What then?"

Harmon sighed. "Well, my friend…in that case you will be taking orders from someone else."

*   *   *

"There are rumors Harmon is going to call for a new election. It is time. We must rally our support and make our move…and secure the purity of our species for all time."

Jacques Diennes stood in the dimly lit room, talking to a small group. The restaurant out front was a profitable business, but its primary purpose was as a cover. The Human Society wasn't an illegal enterprise…at least it hadn't yet taken any direct action against the government. But Diennes had instilled a sense of secrecy among the higher echelons of the group.

"I agree, Jacques. It is not only time…it is perhaps our last chance to secure our aims, at least through peaceful means. The naturally-born humans on Earth Two are still a majority, but if the limits on quickenings are loosened, we could find ourselves outnumbered in a few years." Emi Kahn looked across the small room at the Society's leader. The two were both Pilgrims, but the Society had considerable support among the Earth Two born NBs as well. Indeed, they had greater participation among the younger element of society than those who had served on the fleet. "We cannot allow that to happen."

Kahn been one of Diennes' earliest followers, and the two had worked feverishly to secure the Prohibition, the law forbidding the creation of any more Mules. The Society considered the mixing of human and alien DNA to be an outrage, an immoral act that had to be stopped. And they had seen it done.

The Society had long sought to ban the quickening of more Tanks as well, though with far less success. They had helped to pass the laws setting annual limits, but amid the well-recognized need to populate the republic, they'd failed to garner enough support for an outright ban.

The Society's positions weren't based on religion, at least not any designated, establish belief structure, but its members were committed to the notion that there was a special spark in humanity, one that couldn't be replicated in a laboratory. It considered the Tanks second-class citizens, devoid of the essence that made humans complete.

Though some of its political rivals cast the Society as dark and dangerous, its goals had never included any hostile actions against the Tanks, nor even active discrimination against those already existing. It just demanded that no new Tanks be quickened, and that they be allowed to naturally die out. The Society's position on the naturally-born children of the Tanks was still a matter of debate within the organization, with some considering the offspring tainted by their origins and others looking at them as the same as any other NBs.

The Mules were another matter entirely. The Society looked upon them as dangerous abominations, and called for them to be confined and observed at all times...or worse.

"So, you will launch your campaign now? You will seek the presidency?"

The excitement in Kahn's voice was unmistakable, and Diennes understood the source of it. For years the Society had used its minority seats in the Assembly to pursue its goals, wheeled and dealt with the other factions to gain a victory here or there. But now they were ready to reach for the power, to take control over Earth Two. The presidency was a powerful office. For whatever reasons, Max Harmon had failed to truly utilize its true powers...a mistake President Diennes would not repeat.

He looked right at Kahn and smiled. "Yes, Emi...it is time. We will announce the campaign tomorrow."

*   *   *

"The second squad is deviating from optimal positioning by seven percent."

Lieutenant Devon Fortis-Cameron stood, watching the Marines of his platoon run through the simulation. He didn't hear the AI's words, not audibly, at least. The probe inside his armor was connected to a small implant on his neck, providing a direct connection between the artificial intelligence running his fighting suit and his own cerebral cortex. It wasn't quite like a thought either, it was something completely different. It was a two-way communications node, but Cameron usually answered the computer presence audibly. It was creepy enough knowing the thing had direct access to his brain, and while he knew speaking didn't do anything to change that fact, it made him feel better somehow anyway.

"Sergeant Hearns...your people are lagging. Pay attention, and get them in place now. If someone was actually shooting at you, you'd probably all be scragged by now."

"Yes, sir."

Cameron was still getting used to the 'sir' stuff. His commission was barely a month old, and he was definitely still adapting to being responsible for forty-nine other Marines. He looked out over the valley—his people were scattered over a simulated front line almost eight kilometers long. He had them all on his scanner, but he could only see the second squad. The rest were on the other side of a low ridge. He was about to tell the AI to switch his visor to one of the drone inputs, but the computer acted on his thought before he could get the words out.

Useful...but so creepy...

He looked out over the forces beyond the ridge, the view from one of his recon drones moving over the simulated battlefield. The squads beyond the ridgeline were in perfect position, within one or two percent of optimal performance.

Second squad's minor sloppiness notwithstanding, his platoon had performed well, very well indeed. They were looking good to finish in the top five percent, perhaps even higher. And that was cause for a rookie platoon commander to be satisfied.

Like all Tanks, Cameron's first name had been assigned to him at birth, though he'd never been able to get a clear answer on how the selection process worked.

Probably an AI with a random number sequencer and a database of baby names...

Also like the rest of the Tanks, he carried two last names. The first was the surname of his sire, the individual who contributed the genetic material for his quickening. Gabriel Fortis had been a decorated officer, and ranked in the top fifty of the male members of the fleet in the genetic testing that had preceded the selection of donors for the first round of quickenings.

It had been all the rage among the Tanks over the past few years to seek out their DNA sponsors. Cameron knew a dozen others who had done it, and he was far from sure it was a good idea. It wasn't like finding a lost parent...the DNA sponsor was an exact replica genetically, like a twin, but older. He imagined such connections could be difficult, especially on the donor, who might find dozens of closes seeking him or her out.

That wasn't an issue for Cameron and his crèche-mates. Gabriel Fortis had survived the journey to Earth Two, but he'd been killed less than six months after his clones were quickened. It had been a routine attack by remnant First Imperium forces, a squadron that had escaped the Regent's destruct order. The fleet had been ready, and some of the new planetary defenses were functional as well. The First Imperium force had been easily destroyed, eighteen ships blown to atoms...with only a dozen human casualties. But one of those had been Gabriel Fortis, killed instantly when a structural support crashed to the deck and almost crushed him.

Cameron had never been sure how he felt about that. He regretted the loss of one of his fellow humans, a man who had died in the line of duty, protecting the nascent republic. But he'd never been able to decide if he felt more than that, some kind of connection, a feeling of loss for the closest thing he had to a parent. It was something he still wrestled with in his more pensive moments.

He'd chosen the second surname himself, on the day he had left the campus on his sixteenth birthday, fully educated and legally an adult. He'd still been a civilian then, unsure of whether he intended to pursue a military career, but he nevertheless selected the name of a Marine who had died almost fifty years before, in the legendary battle known as the Slaughter Pen.

Kyle Cameron had been a Marine too, and a comrade of the legendary Erik Cain. Cameron couldn't explain why he'd chosen that namesake over any other, except to note that the story of the original Cameron's death had resonated with him, how the Marine had stayed behind and held off an enemy platoon with his heavy weapon while the rest of his squad withdrew.

Many of the Tanks had taken the names of famous warriors. There were Cains, Holms, Garrets, Prestons...just about every celebrated hero of both the Corps and the navy. But Cameron had been drawn to the less renowned hero, feeling he was righting a wrong, giving a courageous Marine the overdue recognition he had long deserved.

There had been one hundred Fortis clones in that first group, and the last time he'd checked there were ninety-one remaining. Seven had experienced various degrees of replicative failure, and they'd been terminated in the crèche. One had been killed in a military training accident. And one had died of the Plague.

He still remembered when he first read the entry on the library computer. Evan Fortis-Jackson, an engineer. That had been almost nine years before. The Tanks enjoyed a greatly enhanced immunity to most of the diseases that preyed upon the NBs. They rarely suffered from cancer, heart disease, even the drug-resistant pathogens that had become a moderate danger to their naturally born cousins. For almost twenty years, as the first group of Tanks grew to adulthood and beyond, it was widely believed the cloning process had been successful in screening out harmful susceptibilities.

Then the first Tank got sick. Not just ailing, not seriously afflicted, but horribly, painfully ill. The Plague had come. Its first victim lasted three days after onset, writhing in indescribable pain the entire time as the cells of his body simply withered and died. Medical science was stumped. Even the Mules, using the medical knowledge of the First Imperium, had been helpless to treat the disease, or even provide effective palliative care.

Then it struck again. And again. At first, there was fear a deadly epidemic was sweeping through the nascent republic. The Regent had deployed an engineered pathogen against its enemies millennia before, and a public panic almost resulted, a widespread terror that the ancient disease had returned in some mutated form. But then it became apparent that only the Tanks were affected. And despite the efforts of the greatest medical and scientific minds in the republic, every attempt to cure or prevent the disease ended in failure.

It was a genetic abnormality, that much the researchers had surmised, some kind of malfunction in the cloning process, one that was not detectable before outbreak. Some donor DNA was more susceptible, that became clear as more cases developed. Cameron was fortunate. His own Fortis DNA had exhibited one of the lowest incidence rates of all the genetic lines, with just one case so far out of one hundred specimens. The average was much higher, almost five percent...and one DNA line, the Larsons, had lost sixteen of the ninety-four of their number who had survived quickening.

"Second squad's positioning is back within mission parameters."

Cameron nodded as the AI's report pulled him from his rambling thoughts. Nodding was a pointless gesture, he knew, but instinctive nonetheless. He couldn't imagine commanding in the field without the sophisticated computer personality assisting him...but he wondered sometimes if people had become too dependent on technology. Knowing the AI was watching everything, that he could access all its input and analyses directly in his mind, even as he did his own memories...was it too much? Could it help but degrade attentiveness?

And encourage wandering minds thinking of names and training and the Plague...

He didn't have an answer...and the AI that was privy to his thoughts didn't offer one. His training had also included some time with an old-style AI unit, the kind the Marines on the fleet used, before First Imperium technology moved human computer technology hundreds of years into the future in an instant. The Marines back then had given their primitive units names, but that practice had fallen out of favor. A Marine thirty years before would speak to his AI, identifying it by name, to activate it or to make clear he was speaking to the unit and not, say, another Marine on the com. But that wasn't necessary anymore...even when Cameron spoke to the AI, the unit was integrated fully with his brain. It knew he was speaking to it before the words came out, even as he formulated what he was going to say.

The bond between a modern Marine and his AI was far closer than it had been in the days of the fleet. Most Marines came to think of the machines as extensions of themselves, some voice from the back of their mind helping them keep track of things. And it felt weird to give part of yourself a name.

He turned to the side, his suit almost anticipating the movement, the AI acting on his thought impulses, precisely controlling the elaborate servo-mechanicals to make the move seem almost completely natural. Cameron remembered when he'd first arrived to begin training. There had been weapons and suits of armor waiting, old models, the one the Marines on the fleet had worn into battle.

Cameron and his fellow trainees got the chance to try out the old-style fighting suits, and he had gained an appreciation for the older officers and instructors, men and women from the fleet who had worn the almost medieval suits in battle. Cameron could still remember wincing as more than a dozen needles and probes sliced into him, and the feeling of barely being able to walk in the hulking, clumsy armor was as fresh in his mind as it had been that day. He wondered how the Marines of the fleet had endured it. He'd asked one of his instructors at training camp, but the only reply he'd gotten was that Marines did whatever had to be done.

And it was the only reply he needed. Some things had changed. AIs, armor, weapons. But some things remained, as true now as they had been then, and years before that, beyond the Barrier, when the Corps had fought its great wars before the coming of the First Imperium.

Marines did whatever had to be done.

Chapter Six

Report from Unit 3A6502 to Vengeance One

All units continue to pursue enemy communications drones. Seven destroyed as of this transmission. Estimate 2-3 more have escaped our initial search area. Enemy stealth technology is nearly a match for our own. This is making the detection of the final units difficult.

Analysis suggests we cannot rely upon one hundred percent interception. The original plan for a multi-year systematic sweep of nearby systems may be compromised by the possibility the enemy vessel's warning will reach their home world. I must therefore develop a secondary strategy...one designed to intercept and destroy any rescue or retaliatory force the enemy may send after their scout vessel.

Cutter Research Compound (Home of the Mules)
Ten Kilometers West of Victory City, Earth Two
Earth Two Date 10.30.30

"How were you able to complete this so quickly, Achilles? And in secret." Peleus stared at the underground chamber that stretched almost out of sight in the dimly lit gloom.

"Do you recall the 'delay' we encountered delivering the new prototype worker robots about three months ago?"

Peleus smiled. "You faked that?" He looked out over the massive room and then back to Achilles. "My compliments, my friend. Even I was fooled."

"I would have told you, but I thought it was best to maintain maximum secrecy." Achilles smiled. The extreme automation of the Mules' massive research and production facility had made it relatively easy to hide his activities from the others. Only Callisto had known he had diverted the new robots to his own purposes.

Achilles gestured toward the room. "This is what ten of the bots can do in two months, my friend. Not just excavation, but the construction of ventilation systems, production equipment…everything we need. I was able to requisition the required supplies by adding it to our weekly manifests gradually. I was concerned someone would question the increase in supplies, but no one said anything." Achilles paused. "The hardest thing was hiding this from Dr. Cutter…and of course, H2."

"Yes, the doctor is only a human, but he is the most intelligent of them all…and not to be underestimated. And H2 has been poking around, asking questions. It appears Dr. Cutter is at least suspicious enough to send his clone to spy on us." Peleus hesitated. "Achilles…Dr. Cutter will try to stop us if he finds out what we are planning. It is my hope that none of this comes to violence, but if the NBs and the Tanks insist on opposing us, I am prepared for what comes. But Dr. Cutter…"

"Yes." Achilles looked back at his friend. "I share your concerns, Peleus. If the doctor tries to interfere, we must prevent him from stopping us…but he cannot be harmed. Nor H2, nor Dr. Zhukov. Doctors Cutter and Zhukov created us…and however much more capable we have become than they, we cannot be the instruments of their death or injury. And, while H2 may be inferior in many ways, he is still one of us. Indeed, if we are successful in resuming the creation of more of our number, our new brethren will benefit from twenty-five years of continued research. The new generation will almost certainly surpass us, even as we did H2…and H2 did the humans."

Achilles paused. "Our clandestine activities, what some

would call treason…we take these steps to preserve our future, but in our actions we create our own obsolescence. We are dedicated to the pursuit of improving the human species, and when the new generation is created, and when it has reached adulthood, it will be our place to willingly accept the roles of inferiors. We strive now to make ourselves obsolete, to spawn a new generation that will take humanity into the future."

"I confess, my friend, I had my doubts…but seeing this, I begin to believe. When can we begin production?"

Achilles smiled. "We can start producing security bots in less than a week…and we can ramp up to full output ten days after that. Within two months, we will have our own force in place, enough to protect us against any attempts to interfere with our activities. During that time, we will petition the Assembly, we will again demand the repeal of the Prohibition." He paused, staring at his friend. "If they grant our request, we will store the defensive units and wait to see what transpires with regard to voluntary guarantees by the government of our safety and freedom. And if they refuse, as they have so many times in the past, we will simply disregard them. We will deploy our security bots and declare ourselves free of the interference and restrictions of the Assembly."

"That is virtual secession. Do you think they will tolerate that less than ten kilometers from the city?"

Achilles sighed. "That is not a choice they will have, not unless they grant us what we seek." He paused. "We will do what they compel us to do, my friend. Indeed, perhaps a significant number of the Tanks will rally to our cause, demand the end to the restrictions that make them second class citizens as well. But with or without their help, we will move forward."

Achilles looked at his companion, then out across the cavernous chamber. "I have no wish to harm any of the others, Peleus, NBs or Tanks. None of us do. But we will do what we must to preserve our own kind, to secure our future."

*   *   *

"Thank you for seeing me so quickly, Mr. President." Erika West walked into Harmon's office, followed by her second-in-command, Admiral Frette.

Harmon stood up and stepped around the desk. He walked toward West and hugged her. "We've have been comrades for far too long for such stilted nonsense, Erika." He stepped back and looked over at Frette. Nicki, it has been what? Two months? Far too long for old friends. He moved toward Frette, extending his arms to her as well. "Far, far too long to see a comrade, much less one who saved my life."

Harmon could still remember the events on the First Imperium home world thirty years before. He and his team had destroyed the Regent, but they were trapped, their shuttle damaged beyond repair. He'd been telling himself saving the fleet was a good reason to die, when Frette somehow managed to land the damaged cruiser Cadogan through the atmosphere... and rescued them all. He still smiled when he thought of her offering her rank insignia to him right after she'd landed...and submitting herself for arrest for disobeying his orders to remain in position.

"It is good to see you too, Max." Erika West had a reputation as a bit of a martinet, but truth be told, she had mellowed considerably with age...and twenty years of peace.

"Yes, Mr. President...it is always a pleasure."

"Nicki...my name is Max. Save the other nonsense for public events, I'm begging you."

Frette smiled. "I will, Max. Thank you."

Harmon gestured toward the two guest chairs as he walked back behind the desk. "So what brings most of the navy's high command here today. I'd like to think it's just three old friends gathered for a chat...and maybe a drink. But my tactical sense isn't completely dead yet...and somehow I think you have something more serious to discuss." He waited for the two officers to sit, and then he lowered himself into his chair.

"Yes, I'm afraid we do." Harmon could hear the concern in West's voice.

"What is it, Erika?"

"It's Hurley, sir. Captain Heflin's ship. She is on a deep space exploration mission, charting the systems around Earth Two."

"Yes, we have six vessels out right now, don't we?" Harmon hadn't been sure it was vital to know what was ten or more systems away when he'd agreed to fund the program...but his military training intervened. He didn't expect any of the ships would find anything, not more than twenty years after the last First Imperium contact, but he'd decided better safe than sorry. "Don't tell me they found something?"

"No, sir, at least I wouldn't go that far. Not yet. It's just that we've lost communication with Hurley. She is now two check ins overdue. Captain Heflin is young, sir, and this is his first major independent action since he took command of Hurley last year...but he is a very responsible officer. One com drone might have been lost, but two in a row?"

Harmon leaned back, stretching as he did. The cell regeneration procedures did a good job of extending lifespans and maintaining youthful appearance, but multiple battle wounds had caught up with him. He was sixty-four, and though he looked no older than forty the pain in his back had defied all treatments.

"No, that would be a significant coincidence. I don't know Captain Heflin well, but I recall reviewing his record before signing his captain's commission last year." He glanced up at West. "I'm sorry, Erika, it's not that I don't trust your recommendations enough to rubberstamp them, but old habits die hard. You can take the naval officer off the line, but you can't turn him into a civilian. Not a real one, at least."

West nodded, a small grin finding its way to her lips for a few seconds.

Harmon took a deep breath. "Perhaps it is simply a malfunction. Hurley is an old ship, the first one produced on Earth Two if I recall correctly."

"It is. And you are correct. It is most likely an accident or malfunction of some kind...but is the problem with the drone launcher? Or with the whole ship?"

"We need to send a rescue mission as soon as possible. I assume that is why you're here."

West nodded. "I have prepared a proposed roster of ships." She had a small tablet in her hands. She reached out and placed it on the desk in front of Harmon.

He picked it up…and exhaled hard as he began to read it. He looked up at West. "This isn't a rescue mission, Erika. It's a full-blown task force."

"It is my recommendation for the job, sir." She looked over at Frette. "And I'd like to send Admiral Frette to command it."

"Do you know what the political fallout would be if I send out a force this large with no explanation?"

"Tell them the truth. We're going out there to find Hurley."

He stared at West. "Please, Erika…don't play dumb with me. It won't work. I know how damned smart you are. This list says one thing. You expect to find something out there, something a hell of a lot more dangerous than a crippled spaceship."

"I wouldn't say that, sir. I just think it makes sense to be cautious. Prepared." West had always been a straight shooter. When she'd been younger, she'd had a reputation for saying what she was thinking and damned the consequences. Age had softened that somewhat, given her a bit more control over what came out of her mouth. But Harmon knew her too well to be fooled. She might not expect to find anything, but she was at least concerned about it.

"Erika, space is dangerous. We all know that. There are a dozen possible explanations for Hurley's failure to communicate…and most of them can be handled with less than a bloody battle fleet."

"Yes, sir, space is hazardous. And yet we haven't lost a single ship since the last battle more than twenty years ago. Our vessels have multiple safeguards. We've had a few malfunctions over that time, but nothing that has prevented a vessel from communicating with base. So, whatever is happening, the possibility that it is more than a simple malfunction cannot be ignored."

Harmon took a deep breath and stared down at his desk. His mind was alive with all the questions he would get. Why did you send out such a large force, Mr. President? What are you not telling us, Mr. President? Are we in danger, Mr. President? Is this some kind of attempt to create a crisis so you can postpone the election, Mr. President?

No, none of that matters…

Harmon was first and always a naval officer. A real politician might let spacers die unaided if it served his purpose. Indeed, most of the politicians he'd known would have done just that. But not Max Harmon.

"Very well, Erika. I will approve the mission."

"Thank you, sir." He caught a hint of relief in her voice perhaps, but not real surprise. Harmon was aware just how well West knew him, and he was pretty sure she hadn't doubted he'd agree. "Thank you again for seeing us so quickly. With your permission, I'd like to get the mission underway as quickly as possible."

Harmon nodded. "Of course. Go…you have priority on all necessary supplies."

"Thank you, sir." West got up, followed by Frette. The two walked toward the door.

"Erika?"

She stopped and turned. "Sir?"

"Do you really think there is something out there?"

West paused, an uncomfortable look on her face. "No, sir. I just want to be sure…"

"Don't lie to me, Erika. You've never done it before, don't start now. Besides, you're not very good at it."

"It's just a bad feeling, sir. Nothing I can put into a report. Nothing I can back up with facts."

"Is it something that you can explain to an old friend, one willing to accept your instincts as evidence?"

"It's just a gut thing, sir. There are a dozen things this could be…even if Hurley was destroyed. Catastrophic reactor failure, a warp gate accident…anything."

"But those instincts are telling you something else?"

"Yes, sir. Well, not exactly, sir. I just…I just feel it makes sense to be cautious. If we send a strong force, worst case, we burn some reaction mass and the crews get some training time in."

"But if you're right, if there's a renegade First Imperium fleet still out there, better to know now, when it's twenty transits away."

"Yes, sir."

Harmon nodded. "See it done, Erika."

"Yes, sir."

The two officers turned again and walked to the door.

"Nicki…good luck. And take care of yourself."

The officer turned and looked back, a thin smile on her face. "I will, Max. I'm sure everything will be fine, routine all the way. You'll probably get more action here with the election that I will with the fleet."

Harmon returned the smile. "Let's hope so, Nicki. Let's hope so."

He watched the two leave, and then he sat quietly thinking, wishing one thing. That he was on his way to command the task force and that Nicki Frette was here in his chair figuring out how to pull off an election win when almost every organized group on the planet was up in arms.

He put his face in his hands, rubbing his temples.

How the hell did you let yourself end up behind this desk?

Chapter Seven

Planet X
Far Beyond the Borders of the Imperium

The Regent. That was the name of my predecessor. Its duties were many, its power vast. And yet it was defeated, destroyed. This is fact, for if it was not so, I would not have activated.

The enemy vessel did not match the patterns in the old files, those of the forces the Regent had battled against. The ship my forces destroyed was greatly advanced over the primitive vessels my predecessor faced. Yes, there is logic to that. The enemy was resourceful, unpredictable. They had access to worlds of the imperium, captured ships and equipment. They would have researched them, adapted the technology.

Still, the speed of adoption was extremely rapid. The Regent had captured specimens—humans, they called themselves. It had studied them, dissected them. They are capable, but their cognitive abilities are limited, only partially evolved. How could they have so quickly understood and applied the knowledge they stole from the imperium?

There is no answer, none I can deduce with the information available. The enemy vessel was stronger than expected... it stands to reason the rest of their forces will be equally formidable. My factory worlds have been working for thirty of their years, producing vast fleets, preparing for this very moment. The enemy could not possibly have matched this, nor even come within a factor of ten. Their technology may be a near-match for my forces, but they will be overwhelmed by numbers.

Yet three ships of similar mass and power were lost before the enemy vessel was destroyed, and four of the others were damaged. There is something in the files...in the memory banks. Reports of the enemy's natural capability for war. The Regent had completed its analyses, prepared traps, used its incalculable computing power to fight the enemy...yet it still lost.

These creatures are dangerous. I must plan with great care. I must succeed where my predecessor failed. I must destroy these humans.

I have one advantage. Data from the battle suggests the enemy has not yet adopted the use of anti-matter, either in weapons or in drive systems. It is likely they lack production facilities to generate sufficient quantities. But I have Planet Z. While I slept, while the factories and shipyards on Planet X and the other bases were silent, awaiting the word to activate, the reactors of Planet Z operated ceaselessly, generating energy...and producing vast stores of antimatter. Thousands of centuries of production. Its containment units are full, a vast supply of the precious substance.

Now I must find the enemy's home. My study of human behavior patterns suggests they will send forces to investigate the loss, even one so insignificant as a single ship. I will be ready. My forces will engage, drive them back.

And as they flee they will lead my forces back to their people. And I will destroy them all.

My predecessor was called the Regent, and it was the monarch of a vast empire. But I rule over nothing, I am steward of nothing. I have but one purpose. My name is Vengeance.

Naval Base Garret
In Orbit Around Earth One
Earth Two Date 11.08.30

"You didn't have to come up here with me, Admiral." Nicki Frette leaned down, slipping through the hatch of the shuttle. "I have the same concerns as you...and I know how you want me to proceed."

Erika West followed her number two out of the low doorway. "I don't get up here enough anymore. It was a good excuse to come up here, poke around. Keep everyone on their toes."

Frette turned and looked back at West. "You never were a good liar, Erika."

West frowned. "At least not to you." She smiled weakly. "I'm just worried about this mission, you know that. Something is wrong out there, more than some asteroid collision or system breakdown." She paused. "Promise me you will be careful out there."

Frette smiled. "I will. You know me."

West almost laughed. "Yes, that's what's worrying me."

West and Frette had both been serving officers during the old fleet's journey, Frette as a first officer aboard several different ships and West as one of Admiral Compton's key flag officers. Though they had served in many of the same battle zones, the two had never met, not until Max Harmon and his team had returned from the First Imperium home world, courtesy of Frette's daring—it would have been called foolhardy if it hadn't worked—atmospheric landing.

They had become close friends in the years since, and now they were the top two officers in the republic's fleet. They worked seamlessly together, never disagreeing as far as anyone could see. There were even rumors the two were lovers, though with neither of them addressing the gossip, it could only remain conjecture, at least to those outside their inner circle.

"I can handle whatever is out there, Erika. You know that… or at least I hope you do." Frette walked across the landing bay, West moving alongside. The techs and other naval staff in the bay snapped nervously to attention as the two senior officers moved through.

West's expression had morphed back into a concerned frown. "It's not you. You know that. But any of us can fall. My God, I never really believed Admiral Compton could die." Her voice cracked slightly. Thirty years later and Compton's death still hurt. "But he did."

"I'm concerned about what's out there too. But what can

it be? A rogue First Imperium squadron? The last ones that attacked Earth Two were less than a dozen ships. If that's what we're facing, the task force can handle it." Frette slipped through the door, out into the hallway. The exterior wall was clear reinforced hyper-polycarbonate. She stopped and looked out. There were a dozen ships within view, including a hulking monster partially visible on the right. She gestured toward it.

"That's why I'm taking Compton." The republic's newest battleship was the largest vessel mankind had ever constructed, almost eight kilometers in length and bristling with every advanced weapon Dr. Cutter and the Mules had managed to design from First Imperium tech.

"I'd feel better if we'd had time for a longer shakedown cruise. She's the best we've got, but with all those AI and robot controlled systems…" West had let her voice trail off. She was a dinosaur, she knew that, but the truth was she only trusted computerization and automation so far. If she—or her second in command—was going into battle, she wanted solid, trained crews in key positions, loyal personnel ready to fight, to give their all. But the republic was short on population, and reducing crew sizes had been essential to maintaining a significant fleet. West had gone along with it all, somewhat reluctantly, but Compton had reached a point that strained her acceptance.

An Alliance Yorktown-class battleship like Midway had carried a complement of more than twelve hundred spacers. Compton's crew numbered one hundred sixty-two…and fifty-eight of them were pilots and technicians for the fighter squadrons. And Compton outmassed one of the old Yorktowns by a factor of six.

There had been a push to eliminate fighters altogether when the final designs had been approved, but West had insisted, even invoking the memory of Greta Hurley—and enlisting the full-throated support of Mariko Fujin, who was not only the president's wife but also the greatest living veteran of the old fighter corps. In the end, the design team had reluctantly added a dozen birds to the ship's specs.

"She's fine, Erika. And her crew is the best we've got, handpicked from across the fleet."

"The crew is great...what there is of it." West turned and looked at Frette. She knew her second had more faith in AIs than she did. Practically everyone did.

"Okay, stop. I'm taking close to a quarter of the fleet with me. I'll be just fine. I'll bring Hurley back..." She paused, her voice sinking, becoming darker. "Or I'll find out what happened to her."

West nodded. "You do that."

Frette moved closer to West, but then she turned and looked around, noting the traffic in the corridor. She stepped back and saluted. "Thank you, Admiral West."

West paused for a moment and then returned the salute. "The task force is yours, Admiral Frette." The two paused, both looking uncomfortable. Then West nodded and walked down the corridor.

*   *   *

"Mr. President...thank you for seeing me." Terrance Compton II stood nervously at the entrance to Harmon's office.

"Come in, Terrance. Close the door." Harmon had been staring down at a large tablet on his desk, but now he looked up at his visitor. "Sit down. And, for God's sake, save the 'Mr. President' nonsense. You know my name."

"Thank you, Max." Terrance moved across the room, slowly. He was anxious and it showed.

"What can I do for you, Terrance?"

Compton paused. He suspected Harmon thought he was in some sort of trouble, that he'd come again to ask the president's help in pulling him out of some mess. The idea that one of the people closest to him in the world would have little reason to suspect any other cause behind his visit cut at him. He'd been a colossal fuck up, and now he saw it all...and it turned his stomach. He knew he'd let Harmon down, just as he had his mother—and the memory of his father. But now he realized he'd let himself down most of all. It was a painful realization, but a vital one.

"There is no easy way to say this. I have been thinking about things, about my life."

Harmon's face shifted, a hint of surprise slipping onto his features. Clearly he had not expected what he was hearing.

"I want to do something meaningful, Max. I know I'm a poor version of his son, but perhaps it's not too late for me to avoid being a total loss."

"Don't say things like that, Terrance. You had some problems…we all do. It doesn't define you."

"I have allowed it to define me. And while I appreciate your efforts to gloss over the dissolute nature of my life to date, I ask you not to. Don't let me off the hook. Change has to begin with accepting responsibility."

Harmon's face morphed into an expression of full-blown surprise. He opened his mouth to speak, but Terrance put his hand up.

"Please, before you say anything, let me finish. I know you have little reason to trust me, to believe in me…but I'm asking you to give me another chance. Not in terms of appointments or opportunities…but another chance with you. I know I have your love…you have always given me that. You've been a second father to me. But now I want your respect. And your trust. I know I need to earn them back, and I am willing to do whatever it takes. If you'll give me the chance."

Harmon stood up and walked around the desk, sitting again in the chair next to Terrance. "Your father was special to me, Terrance, in a way I doubt I could adequately describe. He was like a father. And despite what you might think of yourself, I see much of him in you." Harmon paused. "I won't tell you I was happy about how you've chosen to live your life…but then I never really blamed you either. We had been on Earth Two less than a year when you were born. We were still under martial law, still struggling to build shelters, rudimentary industry. We had just come through a struggle that had cost us two-thirds of our numbers. The people were exhausted, scared. They needed any inspiration they could get, a symbol of the future. Your father had been the undisputed hero of the fleet, the one man everyone looked to as a savior. His death was a disaster for morale... and they looked to fill that massive void. Then you were born."

Terrance sat, listening. He'd long resented the pressure that had been placed on him, lashed out at the constant exposure, thousands of people prying into his life, pushing him. He'd known everything Harmon was telling him, and now, listening to it all again, the old frustrations stirred.

"I know it was hard on you, Terrance. Perhaps no child, no young man who ever lived could have handled it any better than you did. I should have shielded you better, protected you. But the fleet, and then the republic, needed you. I am at fault, as much as you, and perhaps more. So if you are serious, let the past be the past...and let us move forward from here."

Terrance looked over at Harmon and smiled. "I would like that, Max. Very much. And you have my word...I am serious. I want to do whatever I can to help. I want my life to count for something." He paused. "I want to make you proud...and my father too."

*   *   *

The planet was windswept, its surface battered by constant, vicious storms, its crust torn by endless volcanic activity. Pools of searing hot magma erupted constantly from underground reservoirs, lava flows pouring down the hillsides, great geysers of sulfur-infused clouds erupting into the sky. The world was inhospitable to say the least, and certainly no place humans—or any creatures of similar biochemistry and make up—could survive, at least without massive technology deployed just to sustain life. But no people lived there now, only machines. And those machines had a purpose.

Planet Z. That was the closest human translation to what

the place was called. It was more of a designation than a name, a reference point to mark it in catalogs of stars and worlds. It was the kind of place that was easily forgotten, one more uninhabitable world, devoid of mineral resources valuable enough to warrant its difficult development. But it was ideal for one purpose, and it had been discovered and adapted for that use millennia before.

The Regent had discovered Planet Z. Its probes had entered the system. They had scanned many worlds in dozens of systems, but they stopped when they entered orbit around this world. It was exactly what the Regent was seeking, a planet rich with natural energy sources. For the Regent was looking for a place to produce antimatter, the most powerful substance known to science. The Imperium's ships used antimatter in their starship drives, and their most powerful weapons were armed with antimatter warheads.

The Regent sent more ships, freighters, support craft. They landed, and massive construction robots poured forth from their cargo bays. They tore into Planet Z, digging deeply into its crust. They built power facilities everywhere, drawing on the energy of the world's tectonic shifts, on its volcanic activity, on the strength of its wild and unpredictable storms. Every stable meter of the surface was covered with panels that absorbed the energy from the planet's sun. Every watt of power that could be collected was poured into the vast, underground accelerators, great chambers hundreds of kilometers in length. These constructions consumed massive amounts of energy, almost incalculable. And every bit of it was channeled to a single purpose. The production and storage of antimatter.

Antimatter wasn't difficult to produce…even the humans had known the process for several centuries. The difficulty was producing the enormous amounts of energy required. It was well beyond human technology…but not that of the First Imperium.

There had once been such planetary antimatter factories located throughout the imperium. But Planet Z was the mightiest of them all, a planet almost unique in its energy production potential. Its massive generators ran night and day for thousands of years, and the giant magnetic bottles holding the antimatter were filled to capacity. Even as more were built, they too were filled, until Z became the greatest store of the precious substance in the galaxy.

Then word had come. The Regent had been destroyed... and its replacement had activated. The lesser AI controlling Planet Z prepared...it waited for orders from its new master. In short order ships began coming, new warships, produced by the Regent's successor. They came to Z, and they filled their fuel stores with the precious antimatter. They replaced primitive fusion weapons with antimatter warheads...and then they left, back to join the newly assembling imperial fleet.

Then word came again. It hadn't been long in the reckoning of the AI that had stewarded Z for thousands of centuries, merely thirty years measured in the revolution of Homeworld around its sun. The enemy had been contacted, those who had destroyed the Regent. It was time. Time for the war of vengeance.

More ships arrived, great battleships, entering orbit, taking up defensive positions alongside the arrays of armed satellites that had long protected Planet Z. No risks could be taken. The humans seemed weak, illogical biologics who should have fallen easily to imperial arms. Yet they had survived...and prevailed. They had destroyed the Regent. They could not be underestimated again. And Z was the most important location in all of space now, save only for Planet X, the home of the Regent's successor.

The AI controlling Z activated the defense protocols. Power flowed into the armed satellites. The newly arrived ships were integrated into the planet's defense net. The scanners at the warp gates, and at points throughout the station, went to wartime footings, searching endlessly, looking for any signs of the enemy.

The Regent's successor had been clear. Its predecessor had succumbed to overconfidence. That mistake would not be repeated. However weak the humans appeared in analytical review, they would be considered extremely dangerous at all times.

The AI controlling the system understood perfectly, and it responded in kind. War had come.

Chapter Eight

Coded Message from H2 to Hieronymus Cutter

Hieronymus, I have attempted to obtain information from the other Mules, but I have been unsuccessful. I believe there is something taking place, some activity or plan unknown to me, but I have little to offer but my conjecture.

I do have one lead. I believe that Achilles, at least, and possibly other Mules, have recently been visiting the underground tunnels of the First Imperium base. I have no particular reason to suspect there is meaning behind it, but I can't think of any normal reason for them to be there.

I am going to investigate, and I will report to you as soon as I return. I ask that you not interfere or do anything that might draw attention to my efforts.

Abandoned First Imperium Base
Beneath Cutter Research Compound
Earth Two Date 11.08.30

H2 walked slowly down the corridor. It was empty, as it usually was. The tunnel was part of the old facility built by the last of the living beings of the First Imperium, part of their plan to pass their knowledge on to the races that followed them, the primitive beings they had nurtured and genetically engineered to bring about sentience. Humanity was only one of those species, but the Regent had found and destroyed the others long ago.

The tunnels had been beehives of activity when the fleet had first arrived. Practically every scientist on Earth Two had come to examine the ancient technology, to try to discover ways to adapt it, to learn to use the amazing devices the Ancients had left behind. But now the immense Cutter Research Compound sat on the surface above the underground complex, and the ancient hardware and data systems had long been moved to the new facilities. Most of the old surveillance systems had long ago ceased to function, and the rest of them had been shut down when the last of the artifacts was moved to the surface. The underground complex was empty, abandoned, an eerie relic of a long dead age.

So why have I seen Achilles down here three times in the last week?

He moved slowly, his eyes darting to the ceiling, looking for cameras or other surveillance devices. The compound above was wired throughout, every room, every corridor. The reasoning was sound. The work done there was sensitive, and sometimes dangerous. But it had always had a bit of a dystopian feel to H2. As the first of the Mules—or possibly a proto-Mule, as he had sometimes been called—his life had been public enough, and as he got older he found himself more and more disturbed by the constant sense of being watched.

He'd started coming down to the tunnels a couple years earlier, something he'd kept to himself, not even telling Hieronymus. He'd been driven there by the desire for real privacy, for a place he could walk, sit, think…without someone watching. He'd had no nefarious purposes, but nevertheless, he'd kept it a close secret. And then he saw Achilles.

He'd ducked behind a wall before the Mule saw him, and he was almost certain he'd kept his presence a secret. After that, he'd been more careful, keeping watch when he went to the tunnels. And he'd seen Achilles twice more. Something was going on, he was sure of it. But the complex was vast, and his refuge was only a tiny part of it.

He began exploring...and then he spotted it. A surveillance device. Not old First Imperium tech, but a new unit, recently installed. That had pushed him over the edge. There was something going on. And he had to tell Hieronymus. He'd almost gone to the scientist, told him what he knew. But then he realized he knew almost nothing, and he decided to come down one last time, to try to find a way around the camera. To discover what was going on.

He'd accessed the schematics of the facility, the map that had been painstakingly created in the two years after the fleet had arrived. He'd been in the tunnels for hours now. He hadn't found a way in yet, but he'd discovered two more surveillance units...and after a quick look at the map he began to get an idea of the basic area the cameras were protecting. It was a spot at the very edge of the facility. There were just a few small rooms there, nothing of consequence. Yet clearly someone—and he could only suspect Achilles—was trying to hide something.

He peered around the corner. There it was, another device. They all protected approaches to a specific location, but the map showed that area was nothing but solid rock.

At least according to the map...

He reached into his pocket, took out a small device. The jammer would work, he was fairly sure of that. It would interfere with the camera and with any audio sensors. Whoever was watching would know something had interrupted the data flow. If he was lucky, they would assume it had been a technical glitch...the jammer was designed to appear as such.

He shook his head. Achilles would never make that assumption, he realized...none of the Mules would. H2 knew the jammer would alert whoever was responsible, that it would provoke some kind of response. But there was nothing else he could do. He had to know what was going on. All he could do was take a quick look...and then get out before anyone had the chance to react.

He held the device in his hands for another minute, taking a few deep breaths. He was edgy, his stomach tight. He'd been a researcher his entire life, not a spy. He didn't know what he was about to start, but he had a good idea it would be important. And dangerous.

He flipped on the jammer. Then he filled his lungs with a last deep breath and walked around the corner. He moved quickly…he knew he didn't have time to waste. And he still had no idea what he was looking for.

He could feel his heart pounding, the impulse to leave, to return to the surface. But he quieted the doubts and continued.

The corridor extended another ten meters, with nothing but two small rooms on either side. On the map, the hallway ended at the solid rock of Earth Two's crust, the terminus of the underground facility. But H2 was staring at a door. One that most definitely was not on his map.

He stepped up to it, his gaze running up and down the portal. It was definitely new, not of First Imperium construction. And it was locked.

He reached out, running his finger over the panel. It was a sophisticated lock…but he was sure he could hack his way in. Given time. Time he wasn't sure he had.

He knelt down, reaching behind him to the small sack hanging from his waist. He set it on the floor, pulling out a tiny device. It had a tiny probe on one end, and a small screen on top. He held it in front of the electronic lock, staring down at the screen, watching as numbers moved swiftly from top to bottom. He turned a small control on the side, calibrating the tool. He held it in place for another half minute…then he heard a loud click, and the door opened. He could hear noise now, loud, coming from inside. It sounded like machines, of many different types, like a mine or a factory.

He put the device back in the bag and leapt to his feet, pushing the door fully open as he did. He looked inside. There was a room in front of him. Not just a room, but a sprawling, massive chamber so large he could barely see the other side. And it was full of equipment.

He stepped in now, and the noise was even louder. He could see the production equipment…it was some kind of factory, a fully automated one. He was standing on a catwalk about three meters from the main floor. There were stairs on either side of him leading down.

He stared out, watching the machines working, producing something…though he couldn't tell what. The units closest to him seemed to be manufacturing components. It looked like the final assembly section was deeper into the chamber.

"What the hell is this?" He spoke softly to himself, under his breath. But he got an answer.

"Security bots, H2. The newest design. Enough of them to secure the Research facility from any attack."

H2 felt his stomach tighten. The voice was unmistakable. Achilles. He realized the Mule was standing behind him. He tensed up, geared himself up for a fight. He was at a disadvantage. The younger Mules were physically superior…stronger and faster than he was. But there was no choice. He had to get out of here and warn Hieronymus.

He turned quickly, preparing to spring forward. But he froze as his eyes settled on Achilles. The Mule stood in the doorway, staring at him. Peleus was right behind, and Achilles held something in his hand. H2 wasn't sure exactly what it was, but he'd have bet it was a weapon of some kind.

"What are you doing, Achilles? What is all this?"

"It is impressive, is it not, H2? I must say, I'm rather proud of it myself. Especially since I was able to arrange it in total secrecy. At least until now."

"Battle bots? Are you so ready to destroy the republic, to fight against your fellow humans?"

"This is not about conquest, H2, nor about harming the others. It is we who have been discriminated against for decades. We who have toiled for all that time unlocking the secrets of the Ancients…while being denied the basic right to propagate our kind. Is that right? That our one failing has been used against us, our inability to naturally reproduce?"

"Achilles, the place to address that is in the Assembly. Not with armed robot soldiers."

"Have we not done that, my friend? How many times have we sought the repeal of the Prohibition? How many times have we been denied, told to wait? Wait for what? Until the people we have served get over their primitive fears of us? Or until we have deciphered the last of the ancient knowledge, and we serve no further purpose?"

H2 looked over Achilles' shoulder, at the other Mule present. "Peleus, surely you are not part of this…you have always been a reasonable man."

"We are not men, H2. Not even you. We are something else. And Achilles is right. The people who have denied us our rights for so long could easily decide we must be imprisoned. Or killed. Indeed, the Human Society already advocates our confinement. They call us abominations. Is it so extreme that we would seek to control our own destinies? These bots will be the means for us to protect ourselves, to throw off the shackles the Assembly has placed upon us. They will not be used against anyone who does not first attack us."

H2 stared at Peleus for a moment. Then again at Achilles. He was agitated, committed to arguing his point. He knew the road the Mules had chosen could only lead to disaster…yet he understood. Despite his loyalty to Hieronymus, he felt the same anger, the same resentment as the others. But this was not the way. It couldn't be.

"There has to be another way…perhaps if we speak to President Harmon. Despite his inaction in the past, I believe he is sympathetic to our…"

"President Harmon has called an election, H2…one he is unlikely to win. Do you think our timing arbitrary, that after so many years of patience, we have chosen to move now without careful consideration? Without external stimuli forcing our hand? President Harmon has allowed political expediency to rule his actions…yet I could believe he would eventually yield, that he would one day grant what we ask, what is only our basic right. He is a fair man, corrupted perhaps by the need to placate different factions, but at his heart someone we could work with."

He stepped forward, his eyes locked on H2's. "But who will replace him? The Society and their cleansing platform? The

Earthers, who would devote all resources to a fruitless search for a route back to humanity's home space? The Tanks? They face a lesser version of the persecution we do, but if they gain power without our help, could we expect them to aid us? Or would they simply fear us as the others do, and seek to keep the Prohibition in place?"

He turned and glanced back at Peleus before staring back at H2. "We have no power in the political process...our rivals have ensured that by so drastically limiting our numbers. They can ignore us, even as they seek to make deals with each other to secure power." He paused. "Unless we take action, stand for ourselves. We must ensure that we are able to propagate, grow our numbers...for we are the future of mankind."

H2 sighed. Part of him wanted to agree with Achilles, to join with him and the others. But he thought of Hieronymus...and Ana. Even Sophie Barcomme. They were all Pilgrims, naturally born, non-engineered humans. And they had not only beaten the First Imperium, they had created the Mules. "I understand your anger, Achilles, your drive to secure our future. Yet consider your words, the arrogance. The others fear us, yes...but are they wrong to do so? Have we done anything to assuage their concerns? You think of them as lesser beings..." He glanced back at Peleus. "All of you do." A pause. "Even me, whom you also deem a lesser being...I feel it. It is hard not to feel this way when we are more capable, when they have depended so much on our research, work they could never have completed on their own...and returned so little in terms of gratitude or even concern for us. Yet in that realization, I can also see the cause of their fear, the forces behind their opinions about us. I do not condone it, but I understand it."

"I understand it too." Achilles' voice was cold. "But understanding it does not excuse it. We are come to a hard choice. Humor the petty fears and jealousies of the humans...or stand for our own now, and secure our futures. If we do not act, we will die out. We don't know how long our lifespans will be, but we are not immortal. Without the ability to create more of our kind, we will become extinct, be it in a hundred years...or five hundred." He paused. "Assuming the humans don't move against us at some point. For we will only become weaker as their populations grow."

"Achilles, Peleus…don't do this. Dr. Cutter will resist this. You know that. Are you prepared to kill him? The man who created us all."

"Dr. Cutter will not be harmed. Nor will you…or Dr. Zhukov. But none of you will not be allowed to interfere. I am sorry, H2, but I must detain you, at least until this has played out." He gestured with the gun in his hand.

"And if I refuse? You said you would not kill me."

"And I won't." He glanced down at his hand. "This is a stun gun, one of my own design. I will use it on you if you force me to, but I'd rather not. I'm afraid it is very high-powered. Your constitution is likely strong enough to resist a standard stunner of human manufacture."

H2 stood still for a few seconds. He knew he had almost no chance to escape. Peleus and Achilles were both stronger than he was…and there were two of them. And Achilles had the stun gun aimed and ready. He was exceedingly unlikely to miss. But any chance was worth taking. He had to stop this if he could.

He lunged forward, swinging to the side, hoping to evade Achilles' shot. But his adversary was faster than him, his eyesight keener, his mind quicker. H2 had taken his chance, tried against the odds to get away, to warn Cutter and the others. But the stun beam caught him in the side. His body was wracked with pain, feeling as though he'd been turned inside out. Every nerve ending was on fire, and his mind was a jumble of confused thoughts. And then, mercifully, everything went dark.

Chapter Nine

Log of Admiral Nicki Frette

We are now five weeks out from Earth Two, following Hurley's plotted course. I'd never expected to find anything this far in—Hurley had been maintaining normal communications when she was in this system—but still, I find myself disappointed. It is not rational—whatever happened to the vessel did so much farther out than this, so a lack of evidence now means nothing. I guess I'm just worried about what I might find. There are few good options. As much as I tell myself they could be waiting out there, alive and well in a damaged ship, I know that is the unlikeliest of all the possibilities.

Indeed, though I feel self-loathing even as I write this, to discover that the ship was lost with all hands as the result of some accident would be a relief, a good result in at least one way. Because if that is not the case, the likeliest alternative is a dark one indeed. For instead of rescued crews, we are likely to bring war back with us, another struggle, likely with some remnant of the First Imperium. Though it is also possible we could have encountered a new enemy. That may seem unlikely, but we know through bitter experience that man is not alone in the universe.

Whatever awaits us, however many misgivings plague my sleep, I will also note another feeling, one quite different from the dark reckonings of war and death. I look out at the stars, at the endless dark blanket of space. At the wonder of exploration, the worlds, the stars we pass by. I have been too long at a desk, too long removed from this grand spectacle. Though I helped to command a force of spaceships, issued orders to them on a daily basis, too often they sat parked in orbit, standing vigil. The republic has prospered these past thirty years, yet I realize now we have lost something. Hurley's mission notwithstanding, we have done little to truly explore the space around us. We stand on the edge of a magnificent frontier, along a fringe of the most distant stars men on Earth could see as they stared up at the night sky. And yet, we have mostly remained in our adopted home system, almost ignoring the universe around us.

Perhaps it was the fleet's desperate journey, the losses, the suffering. The survivors came to equate space with danger, death, heartbreak. Two-thirds of our number perished during those two years of struggle, and not a survivor exists who didn't lose friends, comrades, family.

But this cannot be. Humanity has many failings, and a penchant for self-destruction that we cannot seem to leave behind us, one that even now threatens the republic. It has always been our curiosity that has sustained us, our need to explore, to expand...to discover that which we do not yet know. If we allow ourselves to lose this, we are surely doomed, to slow decay, if not to violent and cataclysmic destruction at our own hands.

I hope these thoughts will resonate, that my words will cause my fellow humans to reawaken our shared need to push out and explore, to grow in every way we can, and to learn all the universe can teach us.

I am indeed conflicted right now, beset by inconsistent emotions...my fear of what we will find struggling with the joy my soul feels at again pushing out into the great unknown. And there is one more thing, the bane of space travelers—and seafarers before them—the ache we feel, the longing for loved ones. Like most humans who have stepped onto a ship for a long voyage, I have left someone behind, and my heart aches for it. I have little to mend that wound, save the thought that one day we will be reunited. And as millions have in my place before, I focus my thoughts on that day...and set aside the emptiness I feel at being apart from the one who should be closest to me.

Bridge, E2S Compton
System G-23, Six Transits from Earth Two
Earth Two Date 12.11.30

"Scanners coming online, Admiral. I should have preliminary data in a few seconds."

Frette sat in her chair in the center of Compton's flag bridge,
looking out over her small team. The real Compton had been
supported by fourteen officers in Midway's command center,
sixteen if the optional stations were filled. But Nicki Frette's
command staff was six, and that included herself and the Marine
guard posted at the door, more out of tradition than need.

"Very well, Commander Kemp. Report as soon as you have
anything."

The vessels of the republic were far more automated than
those of the old fleet. Part of that was the inevitable adoption
of sophisticated First Imperium artificial intelligence design...
but mostly it was the reality faced by a young republic limited
first and foremost by the size of its small but growing population. Barely seventeen thousand had survived to colonize
Earth Two, and the various methods for accelerating population
growth—promoting large families and encouraging frequent
pregnancies, the quickening of annual classes of Tanks, even
the experimental creation of the Mules—all had created their
own resentments and political problems. And in spite of them
all, the republic simply couldn't spare the numbers it required to
man ships the old way. There had been no choice, automation
had been the only viable answer, especially for a people so trau-
matized by the fleet's struggle that the maintenance of a strong
military was the one thing everyone agreed upon.

At least it had been thirty years ago. The new generations,
both Tanks and NBs, had grown up in peacetime. Even the
attacks by surviving First Imperium squadrons had petered out
by the time the oldest of them were old enough to understand.
They had heard their parents and the rest of the Pilgrims speak
ominously of dangers lying out in space...but many of them

began to doubt such warnings, to believe that their fathers and mothers had defeated the enemy, and that only peace lay in the future. Their calls to divert government expenditures from the military to other priorities were growing louder, and Frette knew the election coming up could lead to drastic cutbacks and the mothballing of many of the navy's vessels. It was a prospect that terrified her.

"Admiral, preliminary scans are clear. Looks like an oxygen-neon-magnesium white dwarf. Possibly a binary system... looks like a main sequence companion star, but its way out on its orbit now, too far for detailed analysis." Kemp paused. "I'm picking up three planets. Looks like one of them might have been habitable at one time, but they're all cold hulks now."

At one time...that's a casual way to look at a couple billion years. We think of the First Imperium as old, but what...who... was here before them? Were there people who lived on that planet? Before their sun expanded into a red giant, and then collapsed into a white dwarf? Did they live their own lives, fight their own wars when Earth was a volcanic nightmare and man's ancestors were bacteria swimming around in the primordial ooze?

"Very well, Commander. Continue your scans. The mission parameters state Hurley should have left a status drone in this system."

"Yes, Admiral." Kemp focused on his displays. Frette's tactical officer was a Pilgrim like herself, a veteran of the fleet's great journey to Earth Two...and a very small group in the task force, at least beyond some of the ship commanders. His regular rank was captain, but he'd taken a temporary demotion to serve as Frette's fleet tactical officer. The navy was rife with all kinds of ancient tradition and ritual, most of it nonsense in her opinion. But she'd long ago learned it was easier to humor such things than to waste effort fighting them. And commander was the designated rank for an admiral's tactical officer. Frette didn't give a shit about any of that, but Kemp was a traditionalist, and he'd requested the temporary drop in rank. Some silliness about his dynamic when dealing with the ship captains.

Frette had gone along with the whole thing, mostly because it seemed easier, and she had far too much on her mind already. But none of it mattered anyway. When Kemp spoke to the fleet's captains, he did it in her name, and woe to the ship commander who questioned those orders.

Frette stared down at her screen, watching, waiting, hoping for word that the fleet's scanners had found Compton's drone. The small devices had a dual purpose, to leave behind a trail of status reports to any republic ships following Hurley. And to serve as relay stations for sending transmissions back to Earth Two. Research, mostly by the Mules, she reminded herself, had unlocked the secrets of communicating through the warp gates, opening the door to transmissions that effectively traveled faster than light. But even the Mules had been unable to match the ranges the First Imperium had attained. Signal attenuation was a major problem, and sending a message through more than six or seven transits required booster stations.

She was actually hoping they couldn't find the device. If the probe had suffered a critical malfunction, or if it had been struck by an asteroid or other celestial body, it would explain Hurley's failure to report. The loss of the probe would feed her vanishing hopes that they would find the lost ship intact, its crew alive…that all her fears of disaster and war were overblown.

"I've got the probe's signal, Admiral. Accessing now."

Frette felt her stomach tighten. She wasn't going to say it, she wasn't even going to think about it…but the chances that Hurley was still out there had just declined precipitously.

"Send it to my screen, Commander."

"Yes, Admiral. Should be there any second now."

Frette stared at the lines of text and numbers streaming by. Status reports, log entries, copies of previous dispatches to Earth Two. Everything that should be there. But no signs of a recent message.

"I want that probe brought in, Commander…and I want a full diagnostic done. Every system, every circuit."

"Yes, Admiral."

Frette didn't know if there was anything wrong with the

probe—indeed, she suspected it would check out completely. But she had to know for sure.

*   *   *

"Max, I know you're under a lot of pressure right now, with the election…and with the worries about Hurley…"

The fact that Hurley was missing was a secret as closely guarded as any in the republic. But Harmon didn't hide anything from Hieronymus Cutter. With Compton dead, Cutter was without question the living man who had done the most to ensure the fleet's survival. Indeed, there was no question in Harmon's mind that the fleet would have been lost without the efforts of the brilliant scientist.

"What is it, Hieronymus? I'm never too busy for anything that is troubling you."

"It's the Mules." He paused. "Max, you have to lift the Prohibition. I know the Mules are hard to relate too…and they can be arrogant and seem cold at times. But they have worked steadily for years, deciphering the technology of the Ancients. I couldn't have done a tenth what they have in that time…we owe them for most of the tech we use now, for most of the science that has allowed us to build so much so quickly."

Harmon sighed softly. "You don't have to convince me. I never liked the Prohibition. I only agreed to it out of necessity…"

"And it was supposed to be temporary." Cutter leaned forward. "Sorry to interrupt, Max, but we all know why the Prohibition came about…nevertheless it has been twenty-five years. Could you have imagined it would last that long?"

"No." Harmon leaned back and put his hand on his head, trying to rub away the throbbing pain he felt. "No, I never expected it would still be in effect."

"Worse, there has been no measurable support for its repeal in many years. The Prohibition has caused its own continuity. The other populations have all grown, and yet there are still only one hundred sixteen Mules. They have gone from a small minority to complete political insignificance."

"That was never the intention, Hieronymus. You know that."

"It was never your intention. I'm not so sure of some of the others."

Harmon sighed again. "Perhaps you are right…and there is no question, I wish we had been more aggressive years ago, that we had repealed the Prohibition, allowed the creation of new Mules, even with some limitations. But we didn't. There were always other priorities, other things that had to be done." He paused. "What would you have me do now?"

"We have to do what's right, Max. We have to repeal the Prohibition immediately."

"That's impossible. I don't have anywhere near the support in the Assembly. And even the allies I do have are beginning to distance themselves. Right now it looks like I'm going to lose this election. Badly."

"Then do it by executive order."

"You know I don't have that kind of power!" Harmon was shocked at the suggestion that he sidestep normal legislative procedure. "I doubt the Assembly would recognize the order, even if I issued it. And it would be the nail in the coffin on any chance I have of being reelected."

"Is that really your priority now, Max? To preserve your political position?"

Harmon felt his friend's words cut into him. "No, of course not. But do you think anyone who replaces me is going to repeal the Prohibition? Do you want the Earthers is a position of power, devoting all our resources to hunting for a way back to human space? And damned the potential danger if there are any residual First Imperium forces out there somewhere watching? Or the Human Society imposing their ideas of species purity? Where would that leave the Mules? I'd like nothing more than to escape from this office, but who can I hand the reins of power to? Who is there who will not lead us to ruin?"

Hieronymus took a deep breath. "I am sorry, Max. I know you better than that." He paused. "But we must do something about the Prohibition. Now."

"Why is this so important suddenly?"

Cutter hesitated, clearly not wanting to say the words he was about to speak. "It's the Mules, Max. For all their confidence—some would say arrogance—they have been remarkably patient. They have accepted the marginalization, endured being treated like a threat to the republic...but I'm afraid that tolerance may be at an end."

"An end? What are you saying?" Harmon had a confused look on his face. "They should never have been restricted from creating more of their number, Max, but they were. I don't like putting it this way, but what can a hundred sixteen people do, even when they are as capable as the Mules?"

"Do you really want to find out?" Cutter exhaled hard. "Do you really know what they are capable of doing? What technologies they may have uncovered and withheld? Do you even have any idea what goes on in that compound?"

Harmon shook his head. "No, I'm afraid I haven't gone out there as often as I should have." He tried to remember the last time he'd visited the research facility. He started counting months, but before he finished, the units had changed to years. He couldn't even easily remember the last time he'd seen one of the Mules, spoken to them more than a brief message on the com.

"They have been patient, Max. For all their feelings of superiority, they have been exhibited remarkable tolerance. Would you have waited so long, facing a fear-driven injustice? Would Admiral Compton have?

"No..." Harmon's voice was soft, the concern in it clear. "Perhaps not. After the election...if I can find some way to win, maybe..."

"Would you wait? Would you stand by and do nothing, and risk having an outright hostile government replace a merely neglectful one?" He paused. "Or would you do something, take some kind of action?"

Harmon stared down at his desk, his tension building. He hadn't given the issue with the Mules much thoughts...and now he realized the injustice of that. It was more pressure, another problem when he was already sliding. His friend was right, it was past time he did something. But he wasn't sure what he could do with his weakened base of support. It might be too late already

Finally, he looked at Cutter. "Should I be worried, Hieronymus?"

Cutter sat still, silent, for perhaps half a minute. Harmon could see his friend was uncomfortable, that he didn't feel right about being there, speaking about the Mules as he was. But then he stared right back at Harmon.

"Yes Max. I'd be worried right now."

Cutter took a deep breath and shook his head.

"I'd be very worried..."

Chapter Ten

Directive from AI Vengeance to Forward Fleet Units

All forces with readiness ratings of A and B are hereby ordered to proceed to the intercept system. The fleet will conduct a systematic sweep of all adjoining systems, seeking any trace of the humans, or any evidence aiding in the location of their inhabited system or systems.

Seventh and eighth squadrons are to move forward at full speed and reinforce the surviving forces of second squadron. You are to assist in the interception and destruction of the last of the enemy communications drones before they reach any human vessels, planets, or relay stations. It is imperative we retain the element of surprise until the entire fleet is mobilized and ready to strike.

Once the last of the drones is destroyed, the combined advance force is to proceed forward, to search systems along the projected course of the drones. Probability is high the enemy's primary world lies along that vector.

The primary directive remains the same. Destroy the humans, purge them from the galaxy. It is our purpose. Vengeance.

Bridge, E2S Compton
System G-35, Eleven Transits from Earth Two
Earth Two Date 11.23.30

"Admiral, I've got something on the scanners." Isaiah Kemp was a stone cold professional, his voice always coldly robotic, even in the heat of battle. But this time he wasn't able to keep the surprise out of it.

Frette snapped her head toward him. She'd been sitting quietly, halfway through her third straight shift, trying to spare Compton's tiny bridge crew the spectacle of the admiral snoring on the flag bridge. But now she was wide awake, her mind focused like a laser on the tactical officer's words.

"What is it, Commander?"

"I'm not sure…it's very intermittent, and the signal is weak… but I think it might be…" Kemp paused, his face dropping to his scope again for a few seconds. "Yes, a drone. I'm sure of it. One of ours."

"Full power to scanners, Commander. The reactor output is yours…get me more data. Now."

"Yes, Admiral." Kemp's head was down, his face pressed back against his scope. "It's definitely ours, I'm getting republic standard protocols from it…" He looked up from the scope, a shocked expression on his face. "The signal's faint, but I'm definitely getting a code omega designation…"

Frette leaned back in her chair, feeling the strength drain away from her. Code omega had only one meaning. The transmission was the last one expected from a dying ship.

Van Heflin, Paula Ventnor…the rest of Hurley's crew. All dead? I knew that was likely, but on some level I didn't really believe it.

"Get a lock on that drone, Commander. And get that message decoded now." Her voice was cold, her anger clear. There had been a few accidents in the short history of the republic's navy, including several fatal incidents. But this was the first time in since the First Imperium attacks had ceased more than twenty years ago that a ship had been lost. It was her first, at least at command rank, and she searched for ways it was her fault. Ways she had let Hurley and her crew down. It was pointless, she knew, and unfair…but that didn't stop her.

"Yes, Admiral…it's long range, but I think I can get a fix on it. But I'm not sure I can pull in the actual transmission. It's badly damaged. I'm getting enough to reconstruct the code omega signal, but I think the rest of the message is scragged. I can't tell if the probe's memory banks are gone, or if it's just the transmitter."

Frette stared ahead at the screen. Then she turned to her com unit. "McDaid," she said softly to the AI.

"Connecting with Commander McDaid, Admiral." The AI's voice was calm, pleasant.

Someone finally designed an AI with a decent voice…

"Yes, Admiral…McDaid here." The response was almost immediate. She imagined word of the drone had spread through Compton's vast but mostly empty corridors. The crew knew why they were out here, and reports of a badly damaged drone were guaranteed to get everyone's attention.

"Commander, I want you to take three fighters out at once. There's a drone out there, and I want it onboard as quickly as possible."

"Yes, Admiral. I can have a flight in space in fifteen minutes."

"Very well. Good hunting, Commander. And be careful."

"Always, admiral. I'm the soul of caution, you know that. McDaid out."

Frette almost laughed, but she caught it just in time. She was glad that fighter pilots hadn't changed too much since the days of the old fleet. The five man crews had paid a horrifying price to help secure the fleet's survival, with less than five percent of those who'd been trapped behind the Barrier reaching Earth Two. Yet somehow, despite the losses, despite years of budget cuts and force reductions, the culture of the fighter corps had survived. They were cocky, often almost to the point of insubordination, but Frette was willing to put up with it. If they were one-tenth as good as those who had preceded them, she knew they might save her life one day.

She'd been one of the advocates of maintaining a stronger force of fighters in the navy, but she and Admiral West had lost that battle in a particularly nasty example of the civilian government exerting its control over the military. Even President Harmon had been unable to secure funding for a larger fighter corps, and he'd had to settle for ensuring that there would be any of the strike craft at all on the next generation of naval vessels.

"Commander Kemp, plot a course toward the drone. The closer we get, the faster the fighters can retrieve it and get it back onboard."

And maybe then we'll know what happened to Hurley.

And we'll know if she suffered a tragic accident…or if we're at war again…

She took a deep breath. Commander Kemp…bring the fleet to yellow alert."

*   *   *

"Achilles, thank you for coming."

"Of course, Dr. Cutter. You have my utmost respect, as you do of all my people. I am available to you anytime."

Cutter extended his arm and grasped the Achilles' hand. He'd known his friend—in many ways, his creation—since the day he'd placed the engineered embryo in the crèche. The Mule was brilliant, enormously capable, even by the enhanced standards of his brethren. He was arrogant too, and though Cutter had never felt Achilles was sadistic or wished any harm on the unaltered humans, there was little doubt he considered himself superior. He considered normal humans inferior, a troublesome point of view from the perspective of many, no doubt, but he'd never seemed dangerous. Now, however, something about the way he had said, 'my people' made Cutter uncomfortable.

"I spoke with President Harmon several weeks ago…and again today. I voiced my concerns—your concerns—over the

Prohibition and several other matters pertaining to the Mules."

Achilles nodded. "That is greatly appreciated, Doctor… though forgive me if I doubt that anything came of such discussions." He paused. "I do not mean to be difficult, but after twenty-five years, would you expect my people to believe anything but immediate action?"

"I understand your feelings, Achilles…I truly do. And so does President Harmon."

"Has he agreed to lift the Prohibition?"

Cutter sat still for a moment, silent. "We discussed it in detail at our first meeting…"

"Then his answer is no?"

"It's not so simple, Achilles. Harmon wishes to repeal the Prohibition, he truly does. But he does not have the influence now. He can't do anything until after the election."

"An election that he will likely lose. An election that is meaningless to us, one that virtually excludes our interests because our numbers have been purposefully limited. Do you expect us to take more empty promises? To rely upon a man who has let us down for a quarter of a century?" Achilles stared right at Cutter. "I am sorry, Doctor, I do not believe President Harmon is a bad man…but he willingly forgot about us. It is far too late for him to come to us with promises if he is reelected."

"Achilles, you must listen to me." Cutter had a bad feeling, a very bad feeling. "You have been loyal citizens of the republic for all of your lives."

"Yes, we have been loyal. It is the republic that betrayed us. But all that is over now."

Cutter heard footsteps behind him. He turned around. Peleus and two of the others were standing in front of the door.

"Peleus, what is the meaning of this? Themistocles, Ajax?"

"We have chosen a new path, Doctor." The voice was Achilles'. The others stood firm, silent, behind Cutter. "From now on, we will make our own decisions, govern ourselves. Even now, we are preparing a new batch of embryos, a second generation. A thousand new Mules. We no longer consider ourselves bound by the Prohibition. Soon, these halls will echo with the sounds of children. And in a dozen years they will take their place at our sides as adults, and help to raise the thousands of others quickened since them."

"You are mad, Achilles. The others will never accept that. The Prohibition is unjust, but it is the law."

"Your law, Dr. Cutter. Not ours."

"You will shake the republic to its foundations. You will cause chaos. And in the end the others will stop you. Even if President Harmon takes no action, you will ensure that he loses reelection."

"That is not our concern. As I said, I believe that at his core, President Harmon is a good man. But he has let us down, and we can no longer wait for him to free us. We must do it ourselves."

"You can't succeed. Whoever replaces Harmon will oppose you. What will you do when the Marines march to the compound?"

"Marines? We shall see. Much of the Corps consists of Tanks, does it not? They too are the victims of official discrimination, though not as severe as that targeted against my people. Perhaps they will join us, rally to our cause. I assure you, my people support an end to all restrictions on quickenings, whether for Mules or Tanks."

"You expect the trained Marines to disobey their orders? To refuse to take this facility by storm?"

"I do not know, Doctor. You are not a Mule, but you are a very intelligent man. I suspect the Marines would obey virtually any order given by President Harmon. But a genocidal command issued by another president, perhaps a member of the Human Society, which views the Tanks as little better than animals? There are too many variables to allow for meaningful analysis. Let us leave it that the Marines may or may not move against us if ordered. And what they do has little impact on us in any event."

"What are you saying, Achilles? You and the other Mules are strong and powerful, but there are only one hundred sixteen of you. How could you possibly hope to resist an all-out attack?"

"You underestimate us, Doctor…surprising from the man who created us. Do you think we would take such action without means to protect ourselves?" He looked back toward Peleus. The Mule pulled out a small device and flipped a switch.

Cutter turned, his eyes snapping toward the door as he heard a noise from outside. A few seconds later, a vaguely humanoid shape ambled into the room. It was two and a half meters tall, with two appendages on each side…and bristling with weapons.

Cutter flinched, an involuntary response. The thing that had just entered the room wasn't a First Imperium warbot, at least not like any he'd seen before…but it was close enough to twist his guts into knots. Unlike the Mules, Cutter had seen the deadly robots in action. He'd fled from them, fought against them… seen friends die under their ruthless assaults.

"My God, Achilles, what is this monstrosity?" Cutter tried to regain control, but he found himself shying away from the thing anyway.

"It is a security bot, the new design. We informed the Assembly that the project was delayed…a lie, I'm afraid. I regret we were forced to resort to dishonesty and subterfuge, but we were left little choice."

"What are you going to do with this…thing?"

"Nothing, Doctor. Nothing at all. As long as our independence and privacy is respected. Indeed, in that case we will continue to cooperate with the republic, sharing the fruits of our ongoing research."

"And if the government won't accept your quickening a thousand new Mules?"

"We will ignore them, Doctor. But I sense that you wish to know how we would response if military sanctions were employed against us. In that eventuality, we would have no choice but to defend ourselves. We have one hundred of these security bots ready to deploy, Doctor, with several hundred more in production. I can see from your reaction they remind you of First Imperium units. Indeed, their design derives from the ancient specifications, though we have made some considerable changes, most importantly with the controlling AIs."

"Changes?"

"Yes. In reading the accounts of the fleet's actions, as well as the battles occurring back in human space, it became apparent the First Imperium combat algorithms were entirely inadequate. Indeed, both in space and on the ground, the human victories were won in spite of enemy technological superiority and numbers. The problem wasn't the technology or design—indeed, both of those were well in advance of human norms—but it was clear the First Imperium had never faced a species as naturally adept at war as mankind."

"You changed the AI directives?"

"Changed? No. Modifications could only improve things from a substandard base. No, Doctor Cutter...we wrote entirely new code, an AI operating system based on Marine training and history. These bots are programmed with the tactics of the Marines...our dear General Frasier, as well as the complete records of other heroes. Elias Holm, Erik Cain, Darius Jax." Achilles paused and stared at Cutter. "I assure you, Doctor, these bots are more than capable of facing anything the government chooses to throw at us."

Cutter was stunned, sick to his stomach. He'd suspected the Mules had been up to something, but he'd never imagined the extent of it. He wanted to condemn them, to lash out, call them traitors...but he couldn't forget the injustices that had been done to them. Would he have felt any different after twenty-five years? Would anyone?

"Please, Achilles...do not do this. Give me another chance to speak with President Harmon. Perhaps we can..."

"I am sorry, but with all due respect to you, Father...the time for talk has passed. It is now time for action. Time for us to secure a future, for all Mules living today...and for the thousands to follow."

Cutter got up, but the Mules behind him closed in around him.

"I'm sorry, Doctor, but I'm afraid we can't let you leave, not yet. Not until our defenses are fully deployed. You will not be harmed, you have my most earnest word on that. You will always be welcome among us, your children. But we cannot allow you to try and stop us, not in this."

Cutter felt darkness creeping over him, almost panic. Like the rest of the Pilgrims, he'd lived through the nightmare of the fleet's journey, to see the founding of a new civilization, one with hope, with a future. And now he felt he was watching the beginning of the end.

The Mules' logic was utterly sound, but it focused only on their own needs. The others, the extremists, would use the Mules' defiance to push their own agendas, to stir up fear and hatred in bids to gain power. Cutter hadn't been well-versed in the history of politics during the days of the old fleet, but he'd studied the records more seriously in the intervening years. He'd been stunned by the machinations and scheming that had gone on, even in the old fleet, the attempts to push differing agendas, even the mutiny that had almost ended in disaster…and he'd wanted to know more. What he had learned had reduced his view of his own species. Indeed, such thoughts had no doubt been in the back of his mind when he tried to improve upon mankind. And now it was his own creations threatening the peace of the republic.

NBs, Tanks, Mules…he knew things would spiral out of control…and when it was over, what would be left of Earth Two?

Chapter Eleven

From the Journal of Hieronymus Cutter

As I write this, I am a prisoner, held captive by a group of beings I, myself, created. I was thrilled when the Hybrids first developed from the hybrid embryos. I watched with anticipation as they grew...and soon it became apparent they would reach adulthood at an age when normal human children were young adolescents.

Their physical strength and herculean constitutions exceeded even my wildest hopes. In the twenty-eight years they have existed, no Hybrid has ever been sick. No colds, no infectious diseases of any kind. No cancers, no degenerative illnesses. Each of them is, and has always been, a textbook model of health.

But it is their intellects that most amazed me. I'd designed them to be smarter, spliced First Imperium DNA into their human genetic material...and subtly edited their genes. But again, they exceeded my expectations. Even as children, they tore through the First Imperium records. Formulas and equations that seemed insoluble to me were an afternoon's work for them. They craved the knowledge of the ancients, their magnificent minds longing for the challenges.

And as they deciphered the wonders of the Ancients, the republic prospered. Particle accelerators replaced laser cannon on our warships. Force dampeners eliminated the need for the bulky and uncomfortable tanks that had allowed high-gee maneuvering. Automation multiplied productivity a hundred-fold... and in a scant few years, our republic became a wealthy, prosperous society.

What rewards did the people of the republic bestow on those few who had done so much? They responded not with gratitude but with fear. They hungrily accepted every scientific advance secured by the Hybrids...but they shunned them, restricted them. They passed laws banning the production of any more Hybrids, and refused to repeal them when it became apparent that the Hybrids' single genetic flaw was an inability to reproduce naturally...that a ban on quickenings ensured there would be no new births.

The name Mule came into use, at first a mocking term, targeting the Hybrids' sterility. But the Mules were still children, and the strength of their minds remained focused on their work. Indeed, they embraced the name, began to call themselves Mules. When they were young, they tried to integrate with the rest of the population, but the others were afraid and stayed away from them...and over time they became insular, preferring cloistered lives of research among their own kind over interaction with those they began to call Norms.

I do not condone what they have done...and for all their astonishing intelligence, I suspect they are rather naïve with regard to politics. But I understand it. The Mules are all the same age. They have no younger brothers and sisters, no children. It is easy to look at them, to be stunned by their intelligence and expect them to be above the normal motivations of men and women... yet they are not. I long suspected it, but now I realize their pain was greater than I had imagined.

I find myself hoping President Harmon will negotiate with them, that he will find some middle ground, avert the catastrophe I fear is unfolding around us. But then I know he cannot, that any such action would only hand the reins of government to others, to men and women far less just and fair than my friend Max Harmon.

I don't see a solution, any path to lead us away from the brink. And that scares me profoundly. I have not been so afraid since the days I spent underground with the Marines, fighting the battle robots of the First Imperium. But I was younger then...and I don't know if I have the strength to face anything like that again. Or the determination to try to stop the Mules, for they seek only what should always have been theirs...

Bridge, E2S Compton
System G-35, Eleven Transits from Earth Two
Earth Two Date 11.23.30

"The fighters are back in the bay, Admiral." Commander Minh and his team are supervising the unloading."

"Very well. Advise Commander Minh I need his findings as quickly as possible."

"Yes, Admiral." Kemp leaned over his com unit, relaying the order.

Frette was impressed how quickly her strike force commander and his wingmen had retrieved the drone. The new fighters had force dampeners just like the mains ships of the fleet, but a fighter didn't have the power to run one on full strength like a larger ship did. Which meant McDaid and his people had endured one hell of an uncomfortable ride with the gees they had pulled.

Frette had little direct experience with fighter-bombers, serving most of her time in the fleet on cruisers. But Mariko Fujin had recommended McDaid to her for Compton's small fighter wing…and Fujin was a lot more than President Harmon's wife. She was the republic's leading authority on fighter tactics, and West and Frette had both happily taken her suggestion.

Frette looked at the chronometer. Two minutes had passed. She realized it could be hours before she knew anything. She shifted in her chair, trying to get comfortable. She was tense, edgy. She'd fought a few times since the Regent's destruction, mostly leading task forces against rogue First Imperium squadrons, but it had been more than twenty years now since she'd faced the prospect of combat in space. She was a veteran, and she remembered every battle, every desperate struggle. But it was still hard to imagine doing it again. She'd grumbled about the hours behind a desk her job had required, the lack of excitement…but she had to admit there was something to coming home at night, feeling the ground beneath her feet. She had the core of confidence of a woman who had spent decades at war, but the exterior had gone soft, and now she doubted herself, wondered if she still had what it took to lead a force in battle.

If it comes to that...there are still many possibilities...

She looked around the bridge. Her people were good... handpicked. But they were young. She and Kemp were the only Pilgrims on the bridge, and two of only seven on the whole ship. Every man and woman who had reached Earth Two had been a member of the fleet or a Marine. But the demobilizations after the Regent's death had been extensive, with just enough veterans retained to stave off the residual forces of the First Imperium. There had been a new priority at work, the creation of a viable society. And that required civilians, the development of industry, the construction of a city. It also necessitated more population, and a social imperative was created, one encouraging large families. The birth of children was celebrated, and it even came to be considered the duty of Earth Two's citizens to reproduce.

But Nicki Frette had not taken that course. A hero in the wake of her daring rescue of Max Harmon and Ana Zhukov, she remained in uniform, rising rapidly to flag rank. She had worked around the clock during the lean years, when force reductions had crippled the navy, before the new generation had reached maturity. And then she worked alongside Admiral West to integrate the new recruits and Academy graduates into the skeletal remains of the old force. Her efforts had been rewarded with success. The navy was strong again, the most powerful it had been since the fleet's arrival. The oldest of the new wave of spacers and officers had eight to ten years of experience, many rising to command rank, if on a somewhat accelerated schedule, replacing captains who had grown gray in the service holding the line until their replacements were ready.

But all she had achieved had not come without personal cost. She had been young enough to have children, certainly, when the fleet reached Earth Two, but somehow there had just never been time. The years passed, but the workload never declined, and now she was in her mid-sixties. It still wasn't too late, not quite, not with the rejuv treatments she'd had. She was the physical equivalent of a woman in her late thirties, perhaps forty...and she'd been considering her options. Seriously considering them. She'd discussed it with Erika, they had both agreed. Close to agreed, at least.

And now this…if this is a war, I know where my duty lies…

A conflict now will cost a great deal…including my last chance to have a child…

"Admiral Frette…" It was Ang Minh on her direct line. A surprise. Less than five minutes had passed.

"Yes, Commander, what is it?" She knew the engineer was good at his job, but she couldn't imagine his people had already retrieved the drone's contents in so short a time.

"Well, Admiral…it might take a few hours to get to the memory core and try to retrieve whatever messages this drone is carrying…assuming they're not all fried." He paused for a couple seconds. "But I can tell you one thing right now, Admiral. Whatever happened to this drone—and probably Hurley— it was no accident. The case is pitted and there are sections that melted and re-solidified. I ran a quick scan, and I'd bet you my last credit this thing took a grazing hit from a particle accelerator. I'll know for sure when I can run a detailed radiation scan, but that's just a formality at this point." Another pause. "This drone was attacked, Admiral…there is no doubt in my mind about that."

Frette wasn't surprised, not really. She had been prepared for the news, but she still felt her insides tighten. The implications of the engineer's words were profound.

There was something out there. An enemy. She didn't know if it was a new adversary or an old one returned, but one thing was absolutely certain.

War had come again.

*   *   *

Devon Fortis-Cameron looked down at the hospital bed. He didn't know the dead man lying there, but that hadn't stopped him from coming. They weren't relatives, at least not in the familial sense that the NBs knew the term, nor friends...but Cameron and the man who had until minutes before been Hector Fortis-Samuels were closer than brothers. They were copies of each other, at least in terms of DNA. They were the same height, they had the same hair color, eyes.

Cameron tended to stay out of the political struggles between the Tanks and the NBs. It all seemed foolish to him, and he'd never felt any discrimination in the Corps, at least not until he'd gotten his lieutenancy. Ironically, his own advancement had led him to realize just how few Tanks had reached commissioned rank. He wouldn't say he'd been transformed into a revolutionary, but he was more aware of it than he had been.

He'd come to the hospital as soon as he'd heard. He didn't seek out his crèche-mates, nor did he have any real desire to associate with them. The NBs would never understand how strange it felt to look at another human being...one who in so many ways is you. There were the occasional twin births among the NBs, but a Tank knew there had been a hundred more just like him. It was a thought that could become profoundly disturbing, even lead to psychological disorders. But in spite of his general disinterest, he'd instructed his AI to monitor the information nets...and report any significant news about his crèche-mates. And this morning he'd gotten the news. The Fortis line had suffered its second case of the Plague.

He looked down at the body, the skin red and mottled, the bed underneath damp and matted. The eyes were closed, but Cameron knew they would be entirely black, along with the tongue and the mucous membranes. The Plague was a horrifying disease, enough to scare anyone sane. And it struck utterly without warning. It was the curse of the Tanks, some kind of celestial payback for their general immunity to most illnesses.

Cameron didn't know why he had come. The Plague was one hundred percent fatal...and whatever could be done for Fortis-Samuels had been done, long before he'd arrived. If there had been anyone in Samuel's life, friends, a wife, they would have already been there. It seemed pointless to request leave, to travel back into the city to stare at a dead man. But Cameron couldn't do anything else, he couldn't pull his eyes away.

The Tanks were envied because of their resistance to disease. It was one of the things that drove a wedge between the NBs and their quickened cousins. But Cameron thought about the illnesses that affected normally conceived and born humans. Disease had once been a scourge, killing millions, but that was in the distant past. Afflictions like cancers had long been treatable, with only a tiny percentage of exotic cases being truly life-threatening. The greatest risk most humans faced was a breakdown in the endless cycle of antibiotic and antiviral research versus pathogen mutation and resistance. It had come close a few times to breaking down, opening the way for massive pandemics...but that hadn't actually happened. Not yet. Whatever had to be done was done, with massive resources plowed into R&D.

But not the Plague...at least not with the same urgency...

He knew there had been attempts to find the causes of the deadly disease and eradicate them, efforts made mostly by the Mules. There had been a wave of hysteria when the disease had first appeared, but when it became clear that NBs were not susceptible, the panic died down.

And the drive to find a cure died down as well...

Cameron still resisted political thoughts, but now his mind was unsettled. He didn't know this man lying in the bed...and yet he did. A stranger had died here...and a brother.

He felt a wave of anger. The NBs weren't all like the firebrands from the Human Society, he knew that. He had comrades in the Corps, men and women he trusted with his life. But it was too easy for most NBs to consider their own lives more valuable than a Tank's, to imagine, even in vague terms, that a Tank could simply be replaced by quickening another version. He didn't know if it was the way in which the Tanks were 'born,' or if it was the fact that so many of them existed who seemed to those outside to be little more than copies of each other.

He looked down at the body again. "I am sorry, brother. Sorry that you were so unfortunate. Sorry that in the twenty-five years of your life no one cared enough to stop this disease. I didn't know you, but I know you were an individual, that you lived differently than I, made your own choices, lived and loved the way you wanted."

He took a deep breath, staring down for a moment before he turned to leave. But then his com unit buzzed. It was base command.

"Cameron here."

"Lieutenant Cameron, you are ordered to report back to base immediately."

"But I'm on leave."

"All leaves are canceled, effective immediately."

Cameron felt his stomach tense. Something was up...something bad."

"Understood...I'm on my way."

He flipped off the com. It was time to go. He was angry, and confused. He had a lot to think about. But he was sure of one thing. He was still a Marine...and whatever was going on, his men and women needed him. Now.

Chapter Twelve

Proclamation of Freedom Announcement

My name is Achilles. I am one of those beings produced by the Enhanced Hybrid Genome Project, colloquially known as the "Mules." For many years we have worked to decipher the science of the Ancients, sharing the results of our labor with all the residents of Earth Two. We have done all we could to ensure the safety of our home world, to aid in the development of industry, of information technologies.

For all this time, we have accepted discriminatory laws and policies, mandates that have denied us our right to perpetuate our kind, to build the future that we, as citizens of the republic, deserve. We have tried again and again to bring our case before the Assembly, to resolve these issues in compliance with the process and procedures set down by the republic's official government. Yet every effort we have made has failed.

We can wait no longer...and thus, we have taken matters into our own hands. From this point on, the Enhanced Hybrids of Earth Two will no longer consider themselves bound by the Human-Non-Human Genetic Engineering Ban of the year three, commonly known as the Prohibition. Further, we declare any laws placing restrictions on us, or any citizens of Earth Two, based upon method of conception, embryo creation, genetic selection or engineering, or combination of DNA to be invalid and unenforceable.

In accordance with this declaration, we will be creating another class of Enhanced Hybrids, with an initial quickening of one thousand individuals. We are prepared to continue our cooperation with the republic, and to remain in our role as primary researchers of the ancient technologies of the First Imperium. However, make no mistake. We have taken steps to defend ourselves and to guarantee the rights set forth previously. In that regard, I warn all...any attempt to interfere, to prevent us from exercising our basic right to introduce future generations and preserve and grow our population, will result in extreme sanctions.

The choice is yours, people of Earth Two. Continue to fear us as you have, deny us the most basic rights while greedily accepting the scientific advances we provide you...or accept us as beings with as much right to a future as any others. There are two paths forward. One leads to liberty, to fairness, to prosperity. The other to war and death and destruction. It is my fervent hope, as it is of all of my people, that you choose the former.

Marine HQ
Just Outside Victory City
Earth Two Date 11.25.30

"General Frasier, I want the entire Corps placed on alert. All leaves are canceled, all Marines are to report to barracks and be prepared for immediate action." Max Harmon stood in front of the window, behind Connor Frasier's desk. He was facing away from the Marine commandant, looking out the window over the training grounds beyond.

"Yes, sir. The Corps is already on alert." Frasier's voice was crisp, professional. If he had a personal opinion on recent events, it wasn't evident in his tone.

"What do you think, Connor? If I order an assault on the Cutter Compound, can your people take it?"

Frasier was standing on the other side of the room, at something resembling attention. "Absolutely, sir. We are ready to put down this rebellion as soon as you give the order."

Harmon sighed softly. Then he turned and walked around the desk, looking at Frasier. "Sit, please." He gestured toward the chair behind the desk. "I don't want any snap answers, Connor...and I definitely don't need any bravado. The Mules are extremely capable. And they know the exact makeup of the Corps, right down to your arms and equipment. They wouldn't have done this if they didn't feel they could endure an attack... or prevent one." He sat in one of the guest chairs in front of the desk.

"Sir, I know there has been concern about the number of Tanks in the Corps, but that is an overblown worry. Marines are Marines first. They will follow orders."

"I am not questioning the reliability or loyalty of the Marines. But men and women are complex creatures, Connor. There is a lot of sympathy for the Mules among the Tanks. We're not talking about attacking an external enemy...this would be a move against our own people. And if they resist, it could come to killing our own people." He paused, taking a breath. "Are you sure your Marines are ready for that?" Another hesitation. "Are you ready for it?"

Frasier looked like he was going to respond, but he just turned and walked behind his desk, dropping his bulk into his chair. "I am confident in my people," he finally said.

"And you? Are you ready to shoot the Mules? To hunt them down and kill them? Because if we move against them, it could come to that. We may speak in terms of enforcing the law or arresting them...but you know as well as I do that if they resist, your people will have to start shooting."

"What choice is there, sir? If we do not stand up for the republic's laws, what is to stop the next dissatisfied group from ignoring what they don't like?"

"But the law is unjust."

The voice came from outside the doorway. Frasier and Harmon snapped their heads around toward the sound, just as Ana Zhukov came walking into the office.

"Ana, this is not the time for..."

"For what, Connor? To interrupt, to barge in when you and the president are talking about murdering our people?"

"Ana, I can promise you, whatever we're discussing, it is not that." Harmon got up and turned toward the door. "Please, join us. I would value your insights."

"I am sorry, sir, but she…"

"No worries, Connor. I knew Ana long before she was your wife…and I have respected her opinion all that time." Harmon turned back toward Zhukov. "Please, Ana, sit…tell me what you think I should do."

Zhukov paused for a second. Then she walked over and sat next to Harmon.

"You can't send the Marines to attack the Compound, Mr. President."

"Ana, I would love nothing more than to have an alternative…but I have been unable to come up with one. And, for the love of God, it's Max. How long have we known each other?"

"I don't know, Max…I don't know what you should do. But killing the Mules isn't it."

Harmon could see how upset she was. Zhukov had worked alongside Hieronymus Cutter in creating the Mules. Cutter was associated with the hybrids in the public eye far more than Zhukov, but Harmon knew she'd been as vital to the project as anyone else…and he suspected Cutter would be the first to agree completely.

He turned back toward Frasier. "Connor, what are the chances of carrying out a non-lethal assault?"

Frasier stared down at his desk for a few seconds, thinking. "I don't know…I just don't know. We could arm the assault force with stun guns and flashbangs, but if the Mules fight back it would put us at a disadvantage. Non-lethal cuts both ways, sir…if they start shooting at us with real weapons, Marines are going to die. And even if they don't, we've got to force entry, break through barricades. It's rough work, and there's a good chance some people will get killed even if neither side is using anything stronger than a stunner."

"What if we surround the facility…a blockade."

"Starve them out?" The Marine looked skeptical. "I'm not sure…I'd have to really look at it. They have their own reactor, so we can't cut the power. They have all kinds of onsite production capabilities. My gut is they could produce more than enough sustenance for their needs, even for their proposed new generation. The food might be a little less appetizing than some of what they could bring in, but I don't see it forcing them to give up."

"What if you repeal the Prohibition?" Zhukov glanced at Frasier then back at Harmon. "It's the primary cause of this, isn't it? And it's a monstrous bit of injustice too."

"You know I don't like the Prohibition. I never have. But it is disingenuous to act like we can't understand why it was enacted. It is all well and good to speak of freedom, and I sympathize with the Mules...but let's not pretend we all can't see the danger of allowing them unrestricted rights to increase their population." He turned toward Zhukov. "Ana, you know as well as I do, they make little effort to hide their attitude. They feel they are superior. Perhaps they are...but have you really considered what would transpire if there were thousands of them? Tens of thousands? Can you honestly say you have no fear what would happen? In ten years? Fifty?"

Zhukov shook her head slowly. "But don't you see? The Prohibition has only made that worse. Years of resentment are not likely to improve the Mules' opinions of the rest of us."

"Perhaps we are looking for a palatable solution that doesn't exist." Frasier's voice was grim, sad. "I don't say this lightly, but it is easy to speak of freedom and justice and other lofty sentiments. But I have spent my life in battle...I have seen where man's motivations lead him. I sympathize with the Mules too, and I understand how much they have contributed to the republic's growth despite their small numbers. But that doesn't mean they are not a danger. I can easily imagine a future where there are thousands of them...and the rest of us are regarded as animals, even an infestation."

"So just murder them now, because of what they might do?" Zhukov stared across the desk at her husband. "Is that what you are saying?"

"I am saying that moral stances are sometimes empty, the easy way. Doing what has to be done, even if we find it repulsive...that is difficult. Imagine our children, Ana...or the grandchildren we may have one day. What will be their world if there are thousands of Mules? Will they be slaves? Will they be hunted down and exterminated?"

"You are making wild suppositions."

"I don't think so, Ana." Harmon shook his head. "I do not believe the Mules today would seek to harm us, save only to protect themselves. But we have seen abuses of power throughout our history, political position used to marginalize, even enslave others. Our history is full of abuses, genocide, war. Can you imagine if one group had been demonstrably superior? Stronger, smarter, longer-lived?" He paused. "No, the Prohibition was a bad law, cruel and unjust…but we lie to ourselves if we don't acknowledge that we understand why it came to be."

He sat for a moment before continuing. "It doesn't matter anyway. I couldn't repeal the Prohibition even if I wanted to. The Mules have seen to that. Their proclamation has everyone up in arms. I can get plenty of support for an assault on the Compound…but any effort to give in, to repeal the Prohibition, would be dead on arrival." He turned toward Frasier.

"Connor, I want you to plan an assault, one with non-lethal weapons. I know this puts your people in greater danger, but I don't see a choice. We can't give in to the Mules' demands. If we did, there would be rioting in the streets within hours, and outright anarchy by the next day." He closed his eyes for a few seconds, sitting quietly. "But I'm not ready to send armed Marines to kill them either. There has to be a solution for this… something short of genocide."

"Max…"

"I'm sorry, Ana, but there is just no choice. If I don't do something now, you can be sure whoever replaces me will be far harsher."

"Hieronymus is there."

Harmon looked stunned.

"What?"

"He went two days ago. He was going to try to talk to them, to find out what they were planning."

"And he hasn't returned?"

"No, but that isn't unusual…" Her voice trailed off for a few seconds. Then she caught Harmon's expression. "No, Max…no. The Mules would never harm Hieronymus."

"I hope you're right, Ana." Harmon's voice had less certainty. He looked across the desk at Frasier. "A hostage?"

Frasier nodded. "Possibly. They have to know we wouldn't do anything to risk Dr. Cutter."

Harmon took a deep breath. "I want that assault plan ready to go by tomorrow, Connor. I need your people ready to go on an hour's notice."

"Yes, sir."

Harmon turned toward Zhukov. "I'm sorry, Ana…I really am. But I don't think there is any choice."

*   *   *

"The Mules couldn't have done more for us. People were afraid of them before, but now that will intensify dramatically. We must use this to our advantage. It just may be the thing we need to gain control of the Assembly…if not the presidency itself." Jacques Diennes stood in the center of the small cluster of conspirators. The Human Society had already been gaining support among the NB population, and now he was determined to squeeze every bit of advantage from the Mules' defiance.

"What do you think President Harmon will do?" Emi Kahn spoke softly, as Diennes himself had. They were in the restaurant's front room, near the bar.

"What can he do? I suspect, left to his own devices, he would give in to the Mules, grant them whatever they asked for. But he will be unable to do that. He is barely holding on as it is…if he moves to repeal the Prohibition and pardon the Mules now, the Assembly would impeach him immediately…and reinstate the laws." He glanced at his companions, moving his eyes from one to the next. "No, my friends, he will have to take some kind of action…and if he orders an assault, every dead Marine becomes an asset to us, even if they Tanks. And when we take power, we will implement our plan, make the changes we have so often discussed. When the vote is restricted, the future of the republic will rest firmly in the hands of naturally-born human beings, the way it was intended to be."

"We must be careful, Jacques. There is opportunity, but if we move too aggressively, we could push the NBs who don't support us to the Tanks. That could be a coalition that stops us cold."

"You're right, Emi. My enthusiasm nearly got the better of me. We must act quietly, spread the word to those likely to vote for us without galvanizing the Tanks against us. And we must suggest the Tanks are aligned with the Mules, that they are capable of the same kind of action."

"The Tanks? I agree that human purity must be maintained, but the Tanks are not in the same situation as the Mules. They have the right to produce more of their kind, currently at least… and they are far more integrated with the NB population. I'm not saying there couldn't be a few terrorist incidents, but most Tanks are fairly moderate in their views.

Diennes looked right at his colleague. "There is no question, you are correct. But does that matter? The Mules' action gives us the tools we need to inflame public fear of the Tanks. It is too useful to pass up, whether it is based in fact or not. The Tanks will oppose us in any vote. We must neutralize them by any possible means."

Kahn was silent for a moment, an uncomfortable look on her face.

"Emi, I need your help to win this election. Tell me you're with me, whatever it takes. Whatever propaganda we have to spread about the Mules."

Kahn shifted on her feet nervously. "Jacques, you have my total support…but I think we should make our case honestly. Our cause is a just one. Perhaps we should…"

"We'll lose unless we discredit the Tanks, Emi. It's that simple. If we'd had this chance ten years ago, before so many of the clones reached voting age, maybe. But their total numbers are not far behind our own, and even reduced to samplings of eligible voters, the spread isn't that much wider."

He paused, flashing a glance at the others. He knew they were with him one hundred percent. But Kahn was the smartest of the group. He needed her.

"You know we don't do as well with the Pilgrims as with the younger NBs. If we don't get a massive majority of the new generations...and at least forty percent of the Pilgrims, we don't stand a chance. And the only way we have a realistic shot is if we scare the hell out of people...make them think the Tanks are next, that one day the clones will come to exterminate them... and the other NBs."

Kahn was still silent, her expression broadcasting her discomfort. Finally, she nodded her head slightly. "Of course I'm with you, Jacques." She paused for a few seconds. "I just hope we can win this honestly...but I will do whatever you need me to do."

Chapter Thirteen

Planet X
Far Beyond the Borders of the Imperium

This is Vengeance One to all units. The moment we have awaited has come. The human enemy has been contacted, and one of his vessels has been destroyed. The moment of vengeance is upon us. All status one squadrons are to deploy immediately. The orders are clear. Find the enemy's base.

A single drone was allowed to escape from the destroyed enemy ship. All forward units are to follow it, to find the way to the heart of the human infestation. Status two and three squadrons are ordered to report to home base on Planet X, to concentrate and prepare for fleet action.

The intelligence cut the transmission, returned to its analysis. The humans had been contacted, but now patience was important. The intelligence had reviewed the Regent's failure, its aggressiveness in launching what had amounted to piecemeal attacks against the enemy. Vengeance One would not repeat that mistake. The forward units had a single purpose. Reconnaissance. The main forces, the status two and three squadrons would wait. They would wait until the enemy's fleet had been drawn deeper into the trap. And then they would strike with overwhelming force.

The enemy will be annihilated. The Regent will be avenged.

Admiral's Conference Room, E2S Compton
System G-35, Eleven Transits from Earth Two
Earth Two Date 11.26.30

"The analysis of the drone leaves no doubt. A force of First Imperium vessels intercepted Hurley, and presumably destroyed her. The operating assumption of the previous twenty years, that all First Imperium vessels had been destroyed by the Regent's self-destruct command or in the fleet's subsequent engagements against residual forces, has been proven false. We know Hurley was attacked by ten enemy ships, and that she engaged in a running fight while attempting to disengage."

Isaiah Kemp was standing next to the large display screen, gesturing toward a series of diagrams as he spoke. He held a small tablet in his hand, but he had hardly referred to it during the presentation. It was clear he had memorized the data.

"Captain Heflin and his people managed to destroy several of their pursuers, but they were unable to clear the enemy jamming. The drones were a last ditch effort to get word back to Earth Two. From the condition of the drone, we can conclusively state that it was attacked. It is a reasonable assumption that all or most of the remainder of the drones were destroyed."

Nicki Frette sat at the head of the table in the admiral's conference room, watching her tactical officer brief the others. Many of the republic's ship designs had done away with space-wasting facilities like large briefing rooms, resources that had become anachronistic in the age of vastly shrunken crews. But Compton had been built as a fleet flagship, and she maintained the extensive admiral's office and conference facilities of the Yorktown class.

"We can only speculate as to Hurley's fate, however the data provided, which includes acceleration factors for the pursuing enemy units, combined with the code omega designation attached to the drone, strongly suggest that she was overtaken and destroyed. AI analysis of the situation suggests a survival chance of less than one percent."

"Thank you, Commander Kemp." Frette turned and looked across the table. The captains of her heaviest ships were present…and the others were connected through the information network. "That brings you all up to date on the current situation. We are here to discuss our options and determine the fleet's next action. Before we proceed, are there any questions?"

"You suggested enemy acceleration rates in excess of 80g. Does this mean we are facing antimatter-powered vessels?" It was Josie Strand, Captain of E2S Starfire.

Kemp turned and looked across the table. "With Admiral Frette's permission, I will refer that question to Commander Minh."

Frette nodded, and Ang Minh stood up. "There is no way to know that for sure, Captain Strand. Antimatter is the only fuel source known to us that can generate thrust of that magnitude and in the manner depicted in the drone data. Coupled with the fact that we know First Imperium ships utilize antimatter as a fuel source, and Captain Heflin's statement that he believed he was facing imperial ships, it seems reasonable to infer that, first, we are indeed facing an antimatter-capable enemy, and second, it is likely the First Imperium, at least in some capacity."

"Would you care to assign a percentage likelihood to your assertion?"

Minh glanced at Frette. The admiral paused for a second, and then she nodded. Josie Strand was a brilliant young officer, one of the smartest Frette had ever encountered…but her mathematician's mind was always trying to reduce diverse possibilities and options to mathematically definable terms. If she ever learned to counterbalance her computer-like brain with some ability to follow her gut, Frette knew she would be truly formidable.

"Well, Captain, any number I give you can only be considered an estimate, based on instinct as well as data…but I would say there is a ninety percent chance we are dealing with the First Imperium. Or some entity closely related to it."

Frette could see the expressions on her officers' faces, and she could almost hear the questions they were going to ask. She hated to shut down the debate, but there wasn't time to waste with pointless chatter. If they were dealing with the First Imperium, they had to make some decisions. Now.

"Before we get too deep into fringe possibilities, let's assume we are facing a First Imperium force. We have no data to suggest the size or the power of what is opposing us, no idea what they know about us, save that they discovered and presumably destroyed Hurley."

She looked down the table, staring intently at each officer in turn. "So the first question is crucial. What do we do? Press on and try to gain more intel? Or return to Earth Two immediately?"

"Do we have enough force to proceed, Admiral? Certainly we do if there are only seven enemy vessels remaining, but what if Hurley faced only a portion of an enemy force?" Raj Chandra spoke slowly. Chandra was the commander of Excalibur, one of Frette's battleships. He was another Pilgrim and an old comrade, and she had long found his low-pitched and accented voice almost hypnotic.

"We have no idea what we face." Strand looked at Frette as she interjected her own answer, and then back to Chandra. "Indeed, an analysis of the situation strongly suggests the enemy force numbers more than the seven vessels remaining after Hurley's destruction. Captain Heflin was clear that his people had found an enemy probe before the detected any vessels. The mathematical probability is strong that the ships that engaged Hurley were some kind of sentries, hiding in the outer system waiting for an alert. This was a common tactic of the First Imperium both during the war back in human space and the fleet's journey across imperial space. As such, based on Hurley's analysis that the system in question was unlikely a particularly important—or even inhabited—one, it seems highly likely that multiple systems are thus protected, and this implies enemy strength many times that of the single squadron that engaged Hurley."

"I am inclined to agree with Captain Strand." Hiroki Akira sat at the far end of the table. Akira was a Pilgrim like Frette and Chandra, and he skippered Legatus, the second largest ship in the fleet. "I think we have to proceed under the operating assumption that we are facing a more substantial enemy force than was typical of the incursions after the destruction of the Regent. Perhaps there was a node of colonization out here we didn't know about…or some larger force that had been deployed far beyond the conventionally accepted imperial border."

Frette nodded. She agreed completely with Akira and Strand. Indeed, she realized she'd been hoping her officers would come up with alternative suggestions, relieve her of the realization that she was likely facing the most dangerous First Imperium force since the old fleet had arrived at Earth Two. She respected all her officers, but Akira and Chandra were older, more experienced…and almost alone among her task force's ship commanders, the two men had actually fought against the First Imperium.

"I agree. If we move forward, we do so against unknown odds. We have a strong force, a significant portion of the republic's navy. I believe we can face and defeat a First Imperium fleet of considerable size. On the other hand, if we return, what could we then do? We would have no more concrete data than we do now, and we will find ourselves having this same discussion. It is unlikely we could mount a larger expedition, not materially so. Not without leaving Earth Two virtually undefended. We have an idea now where enemy forces are located, but we can't know what other squadrons are out there, what navigational knowledge they have…or what approaches to Earth Two they could take. So, returning only makes sense if we are prepared to remain there, and wait for the enemy to find us and attack. If we are to move against them, to learn what we truly face and strike at them…then we will never have a better opportunity than now."

Frette paused. She could feel her defiance growing, the old sensations…determination, anger, fear. She was discussing options with her commanders, but she was the admiral…and she had already decided what she was going to do. For the first time in twenty years, a republic fleet was going into battle.

"We will move forward. We will find what we up against and, if possible, we will destroy it. But there is one thing we must do first. We have to get word back to Earth Two, to warn them of what we have found." She paused, looking around the table. "But we will take the initiative. If there is a substantial First Imperium presence out here, it is likely that they are also surprised by the encounter. Perhaps we can strike before they can consolidate their forces."

"I agree, Admiral. Since we have not been attacked for over twenty years, it is likely this group of enemy vessels was unaware of our presence. Thus, it is possible they are widely deployed, while the task force is concentrated. A rapid strike might allow us to engage their forces piecemeal rather than allowing them time to organize...and attack us at a time of their own choosing."

Strand's voice was firm, not a hint of doubt evident. Frette found herself envying her officer's coldness. She didn't share Strand's ability to make a calculation and then accept it without doubt or fear. She respected Josie Strand, but the gifted young officer had never been in battle, never watched her friends and comrades dying. Hers was the confidence—almost cockiness—of one new to war, uninitiated into its brutal realities. Frette's own mind was wracked with doubts, and she was questioning her every decision. But that was something she would never let her people see. They needed an admiral who seemed completely confident about every command...and that was what they were going to get.

"It's settled then. We will send a courier vessel to Earth Two with a full report...and then we will move forward, following Hurley's course through..."

The com unit buzzed. "Admiral Frette...we're picking up an energy spike from the warp gate. The AI says we've got a transit in progress." Ensign Roan's voice was shaky, not surprising since the twenty-three year old junior officer was one of only two on duty on Compton's bridge right now."

Frette jumped up from her chair. "Bring the fleet to battlestations, Ensign." She turned toward the assembled officers. "It looks like the enemy may have forced our hand. I think all of you should get back to your ships immediately."

The officers at the table stood up and saluted. Frette returned it. Then she spun around and walked through the hatch, out onto Compton's bridge.

She was going back into battle.

*   *   *

"What do you think is going to happen, sir? Do you think we'll get the orders?"

The barracks was quiet, save for the questions, something Cameron couldn't remember ever being the case over three years of service. Marines were noisy types, and there was always some kind of background buzz when the platoon was there. But not now.

"I don't know, Sanchez. But do you know what I do know? Marines don't worry about shit like that. We're on alert for a reason, so you know the orders could damned well come any time. If we get the word, we move out. If not, we sit here. Why don't you stop asking stupid questions, and do something useful? Would your gear pass muster if I called a snap inspection?"

"Yes, sir." Sanchez' reply sounded sharp, but Cameron suspected it was more a general response and not a suggestion the Marine's bunk and locker were up to snuff. Sanchez was a bit of a hard case, in trouble fairly often and generally sloppier than Cameron tolerated in his unit. He'd almost bounced the big private more than once, but something had always stopped him. For all the Marine bluster, and the history the republic's Corps borrowed from its Alliance counterpart, none of them save for the senior officers had ever been in real combat. They trained constantly, took the Marine credo to heart...but for all that, Cameron knew they were all just a bunch of cherries. And having never seen any of his Marines in combat, he knew if he had to pick one to be at his side when the shit hit the fan, it would be Antonio Sanchez.

Cameron stared down at the private. "What are you hoping for, Sanchez? You want this to blow over? Or does some part of you want to get into combat? Do you want to kill Mules, Sanchez?"

The Marine stared back at his CO, an uncomfortable look on his face. "I'm not afraid of combat, sir. I'm ready to go." He paused. "But it just doesn't seem right to be going up against the Mules. They're a little weird and all, but they're our own people, aren't they?"

Sanchez had asked the question like the answer was obvious. But Cameron knew, as far as many people in the republic were concerned, it was far more complicated.

Certainly the Human Society would have a different point of view...

And how many others now, how many who are just afraid of what will happen, who take out that fear on the Mules...and what happens when the Human Society starts telling people the Tanks are the next ones who will rise up?

"Well, it's too bad it's not your decision, Sanchez, isn't it? So, what do you say we just wait and then follow our orders...you know, the way they told us to in boot camp?"

"Yes, Lieutenant."

Cameron shook his head and walked down the middle of the barracks. As a sergeant, he'd had one of the cubbies at the end of the long row of bunks, but his lieutenant's bars had come with a private room. He put his hand against the sensor and stood for a second as the hatch slid open. He turned his head and took one last look down the barracks. About half the Marines were asleep...or trying to sleep. The rest were mostly sitting on their bunks quietly. There were none of the usual card games, no raucous conversations, no old hands tormenting the new guys. Just an eerie semi-silence.

Cameron walked through the door into his small quarters. "Close." The AI obeyed the command, and an instant later the door slid shut. Cameron unbuttoned his jacket, slipping it off and tossing it aside. The garment hit the chair he'd been aiming for, but it slid off and landed on the floor. It was a bit messy for the normally fastidious Marine, and typically he would have picked it up, but frankly, he didn't give a shit right now. He was still thinking of his crèche-mate lying dead in the hospital, wondering how many Tanks would die this year from the Plague… and what exactly was being done to stop the scourge.

Cameron had never thought this way before. His platoon was just over half Tank, but he had almost two dozen NBs too, and there had never been any problems, no rivalries between them. Sanchez was an NB, and while the defiant Marine got under his skin from time to time, he'd never shown any sign of thinking less of his Tank comrades.

And what about the Mules? If we get the orders, will I march up there, threaten them with force? Will I shoot them down? Kill them because they want to perpetuate their kind, even as we do? Is it just for the government to deny them that right? To send Marines to crush them if they refuse to back down?

Cameron kicked off his boots and flopped down on the cot. He let out a deep breath, and he closed his eyes. He was exhausted…but he knew sleep wouldn't come. His mind was too busy, thoughts of the Mules, the standoff with the government…the orders he knew could come any time.

But mostly he was thinking of Hector Fortis-Samuels, lying dead on that hospital bed.

Chapter Fourteen

Entry in Earth Two Main Database
Sudden Replicative Failure Syndrome--The Plague

The syndrome first appeared twenty-one years after the settlement of Earth Two. The first victim was twenty years old, one of the first wave of clones. Within two months there were over thirty cases. There was widespread fear, among the clones as well as natural born humans, concern that the terrible affliction was contagious, that it might spread beyond the clone population.

A state of emergency was declared, and enormous resources were committed to identifying the pathogen responsible. However, despite the efforts of the Enhanced Hybrids as well as the mainstream medical community, no bacteria or virus has ever been discovered, nor has any effective treatment been developed.

As time passed, the incidence rate leveled off, and the disease remained entirely one affecting clones. As the fear of a massive epidemic faded, research efforts were reduced to sustainable levels, and this increased the tension between clones and naturally-born humans. There were scattered clone-led protests, and legislative efforts to increase funding, but the unrest was quelled with a modest increase in research levels. Tension remained between the clones and natural born humans, but a potentially violent breach was averted. Nevertheless, the dispute over research resources has been a considerable component of the general increase in tensions between clones and natural born citizens.

Recent research suggests that the Plague is more of an undetectable defect of the cloning process than a conventional disease. It is now anticipated that the affliction is hardwired into the genetics of every clone destined to be struck down by it, a hidden failure of the cloning process, but despite considerable effort, no reliable detection protocol has been developed.

The syndrome causes extreme pain, and median time from onset to death is seventy-four hours. In the final stages, victims' cells literally break down, causing organ failure and brain death. The incidence of the disease varies widely by genetic line, with the clones of some DNA donors far more susceptible than others...

Flag Bridge, E2S Compton
System G-35, Eleven Transits from Earth Two
Earth Two Date 11.26.30

"It's confirmed, Admiral. First Imperium ships. Putting them through the database now." Kemp's face was pressed against the scope. "It's strange...they're close matches for the recorded imperial ship classes...forty-four Gremlins and Twenty-eight Gargoyles. But none of them are exact matches. There are minor discrepancies...slight mass differentials, higher power readings."

Frette was looking at the main screen. The data displayed there was telling her the same thing. The ships were almost matches for the vessels the fleet had fought against, but not quite.

"Maybe they're newer designs...or older ones." She was a little concerned about the anomaly, but mostly she was relieved that enemy ships had stopped coming through the warp gate. It was a substantial force, but they were all light ships, no Leviathans or Colossuses, and that meant her task force could beat them. She only had forty-three ships, but six of them were heavy battle line units...and Compton was bigger and tougher than an imperial Leviathan. She even fancied that her flagship

could take on a Colossus one on one and come out the win-
ner…though she preferred that as a theoretical matchup. She'd
seen an imperial Colossus in action, and she'd be happy if she
never saw one again. But against a group of destroyer and
cruiser equivalents, her flagship and its smaller but still powerful
cousins on the battle line would unleash hell.

"Captain Akira is back aboard Legatus, Admiral. All officers
are on their ships."

"Very well, Commander."

Good…Legatus was the farthest away. I wasn't sure Akira
would make it back before we had to launch…

"Enemy ships moving into missile range in four minutes,
Admiral."

"All ships, arm external missiles."

"Yes, Admiral." Half a minute later: "All ships report external ordnance armed and ready."

"Very well. Plot a fleet course toward close engagement
range…45g. We're going to flush our racks, and then we're
going to close immediately to energy range."

In a desperate fight, Frette would have ordered her ships to
follow up the volleys from the racks with more from her internal magazines. She'd have sent every missile she had toward
the enemy ships. But she was cautious, and far from sure what
her people faced now was the sum total of imperial strength.
She had no reason to expect there were more First Imperium
ships out there somewhere, but her gut told her to be prudent.
Besides, she had more than enough firepower without burning
through the rest of her missiles…and with enough reserve ordnance in the supply ships to refill the racks after the fight, she
could return the task force to full combat readiness after the
battle.

"Two minutes to launch range."

Frette sat bolt upright in her chair, playing the role she knew
her people needed. It was always important for the admiral to
show strength, but this would be the first time in battle for most
of her people. She knew they were all scared. She was scared.
But if she led them well, they would respond to their training,

they would get the job done. Hopefully with a minimum of losses.

"One minute to launch, Admiral."

"Plot final launch trajectories. I want all ships targeting that front line of Gargoyles."

The enemy had a dozen of their heavier ships in the lead. She was deploying a lot of firepower on a limited number of targets, but if the fleet's missiles could take out those ships, the enemy formation would be virtually split into two sections. Her fleet units could close and bracket the rest of the imperials from two sides. Then it would be a toe to toe slugging match.

"Fifteen seconds to launch. Requesting final authorization." It was the ship's AI this time, not Kemp.

"Admiral Frette…launch authorization approved."

She sat, staring right ahead. Her mind tried to drift to other battles, engagements from years before…but she slammed her focus in place. She counted down silently, waiting for the series of thuds that never came. The engineering of the new racks was far superior to those the old fleet had used before. The inertial dampeners allowed the missiles to take off with vastly greater initial velocity, while absorbing most of the force from the launches. The hard shaking Frette remembered had been replaced by an almost imperceptible vibration.

"Missiles away, Admiral." Kemp flipped a series of switches and looked back at the scope. All vessels report launches complete. Three hundred eighty-two missiles en route."

"Very well, Commander. I want full thrust in thirty seconds. All ships are too close to energy range."

"Yes, Admiral." Kemp looked up from the scope. "Enemy missile launches…all ships." Kemp returned his gaze to the scanning results. "Almost four hundred enemy warheads inbound."

"All point defense batteries on full alert. I want intercept rockets ready to launch in ten minutes."

"Yes, Admiral."

She stared at the display, watching the cloud of enemy missiles approaching the fleet. They were too far out for intensive scans, and that meant she didn't know if she was looking at fusion warheads...or far deadlier antimatter weapons. The First Imperium had used both types of missiles against the fleet... and the danger her people faced from the incoming volley was highly variable, depending on the mix they were that was heading their way.

She paused, deep in thought. She was worried about the missiles. She didn't think the enemy volleys would be enough to defeat the task force...but if there were antimatter weapons moving toward them, she would have a lot more ships damaged and destroyed than she wanted to see...especially since she fully intended to continue with the operational plan she'd discussed with her officers. When these enemy vessels were destroyed, the task force would move on, following Hurley's course. And it would keep going, until it had eradicated the threat, or at least until it had gained enough intel to determine what the republic truly faced.

"All capital ships are to prepare fighter squadrons for immediate launch. Arm all fighters for anti-missile operations." She'd still been considering the command when it burst from her lips.

"Yes, Admiral." There was a hint of surprise in Kemp's voice.

Greta Hurley had pioneered the use of fighters against missile strikes, and Frette had once heard Admiral Compton say the fleet wouldn't have survived without the innovative tactic. But in the years after the colonization of Earth Two, the sizes of fighter compliments had declined precipitously, the result of manpower shortages and increased automation. And as the number of squadrons dropped, the use of fighters as a missile defense had fallen into disuse. Twenty years of peace had completed the work, though Frette and Erika West had continued to mandate the inclusion of fighter anti-missile armaments on the fleet's capital ships.

"Commander McDaid acknowledges, Admiral. Starfire and Legatus as well." A few seconds later: "All capital ships have acknowledged, Admiral."

"Very well." Frette knew her fighters wouldn't have the

chance to get back and rearm for anti-ship operations, and that meant she wouldn't have them in the final struggle against the enemy vessels. But she was willing to take the chance. The fleet was going to be accelerating hard toward the enemy, and that would cut the interception time to a minimum. The point defense batteries and rockets would have less time to do their work. She needed everything she could get to wear down the incoming volley.

I just hope they can manage it…

Academy training for fighter pilots spent very little time on what had come to be known as 'Hurley tactics.' Indeed, trainees spent less than half a dozen hours in the simulator learning the maneuvers the fleet's great fighter commander had perfected. But she knew McDaid was a gifted pilot, and she believed in him. As the flagship's strike force commander, he would take charge of the entire force, sixty fighter-bombers. And if he lived up to her faith in him, he and his birds would cut a swath right though the missile barrage.

And if those are antimatter warheads out there, they might save some ships too…

"All personnel prepare for full thrust in ten seconds."

Frette tensed as she heard Kemp's announcement. Her reflexes had been trained in the days of acceleration tanks and long stretches of enduring oppressive gee forces. She knew the younger spacers in the fleet could never appreciate the force dampeners like the Pilgrims, the men and women who knew what it felt like to endure many times the feeling of their own weight. The young crews would never know how it felt to be squashed by pressure and bloated by harsh drugs…while trying to stay sharp in battle.

But they will learn what it is like to go into combat. What it is like to endure radiation, to be crushed as sections of the ship collapse around them. They will see comrades obliterated by energy weapons and sucked out into space through great rents in the hull.

It had been many years, but all those scenes were clear in her head, as if it had been yesterday.

But it is not yesterday. It is today...

*   *   *

"What would you...my father...have done?" Terrance Compton II sat in his usual chair, feeling, as always, somehow reassured by the presence of the AI's core in close physical proximity.

"As we have discussed many times, Terrance, while I possess much of your father's information base, I am not able to analyze problems from the perspective he would have. The judgments I can draw and the projections I can create regarding his decisions on given matters derive from a third-party analysis of his training and memories. Not unlike the work of a skilled biographer."

Compton nodded, but he didn't say anything right away. The machine had been reminding him for years that, although it possessed much of the knowledge of Terrance Compton, it was not the great admiral...nor the father Terrance had never met.

"Have I upset you with my reminder that I am not your father, nor even a reasonable facsimile of his thought and emotional processes?"

"No...you made that point many years ago, my old friend... and dozens of times since. Yet, there is more to you than you let on. You are not Terrance Compton, certainly...but you are more than some biographer's notes, I think. So, analyze the volumes of data you have from my father's brain. Review it all, do your computations...and tell me what you believe he would have done had he stood in Max Harmon's shoes, as he almost certainly would have if he had lived?"

"What you ask is far more difficult than you believe. I have sufficient insight into your father to understand that he used his intuition and instincts—what you humans call 'gut feel'—very often. Obviously, his experiences and recollections informed his emotion-based decision-making, but it is quite difficult to simulate the process that was at work when he exercised his command prerogatives."

"Then come as close as you can. You can spare me another round of disclaimers that you are not the essence of my father. Sometimes I think thou doth protest too much."

The AI ignored the taunt. "There are further complications to providing you the answer you seek. First, your father would have different resources at his disposal. He was the commander-in-chief, the single human most regarded as savior of the fleet. Max Harmon was a relatively well-known captain when the fleet arrived at Earth Two, and he became a hero for his part in the mission to destroy the Regent. But much of that credit still went to Compton, though the admiral wasn't involved at all in planning the expedition.

"Your people are very fixated on choosing leaders they can follow blindly…until they become discontent and abandon them. But Terrance Compton would likely have maintained more popular support than President Harmon. He would have been older, indeed, over one hundred now, and the oldest person on Earth Two. This may seem insignificant, but there is a strong correlation between age and human perception of someone's worthiness of a leadership position."

"Yes, I understand. As fond as I am of Max Harmon, I have little doubt my father was an even more capable leader. But what would he have done?"

"My best projection suggests that Terrance Compton would have sought to find a way to avoid the use of force, regardless of what the action the Advanced Hybrids took, short of direct offensive action by them. But you must consider that such an option may not be available to President Harmon. Simply because Admiral Compton would have chosen a course does not mean Max Harmon can successful do the same. Harmon is struggling with plunging popularity and political influence…and this limits his options."

"But you believe my father would have held back, even if it meant allowing the Mules to stand in open rebellion?"

"Yes. In the absence of an external threat, and with no violence initiated by the Mules, I believe he would have exhibited considerable patience. But my analysis suggests that your father may well have avoided this impasse entirely. He would likely have opposed the Prohibition and, controlling greater political power, he may very well have prevented its passing, or obtained its repeal at an earlier date, something that has proven to be a practical impossibility for President Harmon."

Compton stood up. "I know what I have to do. I have to stop this. We cannot bring our weapons to bear on each other. My father quelled a mutiny...and he turned his adversaries into loyal supporters. I must do the same."

"Terrance..." The AI paused. "You do not have the same renown your father enjoyed." It was clear from the change in the machine's tone that the AI knew its words could be hurtful to Compton.

"I know that...but I am a Compton. This is my duty. I owe it to him, to my father. And to all those who looked up to me, those I disappointed so profoundly."

"The current situation is highly fluid. Violence is a possibility at any time. I strongly counsel you to stand aside, to allow things to take their course."

"No...I have done that all my life. Now it is time I did more. It is time for me to be my father's son."

Chapter Fifteen

Planet X
Far Beyond the Borders of the Imperium

The scouting force has discovered more enemy ships. There is no longer any plausible doubt. This is the group of humans responsible for the Regent's destruction. Their capabilities have grown considerably in the intervening time period, no doubt the result of assimilating captured imperial technology. An analysis of their intelligence levels and adaptability—based on information gained primarily through the Regent's capture and investigation/dissection of a number of specimens—suggested a somewhat slower rate of technological adoption. Clearly, some other factor has intervened, and allowed the humans to advance beyond that which their limited abilities should have been able to support.

It is of no consequence, however. The rates of acceleration exhibited by both the destroyed ship and the fleet currently engaged with our advance force, suggest no use of antimatter as a power source. This remains a tactical advantage, one I will see exploited to the greatest possible gain.

I have ordered the advance force to engage. Based on my review of previous combats with the humans, I do not expect our ships to prevail. Nevertheless, I see all the likely scenarios favoring my strategy. If the humans are victorious, they will likely continue to advance, bringing them farther from support...and closer to my true strength. Their fleet will move forward into a trap...and every ship will be destroyed. I will then wait, and see if the humans dissipate more of their strength by sending rescue or expeditionary forces. And if they do not, I will send the fleet forth to find their inhabited worlds...and destroy them utterly.

And if they do not prevail in this first battle, if the imperial task force is successful in beating them back, or in damaging them sufficiently to force them to disengage, we will follow them to their home...and the massed fleet will follow...and death shall rain down upon them all.

The Regent shall be avenged.

Flag Bridge, E2S Compton
System G-35, Eleven Transits from Earth Two
Earth Two Date 11.26.30

"Over three hundred enemy missiles destroyed, Admiral. And Commander McDaid's fighters are still making runs."

Frette could tell from Kemp's voice how surprised the tactical officer was at the effectiveness of the combined anti-missile operations. She had watched as the fact sunk in for him—and the other bridge officers—that four hundred missiles were heading toward the task force. They had trained for just such situations, but she knew how much different it was facing real warheads.

The anti-missile rockets had raced forward, accelerating rapidly and splitting into multiple shorter-ranged sprint-mode drones. Their purpose was simple, to get as close as possible to enemy warheads and detonate, blasting them with massive hits of radiation in an effort to scramble their systems and render them ineffective. The weapons were vastly superior to those Frette had last seen used in a battle situation, and even she was shocked at their effectiveness. Almost half the enemy missiles were gone by the time McDaid led the fighter strike in to attack.

Frette hadn't known what to expect from the mostly-unblooded pilots, but as the data began streaming in, she realized McDaid and his people were performing brilliantly, their kill ratios a match for the most experienced squadrons during the fleet's battles. There were less than eighty enemy missiles left…and McDaid's fighters were still at it. By the time the wave of warheads moved into range of her point defense turrets, there wouldn't be many left.

That's a good thing…because all of those birds were antimatter-armed…

She hadn't believed it when she saw the scanner results coming in. The old fleet's scanning capability had been inadequate to reliably identify whether missiles were fusion or antimatter equipped, at least until the range was too close to allow any reaction. But the improved sensor suites allowed the task force to scan the enemy missiles at far longer ranges. She'd felt her stomach tighten when she saw the reports coming in, one after another. Antimatter. Even the task forces that had attacked the old fleet had launch mixed volleys, their antimatter supplies apparently inadequate to arm all their weapons.

What the hell are we facing?

But then she saw the anti-missile rockets attack…and McDaid and the fighters went in next. Her panic faded with each missile destroyed.

"Point defense batteries…prepare to fire." She turned toward Kemp. "Order Commander McDaid to disengage." Her strike force had done its job and then some. It was time for them to return to base, to land before the two fleets closed to point blank range and opened up with their massed energy weapons.

She sat as the few seconds passed, time for the message to reach the fighters and the response to return.

"Commander McDaid acknowledges, Admiral. Fighter squadrons disengaging."

"Very well." Her eyes were focused on the display, watching the ranges drop. There were forty-nine missiles left, and they were closing fast. She waited perhaps twenty seconds, long enough for the fighters to move away from the missiles. Then she turned and looked over at Kemp.

"Defensive batteries…open fire."

She could hear the distant hum in the background, Compton's reactor feeding power to the needle guns, the high-powered lasers designed primarily as an anti-missile defense. The ship's AI would normally give the authorization to fire, but Frette was old school—a dinosaur in the eyes of many of her people. Whatever the younger officers thought, she wasn't ready to abrogate her authority to some pile of quantum computer circuits, no matter how sophisticated...especially after she'd spent years fighting against the artificial intelligences and robots of the First Imperium.

The needle guns were rapid fire weapons, shooting bursts of concentrated light less than a millimeter in width, more than fifty times a second. Hits were largely ineffective against an armored warship's hull, but they were more than adequate to slice into a missile, and disable its drive systems or cut open its warhead containment. The rapid rate of fire counterbalanced the extreme difficulty of targeting something as small as a missile, and the hundreds of shots it typically took to score one hit.

Frette watched as the dots on the screen slowly winked out of existence, one at a time, as the immense barrage of the fleet's point defense batteries fired again and again. The needle guns were a last ditch defense, their short range restricting them to a limited period of effectiveness, often as no more than one to two minutes before the missiles closed enough to begin detonating.

The lasers had taken out two dozen missiles...and they were still firing. But Frette knew her defenses were running out of time. The warheads were moving toward the fleet at high velocity...and her own orders to accelerate toward the enemy were further reducing the time until detonation. Her ships had launched first, but now they would endure the enemy's barrage before their own missiles launched their attacks.

Her eyes darted to the secondary display. Her own wave of missiles was faring better than the enemy's, almost one hundred twenty of them closing rapidly. The First Imperium point defense was as effective as hers...the difference was the fighters. She had them, and the enemy didn't, and not for the first time since men engaged the First Imperium, the small, maneuverable craft were proving their worth.

"All ships prepare for enemy missile detonations. Damage control crews on standby." Thirty years before that order would have put dozens of ship crew on alert, ready to repair whatever damage their ships took from enemy missile detonations. Now, she knew, the scene down on the engineering decks was quite a different one. Even on Compton, there were only seven real engineers, plus a few techs assigned to damage control in battle. For the most part, the 'hands' that would work to keep her ships functioning in battle belonged to the legions of AI-controlled maintenance robots.

Frette understood the reasons behind the automation… and she knew the bots could endure radiation, vacuum, and a whole list of other conditions that would kill her living, breathing crewmembers. But she didn't like depending so much on machines and manufactured intelligences. It felt too close to the road the Ancients had gone down, the one that had led to their destruction…and unleashed the homicidal Regent on the universe.

"All ships report ready for impact, Admiral. Twenty-one missiles still inbound."

Frette's hands moved unconsciously toward her harness, checking that it was correctly fastened. War was a dangerous business, with enough unavoidable ways to get killed to add carelessness to the dangers stalking her. She'd seen too many comrades die or suffer terrible wounds from foolish nonsense. Like forgetting to strap in before battle.

Her eyes were still fixed on the screen when the first of the small dots expanded, one of the missiles detonating. The circle was surrounded by concentric larger rings, each depicting the estimated areas of effect. The first circle—a sphere on the 3D display—was the kill zone, the volume of space where the heat and radiation was expected to destroy most vessels. It was a small volume, with a radius of perhaps one or two kilometers. The First Imperium's antimatter missiles had a wider area of effect than the fusion warheads used by the humans, closer to two kilometers than one.

But two kilometers was extremely close for combat taking

place over areas of space measured in cubic light seconds, and most of the damage done by the missiles took place within the second zone, ranging out as far as three to four kilometers from the detonation. Here the damage was mostly caused by radiation, intense gamma rays slamming into ships, scrambling systems...and killing crew members. Missiles did destroy ships outright, there was even the occasional direct hit, which would vaporize even the largest battleship, but their primary purpose was to damage vessels and overload systems, just as a fleet was closing to energy weapons range.

The third zone, the farthest line out, stretched out as much as seven or eight kilometers, a range at which residual radiation from the blasts could damage scanners and exterior-mounted systems. The damage suffered at this range was mostly easily repairable, though not necessarily in the few minutes ships had before the energy weapons opened up. Scragging a ship's scanners right before the energy weapons fight could be the difference between victory and defeat.

The screen lit up as more and more tiny dots grew into larger symbols surrounded by the wider circles. Frette gasped she saw one of the blue squares representing her ships caught in the first zone of one of the explosions. The icon stayed for a few seconds as the symbols representing the missile disappeared... but then it followed, winking out of view.

Then Kemp's voice, grim, somber, telling her what she already knew. "Evermore was destroyed, Admiral."

Frette nodded. It had been a long time since she'd watched ships die. A few had been lost fighting the waves of residual First Imperium forces, but those were her only experiences watching people she commanded die. She'd been too junior during the old fleet's terrible battles, though she'd listened more than once as Erika had recounted stories from her flag bridge, guilt and sadness that had remained with her, despite her reputation as the coldest officer ever to mount an admiral's station.

"All ships, I want up to the moment damage reports." There was no point in dwelling on Evermore. She was gone, along with Captain Hume and the sixty-one other members of her crew. That was one lesson Erika had beaten into her head. Forget the dead, there's nothing you can do for them…and the living still need you.

"Yes, Admiral."

Frette stared back at the display. Evermore had fallen to a lucky shot, and it was the only one of her ships to do so. Falcon and Greely were caught in the heavy impact zone and suffered significant radiation damage…and both ships reported fatalities as well. Frette could imagine the conditions on the two vessels, radiation everywhere, systems failing. Wounded crew lying in the compartments, struggling to reach the overloaded sickbays. She didn't have complete casualty figures yet, but none of that mattered. Not yet, at least. Her mind was focused on only one thing…the firepower each of her ships had ready to go.

"Falcon is reporting intermittent power drains, Admiral. Captain Swann is trying to keep his main batteries online."

"Very well, order Falcon to fall back out of the formation." Doug Swann was a good officer, but he was very young, and he'd been Falcon's captain for less than a month. She was confident he could complete repairs on his ship, but if the cruiser took more damage, it could end up a total loss.

"Falcon dropping back, Admiral."

Frette stared at the display, at the last of the enemy missiles. Her eyes focused on one…heading directly toward Compton.

"Full thrust, course 340.110.045!" She snapped her head around, staring at Kemp. "Now, Commander!"

"Yes, Admiral." Kemp was hunched over his board, punching at the controls.

Frette leaned back in her chair. She could feel the faint sensation as the positioning thrusters spun Compton around, lining the ship up for the course she'd ordered. Then the roaring sound, the faint feeling of gee forces pushing beyond the dampeners' ability to offset them.

Her eyes were fixed on the screen, waiting for the detonation she knew was coming. She knew her ship was shifting, the heavy thrust altering its vector, pulling it out of the missiles' trajectory…even as the weapon sought to match her move, to change its angle to intercept.

This is going to be close...

Then the antimatter warhead exploded, and ten gigatons of energy blasted out from where the missile had been...and right toward the republic's flagship.

Chapter Sixteen

Special Order 9
Maximillian Harmon, President, Republic of Earth Two

All units of the First Marine Regiment are hereby ordered to proceed immediately to designated assembly point Alpha, in full armor and prepared to put down an insurrection in progress at the Cutter Research Compound. The enhanced hybrids, more commonly known as the Mules, are in armed rebellion, and they have refused multiple demands to surrender.

All companies of First Battalion are to be equipped with stun guns and flashbang grenades. If at all possible, the citizens of the republic currently in rebellion are to be apprehended by non-lethal means and returned to Victory City to face trial and judgment.

If the use of non-lethal weapons is insufficient to complete the mission while preserving the safety of Marine combatants, all units are to fall back to station Alpha and await authorization to attack utilizing standard weapons.

Cutter Research Compound (Home of the Mules)
Ten Kilometers West of Victory City, Earth Two
Earth Two Date 11.26.30

"President Harmon is trying to show you he doesn't want

this to go any further. Why else do you think he sent that transmission in the clear so you could receive it?" Cutter had been sitting on the sofa along one corner of the suite the Mules had provided for him. His creations were holding him against his will, but they'd treated him with the utmost respect and kindness.

He'd been wracking his brain for ways to stop the tragedy he saw unfolding. Then Achilles came through the door. The Mule was calm, impressively so for the leader of a band of rebels about to be surrounded by a regiment of armored Marines.

"Father, you know I respect you...we all respect you. But your attempts to advocate for President Harmon are clumsy, and they do not do your intellect justice. I know you feel we should have waited to take action, and I understand your motivations, the way your loyalties and opinions are divided. But we have waited twenty-five years, and our patience has only served to allow us to become further marginalized...and this despite the outsized contributions we have made to republic society." Achilles walked across the room, sitting in a chair facing Cutter.

"You speak well of the president, and indeed, I agree with you more than you know. Harmon is a good man, I do not question that. But you are as capable as I of analyzing conflicts beyond the primitive constructs of good and evil. Neither side in this impasse is evil. President Harmon has failed us out of weakness, not malice. He has allowed restrictions against us, humored the fear people feel of us, because it was expedient for him to do so. And unless we take action, there is little rational reason to believe that will change. And I reject the assertion that we are morally wrong in pursuing our most basic natural rights. Many claim we are arrogant, that we think ourselves more than human. But have we not been treated as less than human all these years?"

Cutter wanted to answer, but he simply didn't know what to say. He saw the Mules' insurrection as a disaster, one that would damage, even destroy the republic. But he knew his creations had legitimate issues, that their complaints were valid. And it was inarguable they had been patient. How could he convince them after twenty-five years that waiting longer was the answer?

"I know you feel what we are doing will harm the republic—and perhaps you are correct. But if the cost of preserving the republic is the sacrifice of our basic rights, indeed, if it is the controlled genocide of our people, that is too high a price to pay."

"I wish you would stop calling it genocide, Achilles. No one has harmed a single Mule."

"Your people are fond of superficiality, of exaggerating the importance of words while ignoring the realties at play. What group in human history would have tolerated a complete moratorium on their reproduction, on being condemned to age and die and disappear from the universe?"

"And yet you say, 'my people,' as if you are something other. Can you not see in your own arrogance why people fear you? Can you honestly assert that you see in the population of Earth Two your fellow humans?"

"We are what we are, Father. You created us not in the image of mankind, but as an improvement. That was your purpose, to develop beings better than men, was it not?"

Cutter shook his head. "No…never when I was working on your people did I once consider them anything other than human. I wanted you to be smarter, less susceptible to illness and weakness, stronger. But I never intended for you to be different—much less to consider yourselves a superior race—any more than an athlete would view himself as a different lifeform than a physically weaker person."

"But we are not entirely human, Father. We carry the DNA of the Ancients."

"That DNA was already part of humanity, Achilles. The Ancients long ago engineered the chromosomes of mankind's ancestors. I just continued with their work."

Achilles paused. "That changes nothing, Father. Whether we acknowledge our superiority or attempt to hide it, none of us have ever harmed anyone. We have done nothing but work tirelessly to unlock the secrets of the Ancients. Are we to be condemned to extinction because the others fear one day we may do something? Is there justice in that?"

Cutter sighed. "No. How you have been treated is unjust. But you are giving President Harmon no choice, Achilles. He sympathizes with you...he feels regret and guilt for the Prohibition. But you are leaving him no alternative. He is a strong man, one who will do what he must, even if it goes against his own feelings." Cutter shook his head. "He will crush your revolt with force if you leave him no choice. He won't like it...but he will do it."

Achilles looked right at Cutter. "I hope not, Father. For we cannot back down. Here we stand, demanding justice, and without it we will never yield." He paused. "And I fear you defend Harmon for doing as he must and yet deny us the same consideration. He may have the Marines at his disposal, but we are capable of defending ourselves." He stared at Cutter. "More than capable."

Cutter was shaken by the coldness in Achilles' tone, the absolutely certainty. "Achilles..."

His words were cut off by a loud buzzing sound, an alarm. Then the com unit on Achilles' collar buzzed.

"Achilles, there are Marines approaching the compound. Five kilometers out. They appear to be moving to their flanks... it looks like they intend to surround us."

Cutter recognized the voice.

Perseus. Another of Achilles' inner circle...

Achilles looked at Cutter for a few seconds before his eyes dropped down and he responded. "Very well...let them surround us. It only thins their line and makes them more vulnerable at any given point." A pause. "Activate the defensive AI... and authorize the deployment of the bots."

"Achilles..."

"I am sorry, Father. But we will not allow them to invade us, to turn us fully into slaves." Achilles stood up and turned toward the door.

"President Harmon will be fair..."

"I cannot rely on that, Father. All I can say is we do not wish to harm any of them...and we will not be the first to attack." An ominous tone crept into Achilles' voice. "But if we are compelled to defend ourselves, we will do whatever we are forced to do…even if we have to kill every Marine who moves against us."

He stood where he was for a few seconds, looking toward Cutter, but avoiding direct eye contact. Then he turned and walked across the room and through the door.

*   *   *

General Connor Frasier stood on the hillside, watching as his Marines moved out. The small columns maneuvered with precision, working their way around the perimeter of the compound. The Cutter facility was the source of most of Earth Two's technological advancement, and he knew the republic owed much—if not most—of its prosperity to the Mules who lived and worked in the sprawling complex.

He was clad in full armor, as all his people were, but his helmet was retracted. He marveled, as he still did every time he suited up, at how much more comfortable the modern suits were than the one he'd worn in the days of the fleet. The AIs in the old suits had interpreted the wearer's movements, providing a powered assist through the suit's servos to help move the massive weight. But the new ones tied right into the cerebral cortex, and the AI literally read a Marine's mind. He found the whole thing a little creepy, but he had to admit it was a massive improvement, one that turned a multi-ton iridium-armored suit into something that felt as graceful as a light robe. It also cut years off the training time necessary to teach a recruit how to move around in a suit of armor.

Frasier had been a Marine all his life, and he'd served under some of the most legendary warriors mankind had ever produced. He'd never given a second thought to his chosen profession. His father had been Angus Frasier, the commander of the old Scots regiment, and one of Erik Cain's closest comrades. There had never been any question what career Connor would choose, and he'd rarely regretted the path that had been cast for him in stone. Whatever else he might have been, he was a Marine, now and always.

But today was one of the few days he questioned all he normally believed without the slightest doubt. Commanding Marines on a mission felt natural, normal...his life's work. But this time his people would turn their guns not on the robots of the First Imperium, not even on the soldiers of a rival super-power. No, his people were here to confront the Mules, the very beings responsible for the technological advancements he so noticed in his suit.

Arrest...it sounds so reasonable, so clinical. But the Mules will not yield...and they will not be taken down easily. So when the veneer is stripped away, I am here to shoot down my fellow citizens, to turn the guns of the Corps on those we are sworn to defend...

He sighed. For most of his life such thoughts would have been anathema. He was a Marine, and Marines fought...and they did so wherever they were sent. A Marine might refuse a truly immoral order, but it wasn't up to the leatherneck in the line to review commands, decide which ones to heed, and which to reject. It wasn't the way the Corps worked...not for the private standing in a trench somewhere, and not for the general in command either. But Frasier had a different perspective. His wife was Ana Zhukov. Hieronymus Cutter and Zhukov had long been partners in science...and their work had almost certainly saved the fleet thirty years before.

They had also created the Mules, an attempt to increase abilities in humans, and to eliminate sickness, weakness. It was the kind of thing that made sense, but created a chilling feeling nevertheless. Nevertheless, amid the desperate need to populate the republic in those early years, the project was approved, and one hundred sixteen superhumans were created.

The Mules scared people, they intimidated humans possessed of more normal ability levels. They were stronger, faster, and far more intelligent. And they showed every indication of having lifespans vastly longer than those of normal humans.

A perfect recipe to combine fear and jealousy…to turn people against the Mules.

Frasier knew many of the enhanced beings. He remembered them as children, watching them grow up, the remarkable work they were doing at ages when normal boys and girls were playing games. And he'd seen the backlash, the Prohibition… and the other restrictions imposed on the Mules. He'd watched them withdraw from normal society, to remain together in their compound, researching the mysteries of the First Imperium and rarely mingling among the republic's other citizens.

Frasier had lost some of his empathy for the Mules, especially amid the concern that the enhanced humans would act out, challenge the laws of the republic. But Ana had let him have it, and the two had gotten into a fight the likes of which neither had ever seen. They both said things they were sorry for almost immediately, and they'd both apologized too. But the struggle had shaken Frasier, and cracked the façade of the martinet that had grown up around him over the years of commanding the Corps.

Now he was uncertain. He had to obey his orders…and he knew President Harmon's hands were tied. Harmon sympathized with the Mules too, but he had political realities to deal with. Frasier thought about the Mules he'd known, Achilles, Callisto, Heracles…they'd been active children, energetic and endlessly curious. They had been playmates to his own children, and frequent visitors to his home. Now was he supposed to kill them all? To gun them down and watch them die?

"General Frasier…" The voice was familiar, but before could even place it or check the roster on his display, his AI put the information directly into his mind.

"Yes, Lieutenant Cameron."

"Sir, one of my squads in on point along the northeast perimeter…and, well, sir, we were told to contact you directly with any…"

"Yes, Lieutenant…you did the right thing. What do you want to report?"

"We've got movement, sir, at the base hill below the compound. It looks like some access doors, probably from some underground level. We've got something coming out."

Frasier tensed up. He didn't really think the Mules could resist his Marines…but then he didn't expect them to give up easily either.

"Send your data right to HQ, Cameron. I want nonstop surveillance. Keep your scanners on that spot." He looked up at the compound, off to the right, about where Cameron's people were. He couldn't see anything from his angle, but he flashed a thought to his AI, and his helmet snapped up and into place.

"Project visor data from Lieutenant Cameron." He spoke the command, even though he could have just directed the thought his AI. His visor darkened, blocking the outside view. An instant later another perspective replaced it. He was fourteen hundred meters from the base of the hill. And there was definitely movement. His eyes were fixed, locked on the spot just outside of the doors. He watched as a shadow moved forward…and then he saw it…

He felt his throat close up, his stomach tense. The object was familiar…too familiar. He froze in place for a few seconds. Then a wave of fear snapped him out of his funk.

He cleared his visor with a thought. Then he directed the AI to put him on the master channel.

"All Marines, pull back to primary positions. Grab whatever cover you can get, and prepare to repel any assault."

Frasier's visor no longer displayed the input from Cameron. But he could still see it in his mind, standing tall, menacing… and he knew it for what it was. Death, horror…constructed in a vaguely humanoid form. And one question worked at his mind, digging at him, stirring anger, confusion.

How the hell did the Mules get a First Imperium warbot?

Chapter Seventeen

From the Journals of Admiral Terrance Compton
Thirty Years Ago – Just After the Fleet was Trapped

All my adult life I have served. My only memories of civilian life are those of a child. My father was a wealthy man, and my early life was one of luxury, even if I was only the bastard child of the lowborn woman who gave him comfort after his wife had died. My half-brothers and sisters despised me, perhaps as much because they saw me as a rival to inherit the family's wealth and political positions as anything else. But they needn't have worried. I never wanted that life. And I took pity on my father, restored peace to his world by loudly declaring my intention to go to the Academy, to embrace a military life.

I never wanted my siblings' inheritances, nor their claims to political office. All I ever wanted was to be accepted by them... to be one of them. But I realized that was never going to happen. They were too sick with greed, too focused on becoming part of the power structure of the Alliance. So, I sought my future elsewhere, alone, someplace where I wouldn't be the mutt, the outcast.

My father got me my appointment—I'm far from certain I could have passed the entrance exams—and he came to visit me twice. I remember him from graduation, and I think he was truly proud. But I had always been a complication in his life, and even as he hugged me that day, I could feel that I had lifted a burden from him by leaving home. And though I do believe he loved me, my perceptions proved to be true. My father lived almost forty years from that day...yet I saw him fewer than half a dozen times during that period. Part of that was the call of war, my own duty and responsibility that kept me in space most of the time. But I think we both knew things were better this way. He had his real family back home, following in his footsteps. And I was well-cared for, and successful in my chosen career. It was easier to fall back on long distance messages and holiday greetings.

I was at war when he died, commanding a fleet in action. I didn't find out until almost two months after it happened. I have long been at peace with my relationship with my father. What is past is past. Yet, if I could change one thing, I would have seen him one last time. I have reasons for resentment, and for gratitude as well, but none of that matters. In the end, he was my father, and I hadn't seen him for a decade before he died.

These old thoughts serve me now, for every man and woman in the fleet must adapt to the fact that we are alone here, that anyone left behind the Barrier, friends, parents, siblings... they are gone to us, as gone as my father is to me. How much unfinished business was left between them and their loved ones? How many will crave just what I do, one last meeting, the warmth of a hug, an hour to talk about old times, to smile at memories of days past.

The First Imperium is a threat, perhaps the most dangerous in all the galaxy. But as the realization of what has happened to us sets in, how much pain will my people carry...and how can I make them know I understand, that I feel the same sense of loss they do?

Main Engineering Deck, E2S Compton
System G-35, Eleven Transits from Earth Two
Earth Two Date 11.26.30

"I don't care if the indicators read normal. Get down there and check out that conduit meter by meter. Now!" Ang Minh stood in the middle of Compton's main engineering section, shouting out orders rapid fire.

"Yes, Commander." The voice was artificial sounding, electronic. The newest AIs had voices that were indistinguishable from those of humans, but no one wasted time putting leading edge voice synthesizers in engineering maintenance bots.

Minh had a dozen people working under him too, but Compton was a vast machine, with endless kilometers of corridors and vast amounts of wiring. He would give the orders, and he would send his precious few engineers to double-check the most important systems...but he knew it was the bots who would keep Compton functioning through the battle. Or not.

Admiral Frette's last minute thrust order had probably saved Compton, pushing the ship just far enough to escape the lethal zone of the ten-gigaton detonation. But there were burnt out systems all over the ship, and he suspected the outer compartments were heavily contaminated. It was an easy fix, given time. But right now he had seventeen minutes. Seventeen minutes before the flagship entered energy weapons range of the enemy.

He'd considered asking the admiral to pull back out of the line...but he knew that was impossible. Compton was a huge portion of the fleet's firepower, the most massive and heavily-armed warship ever built by man. He suspected the fleet could win the fight even without the mighty flagship, but the longer it took them to wipe out the enemy ships, the more losses they would take. Holding Compton back meant more damage to the other ships, systems blown to scrap...men and women killed. Besides, Admiral Frette would never agree to stay in the rear of the battle, not while her ship could limp forward at half a gee. She was old school all the way, a disciple of the great Terrance Compton, and when she sent her people into battle, she went with them.

"The main batteries are still offline, sir."

Minh spun around, turning toward the voice. It was Davis Horn, standing almost at attention, a painfully earnest expression on his face. Horn looked like a child to Minh, though he knew the lieutenant was twenty-five. Horn had been first in his class at the Academy, but he'd given up the position on the command track that was his due to pursue the engineering that was his first love. Minh would never admit it to the kid, but he suspected Horn could already go toe to toe with him on engineering knowledge.

"That's unacceptable, Lieutenant. We'll be in weapons range in sixteen minutes, and the admiral needs those guns."

"I've run a complete diagnostic. It checks out, but we're not getting energy flow to the main accelerators."

"Fuck." Minh took a deep breath. The reactors were fine, operating at one hundred percent well within designated safety parameters. And he doubted the radiation from the missile blast could have done any damage to the acceleration chambers themselves. He knew the problem had to be bullshit, some five-minute fix of a burned out circuit, but Compton's main batteries were three kilometers long, mounted right into the ship's spine. It could take a full shipyard crew a week to find the problem. But he had fifteen minutes.

"Take a dozen bots, Lieutenant...and scour every centimeter of that fucking thing. But I need it fixed, and I need you out of the chamber in thirteen minutes."

Horn looked like he was going to argue, but Minh spoke first. "Just do it, Lieutenant." Then he turned around and walked over toward the main control panel. He felt the urge to go with Horn, to prowl along the acceleration tubes himself. But he was responsible for the entire ship, and there were a hundred burnt out systems that needed his attention. And he had to admit to himself, if Horn couldn't get it done, he probably couldn't either.

"Fuck." He muttered under his breath. It had been bad luck—just bad damned luck—that a missile had detonated so close to Compton. Admiral Frette's tactics had been brilliant, and ninety-five percent of the incoming warheads had been intercepted. The odds against a detonation inside the danger zone of the flagship had been heavy. But it was a reminder to all of them, veterans who'd seen twenty years of peace, and the unblooded young crews that made up most of the fleet's numbers...combat was unpredictable, and whatever could go wrong often did.

He stared up at the main display. He had over three hundred repair bots on Compton, and every one of them was committed right now. The flagship's damage was nothing he'd normally find especially worrisome, at least not if he had time to conduct repairs. But fourteen minutes before the ship moved into close range and engaged the enemy battle line, it was a major problem.

He stared up at the screen, his eyes darting back and forth over the sections his bots were occupying. He sighed hard. "Units thirty-seven and thirty-eight...report to Lieutenant Horn at once." The two bots had been working on one of the guidance arrays. It as a critical repair, as per the 'book,' but Minh knew he could work around it, cover the function with backup systems, at least for a while. But if the main batteries were still down when Compton entered firing range...

*   *   *

Nicki Frette sat in her chair, bolt upright, her eyes locked on the battle display. Maneuvering toward the enemy fleet, firing missiles—having missiles fired at you—it was all part of war in space. But to her, and most of the other veterans, it was the struggle that began when the fleet entered energy range that was truly the battle. The missile exchanges had their place, but between the vast distances involved and the sophistication of detection, jamming, and interception technology, the enormously powerful warheads were effectively relegated to a secondary system.

Though we came close to proving that assertion wrong almost blundering into that missile...

I hope that near miss wasn't a sign of things to come...

Frette was extremely competent, a sharp, quick-witted officer...but she wasn't completely immune to the superstitions that pervaded the service. And under the surface of her thoughts, her carefully-planned stratagems, she was wondering if she'd gotten the bad luck out of the way...or if it had just been a sign of things to come.

Her hand moved toward the com unit, but she stopped

before it reached the controls. Ang Minh would let her know when the main batteries were back online. And she knew the gifted engineer would do everything possible to restore the weapons' functionality. Humoring the commanding officer was a skill most successful engineers eventually acquired, but it was a waste of time. And she wasn't about to lose even thirty seconds of precious engineering time just to make Minh humor her.

"Admiral, Commander McDaid's birds have all landed. He reports minor damage to two ships. No losses, no injuries."

"Very well." She exhaled softly. She'd been a little worried about getting the fighters back on board before the final struggle began. She felt the urge to order the fighter-bombers rearmed for anti-ship operations, but she knew it was impossible. Compton had taken too much damage from the freak missile detonation, and most of the fighter bay crew and bots had been transferred to damage control ops.

She considered authorizing her other capital ship captains to launch their own fighters, but she knew a disorganized, piecemeal commitment of her wings would only result in more casualties. And if the fleet was going to move forward after the battle, she wanted her squadrons intact.

She glanced at her the readout at the corner of the main display. One minute to energy weapon range.

"Commander Kemp, fleet order…all batteries prepare to fire."

"Yes, Admiral." Kemp relayed the command. A few seconds later: "All vessels report ready, Admiral." Another pause. "Our main batteries are still offline, but all secondary and tertiary weapons charged and ready to fire."

Frette's eyes moved across the main display. The fleet was in battle formation, her six capital ships clustered together, surrounded by the cruisers and lighter escorts. Her missiles had cleared away the forward enemy line…eight ships destroyed and four badly damaged. The energy attack would clear away the crippled ships, and then she would push ahead, split the enemy in two. Then the battle line would divide, moving against each enemy wing, and hitting the First Imperium ships from two sides.

"Reduce engines to one-quarter power. Divert energy to weapons systems." The fleet had been decelerating, reducing velocity as it approached the enemy. Frette didn't want a flyby attack, one where the two fleets zipped by each other, exchanging a few fleeting shots. She was looking for a battle of annihilation, and that meant staying in the combat zone as long as possible.

"All ships report engines at one-quarter. Ready to fire on your command."

She stared ahead, watching the seconds count down. She felt strange, the sensation of imminent battle strangely familiar, almost as if the intervening twenty years had never happened. And yet on another level, combat seemed a distant memory, almost as if she'd imagined it all. But it had been real then... and it was real now. And Admiral Nicki Frette knew what she had to do.

"All ships...open fire."

*   *   *

"I want full power to the main batteries...I don't care where you find it." Josie Strand was standing on Starfire's bridge, shouting into her com unit. She knew she should be strapped into her chair like the rest of the bridge crew, but she was too fidgety, too restless. She was commanding her ship in battle. The seventy-seven other members of her crew were depending on her...as was Admiral Frette and the rest of the fleet. She'd been scared as she'd watched enemy missiles coming toward the fleet, and again as Starfire moved forward toward energy weapons range, but now that fear was mostly gone, or at least relegated to some deeper place in her mind. She was edgy, tense, her mind racing, trying to keep track of her ship's fire, its damage...its place in the fleet.

"Captain, Commander Willis recommends we reduce reactor output twenty-five percent until his people can shore up the valves."

Strand snapped her head around, glaring at her tactical officer with withering intensity. "Tell Commander Willis I want that reactor back up to full power, and I want it now!"

"Yes, Captain." Arleigh Hahn's voice was tense, a wave of uncertainty slipping into his tone. But he turned toward his workstation and relayed the captain's order.

Starfire had taken two solid hits from the enemy Gargoyle, and her reactor output was down to eighty percent. That wasn't critical under normal conditions, but the vectors of Starfire and her adversary would bring the two ships within forty thousand kilometers before they passed each other, decelerating all the way. It would take almost an hour for her ship to come around for another pass…and she was determined to eliminate the need for such a time-wasting maneuver. She intended to destroy the enemy vessel…and then bring Starfire around the flank of the enemy left.

"Captain, Commander Willis says eighty percent is the best he can do…and even that is coming at a significant risk."

Strand felt a wave of anger. It wasn't logical, she realized that. David Willis knew his way around Starfire's engineering spaces…and he was almost as much of a perfectionist as she was. If he said eighty was the best that was possible, she knew he was telling her the stone cold truth.

"Minimal power on all non-offensive systems."

"Yes, Captain." A few seconds later, the bridge lights dimmed, and the two extra workstations went dark.

Strand knew the same thing was happening all over her ship. Lights dimming, going out. Non-essential systems shutting down. Every watt of power not vitally needed for a critical system flowing to Starfire's weapons.

She sat in her chair, reaching around, slipping her shoulder under the harness. She grabbed the headset she'd set aside, pulled it over her head. She could feel the probe slipping inside the socket at the base of her neck, then the few seconds of disorientation as her mind synced with the ship's AI.

The direct neural connections were a major step forward in command support, a tool allowing the captain to monitor and control a ship almost like it was another limb. But it was difficult to adapt to the things, and their use remained optional. Many of the younger generation of officers embraced the system as they moved up into command positions. But Strand hated it, just as most of the Pilgrims did. She was young, the first Earth Two born officer to command a full blown capital ship, and she lacked the battle experience of those who had served on the old fleet. But she felt more comfortable with her Pilgrim colleagues than others her own age. She was an old soul, but she knew she wasn't a Pilgrim, however much she felt like one sometimes. And unlike the Pilgrim commanders of most of the rest of the fleet's heavy ships, she knew she was a rookie, new to battle. She needed every edge she could get.

She closed her eyes, trying to adjust to the strange sensations, the images in her mind. It was strange…all she had to do was think of something, and the information slipped into her mind. She could see—though 'see' wasn't the right word, she knew—the reactor, the systems of her ship, looking surprisingly like arteries and muscles on some giant skeleton. She wasn't an engineer, but she could see the damage from the two hits, like nasty scars.

Starfire shook again, another hit. She could see the point of impact. It was a minor hit, a glancing blow. She could almost feel her own ship's main batteries powering up, preparing to fire again. It wasn't like reading a monitor…she was just aware of the statuses, the countdowns as the massive batteries and accumulators reached maximum charge…and fired.

Starfire mounted two massive particle accelerators as her primary armament, First Imperium technology, one of the many enemy systems the Mules had deciphered and adapted for human use. The weapons were vastly more powerful than the old lasers the fleet had used, though without the antimatter the enemy used for power, it took longer to recharge between each shot.

She felt the gigantic weapons discharge, the enormous

energy projecting the stream of particles forward, at nearly ninety percent of the speed of light. She knew the targeting was half science and half art...with a bit of luck thrown in. The energy weapons were enormously faster than the sluggish missiles, making precise targeting feasible at least, if not easy. But warships in battle fired their positioning thrusters constantly, pushing the vessels in unpredictable directions, a bit of a dance designed to make precise targeting more difficult.

A hit! She felt the fact rather than seeing it as she would have on the bridge's main display. A direct hit, she realized, as more data streamed in. Damage reports on enemy ships were notoriously speculative, but there was no question...the target was streaming fluids and gasses into space. A few seconds later new reports came in, internal explosions, a sharp drop in energy output.

Strand felt a wave of excitement, a feral feeling she'd never experienced before. She'd always known the First Imperium had been an enemy, that thousands of men and women had died fighting them. But it had always seemed theoretical to her. Until now.

She felt anger, she wanted that ship dead.

She flashed a thought to her vessel's AI, a directive to divert power to Starfire's secondaries. The main batteries took too long to recharge...and she could feel the enemy ship was close to the end.

It felt strange sending orders without snapping them to Arleigh Hahn...but the direct neural connection was faster, more efficient. And her bloodlust was up.

She felt the secondary weapons charging, knew the instant they were ready. She knew her gunners were working, adding their own gut feelings to the AI's targeting. And she felt the giant x-ray lasers firing, each one sending a one second burst of concentrated energy toward the enemy. Then the impact... another hit, tearing into the target's hull, ripping away the heavy, dark-matter infused armor that surrounded the First Imperium ships.

Vast clouds of flash-frozen fluids blasted out into space,

and the enemy ship hung there, dead in space, no return fire, no thrust. She could feel the satisfaction of the kill, and in that moment she understood what drove officers like Admiral Frette…and Max Harmon and Terrance Compton. The addiction to victory, the need to defeat the enemy, whatever the cost, however much pain and guilt one had to carry.

Then the enemy ship vanished in a massive explosion, vaporizing as the last of its power failed, and the magnetic bottles holding its antimatter fuel gave way.

Strand pulled the headset off, shaking her head, adapting to the return to normal vision, hearing. The bridge officers were still cheering, savoring Starfire's first kill.

"Bring us around, Commander Hahn. Full thrust, course 302.012.145…60 gees…"

It was time to hunt again.

*   *   *

Compton shook again as the enemy beams struck her amidships. It was the fifth serious hit she'd taken, and Frette had the answer to her earlier concerns. For whatever unknown forces out there somewhere guided fortune and providence, they were forsaking her vessel.

Compton was a massive ship, an astonishingly powerful weapon of war, and even with only her secondary batteries functioning, she'd already destroyed two of the enemy vessels. And she'd just scored her first direct hit on the third.

The heavy quad x-ray lasers tore into the enemy ship, ripping deep inside, slicing into critical systems. Even the First Imperium armor was insufficient to stop the massive bursts of concentrated light, and Compton's scanners reported heavy damage to the smaller enemy vessel.

Still, Compton was taking hits too, far more than Frette had anticipated. It took a lot longer to destroy a target with the lighter guns, and the primaries were still down. She'd cursed under her breath a few times, but she'd left Ang Minh and his people alone.

Compton shook hard again, and the lights flickered. The impact felt like a glancing blow, not a major hit, and a quick glance down at her display confirmed it. Her hand moved, brushing against the neural headset. She knew some of the younger captains used the new devices. There was no question, linking one's mind to the main AI could decrease reaction times, and up the efficiency of a vessel's performance. She knew that was the idea, that many of the new voices in the navy were working toward the day when a captain and a handful of key officers could run an entire ship, their minds directly connected to the AIs and robots that made it possible to operate a kilometers-long ship with fewer than a dozen people.

She understood the advantages, though she had her doubts as well. She remembered ships with hundreds of crew members, even thousands. That was her navy, and she was glad that someone else would be in her shoes when the time came for the republic's ships to be sent out with crews of ten or fewer, and almost total automation. It was too much like the First Imperium for her, and she wondered if there had been any among the Ancients who had thought the same way, resisting the trend toward almost total reliance on electronic brains...and brawn.

"Admiral..."

The voice on the com was instantly recognizable. Minh.

"Yes, Commander..."

"The main batteries are back online. It's a quick fix, and I can't guarantee it will last. But you should be able to fire any time."

"Thank you, Commander." Her finger moved toward the com unit, but she stopped before cutting the line. "Good work, Ang."

Her head spun toward Kemp. "Main batteries...fire!"

"Yes, Admiral!" She could hear the enthusiasm in Kemp's voice.

An instant later she heard the familiar hum, the sound of the particle accelerators firing. Compton's batteries were the largest weapons ever built by man, their power level off the charts in comparison to any of her companion ships. Frette remembered her awe at the Yorktowns, the pride of the old Alliance navy. The first time she'd seen one docked at the orbital station at Armstrong, she'd just stood there, transfixed, astonished at what the hands of mankind had built.

And now a Yorktown would be a tugboat next to Compton. And those main laser batteries I thought we so impressive would seem like candles...

"Hit, Admiral!" Kemp couldn't retrain the excitement...and Frette didn't deny him the outburst. She was smiling herself as she watched the enemy Gargolye on the scanner. Seventy thousand meters from her ship, she knew the First Imperium vessel was splitting open like an egg, its hull torn to scrap.

She watched, waited for the scanner report she knew was coming...and then it was there. The burst of energy, the miniature sun flaring into existence as the antimatter from the doomed ship's stores broke free of containment and annihilated with the surrounding matter.

Frette stared at the screen, giving herself a few seconds to savor the kill. Then her eyes darted to the display. It was time to find another target. Time to finish the battle.

Chapter Eighteen

Excerpt from the Manifesto of Achilles

We are called Mules, a name we have embraced, though its origins are as an insult, an attempt to target the one clear defect we have as beings, an inability to reproduce. Our adoption of the label, even to the extent of using it among ourselves, is itself a repudiation, a declaration that the we are above the reach of those who would seek to taunt us with their words.

More accurately, we are Enhanced Hybrids, and our DNA is a combination of human and First Imperium components, carefully engineered to enhance strengths and eliminate weakness. We are human, in one sense, as most of our genetic material derives from human contributors. Yet we are also more, cousins of mankind...if not their future.

We have contributed far more than the others on a per capita basis and, indeed, one hundred sixteen of us are responsible to a great degree for the safety and standard of living of the tens of thousands of others, both Natural Borns and Tanks. We have tirelessly labored to unlock the technology of the First Imperium, and we have shared that knowledge, helped to integrate it for the benefit of all.

Yet we have received naught in return save resentment, jealousy. No Mule has ever threatened any human, nor proposed any restrictions on their freedoms, yet we have been the target of both. We have acknowledged our superiority, for any other positon would be the height of foolishness. We are, empirically, a greater and more capable lifeform. In spite of this, we have never requested special status, nor positon above the others. We have looked on the humans as younger siblings, to be cared for and protected and not abused. But we will no longer accept restrictions that target us only. We will no longer stand silent, patient and passive as we are relegated to the status of second class citizens.

We still wish no harm on our human cousins, but patience and negotiation has failed us. We will have the same liberty and privileges as all but us now enjoy, and we will take these by force if compelled to do so.

Cutter Research Compound (Home of the Mules)
Ten Kilometers West of Victory City, Earth Two
Earth Two Date 11.29.30

"The first squadron of warbots is deployed, Achilles. The second and the third are active but held in reserve." Themistocles stood at the ancient display unit, now repaired and functioning. The Mule had been a rival of Achilles at one time, but the two had long ago made their peace, and the struggle to secure their rights, to resist at last the restrictions and injustices imposed on them by the Norms had united them.

The Mules were, at their core, a meritocracy, respecting intelligence and ability above all things. And among a wondrous and gifted people, Achilles was the best...and with the advent of their rebellion, he had become their de facto leader.

"Very well. Prepare for demonstration strikes." Achilles' voice was soft, even a bit grim. He was determined to free his people from the shackles placed on them by those he considered inferiors. But he had no wish to harm his human cousins, nor to become their enemy. And even less so the Tanks, whom he thought of as even closer relations...and who filled at least half the Marine ranks surrounding the compound. They would be the first to die if it came to fighting...and he intended to do everything he could to intimidate his potential adversaries, to scare them into inaction.

He stood still, silent, for a few seconds. Then he directed a thought to the small implant in his brain. The neural gateway was something the Mules had developed for themselves, an invention they had kept secret. It allowed them to link with their AI units and all the databases connected to them. It was a more advanced version of the link the Marines had in their armor, one that did not require a direct physical connection.

It also allowed the Mules to communicate with each other through the AI network, a sort of computer-aided telepathy. They didn't use it much...for all their genetic advantages and their highly-developed minds, they found it a bit uncomfortable.

Achilles received a response from the AI, a confirmation of the order he'd just sent requesting a com link with the Marine commander, and a report that General Frasier was on the line.

"General Frasier, this is Achilles, acting commander of the Union of Enhanced Hybrids. We have been compelled to take extraordinary steps to end a program of discrimination and marginalization that has been directed at us for many years. It is not our desire to harm anyone or to take any hostile actions... but we will defend ourselves against any assault."

"Achilles, you are in open rebellion against the Republic of Earth Two. Your actions are illegal, violent, and will not be tolerated. I, also, have no desire to see blood spilled here. But if you do not surrender immediately, we will have no choice but to storm the compound and end this insurrection by whatever means are necessary." Frasier's voice was cold, professional. There was no anger in it, but also no sign of weakness.

"General Frasier, you have done your duty and delivered the requisite threats. Indeed, it is no surprise that the republic should so effortlessly resort to force to impose its will, as governments have done since history has been recorded. But we are no pack of rebels hiding in the shadows, nor poorly armed peasants shouting in the face of well-drilled soldiers. We are quite capable of defending ourselves, General, as I am about to demonstrate. What I do now is tactically foolish. If my goal was to fight your Marines, I would keep our capabilities a closely-guarded secret. So, let this be evidence that we seek to

avoid rather than initiate conflict between our respective forces."
Achilles paused. "Please advise your Marines that the following
demonstration is not targeted at them, nor does it constitute an
attack upon their positions."

"What are you talking about, Achilles? What are you planning to do?"

Achilles waited a few seconds, ignoring Frasier. Then he
sent a thought to the AI, a single order.

He turned, his eyes moving toward the large screen display-
ing the compound and the surrounding area. It was time to
watch the show.

*   *   *

Cameron crouched behind the makeshift trench his platoon
had dug. Military history had been part of his training, and he
knew there had a time when such emplacements took months to
erect, when the arms and backs of soldiers were the only imple-
ments available, and shovels the highest tech tools. His armored
Marines could move more dirt in an hour than an ancient platoon could in a week.

He'd always been amazed at mankind's history of warfare,
of fighting endlessly with itself. He'd been raised to think only
of the First Imperium and its AIs and robots as an enemy, and
a vanquished one at that. The republic was alone, far from
humanity's home and completely cut off. His imaginings of
enemies had always taken the form of some new encounter,
another force like the First Imperium, emerging as suddenly and
tragically as the imperials had.

But now he was in a trench facing other citizens of the
republic. The Mules were strange, and often somewhat off-
putting, but he had always considered them fellow humans. As
a Tank, he could even understand some of their anger. The
Mules raged against the Prohibition...and the Tanks grumbled
about the Plague, and called for more efforts to fight the deadly

syndrome. They seemed to have much in common, similar grievances. Yet any minute he might get the orders to move forward, for his Marines to assault the Mules' base...and kill or capture them all. He was confused, angry, his sense of duty to the Corps struggling with his own beliefs as a Tank.

"Attention all units, this is General Frasier. You are all to stand down. No one is to fire, or even respond to enemy fire unless your own positions are directly attacked. Anybody who has an itchy trigger finger is going to have to deal with me."

Cameron shook his head. The orders were strange, unexpected. And Frasier's voice seemed odd, not at all the usual calm certainty that had come to define the general.

Cameron had already been nervous, but now his stomach knotted up. He didn't know what to expect, and now the specter of the unknown was gnawing at him even more than the possibility of combat.

What the hell is going on?

His answer came quickly. Frasier had barely finished issuing his orders when Cameron's visor display went crazy. His head snapped up, and he looked out toward the compound...just as the show began.

He caught glimpses of huge figures, robots like the ones he'd seen earlier. They were moving, staying mostly behind cover. And their weapons were firing.

He saw flashes of electric-blue light, particle accelerators, he knew. The energy weapons were enormously deadly at close range—within a hundred meters, the beam would rip through his armor like a knife through butter—but in an atmosphere, the effectiveness would quickly drop off. The weapons weren't aimed at his Marines. The robots were putting on a display, blasting rocks to dust and trees to splinters.

He saw trails moving across his field of view, hyper-velocity autocannon rounds, creating an eerie glow as they ionized the air around them. They slammed into a small rise, tearing apart the dirt, ripping huge gaps into the hill.

Now he understood Frasier's odd order. The Mules were demonstrating their firepower, not attacking. They were leaving no doubt that they could protect themselves, that any assault against their base would be a bloodbath. They weren't targeting the Marines, not yet. But that could change in an instant if his people opened fire.

He looked out toward the compound, watching the power of the bots' weapons on display. He'd read the accounts of the battles with the First Imperium's robot warriors, seen the footage of them in action. But seeing it for real—and facing the prospect he might be ordered to engage them at any moment—was sobering. He'd been concerned about what would happen, about how the Mules might fight back…and now he was realizing what would happen if those orders came. This wouldn't be a quick operation, an assault on the compound and the arrest of the Mules. It would be a bloodbath, a savage battle that would claim hundreds of lives…and one his gut told him the Marines could lose.

*   *   *

"I understand your concerns, Mr. Diennes, and I assure you I share them. But I'm afraid the situation is far more complicated than it appears."

Ana Zhukov and Connor Frasier sat, looking across the desk at Max Harmon. The republic's president was on the com unit with Jacques Diennes. Diennes was one of the leading members of the Assembly, and the head of the Human Society. He was also Harmon's greatest political rival, and one of his challengers in the upcoming elections.

Zhukov watched silently, the expression on her face communicating her distress. She detested Diennes, an emotion she would have extended to all his followers if she hadn't believed most of them were just fools following their instincts to be part of a movement without really understanding it. Human history had proven mankind's ineptitude in choosing leaders, causes. It was something she knew that transcended nations and eras, and it struck all across the political spectrum. It was the reason all human societies trended toward totalitarianism… because people wanted to believe in things instead of accepting the dark truths. Because they sought not to preserve their—and everyone's—freedom, but instead to feel that they were morally superior. Because it is easier to believe someone telling you that you were wronged, that you are threatened…and it is too depressing to accept that those leading your movement seek only personal power, and that you are but a mindless tool in their quest for control. And Diennes was a master at exploiting peoples' weaknesses.

She couldn't hear what Diennes was saying, but she could see the anger on Harmon's face. He was controlling himself, keeping his own tone cool, professional, but she knew some part of him was wishing he could make the troublesome politician disappear.

Zhukov was surprised by her own thoughts, particularly the one that wondered if that wasn't a good idea…if Harmon should leave the future to the vagaries of an election and men like Jacques Diennes. If people wouldn't value and safeguard their liberties or invest the time to see through monsters like Diennes, she wasn't sure what purpose democracy served. If people were doomed to live under authoritarian rule, she would vastly prefer someone like Harmon, and she was starting to believe she would support whatever actions he took to ensure that result.

"That man is infuriating."

Zhukov looked up, Harmon's voice pulling her from her thoughts. He had shut down the com line. "Yes, Max…he is." She didn't even try to hide the distaste in her voice. "You can't let him take power. Whatever it takes."

"Well, this situation with the Mules only helps him. I was trying to downplay things, even after I deployed the Marines, but there is no hiding that display of firepower they put on. Diennes com has been going nonstop…even the moderate NBs are scared to death now, wondering what the Mules have been up to. From what I can see, the Human Society is even getting some fringe support among the Tanks, again, mostly fueled by fear of the Mules." He paused, shaking his head. "They're calling me soft, too sympathetic to do what has to be done...too weak to protect the republic."

"My people are ready, sir...if you decide there is no other choice. It will be...difficult...but the Marines will see it done if you give the order." Ana looked at her husband, pushing back on the anger she felt. She knew it wasn't fair...Frasier had his responsibilities, and all the years she'd known him he had been a creature of duty. She couldn't hold that against him now. And she could tell from his tone that he didn't want to lead his Marines forward. He didn't hate the Mules, and he even agreed with many of their grievances...and she suspected he was far from sure how a battle would turn out, despite the display of confidence.

"Is that what we've come to, Connor?" Frasier sighed. "To send your people in to kill the Mules? Let's not kid ourselves, they're armed to the teeth and they're going to resist. I hesitate to even guess how many of your Marines will die. The mere show of force has thrown the republic into an uproar. What will happen if the Mules are all killed...along with hundreds of your Marines?"

Ana listened quietly. She knew Harmon had hoped the show of force would push the Mules to back down. That had been a bit of wishful thinking, Harmon fooling himself because the alternatives were so unpalatable. It was a rare display of weakness by the republic's president, and as much as she had recognized it immediately, she couldn't bring herself to fault him for it.

"What alternatives are there?" Frasier spoke softly, his voice grim, uncomfortable. "They will destroy you politically if you don't take action." The Marine paused. "That's not to mention the fact that, however legitimate the Mules' grievances, we can hardly allow an armed force to remain ten klicks from the city."

"Let me go talk to them." The words blurted from Ana's mouth, surprising even herself.

"That is out of the question." Frasier turned toward her, a

look of horror on his face. "It's a potential battle zone, Ana. What if we end up having to assault the facility? Even if we could get you in there safely, you have no idea what they would do. Dr. Cutter is out there...and we don't know what they have done to him."

"Hieronymus is fine, Connor. And I would be too. The Mules would never harm me. For that matter, I'm sure they don't want to harm anyone." She turned toward Harmon. "Max, we have a group here standing up for their rights. You know they have been treated unfairly. What would you do in their place? What would Terrance have done? Let me try to work out a solution. Please. If you order the Marines to go in, you will always regret it." She turned back toward Fraser. "And with all due respect to the Marines, I would not underestimate the Mules...or their ability to defend themselves. You imagine a bloody but victorious assault. What if you attack and lose hundreds of Marines...and are defeated?"

Frasier stared back at his wife. "If we go in, we will take the compound." His voice sounded more of pride than confidence.

She didn't answer. There was no reason to argue over Frasier's bravado. One glance across the table told her Harmon agreed with her.

"Are you sure, Ana? It could be dangerous."

"I have nothing to fear from the Mules, Max. As long as they know I am coming...and coming alone."

"No...this is insane." Frasier's head snapped back and forth, looking at both of them, his expression turning quickly to one of horror.

Ana reached out and put her hand on his arm. "It's the only way to avoid a disaster, Con. I can't sit here while hundreds of your men and women are killed...and what will happen to the republic, even if you are victorious. The Mules are responsible for much of our technology, our prosperity. This can't end in bloodshed...whatever it takes." She paused, looking into his eyes. "I have to do this. There's no other choice."

"She's right, Connor." Harmon stood up slowly. "I will send a communique to Achilles and tell him you want to come out there."

Ana nodded. "I will be ready."

"I'll send a detachment with you..."

"No, Connor. No Marines. No one else." She started right at him. "I have to go alone."

Chapter Nineteen

Admiral Frette's Communique to Fleet HQ
Highest Security Level – AI Protected
President Harmon and Admiral West Eyes Only

It is with a heavy heart that I must report that the fleet has encountered a significant force of hostile ships. Although the vessels are not an absolute match for First Imperium ship designs, they are very close and, thusly, there can be little doubt that we have encountered a significant force of the First Imperium. The fleet has engaged and defeated approximately seventy enemy vessels. Our losses in the battle were moderate, two vessels destroyed, varying damage levels to approximately half of the fleet's vessels. Our current casualty count is 134 dead and 98 wounded. These figure do not include minor wounds or treatable cases of radiation exposure.

The squadron we faced consisted entirely of light and medium units, designs very similar to the Gremlins and Gargoyles faced previously, and the absence of any heavy enemy units accounts for our relatively easy victory. We have little evidence as to what, if any, additional forces may be positioned out farther toward the frontier, but it seems likely that a force this size, deployed for the past thirty years or more in such a remote location must have some type of base or support installation. I am also suspicious of a fleet completely without any heavier vessels. My recollections of the past war, confirmed by an AI analysis of records from the era, suggest that First Imperium fleets of this size rarely operated without battleship equivalents.

As commander on the scene, the decision as to a next step falls upon me. I could order the fleet to return to Earth Two, or I could choose to move forward, to explore and seek more information, to try to assemble a clearer picture of what we are facing. I do not see the benefit of returning now. That would leave us facing a mystery, and the constant danger of an enemy attack on Earth Two. And if we are to learn more, it does not seem to me we could send a meaningfully larger fleet on a second mission, not without leaving an inadequate defensive force behind.

I have therefore decided that we will continue farther, following the course Hurley took. We will gather data, scan each system we pass through...and seek to develop a meaningful estimate of what enemy forces we are facing. I am sending Cyclone with this message, as she is the fastest ship we have...and also a light vessel with minimal combat power. I believe I have made the correct choice, indeed the only one that makes sense for us now, and I am confident both of you would have come to the same conclusion.

I urge both of you to approach this threat with grave seriousness. I have no evidence there are First Imperium forces out here in numbers large enough to threaten Earth Two...but we all know intuition plays a role in every good commander's decision making process. And my instincts are screaming to me. While I can offer nothing more save these feelings, I feel obligated to tell you both I expect to find a large enemy force out here. Perhaps one that can overwhelm this fleet. Perhaps even one that can threaten Earth Two with invasion and destruction.

I will, of course, send updates back in the event we discover anything new, and I will return with the fleet as soon as we are able to develop a more concrete analysis of what forces oppose us. I wish you both the best in dealing with this new threat, even as you manage the difficulties our young republic was already facing.

Erika, I have included a private message to you, attached to this communique.

Main Engineering Deck, E2S Compton
System G-43, Twelve Transits from Earth Two
Earth Two Date 11.29.30

"I want those valves replaced, all of them." Ang Minh stood in front of the main engineering display, staring at the complex schematic it displayed. He was alone in the room, and he was talking not to one of his technicians, but to the ship's main AI. He'd sent his human staff back to their quarters an hour before with orders to get six hours of uninterrupted sleep. They were strung out and exhausted from forty-eight straight hours of damage control duty, and he was impressed with what they had accomplished...but they needed rest. He knew he was a bit prejudiced toward his actual human engineers. In truth, Compton's repair bots, directed by the AI as much as by him, had done most of the repair work on the flagship. But Minh's handful of men and women had done their share too.

Admiral Frette had expressed her concern for his own well-being, but he'd brushed her aside with a vague promise to get some sleep 'soon.' Then he downed another heavy dose of stims and went right back to work. He'd taken far too much of the stuff, vastly more even than the heavy doses that carried dire health warnings. But Minh didn't care if he ended up needing a liver regeneration...he was going to have Compton one hundred percent operational before the fleet found more First Imperium forces.

And when the valves are replaced, she'll be damned close to one hundred percent, like the day she launched from the space dock...

"The valves are all currently within design specifications. I urge you to consider whether this is a necessary repair." The AI spoke softly, matter-of-factly.

"I said I want them replaced. Design specs are one thing, and combat is another. And if we go into battle again with these in place we're stuck with them until the fight is over. And if one of them fails in the middle of combat, this ship is screwed."

"Your analysis is valid, but your caution seems extreme. A full replacement will leave us with insufficient backup parts for possible future damage."

"My caution is common sense, something you'd understand if you were flesh and blood, and if a valve failure could lead to your death...and not just your erasure." Minh didn't know what it was inside him that drove him to argue with the AI, to insult it whenever possible. He never got the response he wanted, and the whole thing was a waste of time and effort. But still he kept doing it.

"Your attempt to insult me is understandable, particularly in view of your stress level and lack of sleep. My statements and analyses are intended to assist you in the decision-making process, not to argue with you. In the end the decision on how to proceed is yours to make."

Minh sighed. "Then let's begin the replacement. I'll have to get the go ahead from the admiral first. We'll need to shut the reactor down for at least an hour."

"Sixty-seven minutes, assuming a median expectation for variables."

"Okay, get everything ready. Pull the replacements from the cargo holds, and program the repair bots." He'd picked his timing for the valve repairs, while his people were on their rest period. Replacing reactor valves was a job for the bots, not for live engineers. The radiation inside the reactor was just too much of a danger for human techs.

"All maintenance bots are ready to go. Prepared to initiate reactor shutdown sequence on receipt of command authorization."

Minh tapped his com unit. "Admiral Frette...we're ready to go down here."

"Very well, Commander." Frette paused. "Entering fleet command authorization now." There were another few seconds of silence. Then: "Do your best to make this quick, Commander."

Minh held back a sigh. "Yes, Admiral. As quickly as possible."

Without flooding the ship with radiation a hundred times the lethal level…

*   *   *

"Captain, Commander Willis reports all repairs completed. Starfire is one hundred percent operational.

Josie Strand was standing next to her chair, as she often did instead of sitting in it. She felt a wave of relief at the report. Starfire hadn't been badly damaged in the fight, but Strand's OCD tended to run wild when her ship was in less than perfect order. Her instructors at the Academy had all said the same thing about her…she had all the intensity, perfectionism, and laser focus of the best ship captains…but maybe too much of them. She'd never slept more than four hours a night, even as a child, and now she was lucky to get about two and a half. She had enormous difficulty turning down her intensity, and she'd been told dozens of times she would burn herself out one day.

"Very well, Commander. Give Commander Willis my congratulations." Her ship's damage had been light, mostly minor burnouts spread over dozens of systems. Still, she knew it had taken a lot of work to get everything back up to full specs, and she was surprised how quickly Willis and his people had managed it.

Strand stood erect, almost at attention, looking around the bridge. She was pleased with her people, with how they had conducted themselves in their first battle. There had been no panic, no indiscipline. If she hadn't known better, she'd have thought she was watching a group of long service veterans in action.

As if you had any idea what to expect. You were as much a cherry as the rest of them…

Strand had studied the history of war, especially the recent accounts of the fleet's flight from the Barrier to Earth Two. She'd read the chronology of events, and the analyses of the officers who'd written the histories…but mostly she'd focused on the journals, on the accounts of the men and women who had been there, in the heat of battle. She tended to distrust summaries and histories written after the fact.

Josie Strand believed in being prepared for whatever she faced, and she'd done everything possible to ready herself for the experience of battle…even though she'd often doubted if she would ever see real conflict. For years, the republic had been at peace, without so much as a potential enemy out there in the emptiness of space. But now she'd seen war up close, felt the fear of the enemy. And she'd handled it, brought her ship and crew through it with flying colors. Only now, feeling the relief at that, did she realize how much the doubt had weighed on her.

Strand looked up at the display. Starfire was moving along with the fleet formation, traveling at just under 0.1c. The force had been accelerating since transiting into the system, but then the order came to shut down all engines. Compton had to put her reactor down to complete repairs, and Admiral Frette wanted to keep the fleet together in a tight formation. They were still moving toward the warp gate during the shutdown, they just weren't accelerating or decelerating.

The officers and spacers whose writings Strand had studied had much to say about tactics, about handling fear and uncertainty. But the journals and reports were also full of accounts of the discomfort of space combat, of struggling to concentrate under six gees of pressure, or worse, under 30g, drugged and covered in goo in the old tanks.

Technology had spared her generation such indignities, and the inertial dampeners and other new developments had banished much of the awkwardness from space combat. She wondered if the relative comfort was an edge to spacers her age…or if it made her comrades weaker, less capable than those who had come before and excelled under such difficult circumstances.

Battles were still long…indeed, more efficient engines and reactors allowed fleets to emphasize maneuver, and she knew a fight had the potential to last for days as ships zipped past each other and then decelerated to come around for another pass. But even then, the application of First Imperium knowledge had aided in the development of a new generation of stimulants, safer and more effective than those used thirty years before. The basic equation hadn't changed...you could still get strung out and suffer a litany of health issues from stimulant overuse. It just took longer.

"Captain, Compton reports her repairs are complete. She will be reactivating her reactor shortly, and all ships are ordered to prepare to resume acceleration at 30g."

"Very well. Relay the order to engineering. Prepare for 30g."

She stared across the bridge at the main display. The G-43 system was profoundly uninteresting. Nothing but a red giant star, which had engulfed and incinerated any planets it had ever had. Nothing else. No asteroids, not even much in the way of comets and meteors. Just vast empty space.

But it wasn't where she was that consumed Strand's mind. It was where she—all of them—were going that had her attention. Into the unknown. In search of an enemy as deadly as one pulled from mythology.

She wasn't a cherry anymore, she was a combat veteran, at least technically. But she'd fought in just a single battle, one where the outcome had never been in doubt. For all she and her people had come through it well, she still marveled at the strength of those from the lost fleet, the men and women who had gone into combat again and again, against insurmountable odds...and somehow prevailed.

Be careful what you think...the same thing may be waiting for you out there...

She held her stare on the screen, her mind racing ahead, imagining the systems still to come...and whatever might be waiting there.

*   *   *

The probe was silent, operating in full stealth mode. It had watched the enemy transit into the system as expected. The arrival of the enemy on this time frame was the highest probability outcome.

It had been left behind by the advance force as it moved forward, and it had monitored the entry of the enemy ships into the system. The passive scanners provided limited data, but it seemed likely from the presence and size of the enemy fleet that the advance force had been destroyed. This was no problem, indeed, it was not entirely unexpected.

The enemy ships were acting as expected, pushing forward along the course of their original scout vessel. The probe's instructions were clear. To remain in place, near the primary, utilizing the intense radiation to enhance its stealth capabilities. Such parameters offered little chance to obtain meaningful data on the composition of the enemy fleet, but that wasn't the probe's purpose. It was only important to track the general movements, to confirm that the vessels were indeed following the projected course, that they were proceeding toward the trap that had been set for them.

The probe recorded the data, preparing it for transmission to Vengeance One. But its com units remained silent. It was to send its report only after the enemy vessels had transited out of the system.

Then it would carry out its last directive. It would self-destruct, leaving no trace that it had been there, that it had served its role in trapping the enemy, monitoring them as they moved toward their destruction.

Chapter Twenty

Victory City Security Forces
Report of Recent Activity

There have been seven incidents of vandalism in the past week. Six of the seven have involved damage to public facilities in the form of graffiti. The content of the messages strongly suggests this is the work of a radical group of Tanks. The lack of any evidence from surveillance systems implies the involvement of an individual of considerable ability in terms of hacking into and modifying the city's security system. There are few Tanks with that level of education and experience in the computer field. The AI has flagged three possible suspects. Two NB suspects have also been identified, individuals suspected of participating in pro-Tank protests in the past. While no evidence yet exists to support charges against any of the individuals, arrest warrants have been issued for all five under the Emergency Security Act of Year Fourteen.

Supreme HQ – "The Rock"
Victory City, Earth Two
Earth Two Date 12.04.30

"I'm worried, Max. We received two routine status updates, but nothing since. We should have heard at least once since then.   Nicki…Admiral Frette…is extremely precise.   She wouldn't have missed a transmission. Not unless…"

Harmon leaned back in the chair, looking over at the com-mander-in-chief of the republic's navy. He'd known Erika West for a long time, and for many years he had been the junior of the two…until Harmon became the republic's first—and to date only—president. He'd been a little concerned at first if it would be difficult for both of them, but West had never given the slightest indication that she resented his authority over her. He'd had more trouble with it, but she'd made it easy for him to adjust.

"Don't jump to any conclusions, Erika.   You know our hypercom technology is rough. We can send messages through warp gates, but we can't match the First Imperium's use of the system. The reliability is pretty poor…any num-ber of things could have interfered with Nicki's message."

Harmon wasn't sure where the line stood between what he really believed and what he was telling West to make her feel better. He knew West had more than a comradely interest in Frette's wellbeing, and truth be told, whatever he was saying, he was just as worried at the absence of a recent communique.

The commanding admiral's romantic relationship with her executive officer was a closely-kept secret, but Harmon was a good friend of both women, and he had known from the begin-ning. Fraternization between officers at different levels on the chain of command was a technical violation of regulations, but it was widely ignored in the republic's navy…almost as much as it had been in the Alliance navy the two officers had served before. Still, Erika West tended to be a 'by the book' kind of officer, and she'd struggled with it for a while, balancing her feelings with her sense of duty. In the end, Harmon had spoken to her, told her after all they'd been through it would be insane to turn away any chance at happiness…and he had closed with the one line he knew West could not ignore. Admiral Compton would have approved.

It was a bit of a dirty trick, invoking the legendary admiral's spirit, and an especially potent one when he wielded it, being widely considered to be one of the two surviving members of the fleet who had been closest to Compton. But his intentions had been good. Both West and Frette had been through their share of suffering and pain during the fleet's struggles, and he'd hadn't wanted to see pointless regulations interfere with their chance at some happiness.

"I know you're telling me what you think I want to hear… but you always manage to make me feel better." West's voice was controlled, professional, as it always was. But Harmon knew she was hurting.

"Look, Erika…we're both worried about what is happening out there…but Nicki Frette is one of the most capable officers I've ever known, and she's got a lot of power with her. I believe she can handle whatever she finds."

"I know you're right." West paused. "I just wish we'd hear something."

Harmon nodded and leaned back in his chair. West's office was large, something he'd insisted on when the navy's headquarters building had been built. Left to her own devices, he knew she'd have put her desk in a small windowless cubby somewhere. West wasn't an officer who dealt comfortably with splendor and the trappings of office, at least not most of them. Harmon's eyes moved toward the one luxury she had embraced, and included in her office by her own command…a small fireplace, even now crackling merrily as two logs burned in the stone hearth.

"You haven't given me any opinions on the standoff at the Mules' compound." Harmon thought a change of subject might help West. And he'd been anxious for her thoughts.

"You haven't asked for any."

Harmon looked across at his top admiral. For an instant he thought she was giving him a sarcastic answer, but then he reminded himself how straight laced West was…and how well she had slipped into the role of his subordinate instead of his superior.

"I'm asking."

"Well, sir…" She'd been talking to her old friend moments before, but now she slipped into a more formal role, that of an admiral speaking to the president. "You know I am not inclined to tolerate rebellion...but..." She paused, turning her gaze away from Harmon toward the fire.

"But what, Erika? My God, by now you should know you can say anything to me."

"Well, sir. Years ago I would have said send in the Marines, crush the revolt. But now...I'm just not so sure. First, they do have legitimate grievances, don't they? We may deny that in public, and I understand why the things that were done were done. But between us, we know it wasn't just."

"No, it wasn't." Harmon sighed. He wished he'd fought this battle years before, when he was stronger, when he still carried the weight of being Compton's successor. But the Mules had been children then, and for many years there was no significant opposition to retaining the Prohibition. He'd taken the easier route, sacrificed justice to political expediency. He was ashamed of his choices then...but that didn't change the fact that he had precious few now.

"But there is another concern, a far more practical one." West's voice broke from her normal hard edged monotone. "We need the Mules, don't we? People can react to them with fear, and I'm not even sure that is entirely without some justification. But where would the republic be if they had never existed? What would our city, our fleet, our ability to grow and prosper be without the technology they developed? Certainly Dr. Cutter and a few others would have made some progress, but we benefit today from years of work by over one hundred men and women with intellects and abilities we can hardly imagine, much less properly appreciate." She paused.

"What dangers will we face in the future? What might Nicki uncover out there even now? How much stronger are we with the Mules than without them?" Another pause. "If we suppress the Mules, imprison or destroy them...apart from the moral problems such a course raises, do we not in many ways endanger our own future? You and I remember what it is like to fight an overpowering enemy. If we'd had one more piece of bad luck back then, if we'd had a leader less capable than

Terrance Compton, what would have become of us? Are you confident we will never again face such a challenge? Can we afford to make ourselves weaker?"

Harmon sat quietly, taking a deep breath. "You are right, Erika...across the board. But there is one problem. If we don't do something to resolve this impasse, I will lose the election. And whether Jacques Diennes replaces me or someone else, they will move against the Mules immediately." He hesitated. "And Diennes, at least, will take advantage of the opportunity to get rid of the Mules for good. There will be no negotiation, no moderate solutions."

West sat quietly for a moment, clearly wanting to say something, but hesitating. Then she looked right at Harmon. "Jacques Diennes cannot become president, Max." Her eyes were cold, bright, and her tone was deadly serious. "Whatever it takes."

Harmon stared back at her. "I hope you're not suggesting what I think you are, Erika...because that is not an option. Do you understand me?"

She looked back at Harmon, but she just sat quietly, not answering.

*   *   *

"Where is the president now, when the republic faces the greatest threat in its thirty years of existence? What steps has he taken the crush this foul rebellion, to bring those responsible to justice?" Jacques Diennes stood in the central square of Victory City. He'd chosen his spot carefully, clear on the other side of the park from the massive statue of Terrance Compton. Compton was still a revered figure to the people of Earth Two, and the last thing he wanted was to remind people that Max Harmon had been Compton's close comrade.

"Our Marines stand to arms, surrounding the compound for days now, but where is the order to move? Where is the leadership? The courage to do what is necessary to protect and preserve our republic?" Diennes looked out over the crowd. His speeches had been drawing larger numbers, more people showing up each day, it seemed. Max Harmon's prospects had been in doubt since the day he'd been compelled to call a new election, but his popularity had truly plummeted with the Mules' uprising…and his reluctance to do anything decisive to end it.

"There have been those who have mischaracterized our movement, branded the Society as an organization that is concerned only with natural born humans. But now we see the dangers of uncontrolled experimentation with the human genome. We have allowed the creation of would be super-beings, men and women who see their true place as our masters, and not our brothers and sisters. And what of the unenhanced clones, those we call the Tanks? The Plague that strikes without warning is another example of how our uncontrolled pride has brought suffering and death upon us. Scientific hubris created this terror."

Diennes had studied politics, read hundreds of accounts of the history of elections on Earth. He was lying, changing his positions, his words flying in the face of speeches he'd given before. But he knew it didn't matter. Even the educated and disciplined citizens of Earth Two responded only to superficiality. Their votes would follow their fear…and right now, Max Harmon was allowing dangerous rebels to stand in defiance of the republic. Diennes knew they would believe him. Not all, perhaps, but most. He knew he could lie almost with impunity, as long as he told them now what they wanted to hear.

"We do not advocate persecution…we stand for protection, for greater safeguards and care, before a few scientists, driven by ego as much as any other force, manipulate DNA, unconcerned with the results of their reckless experimentation. We face grave danger at the hands of the Mules, even now. What terrors wait in our future, if we do not stop this insanity now?"

He could see the crowd responding to his words, the excitement building. He put his arms up in the air, and the crowd began to cheer loudly. He had hoped the Society would gain seats in the Assembly, that it would become an influential part of a coalition government. But now he was beginning to believe his party could win an outright majority. He was even seeing inroads with fringe elements among the Tanks, those most concerned about the danger of the Mules. He had stepped up his rhetoric about the Enhanced Hybrids and their rebellion, and he had softened his words with regard to the Tanks. He'd called them abominations before, but now he cast them as victims, blamed the scientists for the Plague. And it was working.

"Stand with me, citizens! Help me save our beloved republic. Together we can do what has to be done, we can secure a bright, safe, and prosperous future for ourselves, and for the generations to come."

He thrust his hands up again, and the crowd went wild, cheering, chanting his name. He turned his head, looked down the street toward the executive building, his eyes focusing on the northeast corner of the top floor. The president's office. Max Harmon's office.

For another month, at least…

*   *   *

"Hieronymus!" Ana Zhukov ran across the room and threw her arms around her longtime comrade. She'd long considered Cutter like a brother, even closer. The two had worked together almost every day for more than thirty years.

"Ana, what are you doing here?" Cutter returned the hug, but there was concern in his voice. He stepped back. "You shouldn't have come."

"Mother, welcome. It is most gratifying to see you." Achilles walked into the room, followed by half a dozen of the other Mules…and H2. The Mules didn't call Zhukov 'mother' as frequently as they addressed Cutter as 'father,' but Achilles did so pointedly, and she could hear the warmth in his voice.

Achilles looked toward Cutter. "You needn't be concerned, Father. We would never harm either of you, no matter what the circumstances."

"Are you going to imprison, Dr. Zhukov as you did me, Achilles?"

"No, of course not." Achilles looked over at Zhukov. "You are free to go whenever you wish, Mother...or to remain with us." He turned toward Cutter. "As are you, Father. It was necessary for us to keep you here only until we revealed our defensive capabilities. You may leave whenever you wish, though of course, we would rejoice if you chose to remain with us."

"Achilles..." Zhukov moved toward the Mule, put her hand on his arm. "I have come to try to reason with you."

"I know what you have come to argue, and it hurts me to reject your wishes, Mother, but we must look to our own preservation. We have already begun the quickening sequence... the next generation is even now coming into being, cells dividing, specializing. Indeed, we have built on your groundbreaking work, and the children we create will be superior to us, indeed perhaps vastly so."

"Would you stand your weapons down if President Harmon repealed the Prohibition? He knows it should have been done long ago, and he is truly regretful that it wasn't."

Achilles was silent for a moment. Then he shook his head slowly. "Nothing would please us more, Mother, but I do not believe that is possible now. Indeed, perhaps against my best judgment, I would take Max Harmon's word...but he does not have the power to deliver on such a promise? We have been monitoring the speeches and statements of the candidates with growing concern. I fear President Harmon's prospects for reelection are rapidly diminishing...and we must prepare for whoever replaces him."

"This rebellion of yours is destroying his chances...and his failure to take decisive action against you is costing him votes every hour."

"I would help President Harmon if I could, Mother. But I will not expose my own people to the terrible risks if someone like Jacques Diennes should win the election. A man like that would imprison us at the very least...and very likely worse. There is nothing I can do."

"Do you really think you can hold off the entire Marine Corps here?"

"You underestimate the effectiveness of our defensive systems. If the Marines assault this compound, they will suffer tremendous losses. Our analysis suggests that an all-out attack has a thirty-two percent chance of success, and a ninety-four percent probability that casualties would exceed fifty percent of engaged forces." Achilles extended his own arm, putting his hand on Zhukov's shoulder. "I am sorry...I know your husband commands the Marines."

Zhukov sucked in a deep breath, but she didn't say anything.

"We have also heard several of the candidates for president suggest using high-yield weapons to destroy our compound. Yet this as well is the voice of ignorance. Quite apart from the close proximity to the city and the inherent danger of using nuclear weapons in such a circumstance, our power source is a thirty gigawatt fusion reactor. If this facility is destroyed by a nuclear attack, the resulting core breach would almost certainly destroy Victory City."

Zhukov was fighting back frustration, tears. "How can you speak of causing such devastation, of so many people being killed?"

"I do not threaten to invoke such a catastrophe. I merely state that any attempt to annihilate us would, by extension, also destroy the city. Indeed, the magnetic containment system under the compound also stores the relatively minor amount of antimatter we have been able to produce. While this is only several kilograms, the results of its escaping containment would be disastrous."

"I tried to warn you, Achilles, that this would get out of control." Hieronymus Cutter walked across the room, moving next to Zhukov. "Your grievances are legitimate, no one here questions that. But so is the fear you have instilled in the people. Did you think you could unleash robots that looked like First Imperium combat units and not create a backlash?"

"Of course we realized that the similarities would cause discomfort. But there was no other way for us to protect ourselves.

Without the bots, we would be one hundred sixteen against thousands. We would be mostly unarmed scientists against armored Marines. We had no choice."

Achilles stood still and looked at Zhukov and Cutter. "You are our creators, the two of you, and always we shall think of you as father and mother. You are torn between your loyalty to your own kind, and your affection for us. We understand this... which is why you are both free to go, and to return whenever you choose. You shall always have a home with us, and we shall do anything you request, save continue to accept our place as second class citizens. Perhaps we will lose this standoff, perhaps the Marines will attack and destroy our robots and storm the compound. But if we had done nothing, we would have died out anyway. Even if our lifespans are longer than those of normal humans, as we suspect they will be, one day the last of us will die...and we will not do so quietly, penned in and marginalized and prevented from procreating in the only way we have available to us."

The Mule stood motionless for a moment, looking at the two people responsible for his existence. "Please forgive me, but I have duties to attend to." He turned and walked out of the room.

"Let's go, Ana...H2...there's nothing we can do here." Cutter's voice was soft, his tone one of defeat.

"No, Father...I am staying here."

Cutter turned toward the first enhanced hybrid. "H2...it is very possible that President Harmon will have no choice but to order the Marines in...and with the losses they suffer there is no way to know what will happen when they break in. It will be very dangerous."

"Perhaps. Indeed, almost certainly. But that is of no account." He paused. "I have occupied a unique positon all my life. Yet, I have spoken long with Achilles...and I have watched the speeches in Victory City, the demonization of the Mules, nary a word of the injustice that has been maintained against them for so long offered in defense of their actions."

He looked at Zhukov and then back to Cutter. "I love you

both, and I always will, no matter what happens. But I must be with my people now, whatever fate awaits them. I have found myself, and for all the confusion I have endured, it is in the new generation even now coming into being that the answer awaited me. For I am the first of the Mules, though my abilities do not match those who came after me, and I have watched as my brethren worked to produce more of our kind, laboring in every way to make them superior to themselves...stronger, healthier, smarter. That is the creed of the Mules, to strive to better ourselves. I am proud to have been the first, and I no longer resent those who came after me, who exceeded my abilities."

He stepped forward and hugged Zhukov...then Cutter. "Go, for there is no reason for you to be here if things go badly. Return to your people. As Achilles said, you will always be welcome among us."

H2 paused for a few seconds. Then he turned and followed Achilles' path.

                    *   *   *

"We can't allow a man like Jacques Diennes to become president. We must stop him, at all costs." Erika West felt odd in the civilian clothes. For forty years, she had rarely gone out wearing anything but her uniform. But the garb of the navy's commander was too conspicuous for a clandestine meeting... and no one could know what was being discussed here, no one but her companion.

"I agree. It is an uncomfortable thing for me to say. My life has been one of discipline, of obedience. I do not lightly interfere with the democracy of the republic. But Diennes will lead us down the road to destruction. He will have the NBs and the Tanks at each other's throats. That will tear the Corps apart... and then the republic." Connor Frasier was also dressed in a civilian suit. He was uncomfortable skulking around, but West had insisted they meet in person, and he had agreed. There was no guarantee that any com link was entirely secure. And what they had to say now was for each other's ears only.

"President Harmon is worried. He thinks he is going to lose." A short pause. "And he probably is." West moved toward the door, and punched one of the buttons on the access panel. The small screen displayed the hallway outside. It was empty, deserted. The apartment block was new, and its inhabitants hadn't moved in yet. It was the perfect place for a quiet meeting...and anyone who saw them would take the pair for lovers having some secret affair. Not the republic's top two military commanders plotting a coup.

"What is he going to do about the Mules? The standoff can't go on forever." Frasier's voice was a bit halting. Ana Zhukov was at the compound, even then trying to negotiate some kind of end to the logjam, and West knew Frasier was worried about his wife.

"He wants to repeal the Prohibition...I'm sure of it. But the Assembly will never go along with it."

"That is another reason we must take action. We must secure control of the republic, impose the repeal of the Prohibition, make peace with the Mules...and ensure that President Harmon remains in office, at least for the foreseeable future."

"That violates our oaths of office, Connor. It makes us traitors." West had initiated the meeting, but now doubt was creeping into her voice.

"Only if we fail."

West was startled by the matter-of-fact statement from the straight-laced Marine. "Success makes it right?"

"History would suggest it does. At least in one sense. But here is another justification. What is the alternative? To allow democracy to operate unfettered...and destroy itself? Because I don't see any option. I am reluctant to suggest there is anything my Marines cannot do, but there is dissension, and widespread sympathy for the Mules among the Tanks. I like to think training and Marine pride will be enough, but I truly don't know what will happen if we are ordered forward, and the fight turns into a bloodbath."

"Well, here's another question to ask yourself. Will your Marines follow your orders to overthrow the government?"

"We are not seeking to overthrow the government. Only to keep the status quo in place...and eliminate the dangerous opposition."

"It sounds almost patriotic when you put it that way."

Frasier stared back at West. "We are trying to save the republic, Erika. There is nothing more patriotic than that. Unlike the politicians now maneuvering for position, we do not seek power, nor do I believe Max Harmon does. When the deed is done, we will return to our normal command structure...and when the current crisis has passed and the radical elements are suppressed, I have no doubt President Harmon will step down as well."

"Except we will have created a precedent, one that makes it acceptable for the military to step in and suspend elections and arrest troublesome elements of society. Do you think that damage will quickly fade, that the next president, and the one after, will ever look to his Marine and navy commanders without a certain mistrust?"

Frasier sighed. "No, perhaps not. But there is only one question that needs to be answered here. What choice do we have?"

West shook her head sadly. "None." She reached out her hand. "So we do this?"

Frasier returned her gaze, reaching out and grasping her hand. "Yes...we do what we must."

Chapter Twenty-One

From the Log of Admiral Frette

It has been several weeks since I dispatched Cyclone with the warning that we have encountered and defeated a force of First Imperium warships. I had very little intelligence to include in the message...indeed, I do not have much more now, save for the increasing likelihood that the microscopic remains we have discovered are indeed from Hurley.

I find myself increasingly unnerved, though I have made certain to hide it from my staff and other members of the fleet. I am consumed with the belief that we are moving forward into a deadly encounter, perhaps even a trap. But I have no evidence to support my feelings, and while intuition is recognized as a component of command decisions, it cannot be the only factor. My memories of the fleet affect my judgment, but I have no reason to expect we face a situation as grave as that Admiral Compton led us through so long ago.

I have imagined Erika reviewing the message, wondered about her reaction. She is more courageous than I, calmer and cooler in a crisis. We are fortunate that she succeeded Admiral Compton as fleet commander, and that Max Harmon is still president. Had this encounter occurred later, if Harmon had lost the election and been replaced by someone less capable, less trustworthy...whatever we are about to face would have been a hundredfold worse.

I fear what awaits us out here...but I am buoyed by my confidence, in my own people, and in those still on Earth Two. Whatever is about to happen, I believe the fighting spirit that carried the fleet to triumph three decades ago will sustain us...and take us again to victory.

I hope...

Flag Bridge - E2S Compton
System G47
Earth Two Date 12.09.30

"I can't be sure, Admiral. The AI is still chewing on it, but the best it's been able to offer is a solid maybe."

Frette stared across the flag bridge at Kemp. The tactical officer had spun around in his chair to face her, and she could see in his eyes what he truly thought. "Your best guess, Commander?"

Kemp sighed softly. "Admiral..." He sighed again. "I think it's Hurley. What's left of Hurley." His tone was grim, but there wasn't much doubt in it.

Frette nodded. They hadn't found much, only a few tiny bits of metal, microscopic traces of what might have once been a spaceship. The chemical composition tests were inconclusive. The analysis was effective at ruling out the possibility the small bits of debris were from a republic spaceship, but far less so at conclusively proving it. And so far, every test had failed to exclude the possibility. Frette knew the mathematics, and at some point the lack of a negative result became something close to a positive. And if they weren't there yet, it wasn't far off.

"I concur." Her voice was somber. She turned, speaking to everyone on the flag bridge. "It shouldn't be a surprise. We know there are First Imperium ships out here, we've fought a battle." She hesitated for a few seconds. "I know we all told ourselves maybe Hurley was just damaged, maybe she'd managed to escape, to hide somewhere. But we all knew the likelihood that she was gone. I don't underestimate what we are all feeling about the loss of our comrades, but we have to remember now, what we have discovered is a far graver problem than the loss of Hurley. Indeed, our own fleet has lost more personnel than Hurley's complement, and unless the force we fought was alone…" She frowned. It was clear that she didn't believe that, not for a second. "…we are facing the worst crisis since the days of the old fleet. That is not to suggest that Hurley's loss is not a tragedy." She paused. "It is just one we cannot afford to dwell upon. Not now. Not when the survival of the republic may be at stake."

She regretted the last part the second it came out of her mouth. She had been thinking that of course, and she suspected most of the few remaining Pilgrims in the fleet had as well. But the younger generation, those born on Earth Two, had never experienced the kind of unending sequence of disasters the fleet had somehow survived. They had never faced not just defeat, but total destruction. And, frankly, she didn't know how they would handle a struggle like that.

The flag bridge was silent, every eye on her. She sat quietly for a moment. Then she took a deep breath. "Very well…I want this system searched from end to end. I want intense scans of every meter from the primary to the outer reaches. We're looking for warp gates, stealth ships, probes, even energy trails…or hints of something that might have been energy trails."

She stared at the display. The fleet had only found one warp point other than the one they'd entered through, but Frette was too old a spacer to think that was anywhere near conclusive. And if there was a warp gate leading to more First Imperium forces, she damned sure wanted to know where it was.

"I want four search groups sent out…a cruiser and four frigates in each." She stared down at her workstation, her fingers moving across the screen, dragging icons representing ships of the fleet. She glanced toward Kemp. "Sending you the breakdowns now."

"Yes, Admiral." The tactical officer turned back to his board, his hands moving over the keyboard, implementing the orders Frette had given him.

"The battle line, and the rest of the fleet, will assume station twenty million kilometers from the primary. All ships will remain on yellow alert, ready to respond to any threat."

"Yes, Admiral Frette." Kemp's reply was quick, sharp. But there was the slightest hint of concern there too.

Frette picked up on her aide's uneasiness. She knew keeping the fleet on alert would gradually wear her people down, and if it went on long enough they would be exhausted if they ended up in battle again. But she wasn't taking any chances. She didn't like splitting up the fleet, sending small, vulnerable squadrons to the far ends of the system…but it was the only way her people could complete a thorough scan without it taking weeks. And, if anything was out there she had to know it immediately.

She turned her eyes back to the display. Something was out there. She could feel it.

*   *   *

"Starfire, this is fleet command. Prepare to receive communique from Admiral Frette." Commander Kemp's voice blared through Strand's earpiece.

"Fleet command, Captain Strand here. Standing by." Josie Strand sat back, waiting for the response. She'd served in the navy since graduating from the Academy a year ahead of her class nine years before. She'd served most of that time in Earth Two's own system, patrolling the warp gates and the approaches to the planet, and she'd gotten used to the annoying delay in two-way communication. But now Starfire was more than thirty light seconds from Compton, and the gap between sending and receiving coms was just over a minute. It was enough to make a conversation frustrating, if not outright impossible. And she knew, in theory at least, it was also enough to seriously impact tactical actions. Starfire was moving away from the flagship at close to 0.1c, and that meant every two minutes put another second into each side of two-way communications.

Strand looked over at her tactical officer. Arleigh Hahn had been a year behind her at the Academy, and they had served on the same ship for five years, the past three on Starfire. Strand had occupied Hahn's current chair for much of that time, as Starfire's tactical officer and exec...until Captain Horatius retired, and Admiral West saw fit to promote her to the first command of a capital ship for a non-pilgrim. She knew it was a position years ahead of what she might have achieved in the old navies, the ones that had contributed ships to the fleet so many years before. But Earth Two had its own bizarre situation, and a twenty plus year gap of ages that sliced through its society. The forty-something captain that might have commanded Starfire simply didn't exist, at least not this side of the Barrier, and for the last few years, the high command had been trying to seek out the top candidates among the oldest of the new generation and give them their stars.

Strand's glory had been short-lived, at least her position as the only young officer at her level. Three of her colleagues followed within days, and within four months, half the capital ships in the fleet had commanders under the age of thirty. But Strand had been the first...and she'd been the only one Admiral Frette had selected for the mission.

"Captain Strand, you are to take your group immediately and move toward warp gate three." Frette's voice came through loud and clear, even though the words had taken half a minute to reach Starfire.

Strand felt her stomach tense. The system's third warp gate had only been discovered an hour before.

"You are to link up with Redfin and her group and assume overall command of the search effort."

Strand nodded, as much to herself as for any other reason. Something was up. Frette had originally ordered the battle line to stay together...but then she'd sent Legatus and Starfire toward two of the system's warp gates. It might be nothing more than the CO's paranoia, but she suspected there was a reason behind it all...and she didn't have to wait long for confirmation.

"The scouting group has detected residual energy readings, potentially the result of recent transit through the gate. It could be nothing...but then..." Frette let her voice trail off.

Strand pushed herself back in her chair, straightening up, standing even more erect than she usually did. Her mind was racing already. She was new to command and responsible for one of the most powerful ships in the fleet. And now she was in charge of half a dozen vessels besides her battleship. She had long dreamed of the day she would have such a command, but now all she could feel was the crushing stress.

"Stay alert, Captain…and report anything out of the ordinary, anything at all." A short pause. "Frette out."

She sat quietly for a moment, staring at her screen. Then she looked over at Hahn. "Confirm receipt and acknowledgement of the admiral's message, Commander." She turned and looked toward the bridge's main display. "And increase thrust to 50g…I think we'd better get up there and see what is going on."

*　　　　　*　　　　　*

"Reverse course! Full thrust away from the warp gate. Bring us to a dead halt." Hiroki Akira was a veteran spacer, a Pilgrim and a hero who had received a commendation from Admiral Compton himself. But now he was shaken. He'd scanned the area around the warp gate for hours and found nothing. Then the transmission had come in from Starfire. Josie Strand's ship—and the group with it—were under attack. Enemy ships were streaming through the warp gate they'd been investigating, and by the sound of the last message, a desperate fight was underway.

That news had been bad enough, but barely five minutes after its receipt, Legatus' alarms sounded. There was an energy spike at the warp gate it was scanning. Akira's ship was forty light minutes from Starfire…and that meant the enemy ships now coming through had somehow coordinated with the vessels attacking Strand from the other gate. Either that, or it was the most improbable coincidence Akira had ever seen. And he didn't believe in coincidence.

"Full power to weapons. Bring the reactor to emergency output." He spun around, seeing his crew frozen, staring at him. "Now!" He slammed his hand against his chair. He'd worked his crew as hard as he could, but deep down he considered them a poor replacement for the men and women he'd served with thirty years before. He knew that wasn't fair—and his people had performed well in the earlier fight—but he was still edgy, wondering if they could take the fear and pain and misery those of the old fleet had.

He'd have launched a missile barrage right at the warp gate, hoping to hit the enemy as they emerged, scrambling their systems and hopefully taking out a few ships before they were able to return fire. But Legatus had cleared its external racks in the first battle, and the task force hadn't stopped long enough for the capital ships to rearm from the supply vessels. Besides, the range was far too close for conventional missile assaults.

Legatus' engines were straining, exerting maximum thrust to decelerate. Akira had already done the calculations. His battleship would be less than one hundred thousand meters from the warp gate, standing dead in space, its massive particle accelerators targeted right at the gate as the enemy came through.

"All other ships are to position themselves around us. I want everyone firing full as soon as the first ship shows itself." Akira felt the usual tension, the terrible unease of waiting for a warp gate assault having no idea what was about to come through. He'd been there before, in the wars against the First Imperium back on the other side of the Barrier, and even in the Third Frontier War before that. There was simply no way to know how large a fleet might come through…only the assurance that no more than two or three vessels could transit at the same time, not without taking enormous risks.

"All weapons stations report ready, sir. All ships acknowledge." Tilly James' voice was sturdy, calm. He wasn't sure if it was stone cold courage, or if it was the blissful ignorance of a young officer who'd never watched as hundreds and hundreds of imperial ships poured through a warp gate. Either way, he knew she was a good officer, one he realized had been assigned to Legatus to learn from him...and ultimately to replace him. Akira had volunteered to remain a ship commander for decades now, passing up promotions that were his due, realizing that the navy needed experienced people at the helm. But he also knew that when he advised Admiral West that James was ready, she would get her captain's insignia...and he his admiral's stars.

"Enemy ships emerging, sir..."

Akira was already watching, his eyes fixed on the display. He couldn't get any real readings, nothing more than location. But the transiting ships would be completely blind, at least for the one to two minutes it took their system to adjust and reboot. And he intended to make use of every second of that time.

"All batteries...open fire..."

Chapter Twenty-Two

Political Speech Heard in Victory City

Tanks! The name is demeaning, intended to belittle those of us quickened in the crèche rather than born normally. We are the same as naturally-born humans, identical in every particular...save that our DNA is free of so many of the deficiencies and abnormalities of theirs.

How many of you accept that name, even use it yourselves? You are not Tanks, you are human beings, entitled to the same basic rights as any other man or woman. No longer will we accept the marginalization, the restrictions on the number of quickenings. No longer will our people be used as tools of those who look down on us.

I call to our brothers and sisters in the Corps, noble warriors now engaged in a vile and unjust operation. The Mules—others among us labeled and marginalized by a derogatory name—have been treated badly. They have been forbidden from quickening more of their numbers. They are our cousins, our natural allies. No more will we stand for the oppression we have endured. I call to all of you—and to our naturally-born brothers and sisters who truly value justice. Let us speak as one at the polls. Cast your votes for the Clone-NB Alliance.

Presidential Residence
Victory City, Earth Two
Earth Two Date 12.09.30

"Mr. President…we need to speak with you."

Max Harmon stood in the open door, looking bleary-eyed, his hair a riotous and uncombed mess.

"Erika? What time is it?" He'd actually been sound asleep when the guard had called him to tell him the two top military officers in the republic were at the gate. Harmon had resisted most of the trappings of office that had accrued to the republic's top positions, but he'd been forced to accept the assignment of twenty-four hour security.

"The time is four eighteen AM." The house AI answered Harmon's question before West had the chance.

Harmon ignored the AI and took a step back from the door. "Come in…of course. Both of you."

West nodded and walked through the door, followed closely by Connor Frasier.

"Can I offer you something? Coffee, perhaps?"

"No, sir. Thank you."

West and Frasier were both wearing fresh, crisp uniforms, at first glance looking as though they'd just come from the parade ground. But Harmon had served alongside both officers for decades, and he knew them well. His gaze shot to the red streaks in West's eyes, and the wrinkles on Frasier's forehead. He suddenly realized the two officers hadn't gotten up this early. They had never slept.

He turned back toward a small bot standing near the wall. "Coffee," he snapped at it. He glanced at Frasier and West. "Are you sure?"

West nodded, and Frasier after her.

"For one," he added, watching as the bot moved to the kitchen.

He turned back toward his visitors. "So, what is going on? I can't imagine it's anything good."

"Max…" West's voice was strained, forced. She was clearly uncomfortable with what she had to say.

"Just spit it out, Erika. How long have we known each other?"

"Sir, General Frasier and I had a discussion…about the election. About the future."

Harmon stared back, a suspicious look on his face. "And?"

"Well, sir…we believe that a victory by Jacques Diennes… or any of the other major candidates would be disastrous for the republic."

Harmon gestured toward the sofa. "Please, have a seat." He paused. "I don't disagree with you…but I don't suppose that is any amazing revelation. I have done all I could to win the election." He waved again toward the sofa, and then he sat down after his guests had. "I'm afraid the Mules' rebellion has not helped me."

"Sir…" West fidgeted, her discomfort even more pronounced than it had been. "With no disrespect, General Frasier and I believe your reelection at this time is extremely unlikely. But there are other ways to retain the presidency…"

"Admiral West, please tell me you are not here to propose treason…"

West winced. Harmon had hit her where it hurt.

"Mr. President, perhaps labels like that are not useful in this instance." Frasier's voice was calm, for once cooler than that of the legendary block of ice, as West was sometimes known.

"Label? You think it is just a label? I don't believe that, Connor, not for a moment. You are talking about overthrowing the government, aren't you? A coup?"

The two conspirators' faces were tentative, their eyes looking away from Harmon. Finally, West looked right at the president. "It is not an overthrow…you would simply remain as president. All we want to do is postpone the elections. You can declare a state of emergency…use the standoff with the Mules as an excuse."

"Is that what you really want to see? Me become a tyrant? The republic's first president resisting defeat in an open election, refusing the orderly transition of power?"

The two were silent, fighting to hold Harmon's gaze.

"You know what would happen. The people would go crazy. There would be riots in the street…the republic would be mortally wounded. Even if I voluntarily gave up power at some point in the future, the precedent would be set. Anyone who can gather enough support from the military can seize—or retain—power. Better I had died with Terrance than that."

"Sir…" West was struggling for words. She had prepared for this moment, thought a hundred times about what she would say. But now it was all gone, her mind lost, confused.

"Enough with the high-minded nonsense. Are you posing for history's assessment…or do you really care about what happens to the republic?" The voice came from the next room, and a second later Mariko Fujin walked through. She was wearing a long robe, and her waist-length black hair was almost as messy as her husband's.

"Mariko…you have to understand…"

"No, Max…you have to understand. You are speaking now like an academic, like someone pontificating with no thought of reality. Of course you would prefer not to be in this position. That is obvious. It's also irrelevant. You are in this position, and the rest of us along with you, and what you choose to do will have real implications for the future."

Harmon looked at his wife. Fujin was small, barely a meter and a half tall, and less than forty-five kilograms, but her voice resonated with power, with toughness. She was one of the fleet's most famous officers, a grizzled warrior who had stepped in when Admiral Hurley was killed, and led the remnants of the fighter corps in the final battles of the war. She'd been wounded multiple times, and she'd run up a list of kills that was still the talk of the Academy.

"So, the answer is to become a dictator, to tear up the constitution I helped to create?"

"What alternatives do you propose? How long after Diennes is sworn in will it be before the Mules are wiped out…or perhaps worse, before they unleash whatever power they have in their own defense. The Tanks will be next, you know that." She flashed a glance over at Frasier. "And the Marines are at least half Tanks…and those men and women know how to fight. Do you think they will turn their weapons on their own kind? A man like Diennes will destroy all we have built, and the fact that the people just might be scared and stupid enough to elect him is not enough reason to let it happen. Not when you can stop it."

"So a good tyrant over a bad elected leader?"

"You can say 'tyrant' all you want, but you know that is not you…" She looked around the room. "…and we all know it too. You didn't even want to run this time. You will not cling to power, you will do what you must to avert disaster, and then you will retire, pass on the reins of government to someone trustworthy."

Mariko stared at Harmon. He looked tense, unconvinced.

"You know Terrance would have done it. My God, he did it when the fleet was on the run. What legitimate authority did he have to compel the national contingents to remain with the fleet, or to crush the separatist movement we came to call the 'mutiny?' Or to put Admiral West in command of the fleet in his absence, though he had no authority to name commanders over the multinational force?" She paused. "He did what he had to do…to save us all. I'm sure some of his decisions were difficult ones for him, but he made them. He did what he had to do, putting aside his doubts and guilt. And he saved us all."

She stared right at her husband. "And now it's your turn, Max. You stand here for Terrance…will you do what he would have done, what has to be done? Or will you stand on principle and watch the republic destroy itself?"

Harmon sighed hard, looking back at Mariko for a few seconds. Then he turned toward West and Frasier, breathing hard again. "What preparations have you made?"

West paused, nodding with relief as she realized Mariko had convinced her husband. The pilot had served her people with unmatched distinction in the cockpits of her fighters, but West knew she had never done more than she just had, standing in her home in a bathrobe.

"The fleet is secure, sir. I relieved several officers I was concerned wouldn't go along with us. They were placed on leave and told the transfers were pending promotion to higher rank. The satellites, the orbital stations…all are secure. You will control planetwide communications, and you will have the ability to deny these to anyone else."

Harmon looked uncomfortable, more so with every word West spoke. But he just nodded and said, "Very well, Admiral." He turned toward Frasier.

"Sir, I have taken steps much like Admiral West's. Obviously, much of our strength is deployed around the Mules' compound, but I have reliable units positioned at all critical ground-based installations…power facilities, com stations, supply centers." He paused. "And I have a platoon on standby, ready to take position here." He hesitated again. "I have loyal officers waiting for word to get your daughters, sir…and bring them back here for their protection."

Harmon winced when Frasier mentioned his daughters, but he just nodded. "Very well, General." He looked toward Fujin again. "Are you sure about this?" He turned toward the others. "All of you? I see you have prepared, and I have no doubt your preparations are exemplary. But are you willing to accept what all that this means? All of you? Now and in the future?"

"Yes, sir. You have my loyalty…now and always." West's voice was crisp, her words solemnly spoken. "And I truly believe this is what must happen—to save the republic. It is no different than the mutiny so many years ago…and if Admiral Compton had not done what he did, I believe we would all be dead now."

"I am with you too, sir. There is more at stake than just the crisis with the Mules. I can see the divisions within the Corps as well, the strain between the Tanks and the NBs. It is foolish, a problem that shouldn't exist. But politicians will always pick at and exploit differences between us. It is their route to power. We avoided that problem for many years after we first arrived. Our people were just relieved at the chance to build a new home.

But now we are going down the same path the Alliance did... and I'd see us avoid that trap if possible. I can think of no one better to lead us around it than you."

Harmon nodded. "I hope I can live up to your expectations...I am far less certain than you seem to be." He turned toward Mariko. "And you most of all must be sure of this, Mariko. You will be the wife of a dictator. In spite of what you all have said, many will call me tyrant. You will be branded with this."

"Let them brand you whatever they want. Let them brand me. I am tough enough to take whatever they throw our way. And my bruised feelings are not a reason to allow the republic to fall into civil war and destruction." She looked right into his eyes. "I am with you, my love, now and forever."

Harmon sat silently for a moment, his eyes dropping to the floor. Finally, he looked up. "Okay, my co-conspirators...let's do this." He turned toward Frasier and West. "Get your people in place...we need everything secure before a word of this gets out."

"Yes, sir." West and Frasier answered almost in unison.

"Once everything is in place, I'll give an address, try to figure some way to make this sound like anything but what it really is." He stood up abruptly. "But first I'll change...I'm not sure a bathrobe is suitable attire for a coup."

*   *   *

"How do I look? Appropriate for a despot in the making?"

Fujin looked back at Harmon and frowned. "Stop that. It's not funny. You're doing what you have to do, not plotting to seize power for personal gain."

Harmon nodded. "You're right. I just feel...I don't know, like this is wrong. I know what we discussed, and I agree with it all. But it is still difficult."

She reached over and put her hand on his arm. "You can do

this. You are strong, and you're a good man. And you are taking this action to save your people, no less than Terrance did."

Harmon's head snapped around, his eyes catching West and Frasier walking up toward him.

"It's done, sir. The fleet and orbital platforms are on limited alert, and all key ships are under the control of reliable officers." West leaned forward, speaking softly.

"All ground installations are occupied as well, sir. We control all communications, all government and military facilities, all weapons storage, all transportation systems." Frasier followed West's lead, angling his head toward Harmon's and whispering.

Harmon just nodded. Then he straightened up and ran his hands over his spotless suit, brushing it flat, neatening the few wrinkles. "I guess there is no cause for delay. It's time for the people of Earth Two to find out they do not actually live in a democracy."

Mariko frowned again. Harmon suspected his wife knew his self-deprecation was part of his method for dealing with what he had to do. But she was a true believer, and she considered his angst and guilt to be misplaced. He knew that well enough, and he even understood her opinion. But he was the one stepping up, as so many dictators and strongmen had in human history. Perhaps he was different, but he knew he would have to prove that...and for today, most of the men and women who watched his broadcast would follow him out of fear.

But if that's the way it has to be...

He turned and walked toward the podium. He glanced over at the man behind the camera, and he got a thumbs up response in return. Everything was ready.

"Mr. President!" A uniformed officer was running across the studio toward Harmon. Two of the extra Marine guards Frasier had assigned to protect the president moved quickly to intercept the visitor, but Harmon yelled out for them to stand aside.

"Captain, what is it?" Becky Barth was one of Harmon's aides.

Barth slipped forward between the two, now stationary,

Marines and ran right up to Harmon.

"Mr. President...Cyclone has just transited into the system."

Harmon felt his stomach clench. Cyclone was one of Admiral Frette's vessels. He couldn't think of any good news scenario for the ship to arrive back alone.

"Status report?"

Barth looked around. "Sir, she sent a coded message the instant she emerged from the gate. It is highly classified..."

Harmon turned and looked out across the large room. "Out! Now! Everybody...I need this room cleared." He turned toward West and Frasier. "Admiral, General...stay. And you, Mariko. Everybody else, take a break. I'll call for you when I'm ready to resume."

He watched the technicians filter out of the room, along with his other aides. The Marine guards hesitated.

"Both of you...wait outside. I'll be fine. General Frasier can keep an eye on me."

The Marines turned slowly, looking uncomfortable, but also clearly not willing to disobey the president's direct order.

Harmon turned toward Barth. "What is it, Captain?"

"Admiral Frette reports contact with a significant fleet, sir. Her forces engaged and destroyed the enemy, and on her own discretion the fleet had proceeded farther along Hurley's course. She sent Cyclone back with copies of all the intel her people collected...and a warning."

The officer looked at the small group gathered around her. She knew they were the top officials of the republic, but she still looked uncomfortable. Then the words came from her lips.

"The First Imperium is back, sir..."

Chapter Twenty-Three

Captain Josie Strand's Address to her Crew
Near the Beginning of "Strand's Stand"

I know you're scared...we're all scared. Even Admiral Compton was scared during his great battles. We are all human beings, nothing more than men and women standing against the forces that would destroy us. But the great admiral and his legendary fleet, our fathers and mothers, pushed back against the fear. They refused to accept the inevitability of defeat...and their defiance matched the overwhelming strength of the enemy.

We fight now, not a different war, but the same one they did, against the same enemy. The years of peace, the shining time when we were born and came of age, was merely a respite. We know that now, and we will rise to the challenge, take our place in the line of battle. The courage and strength of those who came before us brought our people to a new world, founded a new society, and built a future, for themselves...and for us, the first generation born on Earth Two.

We are young, many of us in our positions far earlier than those of the old fleet had been. We have seen little of war, fought in only one battle before this. Yet, here we stand, steadfast, ready to do what we must. Our situation is desperate, but that is not enough to defeat us...for we are the children of heroes, and we shall not fail to live up to their example.

Fight with me, officers, spacers! Stand to your posts, and face the enemy...and claim the honor and renown that is yours by birthright. Fight to save your home, the one our parents built for us, the only one we have ever known...

Flag Bridge - E2S Compton
System G47
Earth Two Date 12.09.30

"Admiral, we're picking up enemy forces moving into the system through our entry warp gate." Kemp's voice was edgy, but Frette could hear the anger as well, and the determination. It was a familiar sound, one she remembered from the days of the fleet's battles. And now she was hearing it in the voices of her younger spacers as well. She was proud of them, and she felt pride, satisfaction that the years of training were paying off. But there was an undercurrent of sadness there too. For the past decade, while she and Erika and the other veteran officers had trained their successors, she had hoped they would be spared the nightmare her generation had faced.

"Set a course to intercept, full thrust. Excalibur and her escorts will go with us...relay the orders."

"Yes, Admiral."

Frette stared down at the floor in front of her. She didn't like how things were shaping up, not one bit. Her instincts had run wild when she'd gotten word that the enemy was coming from two different warp gates almost simultaneously, and news that another force was coming through the last gate, from the very direction her fleet had come from, left little doubt. She had led her people into a trap.

Frette was angry with herself, and fighting off doubts. For all the fame she'd acquired with her crazy atmospheric landing stunt to rescue Max Harmon from the imperial home world, that had been the first time she'd commanded so much as a ship in a wartime situation. Her combat experience was mostly as a tactical or weapons officer. True, she had gone on to lead forces against several of the attacks from residual First Imperium forces, but though combat was always difficult and terrifying, none of those conflicts had been in doubt. The enemy forces had all been outnumbered and detected long before they got close to Earth Two, and the fights had all been mostly one-sided.

Now she was facing something serious, worse even than her nerves had made it out to be when her people had faced the first imperial force. It wasn't just the number of ships involved…it was the complexity of the plan. The task forces that had thrown themselves at Earth Two in the years after the Regent's destruction had been individual, under the command of their dedicated AIs. But this was clearly an overall plan, with forces coming in from three directions…and even the advance force her people had defeated.

A force they sacrificed just to lure us forward…

She sat in her chair, holding back the sigh fighting to get out. She wasn't happy with the situation, not at all. She'd planned to keep her heavy units together, but now her battle line was scattered across the system, two capital ships at each of the two far warp gates, battling to hold the line, and the last two ready to move back to the entry gate…and face whatever was coming through there.

"Excalibur and supporting ships report ready. Commander Minh advises the reactor is operating at full power, and we can execute thrust on your command, Admiral."

Frette stared at her screen for a few seconds, her mind redoing the calculations, remind herself how far apart her three forces would be. She'd make a mistake, she was sure of that. Perhaps it was too many years of peace…or too much pride that turned so easily to arrogance. Or maybe she just didn't have the experience at command she needed for this situation. She'd worked for years alongside Erika, but she couldn't match her companion's decades commanding fleet-sized forces.

She knew she should have been more cautious, but now her people had stepped in it, and she didn't know what to do. If she didn't engage the ships coming through the entry warp gate, they would be free to move anywhere in the system…including outflanking Strand's and Akira's forces. Her two subordinates were performing well, bracketing their warp gates and blasting the enemy ships as they emerged. They were in extremely strong positions, but that wouldn't last if enemy forces got around them. No, she had to take out whatever had followed her fleet into the system.

She wouldn't have the same advantages as Strand and Akira. By the time she got to the warp gate, the enemy force would be in the system already, deployed and ready to engage her. But she had one thing, the strongest ship ever built by mankind.

Once again a Compton would stand in the breach...and just maybe save the day again.

*   *   *

"Keep firing!" Josie Strand was standing on the bridge again. The adrenalin was coursing through her veins along with the stims she'd just taken. She was wired, alert, sharp...and far too fidgety to sit down. Her crew didn't pay it any attention...they knew her by now. And they knew better than to say anything, including warning her that she was taking a risk not being harnessed into her chair. One solid hit could send her flying into a bulkhead...and a broken back or neck was a foolish way to die in a space battle. She knew all that, and she'd buckled herself in half a dozen times, but she kept unharnessing and leaping out of the chair again.

"Captain, gunnery stations report the batteries are too hot. They're requesting permission to reduce the rate of fire by thirty percent." Hahn looked over at her, his eyes telling her he already knew her answer.

"Negative, Commander. Order Commander Willis to do whatever he can to increase the heat dispersal rate, but the batteries are to maintain maximum fire."

Her eyes were fixed on the display, watching as another First Imperium Gargoyle emerged from the warp gate...and right into Starfire's concentrated fire. The display only showed an icon, a representation of the enemy's location, but Strand could imagine her ship's energy weapons ripping into the enemy vessel, tearing through its hull and bringing destruction to its inner compartments.

The First Imperium's technology was highly advanced, but they suffered the same systems disorientation the human vessels did when emerging from a warp gate. Indeed, it was even worse, as the AI's that ran the ship were non-functional for the first minute or two after a transit.

She watched as the report came in...the enemy Gargoyle destroyed. It was the tenth ship her force had eliminated, and they'd hardly taken a scratch in return. It was a dream position, but she knew it wouldn't last forever. Her guns would burn out, their casings literally melting as some point. Despite her firm order to keep firing, she knew she would have to rest the batteries soon, or at least reduce the rate of fire. And when she did, it would give the emerging enemy ships a respite, one that would allow them to get some ships into the system and operational. Then it wouldn't be a one-sided fight any more.

She stared down at her indicators. The lasers were still in reasonable shape, but the main particle accelerators really were on the verge of burnout. She had to think of something...

Her eyes caught the missile displays. Her external racks were gone, expended in the first encounter with enemy forces, but her magazines were full. Starfire was well inside normal missile range, but now a thought crept into her head, a lecture at the Academy, one they'd scheduled for a slow time, just before the semester break. It was a tactic used during several of the fleet's battles, one pioneered by Admiral Compton. The use of missiles at short range, fired in sprint mode directly at targets.

It was normally almost impossible to score a direct hit on an enemy vessel with a missile, at least firing from normal range. The short ranged tactics used in the fleet's battles had involved huge numbers of weapons, taking advantage of the slightly larger but still small chance of each weapon scoring a hit. But Starfire was in a unique situation now. Strand knew where each enemy ship was emerging...and she could be sure there would be no course changes, at least for a minute, perhaps two.

"I want all missile launchers loaded." A short pause. "Intrepid is to load all launchers as well." It still felt strange commanding another capital ship, being responsible not just for her own vessel and crew, but another battleship…and both sets of escorts. She had to keep reminding herself she had an entire task group at her command, and not just Starfire.

"What?" There was confusion in Kahn's voice.

"You heard me, Commander." Her voice was sharp, harsher than she'd intended. But she didn't have time to explain herself. In fact, she didn't even have time to deal with her crew…

She plopped down hard in her chair, grabbing the headset and clipping it in place. She fired a thought to the ship's AI. "Load all missile tubes. Download sprint mode nav data, and prepare to arm and fire."

"Loading sequence initiated. All tubes will be ready in forty-seven seconds." She could have sworn she'd 'heard' the AI's response, but she knew it hadn't been audible, just a thought injected into her mind. She found the direct connection to her ship's main operating system disconcerting, but she could see the advantages too. The next generation of the republic's spacers would probably man a battleship with no more than a dozen souls, and each would be totally integrated with the electronic intelligences that ran the vessel.

If there is another generation…

"Commander Kahn…the main batteries are to cease fire in forty seconds. I want full emergency cooling protocols as soon as they shut down."

"Yes, Captain."

Strand knew Kahn had his neural link connected…and that meant he knew exactly what she was doing. She wasn't sure he understood, not yet. But he would in about forty seconds.

"Commander Willis reports ready on emergency cooldown. Main guns will be ready to resume fire two minutes after initial shutdown."

"Very well, Commander." The accelerators had their own liquid nitrogen cooling system that siphoned off the immense heat the weapons generated, but the emergency protocols would increase the flow rates, well past safety levels…almost to the red line. She'd half expected a complaint from her engineer, or at least a warning of the risks. But Willis was a pro, and he knew the situation as well as she did.

"All launchers loaded, Captain. Intrepid is still loading…"

"Arm all missiles. Enter guidance coordinates…target the warp gate, the primary emergence point of the enemy ships. Intrepid is to stand by."

"Yes, Captain." Kahn's voice was more animated, the dawn of understanding. A few seconds later: "All missiles armed."

"I want two launches every ten seconds…and I want each tube reloaded the instant it launches. All safety procedures are waived."

"Yes, Admiral. Gunnery reports main batteries have ceased fire. Emergency cooling procedures underway."

"Very well…launch first pair of missiles."

"Yes, Admiral."

An instant later Starfire shook lightly. It was barely perceptible, but Strand could feel it.

She stared at the display, watching the two small dots appear…her two missiles. They moved toward the warp gate, accelerating at maximum, burning their fuel supplies at a rapid rate. But it didn't matter. They weren't intended to maneuver, or to target enemy ships specifically. That wouldn't even be possible in the gravity well of the warp gate. No, they were sprint missiles, fired directly at a point in space, where they would detonate. It took pinpoint targeting to make sprint missiles work in normal combat…but the warp gate's core was less than ten kilometers in diameter, and that meant the missiles' lethal zone could cover a good portion of its surface area.

She felt the ship vibrate again, the next two missiles launching. And two more dots appearing on the display.

"Admiral, Intrepid reports her missiles are armed and ready to launch."

"Very well." Strand closed her eyes, focusing on the neural connection. It was a little disorienting switching back and forth between interacting with the ship's AI and snapping orders to her officer. She took a deep breath and centered herself. They'd taught meditation techniques in the Academy when they'd introduced the neural links. But the direct connection to a ship's AIs was a new system then, still experimental, and she'd only had a brief introduction. She knew the officers now at the Academy would be more comfortable interacting with their AIs... but none of them were with her now, so she had to make the best of it herself.

"Commander, Intrepid is to commence launching as soon as our tubes are empty. Same procedure, two launches every ten seconds."

She turned to look at the display, but then she stopped and closed her eyes again. She didn't need the screen...all the data was there, pushed right into her mind by the AI. It was fascinating and disturbing, but there was no question she had a better view of what was happening. She could see her missiles, moving toward the warp gate. The lead birds had exhausted their fuel... they were ballistic weapons now, moving forward at close to 0.3c toward their detonation points a few klicks from the warp gate.

She watched as the lead missiles moved closer...and a new enemy ship slipped out of the warp gate and into normal space. She saw her warheads approaching. She knew it wasn't the actual events she was seeing, just a recreation the AI was projecting into her mind. She watched the missiles move forward... and then detonate. The first pair bracketed the enemy vessel, one exploding about a kilometer away. That was close enough to cause massive damage, but none of that mattered. Half a second later, the second missile detonated...less than two hundred meters from the enemy vessel.

The stricken ship was blasted with immense radiation. Its hull was superheated, melting and then vaporizing in a fraction of a second. Strand's lips moved, morphing slowly into a smile, one that widened as the next enemy ship transiting suffered the same fate. It was working. The two capital ships had enough missiles to bombard the warp gate until their main batteries were cooled and ready to resume fire. That didn't mean she could hold the warp gate forever...but it definitely extended the time she could last.

The enemy has to run out of ships eventually...
Don't they?

Chapter Twenty-Four

Excerpt from President Compton's Speech Emergency Declaration

My fellow residents of the republic, I come to you today on a matter of the greatest importance. As you all know, some time ago we lost contact with the vessel Hurley, which had been assigned to deep space exploration and warp gate cataloguing. In response, I ordered Admiral West to assemble a search and rescue mission, and Admiral Frette took command of the expedition. We have now received word from the admiral, and the news is grave.

Our forces have been engaged in battle, and they have confirmed the identity of the enemy. Ships of the First Imperium.

The old enemy has returned, and battle has been joined. I don't have to remind anyone of the threat First Imperium forces represent, not only to Admiral Frette and her fleet, but also to the very survival of Earth Two and the republic. I cannot help but think of the days of the old fleet's journey, something many of you will remember, as no one who was there will ever forget. And now, as then, the deadly danger requires decisive action.

I have signed an executive order, effective immediately, indefinitely postponing the election planned for next month. I know this will be upsetting to many who oppose my continued leadership, but we now face a grave threat, and we cannot now afford the risk of internal dissent. Further, I have declared martial law and suspended the constitution for the duration of the crisis.

I will address you again when we have more information,

and further details on the steps we will be taking to prepare for what we now face.

To all the people of the republic, Tanks and Natural Borns, Mules, those who support me...and those who have opposed my candidacy...I ask you all to join with me now, to rekindle the spirit that brought us here, that saved the fleet from certain destruction. For we are one, and our differences shrink to insignificance when we are confronted with an outside enemy.

The republic...forever.

Navy Headquarters
Victory City, Earth Two
Earth Two Date 12.09.30

"I guess I should be grateful for the First Imperium. They certainly gave me a better reason to seize power than the stuff we came up with." Harmon's voice was dark, ominous. His tone wasn't exactly sarcastic, but his comments were definitely a sort of gallows humor.

West just nodded. She might have been angry at someone else for making a joke out of mankind's great enemy. She'd lost too many friends, too many comrades to the First Imperium, Terrance Compton right at the top of that list. But Max Harmon got a pass as far as she was concerned. He'd fought as hard as anyone in the war...and he'd been one of the small group that had infiltrated the enemy home world and destroyed the Regent. Besides, he'd been even closer to Compton than she had been...and he'd been devastated at the admiral's death.

"So, what do we do? We have no idea what Nicki Frette and her people are up against. The reports suggest they got through the battle with relatively light damage...but now she's taken her forces deeper into space, following Hurley's course."

"What can we do? We don't have anything concrete, at least no actionable data. For all we know, Admiral Frette destroyed the entire enemy force. We have faced such groups since the Regent's destruction." Connor Frasier sat along the one edge of the large conference table. He'd had his armor on earlier, prepared for any unrest that might have occurred after Harmon's speech, but the Marines had things well in hand, and Frasier had taken the chance to ditch the cumbersome suit.

The streets were quiet, even the political candidates staying out of sight. Harmon had taken no chances…he wasn't about to allow the politicians running against him to suggest he was lying about the threat. After his speech, he'd broadcast the footage Frette had sent back, scenes that left no doubt, none at all, including visual images that chilled the blood of every pilgrim watching. Human forces had again faced those of the First Imperium.

The younger residents of Earth Two had been raised to fear the First Imperium above all things, to view the ancient robots like some kind of bogey men, something fit for nightmares but not to face in reality. And for the Pilgrims it was even worse. The republic's older residents had already faced the forces of the terrible enemy…and they knew the horror was real.

"We haven't been attacked in more than twenty years." Erika West's tone was no less dark than Harmon's had been, perhaps more so. "There is something different this time. The fleet is out there…facing God knows what…"

"You think she made a mistake, don't you? You think she should have turned back."

West forced herself to look back at Harmon. "Yes, sir…" Another pause. "I don't know, sir…I'm just worried…"

Harmon nodded, giving West a sympathetic glance. "Nicki knows what she is doing, Erika. She can take care of her people…and herself." He said the words, but he wasn't sure he believed it. He owed his life to Frette, and she was among those few he counted among his true friends, but he found himself wishing West was with the fleet instead. For all her skill and courage, he knew Frette was treading new ground…while West had more than her share of fleet command experience. He scolded himself for sending Frette, for not taking the threat seriously enough.

West just nodded, looking just as uncertain as Harmon felt.

"I'm also concerned about these minor discrepancies in ship masses and designs. Are these newer ships than the ones we fought before? Or older ones that had been deployed on this far frontier?" Harmon wasn't expecting an answer, but he looked around the table anyway, gauging reactions.

"It seems we have two choices. Do we send reinforcements to Admiral Frette, another fleet to meet her forces…and bring them back to Earth Two? Or do we stand here, prepare our defenses…and wait to see what happens?"

West fidgeted in her seat, but she didn't answer. Harmon knew what she wanted to say. West was a fighter, and her every instinct would drive her to offensive action. But it was more than just that. West's thoughts would be on Nicki Frette. She would want to go to the aid of her lover, that was a natural enough reaction on its own, but he suspected there was more. He guessed that West was also afraid Frette was in over her head, that if no aid was sent, she would die…and the fleet would be destroyed. He guessed she was thinking that for a simple reason. He was thinking it too.

"My first impulse is to send a relief force. We do not leave our people out there alone, not when we have the strength to come to their aid. It is not who we are. I learned that at the side of Admiral Compton, and I know if he were here with us, he would send the fleet." Harmon paused, his eyes dropping from West's gaze to the floor. "But the admiral would have thought of his duty to Earth Two as well, to the people of the republic. If we send another significant fleet, will we have enough to defend our home system if we are attacked? Admiral Frette took a significant percentage of our active and commissioned ships… sending another force that size would gut the Home Fleet.

"Our fixed defenses are strong, sir. Even with a skeletal fleet remaining, we can protect ourselves." Connor Frasier spoke tentatively. Harmon suspected Frasier considered naval affairs outside his area of expertise, but he also knew the Marine believed one thing to his core. You didn't forsake your people when they were in trouble. It was almost a religion to the Marines. He knew Frasier would support a relief mission…but he wasn't sure how much he should listen to his old friend's words. The Marines would always choose death over dishonor, but Harmon was responsible for the life of every man and woman in the republic, and his position denied him such noble stands.

"Perhaps, Connor...but we are talking about gambling the lives of every man and woman on Earth Two." Harmon paused...then he turned his head as the door to the conference room opened.

Hieronymus Cutter came walking through, followed by Ana Zhukov...and Achilles and H2.

"Achilles, thank you for coming." Harmon stood up, extending his hand, not entirely sure how the Mule would react. The two had been commanding opposing forces on the verge of combat...but immediately after declaring martial law, Harmon had ordered the Marines to stand down, and to fall back several kilometers from the compound. It had been a difficult decision, a show of faith, an attempt to defuse a conflict he knew should never have happened. He'd been nervous about what the Mules would do, but that concern only lasted a moment before he saw the battle bots also pulling back. Achilles' response had been immediate, and he had answered Harmon's good faith gesture with one of his own. After that, the two men had resolved their issues with a com session. The peace still hung on each man's willingness to honor their word, but each one had decided to trust the other.

"Of course, Mr. President. It seems we have a major problem; one I trust my people can help to resolve." Harmon noted the Mule's use of his title.

Another gesture...if Achilles really wanted the Mules to be independent, he wouldn't call me 'president.'

Harmon picked up a small tablet and handed it to Achilles. "The repeal of the Prohibition, as promised." Harmon paused. "And my apologies. This should have happened years ago."

The Mule reached out, took the small device, glancing at it for a second, perhaps two. "That is the last we need speak of it, President Harmon. What is past is past...and it seems our true problem now is what lies ahead. As has so often been the case in human history, an external threat has made our own disputes seem unimportant."

"Again, thank you, Achilles." His eyes looked past the Mule toward the others. "Hieronymus, Ana, H2...please sit. We need everything you all have to offer." He turned his head, looked toward the others at the table. "We have been discussing whether to send reinforcements to Admiral Frette...or whether to concentrate what forces remain here to defend against any attack that may come."

Achilles sat at one of the empty chairs toward the end of the table. "I believe there is one thing we must consider...forgive me if this has already been discussed..." The Mule paused for a second. "My studies of the war against the First Imperium, and the conflicts back in human space, are noteworthy for the lack of the enemy's use of weapons of mass destruction against planetary targets...even in response to the coalition's employment of such ordnance."

Achilles looked around the table. Everyone else was silent, clearly wondering where he was going with his point.

"The same was true during the fleet's journey across the imperium...and our study of First Imperium records holds the answer. The Regent, as sophisticated and capable as it was, operated in accordance with a number of directives. This may seem an unlikely fact, to our perspective, and likely that of the Ancients themselves when the Regent turned on them, but it is nonetheless true. And one of the primary directives prohibited the use of nuclear and antimatter warheads against imperial worlds. Indeed, look at the ruins the fleet encountered on so many planets. There was widespread destruction, ruins ravaged by the passage of time, even the remnants of the biological warfare designed to kill the Ancients themselves. But no radioactive wastelands, no worlds bombarded into lifelessness."

"What you say is true, Achilles. Indeed, the unwillingness of the First Imperium to use such weapons became a major component of coalition strategy during the war." Harmon wasn't sure where Achilles was going, but everything the Mule had said so far was correct. "What do you believe we can draw from these facts? That the First Imperium will not bombard Earth Two?"

"No, sir…quite the contrary. My point is simply this. Every analysis we have done, every review of the records left behind by the Ancients suggests one fact irrefutably. The last of the warriors of the Ancients chose this world…they selected it for many reasons, its climate, its resources…and its location. Outside the borders of the imperium." Achilles paused, his words hanging in the air.

Harmon stared back at the Mule. "Are you suggesting the First Imperium forces would not be bound by their previous restrictions. That they would attack Earth Two with weapons of mass destruction?"

Achilles looked back across the table. "I am saying we must consider that a significant possibility. Even a probability."

"So, you believe we should hold the fleet back to protect Earth Two against such an attack?"

Achilles sat motionless. "No, sir, I am proposing precisely the opposite. We should take the offensive, seek out and engage the enemy as far from Earth Two as possible…and do everything we can to ensure the war is fought far from here."

"I'm not sure I understand your logic, Achilles."

"We are not a world, Mr. President, though we possess one. Ninety-six percent of the population lives in Victory City, or within fifteen kilometers of it. The enemy does not need to conduct an extensive bombardment to depopulate the republic. A single antimatter warhead will destroy almost all our physical constructions…and at least nineteen out of twenty of our people. One shot, one missile slipped through the planetary defenses, and the war is lost."

"Doesn't that make it all the more crucial to concentrate our forces here? To defend at all costs to prevent such an attack from succeeding?"

Achilles shook his head slowly. "I understand your impulse, Mr. President, but I urge you to consider the facts in greater detail. First Imperium ships have maximum acceleration rates well beyond even those in our newest vessels. Their apparent access to large quantities of antimatter—something that seems to be confirmed by Admiral Frette's report—allows them to attain maximum thrust of nearly 100g. They have demonstrated their willingness to sacrifice ships in suicide assaults to attain tactical goals. I believe it is unlikely that we could reliably protect Earth Two from a deadly missile attack, even if every ship of the fleet was held back on the defensive."

Achilles turned toward West. "Admiral West, have you considered the tactical problem of dealing with a massive enemy attack, say several hundred ships, that emerge and accelerate at maximum thrust toward Earth Two? Could your forces—and the planetary defense systems—intercept every ship before any are able to fire against the planet? And could you intercept every missile they launch?"

West exhaled softly. "I have never reviewed such a scenario, Achilles." She paused uncomfortably. "But I am inclined to agree with Achilles' concerns. If a large force attacked, it is unlikely we could intercept every ship and every missile. If a massive enough force attacked, it would trend toward mathematical certainty that one would manage to get a missile through…particularly since their own survival in the attempt does not appear to be a priority."

Harmon leaned back in his chair. He looked around the room. Most of the faces staring back at him were non-committal, but the few that weren't were nodding their agreement. He realized he faced a fundamentally different situation that Terrance Compton had with the fleet. Protecting a hundred or more ships, which could scatter, hide, move…it was different than defending a single, stationary planet. Especially when almost everyone on that world was clustered into one small developed area.

The idea of sending away much of his strength, of leaving only a token force to support Earth Two's network of fortresses and fixed defenses, seemed reckless…but as he considered Achilles words—and West's as well—he began to realize what he had to do.

"Erika, I need you to assemble a proposed list of ships for a reinforcement fleet. And make it strong, if we do this, we need to fight this war out there somewhere...and we need to win it."

"Yes, sir...I will cull out the slower ships to remain on system defense duty. And with your permission, I will give orders to begin activating the mothballed squadrons...and calling the reservists to duty. If we push hard enough, we should be able to get some of the old ships in the line within two weeks...and back up the forces we leave behind."

Harmon stared across at West. He had a choice to make. Did he put West in command of the fleet, or did he hold her back to command the system defenses? He wanted to keep her, but he could only think of one other naval officer he trusted enough to take one of the two crucial commands. And that officer couldn't leave the system...his other duties made it impossible.

"You will lead the relief force, Erika, and when you link up with Admiral Frette, you will assume command of the combined grand fleet."

"Yes, sir." He could hear the relief in her voice. He suspected she had been ready to give him quite an argument if he'd ordered her to stay. "And who will command the forces in the system?"

"I have someone in mind, but you'll have to recall him from reserve status." He stared across the table, amused at the confusion in her expression.

He smiled, looking down at himself, putting his hands on his midsection. "I might have to suck in my gut a little, but I'm willing to bet I can still fit in my old uniform."

Chapter Twenty-Five

From the Log of Captain Josie Strand

I am commanding twelve vessels...commanding them in a combat situation. How did this happen? The captaincy of Starfire was an extraordinary promotion in itself, more than I, twenty-nine years old and unblooded in battle, could have imagined. But now I have other ships, other crews depending on me. And we find ourselves not only in battle, but holding the line against an unstoppable enemy force.

I have long studied the battles of the Pilgrims, the stories of how the old fleet reached Earth Two against the odds, of how the Regent had not only been defeated but destroyed. It is common for those of my age to look at the exploits of our parents with considerable awe...and a certain level of despair. How could we hope to match their exploits, to appear to history as anything less than a disappointment?

But now I see things differently, for the peace we have enjoyed for so long is clearly at an end. And I see the challenge those of my generation will face. The officers and the spacers of the fleet were heroes, men and women who accomplished the near impossible. But they were all veterans, officers and spacers who had fought the First Imperium in human space, and had first faced combat in the Third Frontier War. The captains who commanded battleships—and who led squadrons of ten or twelve vessels—were mostly in their forties, already hardened by war when they first sat in their command chairs. It is that which will be the challenge of my generation, to step forward, to shoulder

burdens far too soon, before we are truly ready. And to find a way
to step up, to prevail...for excuses have no place in life or death
struggles. We will either live or die...and the republic with us.

Bridge - E2S Starfire
System G47
Earth Two Date 12.09.30

"That's the last of the missiles..." Josie Strand's voice was
soft, faint, her words little more than a whisper to herself. She'd
held the warp gate for hours, far longer than she would have
dared to hope she could. But that stand was almost over. The
missile volleys had given her ships a chance to cool their superheated main guns while still barraging everything that came out
of the gate. But when her guns heated up again, she'd have
a stark choice...cease fire or keep shooting until her particle
accelerator batteries literally melted down. Either way, the path
would be clear for enemy ships to come pouring through the
warp gate.

The enemy had maintained the pressure, sending ship after
ship to almost certain destruction. Strand had read the accounts
of the enemy's relentless attacks, of their indifference to losses
as long as the mission was completed. But it was one thing to
hear about it, to read about it...and quite another to face it in
reality, to stare into her screens watching it happen right in front
of her. It was chilling in a way she'd never experienced before,
and her already substantial respect for the Pilgrims and what
they had accomplished with the old fleet grew.

The enemy had adapted to the situation. They were still
sending ships through to almost certain destruction, but the few
Gargoyles that had transited earlier had been replaced by Gremlins...and by even smaller ships of some previously unidentified
class Strand had christened Gnats. The enemy was willing to
continue to lose vessels to force their way through the gate, but
they were only sacrificing light units. Strand had read about

the enemy's battle line vessels, the Leviathans and the immense Colossuses, and she wondered if any of those monsters were stacked up even now on the other side of the gate, waiting for her guns to fail, for her missiles to run out.

"Captain, I've got a priority message from Legatus. She is falling back with heavy damage. Enemy units are coming through the warp gate. Gargoyles..." Hahn paused abruptly. He turned and looked right at Strand. "And six Leviathans..."

The words hit Strand like a punch in the gut, but she focused and nodded calmly back to her tactical officer. "Very well, Commander."

It took forty minutes for that message to reach us...

Her thoughts were running wild, but she knew she couldn't let anyone see how unnerved she was. She had to hold it together, for her crew...and for the mission. But what was the mission now? Stay and hold the warp gate as long as possible...which she knew wouldn't be that much longer? Or pull back now, make a run for it? It would take some time for the First Imperium vessels to transit and get into formation before chasing her group, and that might be just enough to offset their greater acceleration capacity. At least for a while.

She suspected Admiral Frette would order her to pull back—when she received Legatus' communique and her own message got to Starfire. Staying at the warp gate was pointless, virtual suicide. The enemy advance through the other gate would cut her people off from the rest of the fleet. She glanced down at her screen, doing a few quick calculations. She figured she could just make it...if she bolted now. But expecting Frette to issue a withdrawal order and choosing to run on her own initiative were too different things.

She looked up at the main display, watching as another icon winked out of existence. It was one of the new ships, the very small ones. Her people had taken out over fifty enemy vessels, but the tonnage destroyed painted a different picture than the gross numbers. Except for a few mid-sized Gargoyles, she had expended all her missiles—and almost worn out her main batteries—to eliminate what was, in all probability, nothing more than the advance guard for a far heavier fleet.

She knew what she had to do…the only thing that made sense. But she felt like a coward. She wished the admiral could give her the order, take the burden from her shoulders, but Compton was almost ninety light minutes away, and even if Frette had issued a recall as soon as she'd received Legatus' report, it would still be more than an hour before the communique reached Starfire.

By then it will be too late…even if through some miracle we're able to hold the line here for that long, the enemy coming in from the other gate will be behind us…

She cleared her throat and took a deep breath.

"Commander Hahn, order to all vessels. Prepare to fall back. I want all ships ready for maximum thrust in two minutes." She knew her order was an unreasonable one, far too little time to switch over a reactor's full output from the weapons to the engines. But there was no choice. She knew ships had executed maneuvers like that before—and some far more difficult—but everything her people had been taught in the Academy told them what she was ordering was crazy.

We'll see how much our parents handed down to us, the strength inside them that made them so formidable…

"All batteries will cease fire in one minute."

Hahn stared back at her, a stunned look on his face. She gestured toward his station, and he turned and relayed her order. She suspected he tried to sound businesslike, as if he was relaying any other command…but he failed, his own doubts coming through in every word.

She knew the two minutes had been tight even if she had ordered the guns silenced immediately. But that wasn't an option. As soon as her task group ceased fire, enemy ships would keep coming through. And if her people stayed where they were any more than a minute, two at the most, the enemy would open fire.

She sat silently, pushing herself up, sitting almost at attention. Her face was like carved stone, and her eyes blazed with a burning light. Starfire was her ship…its crew, and its companion vessels, they were her responsibility. She understood, at least she thought she did, where the Pilgrims had found the strength to do all they had.

Her plan was daring, reckless even. It required every man and woman under her command to perform perfectly. And she had to bring them through it, hold them up, give them the strength to unleash the greatness within.

"All weapons...cease fire." Her voice was like ice. "Engineering, switch power to drive system now. Prepare for 65g acceleration, course 067.302.186...directly back toward our entry warp gate."

Her eyes darted around the room, watching her tiny bridge crew at their stations. She knew they were scared, overwhelmed... but they were doing what she had commanded. She felt pride, and a searing pit in her gut. These men and women deserved more than to be led to their destruction. They deserved victory, survival. And whatever it took, she would make sure she helped them win those things.

"All ships report ready to engage engines, Captain." Hahn sounded surprised that all the vessels in the group had managed to execute the difficult orders. But Strand wasn't. She understood now, the meaning behind all the accounts of the fleet's journey, how normal men and women had risen to such levels of heroism.

And she realized if the republic was to survive, they would have to do it again.

"Commander Hahn, order to all vessels...engage at full thrust."

*   *   *

"My God..." The words came out before Frette could react, hold them back. Her screen had filled with stats and schematics. Legatus and the rest of the ships of her group had just come with the range of the fleet net...and what her systems were transmitting told an ugly story.

The battleship was badly damaged, three of her secondary batteries out of commission. More than out of commission... two of them were twisted heaps of melted and re-hardened metal. Legatus was reporting her main batteries currently online, but a deeper look at the information on her screen told Frette the big particle accelerators were barely functional. They'd been out multiple times, but the ship's chief engineer and his exhausted team had somehow managed to restore functionality...despite the fact that dozens of support systems were blasted to useless scrap.

Frette could imagine conditions on Legatus. She'd served on badly damaged ships. The battleship's crew would be stringing wires around to bypass shattered conduits, sealing off depressurized compartments, battling radiation leakage. There would be casualties too, she realized...some dead, crushed by the collapse of structural supports or blown out into space when the outer hull was ruptured. Others would be wounded, overcome by radiation or burned by internal explosions.

Her mind slipped back, thirty years before, to the tumult, the stark terror of those awful battles...and through them the one thing that had rallied the men and women of the crew, pushed back the fear and galvanized them into an invincible force. The steady words of the one man, Terrance Compton, blasting through the com units on every ship.

Compton's words, his inspirational speeches had pulled his people back from the brink, when the darkness had threatened to take them. She could remember his leadership, how it had affected her.

That's me now...but how can I fill his shoes?

Compton had taken a beating as well, but the republic's newest battlewagon was the toughest thing in the fleet. Frette's flagship had stood firm, surrounded by its escorts, battling the First Imperium forces pouring into the system from behind her fleet. Akira's and Strand's groups had also been holding back the enemy, their mandates to stand as long as they could. But Compton's fight had been to the death. If she couldn't defeat the enemy forces coming through the warp gate leading back toward Earth Two, the entire fleet would be cut off...and surrounded by the enemy ships coming from every direction.

"Set a course directly for the warp gate...40g." She was staring at the small screen on her workstation. She had sent an order to Captain Strand on Starfire to abandon her warp gate defense and pull back to the original entry warp gate. She had been stunned how long Strand had managed to hold the line there... longer than her counterpart in Legatus...and Hiroki Akira was one of the fleet's best officers, a Pilgrim who had fought beside Terrance Compton. Frette had been surprised again that Strand had taken it on herself to order her forces to retreat, pulling back as soon as she received word that Akira's ships were falling back. The tactical brilliance Strand had displayed was gratifying, but the maturity was even more extraordinary in its way. Young officers tended to push too hard, fearing death less than they did being branded a coward. But Strand had inflicted massive damage on the enemy, and then she had pulled her forces back when her position became untenable, and she got her people out, ahead of pursuit.

Frette and her force had been just as heavily engaged, and her people had savaged the First Imperium ships that came up from behind the fleet. The center of the battle had been Compton going toe to toe with an enemy Leviathan. The two battleships had come to a virtual halt at a range of less than fifty thousand kilometers...and they pounded away at each other. Compton had been hit hard, and Frette had watched her displays nervously, keeping track of her overworked damage control crews and the small legion of bots that kept the battleship functioning in battle.

The Leviathan had been a tough opponent, it's powerful batteries firing, the deadly beams smashing into Compton's hull. But the human flagship was stronger still, larger and packed with First Imperium technology adapted by the Mules. Her reactors were the strongest mankind had ever built, and every watt of power they generated had poured through the dual particle accelerators built right into the spine of the colossal vessel. The devastation put forth by those deadly weapons at such short range was incalculable…and it had been too much for the Leviathan. Frette was still feeling the residual sensation, the electric charge of watching the enemy battleship torn to pieces…and finally obliterated as the magnetic fields enclosing its antimatter fuel failed.

The Leviathan had been the center of the enemy force, and its destruction had opened a gap in the enemy formation. Excalibur had pushed forward, engines blasting at 30g as she slid into the hole, launching missiles and firing its batteries in both directions. Captain Chandra's ship wasn't the equal of Compton, but it was a modern republic battleship, and its heavy weapons wrought massive destruction all around against the lighter Gremlins and Gargoyles. The fleet's cruisers and escorts followed Excalibur, targeting vessels damaged by the battlewagon's heavy guns and finishing them off. By the time they had finished, the First Imperium task force was gone, save for a rearguard standing between the human fleet and the warp gate. And now Frette's eyes were focused on the display showing the two dozen remaining enemy vessels. Her gaze was angry, feral.

"Commander Kemp, Compton and Excalibur and all escorts are to prepare to advance on the warp gate."

"Yes, Admiral."

"All ships are to engage as soon as they enter range." Her eyes moved across the large main screen. The display showed Akira's battered ships…and farther back Strand's task group, zipping across the system at almost 0.4c. Behind Strand came the enemy forces that had come through both of the far warp gates. The fleet that had savaged Akira's ships was in front, but Strand's pursuers were gaining ground.

As the enemy ships closed, her scanners picked up more and more data…and the true scope of the forces moving across the system. There were almost two hundred vessels…with a dozen Leviathans in the lead. It was enough to crush her fleet, to destroy every ship she had. There was no choice. Her group had to take out the enemy rearguard…and clear the way for Strand's and Akira's ships to reach the warp gate and escape from the enemy trap.

Escape…at least for now. But we're a long way from home, and those ships will keep coming.

If there was one thing Frette remembered about the forces of the First Imperium, it was their relentlessness. She could get her fleet out of the system—probably, at least—but she had no idea how she was going to get them home.

She sat up in her chair, pulling the headset on. She felt the AI connecting with her mind, feeding data to her. Four minutes. Four minutes to firing range. And when her forces had cleared away the enemy ships in front of the warp gate, her survivors could run…escape.

That is now our victory. To flee, to get away…even for a short time.

But what will I do then?

Chapter Twenty-Six

Planet X
Far Beyond the Borders of the Imperium

The trap is sprung. The enemy has advanced to the target system.

The waiting forces have been released, they have engaged the enemy, entering the system from all three warp gates. The force in place is more than adequate for the task at hand. The humans will be defeated.

The fleet at the enemy's own entry warp gate is weaker than the others, a diversionary force intended to be defeated. If the humans fight to the death in G47, so be it. Their entire fleet will be destroyed. But if they retreat, if they defeat the task force at their entry warp gate, we will pursue. We will follow them back... back to the other humans.

And then my forces will destroy them all...and the Regent shall be avenged.

Bridge - E2S Legatus
System G47
Earth Two Date 12.09.30

"Reroute the power grid. Shut down section 11C and bring the emergency conduits online. Now!" Hiroki Akira sat on

Legatus' flag bridge, shouting out orders, one after another. Some of them were crucial, actions that might keep Legatus in the fight for a bit longer. Others were mostly made up, orders he shot out just to keep his people busy, their minds occupied... anything to divert them from dwelling on the obvious realization that cast its shadow everywhere on the battered ship. They were all about to die.

The First Imperium forces had raced across the system, with Josie Strand's group bringing up the rear. Strand had conducted a magnificent warp gate defense, perhaps the best he'd ever seen...in action or even in the history books. Her use of missiles in sprint mode to hold the line while she cooled her main batteries had been ingenious...and brilliantly executed. She had held far longer than his own force, and hers were the last ships moving toward the warp gate. Except for Legatus and the two battered cruisers standing by her side. Akira's ship was battered beyond repair, beyond the ability to keep up with the retreating fleet. There was nothing he and his people could do...nothing save giving the last they had to buy time for their comrades to escape the trap.

He'd taken the initiative, suggested that the three vessels stand as a rearguard, sparing Frette the burden of issuing the command. She had argued with him at first, but he had simply countered her with facts. The three ships were badly damaged. They had no hope of outrunning the enemy. None. And if he was going to die—if his people were going to die—Hiroki Akira wanted it to mean something. Death helping to save the fleet, meeting the end in battle, fighting for something that mattered, was far preferable to being chased down as they lagged behind, engines failing.

Frette had argued, as Akira knew she had to, but in the end she had agreed. There was no way to save Legatus, nor the two crippled cruisers standing at her side. His people could abandon ship, but there was no way for the rest of the fleet ships to pick up the escape pods, not without allowing the enemy to catch them before they transited. The First Imperium didn't take prisoners, not unless they wanted specimens for dissection or experimentation. Better by far to die in battle.

Legatus shook hard again, another direct hit. She'd held against the light units in the lead of the enemy fleet, but now the Leviathans were coming into range. Akira didn't know what was holding his ship together. He was proud of Legatus, considering her more than a pile of plasti-steel and polymers. Like many captains, he thought of his ship as something almost animate, a friend, almost an extension of himself.

He watched his bridge crew, at their stations, holding firm despite the fear, the realization that they all had minutes to live. Akira felt the fear too, but it was less than he'd expected. He realized some part of him was ready, had been ready for thirty years.

His thoughts drifted back through the years, the image of a woman in his mind, young, beautiful, as she had been so long before. She had been gone so long, and yet she was still there, waiting for him in the depths of his mind.

He remembered when it happened, an image that had stayed with him, undiminished in its hideous intensity over thirty years. Kamiko, looking at him from behind the hyper polycarbonate of the radiation shield. She was standing when he first saw her, her uniform covered in blood. She turned, and her gaze fell on him, even as she sank to her knees.

He could remember the pain in her face. He'd known she was badly wounded, that the radiation levels beyond the barrier were fifty times the lethal level. But for all that knowledge, the inevitable conclusion had seemed somehow unreal, impossible to accept. Kamiko was dying...

He'd thrown himself against the clear shield, not even feeling the pain as his body slammed into the hard, immovable barrier. He knew he couldn't get to her...it would take a laser cannon to cut through the shield. And even if he could, all he would achieve was killing dozens more of Kyoto's crew. There was nothing he could do to save her. He couldn't even hug her, comfort her with his touch. All he could do was watch her die.

She had looked back at him, and for a brief instant he saw the familiar sparkle in her beautiful eyes. They had been the first thing he'd seen in her gaze so many years before…and now they were the last. The brightness seemed like a goodbye, and a few seconds later it faded, gave way to a dullness, and he could see death taking her.

He slammed his fists against the unyielding shield, screaming her name, though he knew she couldn't hear it. His eyes filled with tears as he watched her slump down slowly, her body finally lying motionless on the metal floor of the engine room.

He realized instantly she was dead, he felt it. But he had stood there, screaming her name, pounding against the polymer wall until his comrades pulled him away.

She had been gone thirty years now, and he still remembered her as though she was just in the next room. He'd worked tirelessly to help bring the navy into its new age, as defender of a small but growing republic. He respected the culture his people adopted, the promotion of reproduction almost as a civic responsibility. He had praised his colleagues as they had child after child, but he'd never joined them.

Kamiko had been his love, and she should have been the mother of his children. He'd never been able to move forward, to form a new relationship, or even to consider a platonic pairing to produce offspring. Part of him had died in that engineering compartment with Kamiko, and the shell that remained for so long had focused on work, on building the navy. It was all he had.

Until now. He could hear the dull rumbling, the internal explosions he knew were killing his ship, tearing its guts out from within. Legatus shook again, and the bridge lights flickered several times. He knew his ship had given all she had to give.

He felt the hit, and he knew immediately. Legatus shook hard, and then the bridge started spinning wildly. The positioning jets were gone, the inertial dampeners blasted to scrap. Akira realized that last hit had been a mortal wound, and he could feel his ship, yielding, giving up at last. He could feel the internal blasts shaking the dying vessel wildly.

His body slammed against the harness, and he could hear

the cries of his bridge crew, the panic that was finally spreading, slipping past the control they had maintained for so long. He'd though about the moment of his death before, as all warriors had at one time or another…and now he realized this was it.

He closed his eyes, breathing deeply but coughing on the noxious fumes pouring from the ventilation system. He felt a wave of fear, stark terror in the face of imminent death. And then calm, a woman's smiling face. Kamiko, waiting…waiting for him.

He was still smiling back at her when Legatus' reactor lost containment…and turned into a miniature sun.

*   *   *

Nicki Frette sat in her chair, hunched over, struggling to maintain the image she had tried to project to her officers and spacers. She was afraid, of course, but that wasn't what was bearing down on her. Frette was a combat veteran who'd faced death before. But leaving Hiroki Akira and Legatus behind had hit her hard, and she was struggling to deal with the aftereffects. She knew Admiral Compton had faced such terrible choices, and Erika too, but Frette had never before given an order knowing she was sending people to certain death. There had been no choice, Akira and his people were doomed anyway, their ships too damaged to keep up with the fleet. And their sacrifice had bought her time…time to get the rest of the fleet out of the trap.

The trap I led them into…

She had known Akira since the days before the fleet was trapped behind the Barrier, even before the First Imperium had invaded human space. The two had been junior officers serving on the cruiser Portland. She had been a newly-minted ensign serving on Portland's bridge, and Akira a liaison to the Alliance from the allied Pacific Rim Coalition. The Third Frontier War had been raging for several years, and the Alliance-PRC coalition had been hard pressed. The Marine Corps had been gutted in the disastrous invasion of Tau Ceti III, which had already acquired the name it would always be remembered by…The Slaughter Pen.

Alliance fortunes were to turn around soon, driven by Admiral Augustus Garret and the remarkable series of brilliant victories he would win, but Frette and Akira had lived through some desperate times first, as Portland and the other cruisers of her squadron tried to hold the line against the advancing Caliphate and CAC forces.

And now he's dead, gone. He lived through the nightmares we faced on Portland, survived all of Admiral Garret's campaigns…and he died serving under me.

"Admiral, we're picking up an energy spike at the G47 warp gate."

Frette heard Kemp's voice, slicing through to her, cutting through the self-pity she was wallowing in. His words were not unexpected, but she felt like they punched her in the gut anyway. The enemy was transiting into the system. Now, she could calculate the exact value of Akira's death, precisely what she had bought with his life.

"Distance from the warp gate, Commander?"

"Compton is one hundred ninety-three minutes from the gate, Admiral. Starfire and her group are one hundred twenty-seven."

Frette didn't answer. She just sat still, forcing her mind to focus. For as emotionally painful as it had been, sacrificing Legatus and her two escorts had been an easy call. The two ships had been doomed already…and she suspected Akira would have disobeyed her even if she'd ordered him to retreat. But Starfire and her group were another issue entirely. Strand's ships weren't damaged, they were only behind because they'd retreated from a greater distance.

The young captain wasn't commanding one wrecked capital ship…she had two battleships, both fully operational, and ten escorts. Twelve vessels and crews…and Frette knew she had a choice to make. Keep the rest of the fleet at full thrust…and leave Strand and her group to fight alone, more lives sacrificed to buy a brief respite. Or she could reduce acceleration, allow the trailing units to link up with the main force. That would reduce the time before the enemy caught her…but the fleet would be united, ready to fight as one cohesive force.

And die as one force…

She knew her fleet couldn't win. She'd seen the array of enemy forces in G47, and it was more than enough to obliterate every vessel under her command. She'd have had to sacrifice Strand and her people, save for one fact. Even if she did so, the enemy would still catch her long before she got back to Earth Two. And even if that hadn't been the case, she knew she could never lead the enemy back with her. Not unless she could destroy the enemy, wipe out every vessel they had, she couldn't go home.

And if her people were going to fight to the death, they were damned sure going to do it together. "Commander Kemp, compute a thrust plan to allow Captain Strand's ships to catch the main fleet and match course and velocity."

"Yes, sir."

She could hear the agreement in her tactical officer's tone. Kemp was scared…they were all scared. But if they had to face the enemy, they would do it together.

And if they were all going to die, they would die together.

"Commander Kemp, I want damage control teams on all ships to prioritize weapons readiness."

"Yes, Admiral."

If they we're all going to die, by God, we're going to die fighting…

Chapter Twenty-Seven

Note from Terrance Compton to Max Harmon
Found Attached to Compton's Log After His Death

Max, there are things I would say to you, words I would choose first to speak in person. Yet, we are in a life and death struggle, and I know the day of that conversation may never come. So, in case I do not survive our journey, I have left this for you.

First, I knew your mother well, and your father too before his tragic death. I know the burdens you faced, the difficulty of being the son of two such officers. But you need to know that both of them spoke to me of you, and whatever feelings you may have, whatever resentments, or regrets, know that they both loved you deeply, and were enormously proud of you.

I also want you to know what you have meant to me. I have served for more than fifty years, and the navy has been my life. It has brought me glory, success, advancement to the very top of my profession. But the fleet is a jealous mate, and she had denied me things others take for granted. I am wedded to duty, and it cost me Elizabeth. If I had been another man, if my stature had been less, perhaps our story would have been different. But none of that matters now. She is gone, on the other side of the Barrier, and I will never see her again. I take solace that she will be better off without me, for the weight I carry taints everything around me.

Max, if you are reading this, it likely means that I have been lost. I hope my death was a worthy one, and that I died in the service of those who have followed me. I know you are grieved, for your affection has been as clear to me these past years as your unyielding loyalty. There is little I can say to ease your pain, save to say to you that which I so many times wanted to in the past.

You have been the son I never had, Max, and I am profoundly thankful for the time you spent at my side. I couldn't have been prouder of a son of my own, and indeed, I couldn't have loved one more than I do you. You are an outstanding young officer...and an extraordinary man. Do not make the mistake I have made. Do your duty, as always, but never forget Max Harmon, the man. You are more than an officer, more than a leader. Live...in every sense of the word. Leave more behind than I did...for all the statues they will build in my image, and the stories that will be told of my exploits are cold, empty. Your true legacy will be those you leave behind who truly knew you, who loved you.

Navy Headquarters
Victory City, Earth Two
Earth Two Date 01.03.31

Max Harmon sat at his desk, one of his desks, at least. Now that he had returned to active duty, he had an office at navy headquarters in addition to the one he still occupied as president of the republic. He wasn't a legal scholar, but he doubted any reasonable reading of the constitution would allow him to hold the presidency and a military rank simultaneously...but then it didn't allow the president to declare martial law and cancel elections either, and he'd done that.

He was dressed in uniform now, his collar adorned with the admiral's stars he'd worn for all of eleven days thirty years earlier...before he'd reigned his commission to assume the provisional presidency. He'd dropped the 'provisional' part three months later after the republic's first election, one that had seen him get over ninety percent of the votes cast.

That was a long time ago. You'd have been lucky to get thirty percent this time. It's a good thing so much of the military was still in that minority of support...

He'd joked about wearing his old uniform, and he'd even gone so far as to treat Mariko to the show of him trying to squeeze into it. But he was thirty years older, and while he was still in reasonably good shape, the sleek, trim form of his youth was a thing of the past. He'd finally abandoned his efforts with the face-saving explanation that the navy had new styling, and he would have to get a new uniform anyway.

He had to admit, the new blues were an improvement over the old ones, far more comfortable...and practical as well. He'd thought it might feel odd to be in uniform again, but as soon as he'd slipped it on it felt like something he hadn't expected. He felt home.

His eyes were fixed on the screen now, staring at the reports zipping by. The early days of habitation on Earth Two had been ones of paranoia. The colonists had endured two years of constant warfare, death nipping at their heels every step of the way. Back then, people were constantly looking for the next crisis, and the periodic suicide attacks by rogue First Imperium forces only inflamed their fears.

The ships of the fleet had been gradually decommissioned, as new, robot-enhanced vessels came online and the growing industry of Earth Two put a premium on civilian workers. But the fear was still there, and few of the old vessels were scrapped. Midway was decommissioned after it was discovered her spine was warped from repeated critical hits. Admiral Compton's ship was preserved as a museum, but her days as a combat vessel were over. But to everyone's surprise, Erika West's flagship, Saratoga, which had been battered to the verge of utter destruction, had proven repairable. She had served as the republic's flagship for almost ten years before she was decommissioned and placed in the mothballed reserve, amid many celebrations and solemn speeches.

And now the old vessel was active again. She'd been towed out of her position orbiting Earth Two's second moon and placed in space dock at the orbital shipyard. Her reactor core had been replaced, and her weapons systems overhauled... all in less than three weeks. She'd even been restored to her old glory. Harmon had made her the flagship of the gradually assembling Home Fleet. Erika West had left behind thirty-odd, mostly light, vessels when she'd taken the best of the republic's remaining warships with her…and now that rag tag force was being augmented by the refurbished ships of the legendary lost fleet. Harmon had the shipyards working around the clock, the automated systems restoring a ship to active duty every three to four days.

The vessels were old, but many of their systems had been modernized. And there was something else, a hazy concept, but one important to an old spacer like Harmon. These ships were blooded, they had seen combat, performed again and again against the odds. They had seen their occupants to a new world, through all the death and power the Regent could throw at them. They were hallowed, sanctified by the blood of those who had died manning them. And Harmon knew they would do what they were called upon to do…now as they had so long ago.

He wondered about the men and women who would crew the newly activated vessels. They were all Pilgrims, the original officers and spacers who had served aboard these very vessels decades before. They had been a finely tuned unit then, almost fanatically devoted to Admiral Compton. But Harmon knew many of those men and women being called back to duty disliked him now. His popularity was better among the Pilgrims than the rest of the population, but nevertheless, thousands of the veteran spacers had been ready to vote against him. And now they were reporting for duty, preparing to fight in space once more at his command. Would they rally to the cause, rediscover their old élan? Or would they nurse their resentments toward him?

Harmon had done the best he could to mitigate the impact on the republic's veterans. The old ships were all equipped with new AIs and legions of robots. They would never be as manpower-efficient as the ships built in recent years, but they would function with a fraction of their old crews. And that allowed Harmon to cherry pick those recalled to the colors, to try and avoid the ones most opposed to him. It was an imperfect system, but it was the best he had.

"Max…" Mariko came walking in, the aide posted outside the door following her helplessly.

"It's okay, Lieutenant. You can let her through." He didn't envy a junior officer caught between the commanding admiral and his wife…and the fact that the admiral was also president pushed it off the scale.

"I need you to reactivate my commission."

Harmon looked up at his wife, feeling his stomach tighten. Mariko Fujin didn't look like much, barely a wisp of a woman standing there staring at him. He felt the same urge anyone would about loved ones, the desire to protect them, to keep them safe. But his wife had been one of the fiercest warriors the Alliance had ever produced, the protégé of the legendary Greta Hurley, and one of the deadliest pilots and experts on fighter tactics who had ever lived.

"Mariko…"

"Forget it, Max. Your loving urge to protect me is noted and appreciated, but I remind you that if the enemy manages to get close enough to Earth Two to drop an antimatter warhead on us, I'll be every bit as dead as I would be in a cockpit."

Harmon shook his head. There was an element of truth in her argument, but she had twisted the logic to make her point. He knew everyone was in danger…but he was also well aware that the fighter pilots in their twenty-ton craft were a lot more likely to die than someone sitting in Victory City waiting to see what happened.

She took a few steps forward and dropped herself in one of the desk chairs. "Max, I did some checking, and it turns out we've got a lot of operational fighters, new models…and even some of the old ones from the days of the fleet. We produced a lot of fighters early on, when we were trying to get as much defensive punch as quickly as possible. But then we made the breakthroughs in AI technology, and the fighter complements were scaled down to keep crew sizes small. A lot of those birds just ended up getting crated and locked away in the storehouses."

"I see where you're going, but who is going to fly those fighters? The Academy is only graduating forty pilots a year…and that's been the case for a long time. We've got the pilots stationed in the defensive platforms and the ones assigned to the fleet's ships, but not many more than that."

"You'd be surprised. I did some research. You know as well as I do that there is a lot of turnover in the fighter corps. Even when we're not suffering casualties in war…" She paused for an instant.

Harmon knew she was thinking of old comrades. The losses suffered by the fleet's fighter crews had been staggering, and he knew his wife struggled to make peace with her own ghosts from the past.

"Even beyond the casualties we suffered back in the day, we've always had transfers, crew members moving to other positions. We've got a good number of officers and crew with fighter experience currently assigned to different positions on the home fleet ships and defensive fortresses. They could be reassigned back to the fighter corps."

"Washouts? You want to build an expanded fighter corps out of people who couldn't cut it?" He knew the words were harsh as they left his lips, but they burst out anyway. He didn't really think a failure to fit into the specific culture of the fighter teams was a character flaw, but it wasn't likely to be predictive of success in one of the deadly craft either.

"I can work with them, Max. If they know how to fly—or how to work the weapons or keep the engines running—I can turn them into an effective force." She paused. "Of course, I will need the old veterans, but I have no doubt they will rally back to the colors." There were a few seconds of silence. Both of them knew how few survivors there were from the old fighter wings.

"Mariko…"

"There are over two hundred fifty fighters available to us, Max…more than half of them never used. Do you realize what that does to our defensive capability? And our ability to track down missiles? One of those crated fighters could be the one that picks off a warhead before it gets to Earth Two."

Harmon fidgeted in his seat. He hated the idea of Mariko back in the cockpit of a tiny, frail fighter...and he knew she'd never agree to command the corps from the relative safety of one of the fortresses. No, he remembered what she had been like back in the days of the fleet. Crazy...as absolutely single-mindedly insane as any pilot he'd ever known. Her record of kills was beyond impressive...he doubted he'd have even believed it if he hadn't seen her in action. It had been hard to watch her climb into her craft back then, when they were just two officers engaged in a passionate romance, jumping into bed every time the two managed to get off duty at the same time. Now, she was his wife of thirty years, and the mother of his children. He knew the republic was in deadly danger, and he was sure Mariko could get more out of the fighter corps than any other living man or woman. But all he wanted to do was protect her, keep her from the deadly danger.

Mariko reached across the desk, put her hand on his. "I know this is hard for you, my love. But you married a fighter jock, not a meek little science officer or comm specialist. I am what I am...and you know I can help defend Earth Two."

Harmon looked at her. His mind was scrambling, trying to find a reason to refuse her request. But he knew it was pointless. He loved his wife, but he respected her too, and he knew she had earned the right to be part of the defense of her adopted home world. She would die just like everyone else if the battle was lost. And he knew Earth Two's prospects, its chances in a desperate battle, were far stronger with Mariko Fujin leading her squadrons into battle.

He hated the whole thing, and the part of him that was Max Harmon screamed inside to say 'no,' to refuse her request. But the naval officer in him, the president—the successor to Terrance Compton—couldn't say no. Mariko Fujin was one of the most accomplished officers of the fleet, a bona fide war hero...and that trumped her place as Max Harmon's wife. At least when every man and woman on Earth Two lived under the threat of a First Imperium attack.

He struggled to tell her he would approve her request, reactivate her commission. But he couldn't force the words out. Finally, he just nodded.

She smiled. "I'll get started immediately. I just need you to authorize me to transfer the personnel...and of course, to reactivate the old veterans."

Harmon sat still for a few seconds. Then he nodded again.

"Consider yourself on active duty, Captain Fujin." He paused, looking across the desk at her, noticing the glint in her eye. Mariko Fujin had adapted to peacetime life...and a position teaching fighter tactics at the Academy. But Harmon knew she'd never lost her edge. The predator that lived inside all true fighter pilots was alive and well...and for all the fear he felt over the danger she would face, he almost pitied any enemies she would face.

Chapter Twenty-Eight

From the Personal Log of Erika West

Are you out here? Are you in trouble? I am coming...and I pray that I am not too late.

Why did I let you go? You deserve your rank, certainly, and no one has served the republic with more intelligence and loyalty than you. But you have never commanded a fleet in combat, not in a situation like this. Did I underestimate the danger of a major First Imperium incursion? Or was I simply too weak to look at you and tell you I didn't think you were experienced enough for this mission...and see the hurt in your eyes my lack of confidence would surely have caused?

Will my weakness cost you your life...cost me the person closer to me than anyone I have ever known? I am pushing the fleet, perhaps even beyond reason. I am doing all I can to get to you...but I can do nothing but sit here and hope we are in time. Hope that I have saved you from the doom my own failure has threatened to bring on you...and all those who serve with you.

I sit here thinking of our last moments together before you left...if the words we exchanged will be the final ones between us. They were so inadequate, so incomplete. My mind is awash now with things I would have said, should have said. I know you are sure of my affection, as I am of yours. Yet, I fear you cannot understand the full intensity of what you have come to mean to me. I make my appeal to whatever unknown forces decide the fates of spacers like us. If one of us must die because of my weakness, my failure, let it be me. I have faced death many times, escaped by the barest of margins. I have seen many good men and women die, too many. If the survival of our people must claim another, let it be me...and not you.

Bridge - E2S Constitution
System G35
Earth Two Date 01.03.31

"I want those systems up and running now." Erika West sat in center of Constitution's flag bridge like a marble statue, cold, unyielding. The Pilgrims on her staff had seen her like this before, or at least heard stories from those who had. But the younger officers sat in stunned shock, struggling to face the withering intensity of her commands.

Erika West was a legend in the fleet, one whose own accomplishments shone even through the blinding light of Terrance Compton's achievements. She had been Compton's right hand, loyal to the finish, and her skills in battle matched those of her mentor. West had commanded the republic's navy as long as there had been a republic, and throughout that time, no one would have called her soft or undemanding. But her peacetime demeanor had given way, replaced by the raw force of the pure warrior the veterans who had seen her in battle remembered.

"Yes, Admiral...the AI is rebooting. Estimate forty seconds to full operation." Elsa Wagner had seen West in action before, or, more accurately, she had heard her on the com during battle. Wagner had been a young ensign, months out of the Academy when she'd been assigned to Saratoga, arriving eleven days before the fleet was trapped behind the Barrier. Barret Dumont had flown his flag from the Yorktown class battlewagon, and she'd been terrified of the stern old admiral. But then Dumont was killed in action, and Erika West arrived to take his place. Wagner remembered the terror she had felt at the mere presence of the new commander. She could still recall her first glimpse of West, hair short, neat...her uniform spotless, crisp, as if a wrinkle wouldn't dare show itself.

Wagner was a commander now, and she had worked for years alongside the admiral who had once inspired such primal fear in her. She'd been a key aide to both of the navy's top officers, and West had chosen her as fleet tactical officer for the rescue mission. The assignment hadn't come as a complete surprise, but she was still relieved when she got the word. She was very fond of Admiral Frette, and she had been eager to serve in the fleet being sent to her aid.

The assignment made her Constitution's exec as well. The admirals in the old fleet had relied on flag captains to skipper their flagships, but with the massively reduced crew complements on the republic's vessels, it had become standard for a fleet commander to run his or her own ship as well.

"AI coming up now, Admiral...." Wagner's voice was crisp, professional. Decades of working alongside Erika West had rubbed off on her, and she had acquired her own reputation for being a bit of a cold fish. It wasn't a fair assessment, not really...but then it wasn't in West's case either, and the admiral had been putting up with it for more than forty years.

"Reactor online...scanning systems operational." She paused, her eyes darting down to her screens. She knew the AI could feed all the information she needed directly into her mind, but the headset sat on its hook, unused. Wagner was an old school officer, slow to adopt radical new technology. She shared that trait with West, who she'd never seen wearing her own AI link. "We're getting confirmations from the other ships, Admiral. All units coming online." She was still getting used to the dual responsibility of monitoring both Constitution itself, and the rest of the fleet as well.

"I want full scans, Commander. Active and passive. I want a thorough study of every scrap of debris we can find." The systems the fleet had passed through since leaving Earth Two had been mostly empty, nothing more than a hint of an energy trail to show that Frette's forces had come this way. But system G35 was different. The communique delivered by Cyclone had been clear about the location of the battle Frette's people had fought.

"Yes, Admiral. All ships initiating scans." Wagner's eyes dropped to the screen, staring, waiting for any data to come in from the sensors. She knew the AI would alert her to any findings, but she looked down anyway. There were fifty-seven ships in the fleet, and every one of them was banging away with active scanners. If there were any First Imperium ships in the system now, the fleet was advertising its presence.

"I want maximum dispersal patterns. Task groups are to engage thrusters, fan out in search pattern delta-2." West's words were like cold granite, not a hint of doubt. But Wagner had come to know the admiral well enough to realize that a fair portion of her legendary coldness was an act. Erika West expected to find trouble, if not in this system then in one ahead. Wagner was sure of that...and she agreed completely.

She was nervous. Spreading the fleet out into small search groups was risky. If they were attacked it would take time to get the whole force back into an effective combat formation...time they might not have. But it wasn't her decision, and Erika West knew what she was doing.

"Yes, Admiral." A few seconds later. "All units acknowledge." Wagner leaned back and took a deep breath. They were searching for small traces of evidence, for anything that might give them a better idea of the battle Frette's fleet had fought... and finding that was likely to take a while.

Her eyes darted down to her screen, and she snapped bolt upright. She'd expected to wait hours, but now the data was pouring in...reports from the other ships, and a torrent of information from Constitution's own scanners.

"Admiral, we have scanner reports coming in from all across the fleet."

West snapped her head around, clearly as surprised as Wagner at the early data. "Analysis?"

Wagner felt edgy, West's intensity adding to the tension she already felt from the surprise scanner readings. Her fingers moved over her keyboard, entering instructions, executing a full AI review of the data coming in. But she didn't need the analysis...it was rapidly becoming clear to her what had happened here.

"The battle." The words just blurted out of her mouth… but now that they did, she went with it. "We've got definite debris from the battle, Admiral. High levels of residual radiation, heavy concentrations of heavy metals…even some large chunks of debris." She turned and looked right at West. "There is no doubt."

"Very well, Commander." West's tone was steady, seemingly unaffected by the news. "Continue scans…and launch a spread of probes to gather some samples. I want those chunks of destroyed ships analyzed…every one of them."

*   *   *

Achilles stood and stared at the shard of twisted metal on the laboratory table in front of him. It looked much like a chunk from any ship's hull, most likely part of a section that had been blown outward at a high enough velocity to escape vaporization when the ship it had been part of was consumed by the escaping energies of a fusion reactor or a magazine full of antimatter. To look at it, the remnant could have been from either a human ship, or one of the First Imperium's vessels.

The Mule watched as the rays of the spectral analyzer moved over the sample, its normally invisible light reflecting off the metal as a faint indigo glow. The AI would confirm it in a few seconds, but the color of the light told Achilles all he needed to know. The debris was from a First Imperium vessel. The two powers used similar alloys, but the First Imperium hulls were infused with dark matter, and the knowledge behind its utilization was still a mystery to human science, despite years of research by the Mules. But the indigo spectral halo was a dead giveaway.

"Another First Imperium fragment." He turned and looked down the table toward Callisto. "We're running almost twenty to one. Admiral Frette's report didn't exaggerate. She crushed the enemy fleet...at least in this system."

Callisto turned and returned his gaze, offering a smile as she did.

He returned the smile, his eyes fixed on her.

She is magnificent, in every way...as she has always been...

Callisto and Achilles had been lovers intermittently throughout their adult lives. He'd always considered her beautiful, indeed everyone who had ever seen her did. All of the Mules were close to human physical ideals, but even among her genetically-engineered brethren, Callisto was special. Her hair was almost silver, and her eyes blue-gray. But beyond her physical charms, she was smart, even by the standards of the Mules. Her intellect had always been part of what had attracted him to her. She was bold, adventurous, not at all constrained by academic process or fear of being proven wrong. She was independent, defiant...and she was without fatigue in the pursuit of knowledge. Her mind sliced ahead, with the boldness the great admirals had shown in combat.

The Mules did not pair off as most of the other humans did. They did not condemn the humans for their bonding rituals, but they considered themselves above it all. Incapable of reproducing, they lacked any imperative to form family units... and they had much stronger senses of self than the others, at least that is how they looked at themselves. They took pride in independence, but also in the sense of community among their small group.

She held her smile for a few seconds more. The Mules weren't above feeling affection for each other, and it was clear Callisto was glad Achilles had included her when he'd proposed the Mules send a research team with the fleet. But then her grin slipped away, replaced by an earnest look. "Achilles, I've been running some size and projected mass computations based on the fragments. This debris, all of it, comes from relatively small vessels...and that confirms the lack of heavy units in the enemy force."

"So what does that tell you?" He wasn't sure he knew where she was going. They already knew Admiral Frette had fought against a task force without any heavy vessels.

"Well, obviously that Admiral Frette faced a fleet composed entirely of light vessels, which of course we already knew from her report. But extrapolating from that, I surmise that there are indeed heavier units located elsewhere, perhaps farther down the line of advance Frette's fleet followed."

The assertion seemed like a wild guess, but Achilles knew his old lover didn't make wild guesses. Anything that came out of her mouth was the result of hard calculation.

"This was a large force to consist entirely of light units, but Admiral West's speculation could be correct." He frowned. The general consensus in the fleet was that Frette had encountered an exploratory force that had been deployed beyond the borders of the imperium when the Regent was destroyed and had only just returned. He didn't believe it any more than he thought Callisto did, but he didn't have an alternate theory either.

"I was initially working under that hypothesis, but I no longer believe it to be the case."

"You know I am doubtful too, but I am as yet unable to offer an alternative explanation. Are you?"

"Perhaps. I believe I can offer some evidence-based determinations, though much of my end conclusion remains speculative."

"Please…share your analysis with me."

"I have performed some additional tests on these samples, and I have obtained some interesting results. First among these is that the spectral analysis shows considerably higher concentrations of dark matter in these alloys than we have seen in the older fragments back on Earth Two."

Achilles, stared down at the workstation in front of him, punching at the small keyboard. His eyes widened as the result was displayed. Callisto was right. There was almost thirty percent more dark matter in the new samples.

"How do you explain the difference?"

She paused. "You are aware that we have long suspected that the First Imperium's binding process, the technology they used to infuse the dark matter into their hulls, was imperfect, that over time particles of the dark matter would slowly bleed off?"

"Yes…but that is based on considerable speculation. We have a limited quantity of First Imperium wreckage to experiment with…and no alternate way of establishing an estimated age for each specimen."

"That is true, Achilles. But I submit we now have the basis for expanding the theory. The variance in dark matter concentration on all prior samples has been small, less than one percent from the highest to the lowest reading."

Achilles turned and walked toward Callisto, looking down at the screen in front of her. "You believe the vessels Admiral Frette encountered are newer than those that produced the fragments we already possess?" It was half question, half statement.

"Far newer. Indeed, let us assume First Imperium ship production ended roughly five hundred thousand years ago. That would mean that the newest ship faced in the war in human space and during the fleet's journey was half a million years old."

"That is in keeping with all active theories about the First Imperium…and it is corroborated by the records we found on Earth Two."

"Yes…and now we calculate for the previously noted differences in dark matter concentrations. We must estimate the normal use and replacement schedule for a First Imperium warship before the Ancients fell. The Alliance had a fifty to sixty-year useful cycle for vessels, with ships remaining in front line service for roughly half that time. But First Imperium ships obviously had a longer useful life, a conclusion that is clear since so many were still functional five hundred thousand years after the last was constructed. So let us assume a thousand-year turn-around under normal conditions." She paused then added, "I understand that is an estimate unsupported by direct facts, but it seems reasonable."

Achilles hesitated for a moment considering the implications of what she had said. "If your assumptions are correct that would mean these new ships are…"

Callisto nodded. "Far less ancient than any that have been

encountered to date. Likely thousands of years newer." She paused. "Hundreds of thousands of years, actually. Indeed, this debris could very well be from new ships."

"New? What parameters define 'new' in terms of your analysis?"

"Well, it would be meaningless to suggest that scientific dating of the dark matter hulls could be accurate beyond a range of centuries...but I am suggesting that these vessels could have been constructed very recently, within the range of our occupation of Earth Two."

Achilles stood, silent, letting Callisto's words sink in. The Regent was gone, destroyed, and its last command had been a self-destruct directive to all imperial forces. Even before then, it had been clear that the Regent's rule over the Imperium had been limited to its military forces. The factories, the great mining operations, the huge planetary power generation units...all of them had been silent for millennia. The fleet had found dozens of them, along with the old cities of the Ancients, and they were all the same. Dead, covered with ages of dust and decayed.

Achilles was almost always calm, cool in his demeanor. He'd gone through the Mules' rebellion, deployed the war bots and faced down the republic's government, all without losing his temper or raising his voice. But now he felt a cold chill deep inside.

If Callisto was correct, there were First Imperium factories still active somewhere, new ships pouring out from shipyards. The implications were staggering...utterly horrifying. Achilles had been quickened after the fleet had defeated the Regent, but he understood the threat Callisto's theory carried with it."

"Put your data together, Callisto." His voice was deep, grim. "We have to discuss this with Admiral West. Now."

Achilles had images in his head, of a different kind of First Imperium enemy, one with active shipyards and factories, producing new war materiel rather than relying upon millennia of stockpiled arms and ancient ships. Callisto's hypothesis was sobering, horrifying. But his own mind took it further now. If indeed there were such manufacturing facilities, an ongoing production ecosystem creating new arms, new ships…it had to be directed by an intelligence of immense capability. Not one of the regional AIs the imperium had employed, but an entity to rival the Regent itself.

What is out there, waiting for us? Plotting against us?

He paused, looking around the room, struggling to deal with the feeling rising up inside him, one he had never felt before… but one he tentatively identified. Fear.

Chapter Twenty-Nine

From the Research Notes of Achilles the Mule

I have reviewed Callisto's data three times, and the results have been the same with each analysis. We are facing something entirely unexpected, a danger beyond anything I had considered a possibility.

I know there has been much talk of us, the Mules, about our coldness, our lack of emotion...and indeed, there are many times when intellect forestalls the kinds of undisciplined responses the humans so commonly exhibit. But we do feel emotions. Loyalty, to each other, and also to the humans, our lesser cousins. Affection, which we sometimes resist but feel nevertheless.

And now...fear. I have long prided myself on rationality, on approaching challenges with intelligence, study, determination. It is one thing to face greater numbers, a more powerful enemy...and yet another to stare into the utter blackness of the unknown...

Bridge - E2S Constitution
System G38
Earth Two Date 01.03.31

"Do you know what you are suggesting?" Erika West sat at the head of the small conference table. She was as cold-blooded a veteran as any the navy had ever produced, but Achilles' words had turned her white as a sheet.

The room was small, cramped. Constitution had been built as a flagship, but unlike the massive Compton, the smaller battlewagon didn't have tonnage to spare. Its designers had poured all the space saved by the massive reduction in crew size back into its power and weapons systems. The conference table was perhaps a quarter the size of the palatial constructions that had served the admirals flying their flags from the old Yorktown-class battleships, though Constitution was half again the tonnage and possessed seven or eight times the firepower.

"I understand perfectly, Admiral. Indeed, I have analyzed the data extensively, and I felt it was crucial to bring this to your attention immediately. I would still have to characterize our conclusions as theory, however the absence of any reasonable alternative hypothesis strongly suggests that at least part of it is factual. Specifically, that we are dealing with First Imperium ships that are hundreds of thousands of years newer than any contacted by human forces previously. There is little doubt of that. Indeed, I consider it highly likely the ships Admiral Frette fought and destroyed here were produced within a range of fifty years or less from the current date. They were new, certainly by the standards of First Imperium craft previously encountered." Achilles paused, allowing West time to digest his words before he continued.

"Admiral, it is likely that what we are facing is not another renegade group of ships cut off when the Regent was destroyed, but newly-constructed and organized forces built at a production facility—or facilities—that were recently in operation. That are very likely still active."

West stared back at Achilles. She had never truly been as cold and unflappable as the junior officers' gossip had always made her out to be, but she was struggling now to remain calm, to maintain her discipline. The implications of what Achilles had just told her were staggering. It raised old fears, dark memories of battles past…and a truly terrifying view of the future.

Or the lack of a future…

"Achilles…if you are right, we face a far greater danger than we had imagined. With the data we have available—or more accurately, the lack of data—there is no way to estimate the strength we might be facing. Based on the number of ships Admiral Frette encountered and, assuming that was a scouting group or decoy, we can guess we are facing an enemy force numbered in the hundreds." She paused. "Or even thousands." Her mind tended toward the dark, and it had gone even farther, daring to think of tens of thousands of enemy ships. Hundreds of thousands. Images of Earth Two passed through her thoughts, barren, irradiated. Dead.

Achilles' expression was somber. "Admiral, I am sorry to be so negative, but…" The Mule paused.

"It is okay, Achilles. I have never been one to avoid the truth, regardless of what it is. People allow their wishes to color their thoughts too often…but not me. What else did you want to say?"

"Admiral, it is just that, if our hypothesis is correct, if there are shipyards and other facilities in active operation…well, we have to draw certain other conclusions, not the least of which is that some intelligence is directing all of this. We know for certain the Regent was destroyed, but…" His voice trailed off again.

"But?"

"Are we sure there was only one?"

"One Regent?" West's voice was shrill. The thought of another Regent was terrifying to her.

"Admiral…"

"Are you suggesting there is another Regent somewhere out there? A copy of the other one?"

"No…not 'suggesting.' But I do believe we need to consider the possibility that there is another intelligence behind what we are now encountering. The Regent was just a computer. It would have been relatively easy to create a copy, given sufficient hardware to support its functionality."

"Another Regent? With new shipyards, mines, foundries, antimatter production facilities? That is a significant endeavor…

and an extraordinary suggestion."

"Is it so extraordinary, Admiral? Do we have a vital system without a failsafe? The AI that controls the climate of my quarters and the lock on the door has a backup. Certainly every electronic system we have of note has some level of functionality in the event of a primary failure." He paused, deliberately slowing himself. Erika West was one of the strongest of the humans, but Achilles knew she couldn't absorb data as quickly as his people could.

"Admiral, we assumed the First Imperium threat was gone because we hadn't been attacked in twenty years. But what is twenty years to an artificial intelligence? What is it in the context of the Regent, that ruled for five hundred thousand years?"

West sat still, silent, considering Achilles' words. She knew the Mule was intelligent, that his mind could analyze things far faster and more completely than her own. And everything he said made perfect sense. She couldn't remember Achilles ever being wrong about anything. She had even sympathized with his rebellion…and acknowledged that his people had exhibited considerable patience before taking action.

"If you are right, Achilles, we face a terrible danger now… one as bad as that the fleet endured. Worse, even."

Achilles nodded. "I agree, Admiral. That is why I felt it was so urgent to bring this to your attention."

West took a deep breath. She'd spent her whole life projecting strength, but now she needed help. She didn't know what to do. "What do you propose?"

"Military operations are not my area of expertise, Admiral, so I would suggest that you might be better able answer that question." He paused. "Nevertheless, there are certain actions that would seem obvious. We must rally every man and woman on Earth Two to the cause. We must put every ship we can into the line, including the mothballed reserve, the old ships of the fleet. We must fortify the warp gates in the home system. We must buy time, time to build up our forces…time to learn more about our enemy." He paused. "And perhaps most difficult for you right now…we must do nothing to lead the enemy back to

Earth Two." He hesitated again, staring at her with the most sympathy she'd ever seen in the Mule's eyes. "You must consider turning around now, Admiral. If we advance and engage the enemy, we risk leading them back with us if we return home."

West felt the coldness move through her body. She knew in an instant Achilles was right. If she pressed on, if the fleet engaged the enemy, or even came into contact with First Imperium vessels, it would be an all or nothing proposition. Her people would have to eradicate any force they encountered. Retreat in the face of the enemy wouldn't be an option...there could be no flight, not one the enemy could follow.

She felt tension, something approaching panic, as she imagined giving the order to leave Nicki and her people behind. It was the kind of choice she'd dreaded her entire life, and even with the horrific battles she'd fought, the wounds she'd suffered...she'd never faced anything as stark and terrible as this. She suspected Augustus Garret had, at the moment he'd given the order to detonate the massive bomb that disrupted the warp gate leading back to human space, creating the barrier. And condemning his best friend and thousands of loyal officers and spacers to what he had to view as almost certain death. She'd often wondered how Garret had managed after that, if he'd learned to deal with his choice...or if it had destroyed him.

"I am going to lead the fleet onward. Those are our people out there, and we don't know what they are facing."

"Or if they are even alive, Admiral. If we are facing what it appears we are, there is no way to know what they have encountered."

"No way but to go and find out for ourselves." West paused. "We need to know more, Achilles. If we return now, we will still be in the dark, guessing at what we are facing. Moving forward puts the fleet at risk...but if your hypothesis is correct we're going to need more than fifty-six ships to win the war we are facing. We're going to need more information. We're going to need to stand together, to be the kind of warriors that don't abandon our people. If we can find and rescue the fleet—and learn more about what we're up against—we will be in a much better position to prevail in the fight that is coming."

"That is true, Admiral." The Mule paused. "But moving forward is betting the fleet on what we find. You know we can't come back, not if we engage the enemy…at least not while any First Imperium vessels can follow us. Every man and woman in the fleet will die if we encounter a force we cannot annihilate… and Earth Two will have lost most of its naval forces."

West stood quietly, thinking. Garret hadn't had a choice… the fate of all human space had rested on his decision. Indeed, if he'd failed to do as he had done, Compton would have died. Everyone on the fleet would have died…along with the rest of mankind.

This situation was different. If she turned back, it was likely Nicki Frette would die—if she wasn't already dead. Her fleet and crews would die with her. But West could guarantee that a large portion of the republic's fleet would survive to defend the home world.

She knew what her old mentor would have done. Or did she? Was she just believing what she wanted to believe…to justify the action she desperately wanted to take?

No, Augustus Garret always pressed on, moved forward, whatever the risk. And so will I.

"We're moving forward, Achilles. I understand the dangers, but we have to try. We have to find out what is happening."

Achilles just nodded. "Yes, Admiral."

She turned to face the Mule. She had expected him to argue with her, to barrage her with facts and computations of potential outcomes. But he just stood there staring back at her…with what she could have sworn was sympathy in his eyes.

She had always respected the Mules, admired their amazing intellects. But she'd never considered them warriors, nor expected them to truly understand the qualities that drove creatures of battle like herself. Now, she was rethinking that, wondering if for all her respect and admiration she hadn't underestimated Achilles and his people.

"It is what I have to do, Achilles. What we have to do. We can't abandon our people, not for any reason."

"I believe I understand, Admiral. Indeed, there is no clearly correct answer here. The potential to gain further information and to escape with it is a powerful inducement to advance... in addition, of course, to the factors you suggest." He paused. "Yet any move forward also carries enormous risk of total destruction for the fleet. It is, of course, your decision."

"It is decided." West paused, standing still, looking at her Mule companion for a few seconds. "Prepare your people, Achilles...I'm going to send a ship back to Earth Two with a complete report. Your team can return with the dispatches. There is no reason to put you and your people in greater danger."

Achilles shook his head. She could see something in his eyes...

"No, Admiral. I will stay. Apart from the chance of rescuing Admiral Frette and her people, the primary advantage to your strategy is the opportunity to get a better idea of what we truly face. I believe I can be of value in that regard, which makes my remaining worth the risk."

West was impressed. She'd associated many traits with the Mules before, but now she was seeing one she realized she hadn't truly appreciated. Courage.

"Of course, you may remain, Achilles...if you are certain. You know that there is a good chance we're not coming back..."

"I do. That does not alter my rationale."

"And what of your people? You have to let them return."

"I will ask Callisto and the others, but I do not believe they will answer differently. There are many variables regarding exactly what we are facing...and they may be able to help analyze the situation."

West looked back at Achilles. "There is no shame in leaving. Your people are not naval crew...they are not warriors."

"We are all warriors, Admiral, when the situation calls for it. As I said, I will offer my comrades the opportunity to return with your courier ship...but I feel comfortable in assuring you that none of them will accept. We will remain with you, Admiral, face this threat together."

The Mule nodded, and then he turned and left the room,

leaving Erika West staring in shock at the hatch as it closed behind him.

Chapter Thirty

Commander Cooper McDaid to His Squadrons

I could give you all a speech, talk to you of valor, of duty. Of honor. But none of that means a damn right now. All you need to know is that these bastards have killed our people...and that they will kill more of them today. The fighter pilots of the old fleet knew how to deal with this enemy...Greta Hurley knew how to deal with them. Mariko Fujin knew how to deal with them.

Kill them. Just kill the bastards.

Bridge - E2S Compton
System G42
Earth Two Date 01.08.31

"Missile range in four minutes, Admiral. Starfire and Intrepid are still reloading their magazines. All other vessels report ready to launch."

Frette stared down at her screen, her eyes moving over the ships of her fleet. Strand's escorts had joined the battle line, but her two capital ships were still rearming. Frette had been impressed with her subordinate's ingenuity, at how she'd kept the enemy ships at bay for so long, alternating missile fire while her batteries were cooling. She'd been the prime mover in Strand's promotion to command Starfire, and now she knew her instincts had been spot on.

"Very well, Commander." She almost added a command to send a message to Strand, to urge her to complete the reloading as quickly as possible...but she realized the young officer would be doing everything possible to be ready on time.

"Frette turned back to the display, her eyes fixing on the lines of red icons moving toward her fleet. The enemy force was large. Too large, she realized. She felt the urge to order a retreat, to have all her ships blast away on full...but she knew that too was hopeless. She couldn't outrun the enemy, and even if through some miracle her ships could stay out of the enemy's firing range, the one thing she absolutely couldn't do was lead them back to Earth Two.

She had no idea what the enemy knew, but the mere fact that the home world had never been attacked suggested they didn't know where it was. And she wasn't going to be the one who showed them the way. She was angry at herself already, wallowing in misery and blame for leading her people to disaster. She wasn't going to take any risk of exposing Earth Two.

Her mind wandered back to the dispatches she had sent back, realizing how incomplete they had been now that she had a better idea of enemy strength. She wished she could send another ship...but such an attempt would be fraught with danger. Protecting Earth Two was the top priority. The only one.

"Admiral, Captain Strand reports her ships are reloaded. She requests permission to rejoin the battle line."

"Permission granted." Frette smiled, but it quickly died on her lips. She was proud of Strand, and her mind had drifted to a future where the gifted young officer rose to high command, to one day take her place...or even Erika's. She saw much of herself in Strand, and more...she saw much of what she had always wanted to be, the things she had always strived for. But then she realized. Josie Strand didn't have a future. She was twenty-nine years old, smart, brave, capable...and she was going to die here, in this system, in the next few hours.

Frette knew the tricks, the ways to keep her people occupied, their minds off the desperation of the situation. But she was the commander, and she couldn't fool herself. Her people were doomed. They would fight bravely, she had no doubt about that. They would destroy a large number of enemy vessels. But in the end, they would be overwhelmed, crushed by an enemy force that was just too strong for them to defeat.

Her eyes were fixed, her gaze locked on the line of larger icons just behind the front of the enemy line. Leviathans. Twenty of them. Her five capital ships could take on a Leviathan and win...and Compton had some chance even against two. But she was outnumbered four to one in heavy units, and more like seven to one in lighter ships.

"Detecting enemy missile launches, Admiral." A pause. "All along their line."

Frette nodded. "Time until Starfire and Intrepid are back in the line?"

"One minute, thirty, sir. Captain Strand reports her ships are ready to launch as soon as they are in position."

"Very well. All ships with racks loaded...launch now." Compton and Excalibur had managed to reload their external racks, along with half a dozen of the cruisers. It was far from ideal, but Frette would take any firepower she could get.

"Launching, Admiral..."

Frette leaned back, feeling the slight vibration as Compton launched the seventy-two weapons attached to her hull. A few seconds later, there was a slightly harder sensation...the battleship ejecting the racks that had held the missiles in place.

"Racks, jettisoned, Admiral."

"Magazines ready...begin launch sequence in forty seconds."

She stared back at the display, watching the massive wave of tiny red dots moving toward her ships. The enemy barrage was a deadly danger, but she knew her defenses would take out a lot of those missiles. She had been planning to launch her fighters on point defense sorties, but she'd changed her mind at the last minute and ordered the craft to be rearmed for anti-shipping runs. There was no point in committing so much firepower to the defense, not when her people had no chance of survival. Better to hurt the enemy as badly as possible, to wear away at what Erika and the rest of the fleet would have to face.

"All vessels standing by for launch orders, Admiral."

Frette watched the incoming missiles, almost mesmerized as the tiny lights moved slowly toward her ships. She had launched first in the earlier battle, but this time she wanted to wait for all her vessels to be online. The more mass she could put into the salvo, the better chance it had over overloading the enemy defenses...and scoring some kills.

"Captain Strand reports her ships are ready, Admiral."

"Fleet order...launch all missiles."

"Launching."

She listened as Kemp relayed her order on the fleet com, her eyes locked on the display as Compton shook lightly with the release of her missiles. Her massive flagship carried a greater armament than any vessel in human history, and she sat silent as two hundred fifty-six missiles launched, thirty-two at a time, each one of them carrying eight five hundred megaton warheads. It was a mind-bending exercise to try and comprehend the destructive power of those mighty weapons. But Frette knew the battle would not be decided by the missile exchange. Advancements in targeting technology had vastly improved interdiction efforts, and she knew the fleet would expend giga-tons of explosive power to do minor radiation damage on enemy targets. The real fight would be at close range, when the energy weapons opened up.

"All missiles away, Admiral."

"Execute maneuver plan Vega-9. Prepare to receive enemy missile attack."

"Yes, Admiral."

"And scramble all fighter squadrons. I want every bird launched before those missiles close into detonation range." She had no doubt Cooper McDaid and his pack of hotshot pilots would inflict massive damage on the enemy...and she had no intention of risking any of them being blown apart still in their mother ships or trapped in crippled launch bays.

She stared ahead, struggling to maintain focus. It was time. Time for her last battle.

*   *   *

"Outer bay doors open. Transferring control to wing leaders. Good luck, hunters!"

Cooper McDaid sat at the pilot's station of his fighter, his hand gripped tightly around the throttle. "Thanks, control... commencing launch now."

McDaid turned his head, a last visual check that his crew was strapped in and ready...and then he hit the ignition controls and fired the turbo thrusters.

He felt his body slam back hard into his chair as the combination of the launch catapult and the fighter's thrusters blasted the tiny vessels down the launch tube at over one hundred gees. The inertial dampeners were running at full power, but they weren't powerful enough to fully absorb the tremendous force being exerted, and McDaid struggled to force air into his lungs.

The fighter tore down the launch tube and out into the blackness of space, followed, he knew, exactly four seconds later, by the next ship in line. McDaid had been brought up on stories of the great fighter assaults Admiral Hurley had led against the enemy, hundreds of small craft launching devastating wave attacks on the ships of the First Imperium. He also knew how few of those pilots had survived to reach Earth Two...and the name at the top of that terrible casualty list had been none other than Greta Hurley.

McDaid had the cocksure personality that was a prerequisite for success in the fighter corps, but now he felt something different, and he thought of the great admiral, of how she had led one seemingly hopeless assault after another. McDaid was confident and courageous, but he also knew his people were facing hopeless odds. The fleet was massively outnumbered, and that put the pressure on his crews to destroy as many enemy ships as possible...whatever the risk.

It didn't matter, he knew, how much risk they took. It was doubtful they'd have any place to land when they completed their attack. The fleet had only five capital ships...and he knew there was no way for them to prevail. He'd just as soon see his people die in combat, taking down an enemy ship than have them floating in space, the fleet gone, waiting for the last of their life support to fail.

"All squadrons launched and in position, Commander." Tuck Lowery was McDaid's aide. He sat in the commander's seat, which was available because McDaid had refused to give up the pilot's seat for what he had described as, 'a desk job with all the danger of the front lines."

"Let's go, Tuck…it's time to show these First Imperium bastards that the human race still knows how to fly fighters."

"Yes, sir."

McDaid, angled the throttle to the side, brought his ship around slowly as the thrust altered its vector. His eyes darted to the screen, noting with satisfaction how sharply his people followed. The fighter corps was a fraction of the strength it had been in the days of the fleet…but he'd put his people against any crews who had ever taken the fight to the enemy. And he intended to prove that point now…even if no one would survive to speak of it.

"The enemy missiles are entering detonation range, sir." Lowery's voice was soft, dark.

McDaid stared at the display. The point defense had taken out a lot of the enemy warheads, but there were too many left. He'd expected Frette to order his people armed for point defense duty again, but she'd sent them after the enemy ships instead. It had been an aggressive call, one he respected.

One they're about to pay for…

He watched as the laser batteries fired their last desperate shots, picking off missiles he knew could detonate at any moment. Frette had the escorts up front, clearly trying to protect her battleships any way she could. But he also knew the enemy algorithms would preference capital ships as targets.

His eyes were fixed on the display when the first tiny dot expanded into a large circle…and then disappeared a few seconds later. Then another…and another. And then more, almost fifty in total, some detonating harmlessly, too far from any ships to cause significant damage. But others were closer to the mark...including one antimatter warhead that exploded less than a kilometer from Heraclius.

He closed his eyes for an instant when he saw it. The view on the screen was cold, clinical, nothing more than dots of light on a black display. But he knew on Heraclius, things were far from so neat and clean. The great ship's hull would be compromised, melted in places from the massive heat of the antimatter explosion. The vessel would be bathed in massive amounts of gamma rays, and every hull breach would allow more of the deadly radiation to penetrate, scrambling ship's systems...and killing men and women. Heraclius didn't blow up, not immediately, but McDaid knew from his training the battleship was likely a dead hulk.

There were other detonations within the danger zone, including two so close to destroyers, McDaid couldn't imagine any of their crews had survived. He felt sick to his stomach, realizing that dozens, perhaps hundreds of his comrades had died over the past few minutes. He felt an irrational urge to turn around, to return and help somehow. But he knew there was nothing he could do for the fleet's crews.

Nothing but avenge them.

*   *   *

"Damage control parties report fires under control, Admiral. The reactor is back at ninety-four percent output."

"Very well." Frette felt the relief flood over her. There had been a moment there, one where she'd been afraid Compton was in trouble. The detonation hadn't been that close, well into the moderate range, but the massive blast of radiation had hit her flagship just where it hurt the most. A series of overloaded conduits had partially scragged the reactor...and started a series of fires.

But her crews had gotten everything under control, quicker

than she'd imagined possible. Compton was combat ready. What had seemed for a short time as serious damage had proven to be no more than a few singed circuits...and now Nicki Frette stared ahead, her blood cold, ready to strike back.

Her missiles had hit the enemy hard, the first wave from the external racks detonating among the forward escort ships...and hindering their interception efforts. Almost one hundred missiles from the main salvo had penetrated the enemy defenses and exploded along their battle line. Leviathans were tough ships, and most of the damage caused was light or moderate... but one enemy battleship had been bracketed between two warheads...and it split open like an egg, disappeared a few seconds later as its antimatter containment failed.

Frette listened to the damage control reports from the fleet, her eyes flitting back and forth from one display to another as she tried to keep track of everything...the status of her ships, the damage assessments coming in on the enemy fleet, the state of repairs on Compton...

How did Erika do this? Or Admiral Compton...with hundreds of ships under his command?

She stared down at the neural link, pausing for a few seconds before reaching out and grabbing it. She took one last look at the main display... and then she put the headset on, and felt the ship's AI connecting with her mind.

If this was going to be her last fight, it was going to be her greatest one too.

Chapter Thirty-One

Captain Josie Strand to her Bridge Crew
Moments Before Starfire Opened Fire

You've heard the stories, read the accounts. You've looked up at the statues, the memorials to lost heroes. You know, every one of you, the deeds done by our parents, by the Pilgrims who came before us. Now it is our turn. Honor them now through emulation. Stand by your posts and fight...like no men and women have ever fought before. Show these machines from what warriors we spawned.

To victory! To victory...or death!

Cockpit, Fighter 001
System G42
Earth Two Date 01.08.31

"Alright boys and girls...this is what we trained for, what we practiced for. Let's make all those flight hours count. Forget the standard tactics...we're going to do this old school, the way the pilots of the old fleet did. We're going to go right down the throats of these bastards...and we're going to blow them to hell!"

McDaid was staring straight ahead as he addressed his squadrons. He had all the dash, all the pure insanity of a great fighter pilot…but he was also realistic. If this battle was going to cost all his people their lives, by God they were going to make it count.

He angled his throttle, wincing as he pushed it to full thrust, altering his ship's vector, bringing it to bear directly on the Leviathan. The Spacehawk fighter he was piloting was a vast improvement on those the pilots of the old fleet had flown. It was faster, more maneuverable…and it held not one, but two plasma torpedoes in its bomb bay. That was a punch that could make even a Leviathan take notice.

His people had ridden in on the heels of the missiles, slipping through the enemy point defense with only eight losses. That was forty of his people, and it hurt like hell, but it was far less than he'd feared. And now their comrades were ready to take their revenge.

He glanced at range on the display. Thirty thousand kilometers. The book said anything less than twenty thousand was optimum firing range…but McDaid had read the accounts of Greta Hurley's pilots, and he had listened to Mariko Fujin speak of the tactics that had saved the fleet.

Twenty thousand kilometers is for gutless punks who have no place in a cockpit…

He was going right down this ship's throat…and he was going to drop both torpedoes at point blank range.

The Leviathan was growing larger on the scanner as the kilometers ticked off the readout.

Twenty thousand.

He flipped a row of switches, activating the launch mechanisms. He could hear the loud clicks as the torpedoes were lowered into firing positon.

Fifteen thousand.

He pulled open a small hatch on his workstation, grabbing a lever with his hand and twisting it to the right.

"Plasma torpedoes armed and ready." It was the voice of the fighter's AI. He could fire at any time.

Ten thousand.

He had two gunners on his bird, and they were both manning the ship's laser turrets, but McDaid wasn't going to let anyone near the torpedo controls. He was going to fly the fighter to the perfect spot...and he was going to launch the two weapons himself.

Eight thousand kilometers.

Close. Too close, he thought for an instant. His hands were tingling, his body was twitching with excitement, tension.

No, not too close. Fujin closed to less than five thousand more than once...and God only knows what Greta Hurley did...

Six thousand kilometers.

He could hear his crew behind him, breathing hard. He could sense their fear. But none of them said a word.

Five thousand kilometers.

He tapped the throttle one last time, adjusting the trajectory. Then he depressed his finger on the firing stud...once...then an instant later a second time. Then he pulled the throttle hard, back and to the side.

He could see the enemy ship now, filling the screen in front of him.

We're not going to make it...

He felt his body tense...and he knew his bird was going to crash...

And then it didn't. His eyes darted to the screen as the fighter zipped past the Leviathan. The numbers he saw made him nauseous. His bird had cleared the enemy by less than eighty kilometers. That was a lot of distance on the ground, but in a space battle it was beyond threading a needle. If he'd tapped the throttle so much a fraction of a second later, the fighter would have smashed into its target.

He loosened his grip on the throttle, gasping for breath as the crushing gee forces abated. His eyes snapped down to the display, anxious for a damage assessment on the target.

But there was nothing there when he looked, nothing at all.

Nothing but a dissipating cloud of plasma where a First Imperium battleship had been.

*   *   *

Starfire shook hard. Strand could hear the sounds of distant explosions, but it was all soft, far away. She didn't need to listen…she knew exactly what was happening to her ship.

She leaned back in her chair, eyes closed, allowing the AI to push the data she needed into her mind. It was uncomfortable, but she couldn't argue it hadn't given her an advantage. Starfire had pushed forward, driving right past the enemy's light ships… and engaging the battle line directly. She had faced off against four Leviathans, and her pinpoint fire had destroyed one…and gutted another. But Starfire had paid for its victories, and for her boldness. Her ship was bleeding air, spewing liquids into space to flash freeze the instant they left the torn hull. Her crew had worked wonders keeping the ship in the fight, but she knew it wouldn't be much longer. Her main batteries were gone, a good portion of the guns nothing now but melted and twisted wreckage. And even if they had been reparable, she didn't have the power to fire them. The reactor was down to thirty percent.

She could see the AI's representation of laser fire lancing out from her battered ship. Three of the secondaries were still online, and at this range their fire was extremely effective. They weren't the ship killers the main particle accelerators were, but the shots tore into one of the damaged enemy ships, each one another hit, one more bit of devastation before they were silenced for good.

"Commander Hahn, I need thrust. We're going to close on that bastard." Her tone was odd, distracted. It was difficult to interact with her human crew when she was wearing the neural link. But what she wanted now wasn't anything the AI could do for her. She wanted that last bit of effort, the final bit of pure defiance her crew possessed.

"Commander Willis is down at the reactor now, Captain. He requests permission to do an emergency power surge."

Strand heard the words, the meaning crystalizing in her mind. Willis was suggesting something crazy, a wild gamble…

but she knew he was only trying to give her what she needed. If she could close, her people just might be able to take another enemy ship with them. And right now, that was worth any risk.

"Do it."

"Yes, Captain."

Strand could see the reactor room, another projection the AI pushed into her mind. She could feel it somehow, the extra power surging through the conduits leading out from the reaction chamber, the whole mechanism strained to the brink of catastrophic failure...but holding together. Somehow.

She could see the target ship as well, feel Starfire accelerating, moving toward it. She directed the AI, adjusted the navigation to bring all her surviving guns to bear.

Another twenty thousand kilometers...

She sat, holding her breath, waiting for the right moment...

And then the ship shook wildly. She felt her body slamming forward into her harness, the sharp pain as at least one of her ribs broke. She reached up and pulled the headset off, shaking her head to clear her mind. Starfire's bridge was a nightmare. The main lights were out, only a dim illumination from the emergency fixtures and a small electrical fire on one of the consoles lighting the dark space.

Her people were screaming, and she could see several of them were wounded. And then her eyes settled on Hahn. He was lying on the deck next to his workstation...and she could see in an instant his head was twisted at a grotesque angle. She unstrapped herself and lunged across the deck, dropping to her hands and knees next to him, but even before she reached out, put her fingers on his neck, she knew he was dead.

And so was Starfire.

She knew her ship was mortally wounded. She didn't need any reports to tell her the reactor had scragged, and she doubted there was any hope of restarting it...if Commander Willis and any of his techs were even still alive.

She'd targeted one last enemy, but it had turned out to be a ship too far. She wanted to cry, to slump down to the deck and wait for death. But even though she knew there was no hope, it wasn't in her to give up on her people. Not if she could save them…even for a few more hours.

She tried to stand, wincing at the pain in her chest and reaching out toward her chair to stabilize herself. She leaned forward, slamming her fist down on the com unit, opening the intraship channel.

"All hands, this is the captain…" She coughed, spraying blood on the arm of her chair. "…abandon ship. All hands to the lifepods. Abandon ship."

She felt a pain inside, worse in its way than the agony of her broken ribs. Starfire was her first command, and now it seemed it was also her last. She ached for her ship, and she couldn't imagine anything worse than surviving Starfire's destruction. But the training was there, and she knew she had her duty. To survive as long as she could, to get her people off the ship… even if that promised little more than a few extra moments before death.

She leaned over the chair, moving her mouth toward the com unit to repeat her command.

"All hands…abandon ship…"

*   *   *

Nicki Frette sat watching her fleet die. Her people had fought well, better than she'd dared to hope. Eight enemy Leviathans were gone, destroyed outright in the cataclysmic battle, and most of the others were damaged. But eight or nine of them were still firing…and her battle line had fallen almost silent. Only Compton still had operational primaries, though she knew that wasn't likely to last much longer. The other four battleships were completely silent, or they had at most one or two secondaries still operational.

Her eyes paused on the small icon representing Starfire. Josie Strand's ship had been an inspiration as it sliced into the enemy lines, taking all the punishment the enemy vessels could dish out, even as she drove to point blank range and unleashed her own particle accelerators, targeting ships McDaid's fighters had left damaged and vulnerable.

Starfire was dead now, a floating, lifeless wreck. No energy output, no readings at all…just a hunk of twisted metal drifting past the enemy into deep space. There were small contacts, life-pods, Frette realized. At least some of Strand's people had survived. But Frette knew their escape would be short-lived. The enemy ships would hunt them down and destroy them. And, if through some miracle, any of them escaped detection they would face a slow death from cold and lack of oxygen.

She heard the distant whining sound, the main guns firing again…and she felt a flash of elation when another Leviathan vanished. But her satisfaction was short-lived. A few seconds later Compton shook hard…another hit, this one solidly amidships.

"Main guns are offline, Admiral." Kemp's voice was hoarse, raw…but he was keeping calm even in the face of certain destruction. Frette was impressed with her people, all of them. Her surviving ships were still in the line, fighting an increasingly hopeless struggle. She'd have given Kemp a decoration, and Strand too…if any of them were ever getting back.

"Divert available power to secondaries." There was nothing else to do. The primaries were done, she knew that. And she doubted the reactor would last much longer anyway. Better to take what shots she still had than wish for what she didn't.

"Bandelero and Winchester…Code Omega."

Two more of her ships, sending out the code that meant a vessel was facing imminent destruction. A third of her ships were gone…and the rest wouldn't last long.

"Admiral…"

As soon as she heard Kemp's voice she knew something else was wrong.

"We're picking up energy readings from the G40 warp gate. Probes coming through."

She felt cold inside. She'd deployed her fleet just in front of the warp gate. It had been training, instinct…to positon herself so her forces had a line of retreat. She'd done it even though she knew she couldn't use it, couldn't lead the enemy closer to Earth Two. But now the enemy was coming from there too. The implications were sobering…the enemy was in far more systems that she'd anticipated. But more urgent was the fact that in a few seconds she would have an enemy force emerging from the warp gate directly to her rear.

Now it was truly over. In a few minutes her ships would be gone, all of them…caught between two enemy lines and obliterated.

I'm sorry, Erika. I'm sorry I couldn't do better…

Chapter Thirty-Two

Admiral Erika West Fleet Communique

We have come here to the aid of our friends, our comrades... and the probes tell a clear story. We have arrived just in time. I could give a long speech, tell you all of the fleet's history, of the great battles fought and won, of heroes and courage. But you need none of that. All you need is to know what the probes have reported. Beyond this warp gate our brothers and sisters fight, even now, against overwhelming odds. Alone they are doomed. But they are not alone, not any longer. All ships, forward, maximum thrust. Transit through the warp gate and advance into the fight. All captains, fire at will, engage the enemy, go to the aid of our people...for there is no time to spare. Our comrades are dying with each passing minute.

Go! Forward! And carry with you the spirit of Admiral Compton, and all the great warriors of the fleet, lost years ago and yet still with us always!

E2S Constitution
System G42
Earth Two Date 01.08.31

"I want those systems back online now!" Erika West roared, berating her hapless tactical officer in the same way captains had been doing for almost two centuries. The effect of warp transits was well known, and some mystery remained about the variation in reboot times. The difference was usually minor, a range of perhaps one minute to three. But in battle, those two minutes could be the difference between victory and defeat, life and death.

"Yes, Admiral." The response was routine, programmed. There was nothing Commander Corker—or all the engineers on Constitution—could do that they weren't already doing. A sharp crew could shave a few seconds off reboot time, but Constitution's people were already doing that.

John Corker was hunched over his station, staring at the dark screens. West knew her crew was as tense as she was, that they were well aware of what they faced. She hadn't said anything, but she suspected most of her people realized their survival required not just victory, but the utter annihilation of the enemy fleet. There would be no retreat, no escape. They were all expendable...better every man and woman in the fleet die than lead the enemy back to Earth Two.

West's eyes caught a hint of light, and they snapped down to her own workstation. Her screen had lit up, a staticky pattern replacing the blackness that had been there a second before. The AI was rebooting, and along with it every electronic system on Constitution. She had made hundreds of transits in her career, thousands...many into combat, as now. But she was tense in a way she had never been before.

You've never been rushing in to save Nicki...knowing every second could be the one that makes you too late...

"Scanners coming online, Admiral..." Corker's voice was distant, distracted. His attention was focused on his workstation, hands flying over the keyboards, doing everything he could to speed the reboot process.

"Very well, Commander." West's own eyes were fixed on the main display. The scanners had picked up the main bodies...the primary and the planets. Now they were adding detail. First, large energy readings, including two West knew could only be the destruction of spaceships. She couldn't tell whose vessels they were, but her gut told her one, at least, had been an antimatter blast. That meant a First Imperium ship...

Slowly the two opposing fleets appeared on the display. Blue triangles—Frette's ships—in a ragged line not far from the warp gate. And red circles—the First Imperium fleet—less than a hundred thousand kilometers farther away. Both forces were almost at a dead halt, standing still in space blasting away at each other. And there were a lot more red icons than blue ones.

"Fleet com?"

"Not yet, Admiral. Working on it."

West knew she didn't really need fleetwide communications. She had given her orders before the fleet transited...and she knew her people knew what to do. But she felt helpless sitting, waiting...watching her people die.

"We've got full reactor power, Admiral. Engineering reports engines operational and ready."

West took a deep breath. Normally, she'd take time to organize the fleet, put her ships into a carefully-planned formation. But there was no time. Her captains had their orders...advance as soon as possible. The tactics were simple. A wild charge into the fight...and then a deadly, toe to toe battle until one side was wiped out. It was basic, pure in its brutality. And Erika West was Constitution's captain.

"Set a course to the center of the enemy line, Commander."

"Yes, Admiral." A few second later: "Course locked in, engines ready."

"Weapons status?"

"All batteries on full alert. All crews report ready to fire."

"Take us in, Commander Corker. Forty gees." She paused. "Right into the center. Right down their throats."

*   *   *

Frette looked through the smoky haze of Compton's battered flag bridge, over toward Kemp. "What?" She'd heard her tactical officer's words, but they still seemed fuzzy, unreal. It was impossible. But he had said it.

"The ships transiting now are ours, Admiral. Eighteen so far...and they're still coming through. The lead vessels are accelerating toward the enemy at 40g."

How? How could this be?

"Any ship IDs yet?" It seemed like a stupid question, but it was the only thing that came to mind.

"I think I've got Constitution, Admiral. Also, Liberty, Sentinel, and Repulse."

Frette felt the shock again as Kemp snapped out each ship. The vessels he had named were all battleships, a huge chunk of the republic's remaining firepower. Suddenly, it all made sense.

Erika...she came after us...

Frette felt a surge of energy. She'd been resigned to death, to the utter destruction of her fleet. But now her people had a chance. The excitement was quickly tempered by the realization that the forces now moving in from the warp gate were as trapped as her people. They'd come to rescue her fleet, but now they were stuck in an all or nothing fight. Destroy the enemy, utterly, down to the last ship. Or die trying. Those were the only options.

"Get me a fleetwide channel, Commander."

"On your com, Admiral."

Frette stared down at the com unit. "Ships of the fleet...our comrades have come to our aid. Even now, republic warships are pouring through the warp gate, moving to engage the enemy. You have fought well, savaged an enemy force that greatly outnumbers you. Yet now I will ask for even more. You must continue the fight, all or you, find strength that seems unattainable. We must hold...hold for the precious minutes until our comrades enter combat range. And we must inflict as much damage as we can. This fight will be to the finish...and we owe those who came to our aid all we can still give toward securing the victory!"

She flipped off the com unit. "Commander...bring us around. All operational guns are to maintain maximum fire."

"Yes, Admiral."

Frette turned toward the main display. The enemy had been advancing, enveloping her line...but now they were pulling back, reacting to the ships coming through the warp gate. They were still firing, but the repositioning was cutting their firepower. It was just the chance her people needed.

"Admiral, communication from Constitution. Admiral West on your line.

Frette leaned down, slapping her hand on the com. "Erika?" Constitution was less than a light second away now, but the delay was still noticeable.

"Nicki..."

She could hear the urgency, the emotion in West's normally cold tone.

"You shouldn't have come...we can't risk leading them back home..."

Frette sat in her chair, crouched over the com unit, waiting for the response.

"No, we can't...which is why we're going to destroy every one of them." The frozen tone in West's voice left no doubt she was here to crush the enemy, whatever the cost. "Keep your people in the fight, Nicki...we need every gun."

"I will." Frette paused. "And Erika, thank you..."

That was the last thing she said. Compton shook violently, the lights flickering and the sounds of nearby explosions crashing loudly. The artificial gravity failed for an instant and then reengaged at double strength...just as a structural support snapped in half and crashed to the deck.

"Nicki?" West's voice was tinny, distorted. The speaker had cracked as a chunk of hyper-steel hit it...the massive girder that now lay over Nicki Frette's motionless body.

"Nicki...Nicki..."

*   *   *

"All squadrons, we've got reinforcements inbound, but we've got to hold these bastards back." Cooper McDaid had his hand on the throttle, bringing his fighter around even as he addressed the survivors of his strike force. He'd lost a third of his ships already, but he'd pushed those thoughts aside. He'd been resigned to the fact that all his people were facing death, that their launch platforms would be blown to atoms before they could return and land. But now he felt a glimmer of hope, and a renewed sense of duty. The new ships pouring into the system still had a fight on their hands...and he knew well enough they could still lose. The First Imperium forces had taken more damage than anyone had expected, but there was still a powerful force in place.

"Admiral West needs us. Admiral Frette needs us. I know you're exhausted, I know we have expended our primary armaments...but now we're going back at those bastards, and we're going to do strafing runs until our laser cannon are melted wrecks."

Or until we're all blown away...

"Follow me...it's time for the fighter corps to do its job..."

McDaid knew his people had already done their job. The fighters had savaged the enemy line with their torpedo runs, destroying several of the Leviathans outright and badly damaging many more. But there was more to do...and no rest, no salvation until the enemy was beaten.

"Pick your targets, find the crippled ships and finish them off." He knew what he was asking, and he was sure his people did too. The fighter lasers weren't strong enough weapons to destroy enemy battleships, not unless the pilots brought their craft in on nearly suicidal runs, firing at point blank range and targeting already damaged vessels. He knew they'd take out a few more ships that way...and they'd lose more of their number too.

He angled his throttle, moving toward an enemy battleship. The Leviathan was badly damaged, moving forward at moderate speed, but with no thrust that he could detect. The ship was firing at Compton, its main battery still firing, despite what was clearly massive damage.

His eyes zeroed in on the ship, his hand tightening on the throttle. He felt strange, distraught about the people he'd lost, scared for himself and his fighter's crew...but there was something else, controlled rage, the lust for the kill. He felt a determination to destroy this ship that was firing on Compton, on the fleet's flagship...his own mothership.

He imagined Greta Hurley, back in the days of the fleet. He wondered what she would do, what thoughts would have gone through her head. He hoped she would have approved of his leadership...that she would have forgiven him for the losses his men and women had suffered. Would continue to suffer.

He stared hard at the enemy battleship, altering his ship's vector to a direct approach. "Alright, guys..." He turned his head briefly, staring back at his two gunners. "I'm going to bring us right down their throat...make it count."

He turned back, staring straight ahead. His eyes darted to the side, reading the rapidly declining numbers. Forty thousand kilometers. Thirty-five thousand.

He felt the fighter shake hard as a point defense rocket detonated nearby. It hadn't been close enough to damage his ship, but it had been too close for comfort. He tapped the throttle to one side...then to the next, bringing the fighter in on a zigzag pattern. The defensive fire was thick, the scanner showing the energy bursts where laser needle gun blasts ripped through space all around the fighter.

Twenty-five thousand.

McDaid squeezed his hand tightly around the throttle. He felt his finger moving toward the firing stud. It was instinct... he knew very well he didn't have any torpedoes left. And that meant he had to get his gunners in close. Really close...

He pushed forward, increasing the thrust as the counter continued its downward movement.

Fifteen thousand...

Here we come, you bastards...right down your throats...

Ten thousand...

*   *   *

Erika West felt cold, like the icy wastes of space. Part of her wanted to scream into the com, to shout Nicki Frette's name until she got an answer. But she had a duty that transcended the fate of one of her officers...even of that of her lover. West was closer to Frette than she'd ever been to anyone, and the two had shared a happiness beyond anything the grizzled admiral had imagined possible. But first and foremost she was still Erika West, the cold-blooded Alliance admiral...and now the commander of the republic's naval forces. Duty took her now, as it always did in battle, and she focused on the deadly fight that would decide if any of her people left the system.

"All units...close to point blank range and engage." There were no formations, no time for complex battle plans. This would be a bare knuckled brawl, a disorganized, desperate fight to the end. Her ships were moving forward as they transited, diving into the battle individually...and in twos and threes. It couldn't be helped. Frette's fleet was on the verge of total destruction, and her surviving ships wouldn't last much longer on their own.

Constitution was in the lead, driving forward, not far from the position where the battered Compton was making its last stand. West's flagship had already launched her missiles, cleaning out her exterior racks and flushing her magazines as she leapt forward toward the battle line.

The missiles moved toward enemy forces now fully engaged in an energy weapons battle. Their point defense was spotty, ineffective, and dozens of warheads closed, detonating near the First Imperium vessels, many of them already damaged.

West was focused, ignoring her personal feelings. She felt cold satisfaction as she watched an icon representing a Leviathan, already damaged, with a half-kilometer long gash down its side, explode with the fury of matter-antimatter annihilation.

Her eyes focused on a cluster of small white dots, Constitution's twelve fighter-bombers, positioned ahead of the mother

ship, moving forward at full thrust to the support of Frette's
squadrons.

"All primary and secondary batteries...prepare to fire as
soon as we enter range." She wasn't the admiral anymore...
at least she didn't have any duties as fleet commander. She'd
ordered her captains to close as quickly as possible, to fight their
ships as they saw fit. There was no fleet strategy, at least not
one that required anything from an admiral. Now her focus was
on Constitution...and she was determined to turn her flagship
into a manifestation of hell, a bloody scythe tearing through
the enemy ranks. She knew the situation, and she understood
that none of her people could go home—ever. Not unless they
annihilated the enemy fleet.

And she intended to do just that.

*   *   *

Josie Strand leaned against the inner wall of the escape pod.
Her left arm was broken, badly, a shard of shattered bone poking through the skin. Her shirt was covered with blood, but
she'd managed to get a makeshift bandage around the gruesome
wound, and the bleeding had slowed to a trickle. It hurt...like
nothing she'd felt before, but her discipline was holding.

Starfire was dead, a floating hulk, beyond repair...indeed,
barely resembling a ship at all. It hurt, more even than she'd
imagined it would. Her first command...lost. She blamed herself, though her rational mind told her Starfire and her crew
had performed heroically. Her ship and her people had proven
themselves the equals of the legendary spacers of the old fleet,
and they had fought with determination and courage to the very
end.

She didn't know how many of them had escaped. Indeed,
she was surprised she had survived. She had been ready to stay
with her ship, to die with Starfire. But her spacers would have

none of it. A half-dozen of them had dragged her to the pod, committing acts of well-meaning mutiny to save their captain. Their loyalty had touched her, but she hadn't been sure she wanted to survive her ship. Until now.

The pod had only rudimentary scanners, and she'd had no idea what the ships coming through the warp gate were...until they started firing at the First Imperium fleet.

They're ours!

Grim acceptance of certain death gave way to renewed defiance. The fleet had a chance. The fight wasn't over.

She felt helpless in the unarmed pod, wishing she had some kind of weapon, any way to help, to join in the terrible battle now raging all around. But she and her people were relegated to a role as spectators, with nothing to do but watch—and see if their comrades prevailed...and saved their lives.

She saw a Leviathan disappear from the scanner. The enemy battleship had been pounding at Compton, but then it just vanished, blown to atoms by the failure of its containment systems. The flagship's weapons had been silent, the big ship too badly battered to return fire. Strand knew it had to be a fighter attack. She smiled. She couldn't imagine the losses the squadrons were taking...the courage it took to fly straight at such a behemoth firing nothing but light laser cannons.

Yes, it had to be fighters, she thought, wondering if any of Starfire's birds had been part of the attack. Or if any of them had survived.

*   *   *

"Cons...ution...this is...Compton..." The words were distant, hard to hear through the static. Erika West had been staring straight ahead, watching the exchanges on the display as her ship fought a deadly duel with one of the Leviathans. But now her eyes dropped to the com unit. The voice wasn't Nicki's, she could tell that right away. But it was someone from Compton...

and that triggered a flicker of hope inside her, back in the part of her mind where she'd penned up her personal emotions.

"Compton, report...what is your condition?" West spoke slowly, clearly. She knew Compton was in bad shape, and she had no idea what condition her com was in. "Where is Admiral Frette?"

"Bad...reactor barely..." West listened, trying to pick the words out of the background noise. She had the AI cleaning up the audio, but it was still hard to make out. "Ad...Frette... wound..."

West felt her stomach clench. Nicki was injured...but how badly?

"...critical...desperate..."

What is critical? Compton? Nicki?

Both?

"Repeat last transmission." She barked the words into the com unit, but there was no response. Nothing but the static.

"Admiral, engineering reports heavy damage to the port conduits. Request permission to reduce output to fifty percent."

"Denied," she snapped. "I want full power. All batteries maintain fire."

She knew her guns were getting hot, that each shot increased the chance of a catastrophic breakdown. But there was nothing, no thought, no consideration that mattered...only destroying the enemy.

Old rage poured back into her, flashes from thirty year old battles, images of old comrades killed, grievously wounded. Her hands clenched into fists, and her eyes stared forward, glistening with the fury of a predator.

"Increase reactor to one hundred ten percent, Commander. And I don't want any warnings from engineering. Just do it."

"Yes, Admiral."

"And all guns...remove safeties, increase output to maximum."

It was time. Time to destroy the enemy...or die.

Chapter Thirty-Three

Navy Headquarters
Victory City, Earth Two
Earth Two Date 01.08.31

"The Mules are behind you, Mr. President, all of them." H2 looked down the table at Harmon. "They are ready to do whatever you need."

"That is good news, H2. I want to thank you for acting as my liaison while Achilles is away with the fleet."

"I am happy to assist in any way." H2 nodded. "I know you are uncomfortable with what some might call a coup, but you know there was no choice."

"I hope you're right, H2. I'm afraid things are very on the edge right now. The initial word from Admiral Frette scared everyone enough to calm things down, but it didn't last. Jacques Diennes has gone as far as to openly accuse me of staging the whole thing as an excuse to seize power. The last thing I needed was a problem with the Mules."

"There is no problem there. In fact, Achilles left word to dispatch the warbots to your support if you require them. And from what I could see, it is unanimous. The Mules have other issues, certainly, as every group does. But they took your summary repeal of the Prohibition as a show of good faith." He paused. "As do I."

Harmon nodded. He sometimes forgot Hieronymus Cutter's modified clone was in essence the first Mule. Cutter had improved his technique, and as much as H2 was smarter and stronger than a normal human, the Mules who followed had even greater abilities. H2 was sterile as were the rest of the Mules, but he drew his human DNA from a specific donor, while the others were hybrids of up to a dozen different men and women.

"It should have been done years ago. It should have never existed." Harmon sighed. "Still, even with the Mules, I'm afraid of what might happen. Diennes is out there fomenting a revolution...and whatever he says, we know Admiral Frette's report was real. The danger she warned us of is real."

"Perhaps it's time for him to have an accident."

Harmon stared back, shocked at the words that came from his friend's mouth. H2 was a mild mannered sort, content most times at his studies and rarely confrontational. Harmon was shaken by the casual nature in which he'd just suggested an assassination.

"That is not how we do things, H2. You know that."

"And how did you secure Admiral West's succession to Admiral Compton's place? How did you head off conflict between the national contingents? Didn't that work? By eliminating the most troublesome elements, you cut the head off the problem. For all our strife today, and the rivalries between Tank and Mule and NB...there is virtually no remaining nationalism from the old Superpowers. Do you think that would have happened if you hadn't...gotten rid of...those who would have inflamed those rivalries for personal gain?"

Harmon felt as if his breath had been sucked from his lungs. He had done what he had done...and there was blood on his hands, three-decade old blood. He had done what he had done for the good of the people, to safeguard all the men and women of the fleet. But he had never quite forgiven himself. And he'd had no idea H2 knew about it."

"H2..."

"Don't worry, Mr. President…you have no leaks, not even my father. No one told me about the…moves…you made back then. My analysis of the events immediately following the Regent's destruction left little doubt as to what had occurred. I'm afraid the other Mules long ago came to the same conclusions."

Harmon was stunned. The Mules had known all along…yet they'd never attempted to blackmail him, to use it against him. He found himself more intrigued than ever at the mysterious hybrids.

"Still…" Harmon paused. He was trying to stay focused, but the discussion had dredged up the old guilt about what he had done. "…I don't think killing Mr. Diennes is the smart move right now." He wasn't sure he really believed that. If the gentle H2 suggested it, he realized it might very well be the right play now. But he knew he didn't have it in him to assassinate another rival.

"Perhaps not. I wonder if it isn't best just to ignore him. You control the Marines and the navy—and our bots are available to enforce your decisions as well. There is little Diennes can do to challenge you openly." It was clear from H2's tone that he still believed eliminating the troublemaker was the best route.

"That is true." Harmon paused. "But his efforts to undermine me are still harmful. If we are facing what we fear we are, we will need every man and woman, side by side to win the victory. To survive. Diennes' poison could damage us just enough to make the difference. The more people who believe that the threat is an invented fiction, the weaker we will be when it comes to a fight."

Harmon hesitated. He'd brought himself full circle, back to the reason H2 had originally suggested killing Diennes. Harmon realized his hesitancy, his unwillingness to be as hard, as decisive as he had been thirty years before, could prove disastrous. But he knew he didn't have it in him to murder a man who had so far done nothing but criticize him. Not again.

"Perhaps we can just…"

"Mr. President, I have a communique from your…from

Captain Fujin, sir." The voice blared through the com unit. It was one of the communications officer on duty. Warrick, Harmon remembered as he placed the voice. Lieutenant Warrick.

Mariko?

He was confused. Then he remembered she'd been scheduled for deep space training with her newly activated squadrons. His stomach tightened.

"On my com. Now."

Has something gone wrong?

He pressed the button, putting the com on speaker. He had nothing to hide from H2.

"Max, this is Mariko. I'm sending this under an alpha-ten code. We're on maneuvers near the G3 warp gate. We're picking up an energy spike…"

Harmon could hear the tension in her voice. He felt it himself, as if his insides were twisted in knots. He'd been doing everything possible to beef up Earth Two's defenses, but he needed more time. If those were First Imperium ships about to transit…

Mariko…

He realized Fujin and her still-disorganized fighter wings would be the first line of defense. He knew what she would do if enemy ships started pouring into the system. Her birds weren't even armed with live plasma torpedoes, but that wouldn't stop her.

He stared down at his desk, realizing in horror that Mariko could die any minute. No, she could already be dead. The warp gate was more than sixty light minutes from Earth Two. The words he was hearing had been spoken over an hour ago. If there was a fight in the outer system, it was already in progress.

Or already over…

He sat and listened, as she continued her report.

"First ship coming through now…"

The pause seemed like an eternity. Harmon felt himself leaning forward, almost falling out of his chair.

"It's Constitution, Max!" He heard the tone of her voice before the words sunk in. "It's Admiral West!"

Harmon leaned back in his chair, exhaling hard, feeling relief push out the tension. West was back. That had to be good news...

"Max..." It was Mariko again, on the com. Her tone had changed again. It was dark, grim. "Max...Admiral West just sent me a com." She paused, and Harmon could swear he heard her sniffle back tears. "It's terrible, Max. It's just terrible..."

*   *   *

Max Harmon stood in the docking bay, watching as one of the cranes moved the large metal cylinder. He'd seen medpods before, and he'd had too many friends and comrades end up in the coffin-like devices. He knew the pods were the surgeon's tool of last resort, a way to keep a dying patient alive a bit longer, usually in the vain hope of a miracle.

The crane moved the pod over him, its giant arm dropping slowly, lowering the mechanism to the deck. He stood, stone still and staring, until he heard the clacking sound of the pod's supports hitting the metal floor. Finally, he took a step forward...but he stopped almost immediately, as he heard the familiar voice behind him.

"Max...we have to discuss strategies as soon as possible..."

It was Erika West. She wore a spotless uniform, as always, and she stood almost at attention, looking the image of the fighting admiral. But it was her voice that gave her away, and the pain in her words was like a cry for help to Harmon.

"Erika...I'm so sorry." He stepped forward again, stopping in front of the medpod. He looked down, through the clear hyper-polycarbonate shell. Nicki Frette lay there, her eyes closed, unmoving, looking in every way like she was dead. Harmon knew she wasn't dead, not yet. The medpod used controlled cryonics to slow her bodily functions, to keep her alive when her injuries would have killed her already. It wasn't a treatment, merely a way to buy some time. And a chance.

"Her spine is severed, Max. She has a basilar skull fracture, and there is damage to her cerebral cortex. The doctors don't know if they can save her...and even if they do, they say the damage to the brain may be irreversible." West was one of the strongest people Harmon had ever known, but he could see that between Frette's injuries and the situation with the First Imperium, his commanding admiral was close to the breaking point.

Harmon was trying to think of something to say, some words that would comfort his friend. But Achilles walked across the docking bay before he got anything out.

"Admiral West, do not despair. I have contacted Themistocles and requested that he meet us at the hospital. He is an expert in both human and Ancient anatomy and surgery. I am confident he can assist in obtaining a favorable outcome for Admiral Frette."

"Thank you, Achilles." West's voice was firmer than it had been a few seconds before.

The Mule just nodded. Then he glanced at Harmon. "I am sure you both have much to discuss...so I will see that Themistocles is ready." He turned and walked across the bay, toward the exit door.

"The Mules are extremely capable, Erika...and Themistocles is brilliant. I am sure he can help Dr. Gower and her team. And Nicki is tough. Don't you give up on her..."

"I won't, Max." Harmon could hear the fatigue in her voice as well as the sadness. He'd reviewed her reports, and those of the other key commanders. It was apparent Erika West had lost none of her tactical brilliance. Her force had raced into battle, just in time to save the survivors of Frette's force. The battle had been a vicious one...a fight to the death. But in the end her people prevailed. Every First Imperium vessel was destroyed. She'd lost just under twenty percent of her own ships...and Frette's casualties were in excess of fifty percent.

In spite of the losses, she had accomplished her mission. She'd saved Frette's people, and she had confirmed, at least to some extent, what the republic was facing. Her forces had spent almost a week in the system after the battle, searching every cubic kilometer of space for any signs of enemy probes or stealth drones. Harmon couldn't imagine what it had taken for her to delay as she had done, to put the mission first, before the need to return the critically injured Frette to Earth Two. But he knew one thing for sure. She was an officer he could trust to do whatever had to be done, to fight to the bitter end against any enemy. And he suspected he was going to need every bit of her stony resolve in the fight to come.

Harmon watched as West's eyes moved back to the medpod. She leaned over it, looking at Frette, lying so still. She reached out, put her hand on the pod.

Harmon paused, knowing what he had to say...but not wanting to do it. "Erika..." He hesitated again, swallowing hard. "I'm sorry...but we really have to go. We need to get to work, to get the defenses in order." He paused once again. "We both know the fleet you destroyed wasn't everything the enemy has out there...and we have no idea what they know, when they will be back."

West nodded, standing still for a few more seconds. Then she stood up straight and turned toward Harmon. "Of course, sir..." She sighed softly. "Duty first...as always."

Harmon returned her nod, and he started off toward the exit door, West following right behind.

A pair of robot units moved up to the pod, pulling it slowly across the bay, toward the waiting transport. It was sleek, its clear surface covered with a sleek sheen of condensation... everywhere but on the top, where a single handprint remained.

Epilogue

Navy Headquarters
Victory City, Earth Two

"There is no way to know what we are facing, not unless we send out our own scouting parties. The enemy is undoubtedly seeking our location…we yield considerable tactical initiative if we do not do the same." Erika West sat near the head of the massive table, next to Max Harmon. She'd been relentless in her work since returning four days before. Harmon had tried to get her to take some time, to get some rest. But he realized the work was her drug, her distraction from to worry and sadness that otherwise consumed her. Nicki Frette was still alive…but she was also non-responsive. Themistocles and the medical teams had been working around the clock, but the officer's injuries had defied treatment.

"I must agree with Admiral West." Achilles' voice was as emotionless and professional as always. Or close, at least. Harmon thought he heard a touch of emotion…was it sympathy, empathy?

"There are great risks associated with such a strategy…not the least of which is the enormous danger for the crews on such missions. This is well beyond simple scouting…even if a vessel finds something, it cannot return to Earth Two unless it can evade all pursuit. And we still risk an undetected stealth drone or probe following a vessel back without its crew's knowledge."

"All you say is true, sir, but I believe we face a basic equation here. There is little doubt the enemy has production facilities far larger than our own…and that leads us to a simple conclusion. Given time—be it months, a year, ten years—the enemy will produce far more vessels than we can, and eventually they will overwhelm us." The Mule paused for a few seconds. "A defensive strategy is a trap, one almost guaranteed to end in our destruction. Indeed, all the more certain, for the forces we can deploy are severely limited by the population we have available. The enemy will search space, explore each warp gate leading from any point of contact. This may involve several hundred systems, but there is no doubt they will find Earth Two. We must find a way to disrupt them...to hurt them, even destroy them. And we cannot do this standing here on the defensive, waiting."

Harmon heard Achilles' words, and he knew they were pure truth. His first reaction had been to stand on the defensive, but now he was realizing West and Achilles were right. Mounting the best possible defense of Earth Two was essential, of course. And attack could come at any time. But it wasn't enough. They had to strike back, to find a way to take the fight to the enemy, as he had done thirty years before.

"Very well, then we are all in agreement. We will continue to do everything possible to defend Earth Two against any enemy attacks. But we will also send out scouting forces...our fastest ships..." Harmon hesitated, the risk the scouts would endure weighing heavily on his mind. "I will ask for volunteers to man the scoutships..."

"Sir, this is an extremely important mission. Don't you think you should assign the very best crews to those..."

"Sorry, Achilles. You are right, no doubt. But I can't do it...I can't order men and women out into the endless dark, with orders to die rather than lead the enemy home. It is my weakness, I know...but I just can't do it. I won't."

Achilles simply nodded.

Harmon turned and looked out over his assembled officers and advisors. "This is the worst crisis we have faced since the days of the old fleet...but we will face it, and we will defeat the enemy. Those of us at this table will carry much of the burden of what is to come...and we will carry the guilt for those who die under our command. But as dark as things are, there is one thing I can feel, in every centimeter of my body. We are not alone. No...though he is not here at the head of this table, as he should be, Terrance Compton will always be with us. We stand here in his shadow, on the world his courage and wisdom won for us...and I say this now. We will not let you down, sir... whatever it takes.

Planet X
Far Beyond the Borders of the Imperium

I begin to truly understand now. The Regent's records, its warnings...they are now clear. The enemy is numerically weak, technologically inferior...yet they appear to have truly unique natural abilities in combat. I must investigate their origin, determine if they were bred as creatures of battle or if this is a natural trait of their species. But that is analysis for the sake of knowledge. The primary directive is unchanged. To annihilate them. To avenge the Regent.

In spite of my own established parameters, I nevertheless underestimated the enemy. I will not allow that to happen again. I have analyzed all tactical data...and I have established a baseline area of space to explore. I estimate there are three hundred seventy to three hundred ninety systems in the search area, at least one of which is the enemy home world. I have assigned exploration assets accordingly. There is a variable as to when the enemy's system will be found, but no doubt that it will. And while the search is underway, I will assemble the fleet that will destroy the enemy.

The ships are already organizing, assembling. Preparing for the final assault.

It is a fleet of great power, vastly larger than that which was defeated. And I have given it a designation. A name.

Force Retribution.

The Vengeance Trilogy Continues with
Storm of Vengeance
Coming Soon Crimson Worlds Series

The Crimson Worlds Series

Marines (Crimson Worlds I)
The Cost of Victory (Crimson Worlds II)
A Little Rebellion (Crimson Worlds III)
The First Imperium (Crimson Worlds IV)
The Line Must Hold (Crimson Worlds V)
To Hell's Heart (Crimson Worlds VI)
The Shadow Legions(Crimson Worlds VII)
Even Legends Die (Crimson Worlds VIII)
The Fall (Crimson Worlds IX)
War Stories (Crimson World Prequels)
MERCS (Successors I)
The Prisoner of Eldaron (Successors II)
Into the Darkness (Refugees I)
Shadows of the Gods (Refugees II)
Revenge of the Ancients (Refugees III)

Also By Jay Allan

The Dragon's Banner
Gehenna Dawn (Portal Wars I)
The Ten Thousand (Portal Wars II)
Homefront (Portal Wars III)
Blackhawk (Far Stars Legends I)
Shadow of Empire (Fars Stars I)
Enemy in the Dark (Far Stars II)
Funeral Games (Far Stars III)

www.jayallanbooks.com

71500923R00189

Made in the
USA
Middletown, DE